Murder in Greenwich Village

MURDER IN GREENWICH VILLAGE

LIZ FREELAND

KENSINGTON BOOKS
www.kensingtonbooks.com

To the extent that the image or images on the cover of this book depict a person or persons, such person or persons are merely models, and are not intended to portray any character or characters featured in the book.

KENSINGTON BOOKS are published by

Kensington Publishing Corp.
119 West 40th Street
New York, NY 10018

All Kensington titles, imprints, and distributed lines are available at special quantity discounts for bulk purchases for sales promotion, premiums, fund-raising, educational, or institutional use.

Special book excerpts or customized printings can also be created to fit specific needs. For details, write or phone the office of the Kensington Sales Manager: Kensington Publishing Corp., 119 West 40th Street, New York, NY 10018. Attn. Sales Department. Phone: 1-800-221-2647.

eISBN-13: 978-1-4967-1425-1
eISBN-10: 1-4967-1425-3
First Kensington Electronic Edition: June 2018

ISBN-13: 978-1-4967-1424-4
ISBN-10: 1-4967-1424-5
First Kensington Trade Paperback Printing: June 2018

10 9 8 7 6 5 4 3 2 1

Printed in the United States of America

Murder in Greenwich Village

Chapter 1

New York, June 1913

On Thursday nights, my aunt Irene's Upper East Side townhouse hummed with conversation, laughter, and music coaxed from a temperamental old Chickering upright by whatever guest felt the urge to tickle its yellowed ivories. There was no predicting who would turn up on those at-home evenings: writers, painters, theater people, men of business, and even the odd tradesman whom my aunt deemed interesting for her own particular reasons. And me. I had to shrug off my feeling of being an out-of-town imposter as I threaded my way among the second-tier luminaries Aunt Irene's open invitation attracted. Here was a sophisticated world I barely could have imagined as I'd plodded away at the account books of my uncles' fish and butcher shops in poky Altoona. Even after six months, I wasn't entirely convinced I belonged.

Above all else, Aunt Irene wanted her guests to be *fascinating*. I never kidded myself that I was fascinating to her, except perhaps in the way that a scientist might find a specimen under a microscope fascinating. Irene Livingston Green had made her name—and a pile of money—churning out sentimental stories of youth such as *Myrtle in Springtime* and *Pretty Is as Petunia Does*. I suspected I was Exhibit A in her study of Small-Town Girl in the Big City, which was flattering because I had nothing of the heart-stopping beauty, self-confidence, or can-do spirit of my aunt's fictional heroines. I was useful as an extra pair of hands when canapés needed handing around, however, and Aunt Irene was happy to make use of me in that way, too.

Once a guest paid proper homage to the hostess, it was all very casual. People drifted in and out, clumping together between the brocade settee where Aunt Irene held court with Dickens and Trollope, her two toy spaniels, and the point on the opposite side of the room where Walter, the butler, tended bar at the mahogany liquor cabinet. Those uncomfortable with crowds could snatch a moment of comparative quiet in the dining room, which communicated with the parlor but whose windowless, cramped atmosphere discouraged clustering. The space felt dwarfed by a massive dining table and sideboard, and there were nothing but Jacobean high-backed chairs to perch on, with barley twists that seemed specially designed to dig into the occupant's shoulder blades. Only recluses and misfits tended to camp out there.

But I often found glamour even among the dining room castaways. This night, the guest who captured my attention was a young man named Ford Fitzsimmons. From the moment I'd overheard a magazine editor introducing him to Aunt Irene, I'd tracked his orbit around the room and edged closer to him. He clearly wasn't enjoying the party and knew few people here. As the evening progressed, he receded farther from the action, growing gloomier and more inebriated. Once, I found myself next to him, but before I could introduce myself I was buttonholed by a lady who appeared to be in the process of being devoured by the beady-eyed head of her voluminous white fox stole. She'd survived the sinking of the *Titanic* and was grabbing egg-salad sandwiches off my tray as if compelled to bulk up in the event of another unscheduled sojourn on a lifeboat in the North Atlantic. I fed her and listened patiently. My personal disasters hadn't been as newsworthy as the *Titanic,* but I understood about lifeboats. New York City was mine.

Finally free and spotting my quarry alone in the dining room, I sped over with what was left of my plate of sandwiches and took the chair next to him. "Please try to eat something, Mr. Fitzsimmons," I urged.

His blue eyes took in my diminished tower of dainty, crustless offerings as if it were a pile of garden slugs. "I'd rather have another of these." He twirled his drained glass.

"Not until you eat something," I insisted. "Food in your stomach will do you good. I bet you haven't had a real meal in days, have you?"

My tone coaxed a hint of a smile. "No, Mother, I haven't."

I nudged the plate toward him and held it rigid until he dutifully took one and popped it whole into his mouth. "I don't see why you want to starve yourself," I said as he chewed.

He swallowed, and took another. "It's cheaper. Also, one is supposed to earn one's bread. I've barely earned a dime by my own wits since coming to this infernal city."

Small wonder he wasn't a hit at the party. No pep. He needed beefing up, physically and psychologically, and I appointed myself chief pepper-upper. "You had a story in *Gotham Magazine,* didn't you? That's a good beginning."

"You read that story, did you? Well, you have more confidence in me than the rest of the world does."

Tired of holding the plate, I slid it in front of him on the table. "That's because I know your work. It's just a matter of time before you'll be the envy of most of the people milling about here this evening. In a few years, that crowd will gather around you."

I nodded through the opened French doors into the parlor, but his eyes, wide with amazement, remained focused on me. Absently, he grabbed another sandwich and gobbled it down. "Are you real, or is this some kind of fever dream fledgling writers are susceptible to?"

"I'm real, and I have a real job at Van Hooten and McChesney."

"Oh." Gloom descended on him again. "They rejected my book."

"It wasn't on my account. *Live Till Tomorrow* kept me up an entire night reading it. I gave it a glowing report."

He sat up straighter. "Then why . . . ?"

"I'm low man on the totem pole at Van Hooten and McChesney. I was hired to be general secretary and receptionist, but I pestered my bosses to let me read manuscripts that come over the transom." They hadn't required much persuading, actually. Heaven knows my bosses didn't want to read any more than they had to. Sometimes I wondered if either of them liked books at all. "Most of the submissions are pretty forgettable. Yours was that one in a thousand that's truly remarkable."

In my opinion, at least. Jackson Beasley, the editor at Van Hooten and McChesney, had skimmed my report, read two pages of the manuscript, and declared it "amateurish flub-dub." I feared that was primarily because I, a mere clerical underling, had recommended it. Jackson might be an unappreciated editor at a past-its-glory publisher, but he had his pride.

Ford's lips quirked into a bitter smile. "And you're that one in a million who thinks so."

"Van Hooten and McChesney is so . . . well, fusty. Mr. McChesney's tastes in particular are rather outdated." I didn't bother to mention Jackson, or Guy Van Hooten. On work days, the scion of our floundering firm could be found in the city clubs and Turkish baths more often than in his office. No one knew his literary tastes, or if he'd ever read a book more intellectually taxing than *The Rover Boys*. "Our company makes most of its earnings from Bulwer-Lytton reissues. The only new book we've acquired in the past few years that's turned a healthy profit was *The Healthy Effects of Pickle Juice on Digestive Disorders*. All things considered, they might have done you a favor passing on your manuscript."

A mirthless laugh huffed from him. "Many people have done me the same favor. How will I ever repay them all?"

"I didn't mean to be glib," I said. "But please don't feel discouraged. And if you ever want a reader for your work, I'd feel honored."

That perked him up. "Is that offer genuine?"

"Of course."

He looked at me in wonder. "Who *are* you?"

I smiled and offered my hand. "Louise Faulk, lately of Altoona, Pennsylvania."

"Ford Fitzsimmons, of Worcester, Massachusetts." He might have golden boy looks, but his rough hands and a certain hardness in his eye told me he'd worked his way through college—if he'd finished college at all. I didn't think he was much older than I, but my guess was that he'd seen much more of the world. "What brought you to the big city, Miss Faulk?"

"Louise, if you don't mind." I considered how much I should tell and decided, as usual, on the abbreviated version. "Does anyone need an excuse to flee Altoona? I finished a secretarial course and did accounts in the back of a butcher's shop for two years before I remembered I had a perfectly good aunt in New York City whose hospitality I could take advantage of."

"You live with your aunt?"

I shook my head. "That's where I was naïve. I turned up here with my suitcase and she promptly directed me to the Martha Washington Hotel for women. Except for these Thursday nights, Aunt Irene likes her privacy."

"Aunt Irene?" He gaped at me. "You're the hostess's niece? I beg your pardon. I thought you were hired help."

"She has the charming habit of treating the entire world as hired help. But I owe her so much, I don't mind popping round and lending a hand. Without her, I never would have found my job at Van Hooten and McChesney. I'm very grateful."

His gaze strayed to my aunt, ridiculously regal in a dress of drifts of lace with a jeweled headdress that featured a plume that was nearly half as long as the settee. Dickens and Trollope bookended her. The expression on Ford's face spoke volumes about what he thought of her. No one who'd read a title from her syrupy oeuvre would mistake her for a literary giant, and her pretensions at hostessing these soirées probably struck him as absurd. I had my mental dukes up, ready to jump to her defense, and was relieved when he changed the subject.

"Still at the women's hotel?" he asked.

"Oh no. I share an apartment now with a girl I met there."

"Just the two of you?" His tone conveyed surprise, but I didn't read any judgment in his eyes. I was used to my independence raising eyebrows. My boss, old Mr. McChesney, had acted positively scandalized when he found out I was living on my own, and not even in a respectable boardinghouse. I was sick to death of boardinghouses, though, and had little patience with the idea that any woman not living under her family's protective roof or under the watchful eyes of snooping strangers would inevitably sink into a life of sin and dissipation.

"Just the two of us," I said, although that wasn't technically true at the moment. I just wished it were.

I glanced around the room and found Callie. She'd arrived fifteen minutes ago and was now perched on the arm of the chair of the gray-haired man she'd come in with. I was a little nettled with her. I'd been late getting to Aunt Irene's because I'd waited for Callie to meet me at my office as we'd planned, and she'd stood me up. But my irritation was short-lived, especially when I saw the old geezer administer a pinch to her thigh. She often got stuck with my aunt's more tiresome guests.

"There she is." I pointed her out.

"I see." Unlike most males with a heartbeat, Ford uttered no word of admiration. Very peculiar, given that Callie was by far the most dazzling creature in the room. In coloring, she could have been Ford's sister. They shared the same honey-colored hair and blue eyes. Callie's personality rarely ran to gloom, though. She was one of those lucky souls who floated through life on good spirits and optimism, tempered with a grit gained, I supposed, from living in the city a full six months longer than I had.

"Callie grew up on a dairy farm upstate near Little Falls. She calls it Little Yawns. Now she's in the big city, works as a mannequin at a dress house called Solomon's, and auditions for shows on Broadway." So far she'd never been cast, but I was impressed by her persistence.

"Sounds like one of your aunt's books."

"Aunt Irene loves her. She says it's only a matter of time before Callie has the town at her feet."

He glowered as another guest leaned close to whisper something in Callie's ear. "It would appear she's made a good start here today." Before I could respond, he turned back to me. "Where downtown do you live?"

"Bleecker and Tenth Street."

"We're practically neighbors," he said. "I live on Christopher."

"Then if you ever need bracing up, you should drop by. 391 Bleecker. Third floor."

A blond brow arched. "Won't your roommate mind your giving an open invitation to a virtual stranger?"

Callie wouldn't mind a bit, but there was someone else in our apartment who would. Ethel. However, I refused to elevate Callie's visiting cousin to the status of roommate.

"How can we be strangers?" I asked. "I read your book."

A hint of a smile touched his lips. "That's right. I spent an entire night with you, by proxy."

I felt myself blushing, which was so ridiculous and unsophisticated. So Altoona. To cover my embarrassment, I swung the subject back to my roommate. "Anyway, Callie loves company. Though I should warn you to guard your heart. She breaks about one per week."

His mouth flattened into a grim line as he watched Callie extract herself from an unwanted tug toward the piano, where a few couples were dancing to a new rag tune. Everything was a rag now, or purported to be. "The Hungarian Rag." "The Crazy Bone Rag." "The Swiss Cheese Rag." I was in a position to know all about music crazes, since the apartment below ours was inhabited by a saxophone quintet called the Bleecker Blowers. Their foundation-shaking renditions of all the popular songs of the day sometimes made me nostalgic for the Caruso phonograph records my Aunt Sonja would put on the Victrola back in Altoona. Opera was her sole indulgence.

Ford was still eyeing Callie. "No need to worry about my heart. Women are the devil."

From his bitter tone, I surmised he was nursing a wounded heart already. In this he was not alone. Everyone in New York seemed to be suffering from some kind of ailment of the heart. I was no exception—a fact that probably would have surprised most people who knew me. Some days, the ache inside surprised even me. I had no one to pine for, but I'd discovered there was more than one way a heart could break. Back in Altoona, I'd attracted a few louses and even one devoted admirer. A frustrated musician, Otto Klemper had worked as an assistant in Uncle Dolph's butcher shop. But it was impossible to fall in love with a man who made eyes at you over a meat slicer. The most immediate emotion Otto had aroused in me was fear that he'd lose a finger.

"I should go," Ford muttered.

My straying thoughts snapped back to attention. "Already? Are you tired?"

He smiled at me. "You're priceless. It's not bedtime, it's tavern time."

That didn't sound good. "I've failed to give you any encouragement, haven't I?"

"Guess again. You've given me the only shot of cheer I've had in a long time." He stood and bowed with exaggerated reverence. "It was a pleasure to meet you, Louise Faulk. You might be my first real friend in publishing."

"Please stay a little longer," I said. "I'd like you to meet Callie."

He frowned again at my roommate, who at that moment had tossed back her head to laugh at something the man next to her had said. The laugh was too big for the room, and drew other stares, as well.

"No, thanks," Ford said through a clenched jaw. "I feel as if I've already met her."

He turned and left without saying any further good-bye to me, or to his hostess.

Bad manners. And yet, perversely, part of me found his stark lack of susceptibility to Callie's obvious charms refreshing. Maybe I'd discovered the one man in America who preferred bookish brunettes to shapely blondes with dazzling smiles. Not that he'd shown much interest in me, especially. No one could accuse him of being a wolf. But there was something in Ford's brooding genius, his very indifference, that appealed to me. I told myself that my interest in him was purely professional. I imagined taking Ford under my wing and spurring him into further flights of creativity. Then, once he realized to what degree he owed all his great success to me, and how invaluable I'd become to him . . .

From there my usual sensible self gave way to an imagination run amok. I wasn't Irene Livingston Green's niece for nothing.

After the party broke up around nine thirty, Aunt Irene led Callie and me to the kitchen. As far as I knew, these were the only times my aunt appeared in that functional room. Bernice, her dervish of a cook, kept her domain gleaming and spotless, and the cabinets, some of which reached the eleven-foot ceiling, were painted a stark white to match the tile countertops. Compared to my aunt Sonja's kitchen, with its perpetually floury butcher block tables and inescapable vinegar and cabbage smells, this place was as clean and ordered as a hospital dispensary. Aunt Irene navigated it with her usual efficiency, boxing up leftovers for us and fixing herself a pot of coffee on the stove.

Her nightly coffee was more than an eccentricity. Despite what I'd told Ford, I'd spent my first two weeks in New York City with Aunt Irene, so I knew her routine. As soon as we were gone, she would hole up in her study to work as late as 3:00 a.m. At night she wrote at her rolltop desk with pen and paper, Dickens and Trollope snoozing in their baskets nearby. While the city slumbered, she focused without interruption on her imaginary melodramas and rigorously paced herself by the gilded bronze mantel clock with cherubs that struck each quarter hour. The next morning she would wake up late, have breakfast, and then type her pages from the night before. Her output usually amounted to eight pages, give or take a page. Though Aunt Irene projected a fluttery femininity to the world at large, at her core she was a hard worker who kept to her hours as sharp as any miner punching a time clock.

As my aunt waited for the coffee to percolate, she turned to the food. Bernice always prepared too much, and the leftovers were our weekly reward. "You girls were too, too kind to help out." She wrapped a wedge of cheese in waxed paper. "Callie, I could tell you made a few conquests."

Callie, collapsed in a chair by the kitchen table, let her tired legs sprawl out before her. Even in that relaxed pose, she resembled some impossibly elegant creature, like a ballerina, or a giraffe. She blew out a breath of exhaustion that disturbed the blond helix curls of her fringe. "I've never encountered so many gropers in one place. Even buyers in the showroom are less handsy when they check out the goods."

Aunt Irene shook her head at her guests' naughtiness. I suspected there would be a young model being pawed in the next Irene Livingston Green novel.

"What did you think of Ford Fitzsimmons?" I asked my aunt.

"You mean that sad fellow in the dining room?" Her lips formed a moue of displeasure. "Drinking too much is never becoming in a young man. It's rather coarse."

I preferred to think of him as a diamond in the rough. "I read a book he wrote. It was grand."

My aunt stilled before a plate of cookies. "What kind of book?"

"A coming-of-age story. Very tragic."

She relaxed a bit and slid the cookies into a tin. The word *tragic* dissipated any fear of competition. Happy endings, not tragic ones, were her specialty. In Irene Livingston Green's world, unhappy endings only befell villains who deserved a by-gosh good comeuppance. "What became of the book?"

"It was rejected."

She sighed, either in relief at having one less title to compete with, or commiseration, or both. "Poor boy. Well, he's still young. Not long out of college, by the look of him. Plenty of time for him to make his name." Her gaze sharpened on me. "But I wouldn't get involved with a writer if I were you. Especially a struggling one. Artist types make interesting friends, but disastrous husbands."

"I'm not looking for a husband."

"Nonsense," she said. "*Every* girl is looking for a husband, unless she's a fool."

"You didn't," I pointed out.

She aimed a sharp look at me. "Now, how would you know that? Maybe I looked but didn't find." She laughed. "For all you know, I'm still looking. I've even considered writing a book on the topic. *Never Too Old.* What do you think of that title?"

Callie's gaze met mine across the kitchen, and we smiled. Aunt Irene might pine for love, but if she never found it she would compensate herself by using her own private yearnings as fictional fodder.

Walter, who lived in Irene's basement, came back in from walking the dogs. He arched a brow at Callie's and my relaxed postures. "Looks like we're down to the last two scavengers," he told my aunt.

She laughed and let him take over the food wrapping and coffee preparation. Born plain Irma Mayer and raised with my mother and Aunt Sonja by a widowed scrubwoman, Aunt Irene was still too tickled to be in the position of having a butler to take offense at anything he did. To her, Walter was as much the embodiment of her success as her shelf of published books, her healthy bank account, or even this house.

Callie and I knew Walter's return was our cue to leave, so we dutifully got to our feet. I looped my leather satchel over my shoulder, causing Walter to shake his head.

"What?" I asked.

"That *bag*." He all but shuddered. "It always makes me think of the postman."

"You should see the inside," Callie said. "It's a magpie's nest in there."

I bristled a little at the criticism of my bag, which I'd found at a leather goods shop near Sheridan Square and for which I'd paid the incredible sum of eight dollars. It was made of handsome golden leather and was big enough to hold everything I could need while I was out and about. I didn't know how I'd survive in the city without it. Callie never carried anything bigger than a tiny purse she could slip over her wrist, so she never had a spare handkerchief, or a pencil and paper, or a book.

My aunt laughed. "Never mind, Louise. I think it's very modern. Makes you look like a girl prepared for anything."

"Or like someone about to knock on the door and say, 'Special Delivery,' " Walter said.

At the door, my aunt handed us an extremely generous five dollars for cab fare. There ensued a scene so predictable we all might have been reciting from a script.

"It's too much," I protested.

"We're just going downtown," Callie chimed in, "not to California."

Aunt Irene held firm. "If there's any left over, split it and have a little splurge on me. Or put a little something in your hope chests. You girls still have hope chests now, don't you? Althea does."

"Who's Althea?" Callie asked.

"My current heroine." She might be standing at the front door with us, but her mind was already at her desk.

Waved off in a flurry of lace and feathers, Callie and I headed toward Second Avenue, where we could pick up the elevated railway on Fifty-seventh. Neither of us could bear to spend the five dollars on a cab on a fine summer night when legging it to a train would leave us so much richer.

Once out of sight of Aunt Irene's windows, Callie snatched the five dollars from my hand.

"Hey, we're supposed to split that," I said. "For our hope chests, remember?"

My protest was met with amused refusal. "My hope chest needs replenishing now, after you spilled ink on that shirtwaist you borrowed."

This was news to me. "When?"

"Last week." She clucked her tongue. "I swear, you're becoming a hopeless wardrobe marauder. This morning one of my skirts showed flecks of dried mud, and I'd just cleaned it."

"I borrowed your skirt?"

She gave me an exasperated side eye.

It was true that I made too free with her clothes sometimes. She had so much—many of the items samples given to her at work, or purchased at a deep discount—and she was always generous in lending me things. But I needed to take better care. I silently vowed to mind myself around inkwells and puddles.

"What happened to you earlier?" I asked. "I waited at my office for ages before giving up on you."

"Did you?" I was expecting an apology. Instead, she skipped a step ahead of me and then turned back to face me as we walked. Pent-up excitement bubbled out of her. "What do you think, Lou? A producer came in today. Marvin Sanderson! I recognized him on sight, and if I'd vamped any harder around that showroom I would've dislocated a hip. The old goat"—she cleared her throat—"I mean, the *dear fellow* asked me to come round to his office this evening to audition as a replacement in a show of his." She wheeled in glee at the thought and practically skipped to the corner. "It's just a chorus part, but it would be a beginning."

Her face beamed as if she could already feel the heat of the footlights.

It was hard not to be swept away by her optimism, but to me the setup smelled as off as three-day-old fish. "I've never heard of evening auditions."

Her lips twisted into a wry smile. "You really did just fall off the turnip truck, didn't you?"

I caught the gist, and revulsion roiled inside me. In an instant I was back to my top floor room at Aunt Sonja's. Frantic. Unable to breathe. *Stuffy.* It had been a gorgeous afternoon, yet in that room with its cheerful cabbage rose wallpaper, the air was close and fetid. The windows had been shut. That was the detail that made the incident seem diabolical to me now. Had they been closed on purpose, or had I left them that way before I'd gone to work that morning?

"Louise?" Something of the disturbance I felt must have shown on my face, because she took my arm. "It was just a little canoodling. Every girl has to make a few little compromises to get ahead. You don't have to look as if I'd defiled myself."

The last thing I wanted to do was judge anyone. Callie often mistook my worry for prudishness. Now, for instance. "I swear," she continued, "sometimes you're as bad as Ethel."

At the name, a troubled silence settled between us.

Ethel. Callie's cousin from Little Falls. The bane of our existence. A month ago she'd arrived for a short visit to the big, sinful city, and was still with us. Why she stayed was a mystery. From the beginning she'd declared Manhattan to be noisy, smelly, filthy, and corrosive to moral hygiene. She was suspicious of all the inhabitants of our building, particularly Max, the painter who lived above us on the fourth floor with his Italian wife. Despite their having three small children, Ethel was certain the couple remained unmarried, and the patter of little feet overhead seemed to torment her all the more because of their unwed origins.

The trouble was, while Ethel never expressed anything but distaste for the city, she showed a maddening inclination not to leave it. In the first flush of hospitality, Callie had offered Ethel her own bedroom, our best. Now the woman was a permanent installation in Manhattan, like the Flatiron Building. She devoured our food, planted herself in the bathroom half the morning, and did so little housework we might have been her maids. She claimed to be in ill health, and some days truly looked frail and never got out of bed at all. But all my sympathy for her was neutralized by her tendency to sermonize nonstop on the evils of the city. The woman was Cotton Mather in a petticoat, and we were her unwilling congregation of two.

Another sore point was money. Ethel had chipped in very little for expenses. We'd been understanding at first, until in a rare moment alone in the apartment a week into Ethel's visit, Callie had run across a wad of bills in one of Ethel's spare boots.

"It might have been a hundred dollars," she'd told me excitedly that evening as we huddled in bed. "Maybe more."

I suggested we confront her with the fact that she was holding out on us, but Callie had demurred. To tell Ethel we knew about the money, she would have to admit that she'd been snooping. "She's got to pony up sometime," she'd insisted.

"Better yet, she's got to *leave* sometime," I said.

But days and then weeks had gone by, and neither sometime had come to pass.

In our rare moments of privacy, Callie and I wondered what Ethel did all day while we were at work.

"Maybe she's working on a new Methodist women's manifesto," Callie suggested once. Going to church on Sunday was one of Ethel's few regular outings.

"Or maybe she sneaks out and takes dance lessons." We'd dissolved into whoops at the idea of rigid, spinsterish Ethel ballin' the jack and turkey trotting when no one was watching.

The joking had been a couple of weeks ago, when Ethel seemed more humorous and less of a long-term irritant. When Ethel announced that her sister was coming to visit her, we'd rejoiced that our travails were almost ended. Surely Dora, the married sister with whom Ethel had lived most of her life, was coming to fetch Ethel home. But she arrived early one weekday morning, and by the time Callie and I returned from work that evening, Dora was gone and Ethel was still with us, locked in the best bedroom, weeping. Perhaps the sisters had argued. Ethel never said. The slightest mention of her sister's visit threw her into hysterics.

We weren't only tired of her, we were just plain tired. All this time that Ethel had indulged in splendid privacy, Callie and I had been sharing my tiny, airless bedroom. Callie snored, and she claimed I kicked. Neither of us had managed a good night's sleep in a month.

We stopped at Second Avenue and climbed the covered steps to the El platform. "Far be it from me to blame anybody for not wanting to go back to Little Yawns," Callie said, "especially if she and Dora had some kind of falling out. But why our apartment? I've got to get rid of her somehow."

"Anything short of murder will be fine with me."

"If she won't leave, she could at least give us some money," Callie said once we were clattering southbound on the train. "Why should I be responsible for her upkeep?"

We got off at Eighth Street and descended the platform. My worries about growing old and gray with Ethel were interrupted when I looked south at the tower of the Woolworth Building, glowing like a beacon. The nearly finished skyscraper had been a looming presence downtown when I'd arrived in New York, but now it had opened, electrified by a flick of a switch by Woodrow Wilson in Washington, DC, and its cathedral summit haloed in white lights made the stars and moon seem dim, unimaginative things in comparison. It was the tallest building in the world. Gorgeous. Audacious. And to me, terrifying.

Callie followed my gaze. "They've opened the observation gallery up at the top. We could go this Sunday."

Few things in this world frightened me, but heights did. I wasn't wild about elevators, either. "To the top of that thing?" I was still recovering from a ride on The Tickler in Coney Island the previous weekend. "Aren't there any pastimes in this city that don't involve machinery hurling us away from solid ground?"

She laughed, and we zigzagged south on Fifth and then west on Washington Square, facing the magnificent arch. We didn't go through the park but skirted its north end. The late hour meant most businesses were closed except a few restaurants, the corner newsstand, and taverns. The sidewalks were sparsely populated and puddled periodically in darkness where the streetlamps weren't sufficient. Callie and I instinctively linked arms as we strolled. As two women walking alone at night, we attracted a few speculative stares and at least one whistle from a stoop across the street.

Annoyed, Callie muttered "fresh" under her breath, but I hadn't been paying much attention. At every watering hole we passed, I wondered if it was the tavern Ford had planned to visit.

Two blocks from our apartment, someone waited at the corner. Callie's footsteps slowed, but the man, seeing her, rushed toward us. In the dim illumination cast by the streetlamps, his eyes held a feverish gleam.

"Sawyer," Callie said as he stopped in front of us. His appearing out of the blue had robbed her of the usual knowing tone she took with men.

Then again, this man left me a little breathless myself. Sawyer Attinger was a perfect specimen. His tall, broad-shouldered frame had made him a hero on the playing fields of Yale, but his chiseled features and golden hair no doubt would have made him the hero of women's hearts everywhere, regardless of his athletic prowess. In addition to those assets nature provided, he wore the finest tailored clothes and possessed the aristocratic bearing of a man accustomed to the world's bending in his favor. Callie summed it up best: Sawyer Attinger was rolling in dough.

As far as I could tell, the man possessed only one defect, but it was a fatal one. A certificate of marriage.

He reached out and held Callie's shoulders. "I've just been to your apartment. Nobody answered my knock. Where were you?"

Callie, more collected, let go of my arm and drew herself up in a regal stance. In looks, she was more than a match for the blueblood Sawyer—her fine-boned face betrayed nothing of her dairy farm origins. "I was out with Louise. Not that it's any business of yours."

He cut a dismissive glance my way and continued as if I weren't there. "Meeting men?"

Callie's brows drew together, a sure sign that her anger was roused. She slapped his hands away. "Wouldn't you like to know."

"Don't torture me," Sawyer pleaded.

Her rigid posture gave a fraction. "Then don't be a dope. We were at Louise's aunt's house."

"I was worried," he said.

"We didn't have a date," Callie reminded him.

"I know, but I was working late, so I thought I'd . . ." He shook his head. "I shouldn't have presumed, my darling. Of course a girl like you would seek out company."

Out of awkwardness I began to edge away from them, feigning curiosity in a bill someone had posted announcing an upcoming rally for women's suffrage in Union Square. Not that I wasn't interested in gaining the vote, or in seeing Lucy Burns and Alice Paul—suffragists I'd read about in newspapers—in the flesh, but I was much more concerned with Callie at the moment.

She darted out a hand and clamped it around my arm. "Stay,

Louise. Mr. Attinger won't be escorting me home. It's late, and I'm sure *his wife* will be worried."

His gaze filled with longing. "My wife has nothing to do with my feelings for you."

Callie only laughed.

"I've told you that I'll always take care of Margaret," he said.

She lifted her chin. "How generous! Pledging to me to take care of a woman you've already pledged before God to take care of till death do you part."

"Why can't you believe that Margaret and I are no longer in love? We're like two strangers rattling around under the same roof, both lonely."

"Not too lonely. I seem to recall there are two small children rattling around with you." She linked her arm through mine again. "It's late, and Louise and I have to work in the morning. Good night, Mr. Attinger. And good-bye."

We strode past him at a quick yet still dignified pace.

"Callie!" His wail at our backs echoed around the dark block, plaintive and desperate.

"You did right," I said to her under my breath.

"Oh, hang what's right." Callie scowled at the pavement. "I'm not noble. I just don't like liars, is all. A man who would cheat on his wife would cheat on anybody."

Her trembling arm belied her tough tone. After first meeting Sawyer, Callie had been over the moon. A month passed before she'd learned about the wife and children, and that discovery had been through her own detective work, not any pang of conscience on Sawyer's part.

"I'm sure he's got the message now," I said. "You made it plenty clear you wouldn't see him again under any circumstances."

Callie whipped toward me. "Oh no, did I really?"

Her worried expression confused me. "You *wouldn't* have anything to do with him, would you?"

"Well, for instance, if he got divorced . . ."

"You just said you couldn't trust him."

"But if he were to divorce his wife and marry me, that would be a whole different ballgame."

"Exactly. He might cheat on *you*."

"But I would be his wife. I'd have leverage, and security."

"What kind of security can there be in marriage to a man who's already set one wife aside?"

"More security than I've got now, or ever had. Have you ever woken up before dawn on a winter morning to do farm chores? Have you ever had chilblains from milking cows?"

"But you're here now, and you have ambitions. The stage, remember?"

Callie laughed. "When half a million dollars falls in love with you, remind me how much you enjoy being a secretary."

We entered our building, rejoiced that our landlady's son, Wally, wasn't lurking about, and hurried up the two flights of stairs to the apartment. The chorus of "Be My Little Baby Bumblebee" performed by five saxophones accompanied us.

"Still?" Callie hissed as we passed their door.

It *was* late. The Bleecker Blowers were lucky that Mrs. Grimes, the landlady, was stone deaf.

"I'm surprised Ethel hasn't lodged a complaint already," Callie said.

The apartment door was unlocked and a light was on inside, but the stillness around us made it clear that Ethel had already gone to bed.

Peeved, Callie muttered, "Miss Waste-Not-Want-Not wasting the electricity," as she unpinned her hat and hung it on the wobbly coat rack by the door.

I busied myself putting away the leftovers and breathed a sigh of relief when "Be My Little Baby Bumblebee" ended and wasn't followed by an encore. Maybe we'd have a peaceful night after all.

A piercing scream from the next room shattered that hope.

I raced to where Callie was standing in the doorway of what had been her room, the one Ethel had taken over.

"I just pushed the door open," she whispered, her voice a flutter of panic. "Just to check."

It was gaping open now. Inside, Callie's little bedside lamp was on, its green and yellow beaded shade casting a jaundiced glow over a grisly scene. In the center of the bed lay Ethel, facedown, a butcher's knife plunged into her back. A dark stain spread across her nightdress and the bedspread. One of her shoes—one of Callie's shoes, actually—dangled off her foot. On the rag rug lay a pair of once-white gloves now crimson with blood.

Callie's long-nailed fingers clawed my arm. "Send for a doctor."

I shook my head. I kept staring, taking in the gruesome scene, unable to look away. I'd encountered death only under the sedate, controlled conditions of the funerals and last viewings of distant relations, but this was different. The tableau before me was a horror that almost wrenched me from my mental moorings. Even so, there was no mistaking the ruthless stillness of death.

"We need to send for the police," I said.

Chapter 2

I wasn't the only one who'd been alarmed by Callie's scream. When I returned from running downstairs to shout for help, Wally, who lived on the first floor, charged up the stairs after me, followed by two of the saxophonists from the second floor. I didn't know any of the musicians very well—membership in the Bleecker Blowers seemed to rotate monthly—but that didn't stop them from barging right in. Moments later, Lucia from upstairs elbowed her way through in full-throated irritation at all the racket.

"All this noise, what is?" She added something in Italian that was beyond my feeble power in that language, garnered solely from listening to those aforementioned Caruso records. "Finally I put the bambini to sleep, and now—"

Her gaze fell on the bloodstained bed, and her skin went almost as pale as Ethel's. Fearing a faint, I took her arm, piloted her out to the nearest chair with no view of that bedroom, and then hurried to the kitchen and dampened a cloth to make a compress. What was taking the police so long? Mr. Weiss, a man next door who gave voice lessons, had promised to find an officer or a telephone to call the precinct. I'd last seen him running toward Seventh Avenue booming, "Police! Help!" in his stirring baritone.

While I was occupied with Lucia, Wally sidled up to Callie and put a hand on her shoulder. "Is there anything I can do for you?" he asked, practically drooling.

Her gaze could have frozen hot coals. "You can keep your mitts to yourself."

Wally retracted his hand, but I was almost grateful to him for snapping Callie out of the funk she'd fallen into since discovering Ethel. If anyone could do it, it was Wally. He was stout and humpbacked, with skin that had a persistent sheen of sweat. If his personality weren't so repugnant I might have pitied him, but his manner alternated between bossy and obsequious. His habit of lurking in his partially opened doorway and squinting up our skirts as we ascended the stairs made Callie dub him The Troll.

Rebuffed, the man appointed himself interim constable. "Nobody leaves the apartment," he announced.

"It would be better if Callie and I could be alone," I said.

He puffed up. "This is a crime scene."

"*La povera!*" Lucia cried. "And to think, all the while I upstairs, putting my little ones to sleep, she down here and then this." Her fist arced like a knife being wielded by a killer.

The gruesome pantomime sent a shudder through the room.

"How do you know this happened while you were tucking your children into bed?" I asked Lucia.

"I hear the shouting," she said.

Callie froze. "You heard Ethel being killed?"

"What did you hear?" I asked.

"I hear the lady. Even with the noise, I hear." She shook a fist angrily at the men from the second floor, who lingered. "*Sassofoni maledetti!*"

There followed what I gathered was a spew of curses against saxophones and inconsiderate men making noise while hardworking people with little children were trying to sleep.

Much as I sympathized, I had to interrupt. "What exactly did you hear, Lucia?"

" 'Alexander's Ragtime Band,' " she said.

The song was one of the Bleecker Blowers' favorites, but that wasn't what I meant.

"What did you hear Ethel shouting?" I asked.

Lucia nodded, understanding. "The lady shout, 'Stop! Stop!' I thinked she hate the music, too." She buried her face in her hands. "*La povera donna!* Only the devil could do such a thing."

"Then I saw the devil," Wally said excitedly, as if suddenly remembering. "I saw him!"

I turned to him. His skin shone with an extra sheen of excitement. "You saw someone in our apartment?"

"No, but I saw a man lurking in the stairwell. When he saw me, he ran out."

Maybe his trollish ways would prove useful for once. "When was this?" I asked.

"Earlier tonight. Half an hour, forty-five minutes ago. I remember looking out because I'd seen Miss Gail come in not too long before."

"You saw Ethel?" Callie frowned. "Coming in from where?"

He lifted his heavy arms. "How should I know? I'm not a snoop."

No, just a creepy staircase voyeur. "Did Ethel say anything to you about where she'd been?" I asked.

"Nah, she just scooted up the stairs. She's shy with men, I guess." He swallowed, remembering. "*Was* shy. Anyways, I saw her go up, so when I heard someone coming down not too long after, I says to Ma, 'Gee, I wonder if something's wrong with Miss Gail. She's not usually out at this hour.' That's when I looked out and saw the killer."

Callie glanced at me, then back to Wally, a new fear dawning in her eyes. "What did the man look like?"

"An average-sized kind of fellow." Wally wiped his brow with a yellowed handkerchief. "Wore pretty fine clothes. Blue suit, dark hat. But he was fair, with blue eyes."

Every word out of his mouth caused Callie's eyes to widen a fraction more. The description, general as it was, fit Sawyer Attinger. And Sawyer had even said he'd been here. I recalled those feverish eyes and his agitation. But why would he have waited to speak to us at the corner if he'd just killed someone in our apartment?

"Lucia," a deep voice behind us said. "We should go back upstairs."

I hadn't noticed our neighbor Max come in, which just showed how distracted I was. Lucia's husband's six-foot-four frame was impossible to miss, especially in our cramped rooms.

Wally threw his bulk into the doorway. "You can't leave. The police will want to speak to us all. Maybe you saw the killer, too."

"I didn't." Max, towering over him, looked as if he might squish Wally under his boot if he didn't move. "If the police want to talk to me or my wife, you know where to tell them to go."

The double-barrelled statement left Wally's doughy face contorted in confusion, and maybe a hint of fear. Wisely, he stepped aside. Max, a painter, had never caused any trouble in the building, but his imposing bearing and the angry red scar on his cheek bespoke a man who'd survived a brawl or two.

A policeman did arrive shortly thereafter, and Wally tackled him at once. "I saw the man who did it."

The officer hadn't as yet viewed the murder scene, and upon entering the apartment he seemed skeptical that the account of murder that he'd been given so far was actually true. His demeanor changed as he approached the bedroom and took in the scene in all its horror. "My saints," the man mumbled under his breath. "Aw, the poor lady."

I forced myself to stand beside him and look again. Once more, my gaze was arrested by the sight of that knife, and it dawned on me that it was the ten-inch butcher's boning blade from our own kitchen. I'd seen Uncle Dolph use one like it to hack twenty-pound turkeys clear in half, as easily as going through meringue. A set of knives had been his farewell gift to me when I left Altoona. He'd sharpened the edges to razor points, but I wasn't a cook and the ten-inch blade had never been used. Until tonight.

Poor Ethel. Tears welled in my eyes. What must she have gone through? I hadn't liked her much, but I'd never wished any harm on her.

"You knew this lady very well, I take it, miss," the constable said to me in a kindly tone. "She lived here?"

When I tried to respond, my throat constricted like a snake around a mouse. Callie saw, and answered for me. "Ethel was my cousin." She went on to tell him about Ethel's arrival and her prolonged stay. What little there was to tell.

As she spoke, my mind focused on other particulars. Something about the room was different from the first time I'd looked in, but I couldn't put my finger on exactly what. Something missing? The most striking detail was what Ethel was wearing: an ivory satin nightdress. The bloodstained garment belonged to Callie, and it was beyond strange that Ethel would have died in it, or had put it on at all. The matching shoes were also Callie's. And Ethel had blond hair, almost the same shade as Callie's. A chilling realization struck me: Facedown in that flowing gown, she might have been Callie herself.

I glanced over at my friend, and from the confusion in her eyes and the edge to her voice, I guessed she had also noted the resemblance and wondered what it meant.

As another policeman arrived, and then another, Wally regaled them with his account of the man on the staircase, who grew more sinister with each retelling. His third recitation added a new detail. "He was carrying something under his arm. Looked like one of those envelopes. You know—to hold papers. About so big." His two index fingers air-sketched a rectangle the size of the envelopes I handled all day long dealing with manuscripts at Van Hooten and McChesney. They were the preferred packaging of writers who didn't still wrap their manuscripts in butcher paper and string.

A blond man of medium build, wearing a dark suit, carrying an envelope to our apartment. I'd given Ford Fitzsimmons my address, and he'd left Aunt Irene's party at least an hour before I did. Could he have made it downtown in that short time, put a manuscript in an envelope, sought out my apartment, and . . .

I gave myself a shake. Why would Ford want to kill Ethel, of all people? Why would he kill anyone? The disgust on his face as he'd looked across the room at Callie came back to me. *Women are the devil,* he'd said. But disgust wasn't a motive for murder, was it?

Besides, I would have known if I'd been feeding egg-salad sandwiches to a maniac.

The policemen, after listening to Wally, turned back to Callie and me. "Does his description fit anybody either of you know?" one asked.

"Sounds like half the men in Manhattan," Callie said.

The first constable on the scene, a man of about forty, asked in an almost paternal air, "Many gentlemen callers here in the evenings?"

Callie raised her chin and declared, "I should say not," sounding almost as prim as Ethel.

"It's not that kind of house," Wally said. His offended tone might have been more believable if he hadn't been standing in his sweaty undershirt, looking as if he was used to making himself at home in our apartment.

The constable nodded. "No offense, girls. But you can see..." The tilt of his head toward the bedroom door brought it all back. The beaded lamp. Callie's pink tulle curtain rustling in the breeze. The blood-soaked satin nightgown. Blood pooling on the bedclothes. Yes. It looked sordid.

Poor Ethel. She would have been mortified, if she hadn't been dead already.

Soon, coroner's men were in the apartment, too, taking pictures, measurements, sketches. A new menace appeared in the shape of reporters, who were chased out but kept swarming back. How had they heard about the murder so quickly? Apparently newspaper men camped out in police stations waiting for grisly news they could leap on like vultures with notepads. And they weren't the only spectators. Once, I looked out the front window and saw a small crowd milling below. For some, murder was tragedy, for others, entertainment.

Two detectives in street clothes, Muldoon and Robinson, arrived and were set upon by Wally. The detectives dispatched several of their uniformed brethren to other apartments and adjacent buildings to make inquiries. Callie and I hung back, saying little to each other and even less to anyone else. While Muldoon and Robinson heard Wally's tale of the man on the stairs, I studied them. One was an older gentleman whose long face and downturned mouth reminded me of my sweet uncle Luddie, the fishmonger. When I was a little girl, Uncle Luddie used to hold up a fish head to his face and, turning down his own full lips, ask, "Which one's your uncle?" No matter how I answered, he'd burst out laughing. The old detective only bore a slight resemblance to a tuna head, but his face was kind. The other man, Muldoon, was younger, and peered at the world through fierce brown eyes. He wasn't as tall as his partner, but he exuded strength, like a boxer. Like a boxer, he had a crooked nose that looked as if it had been broken a few times.

Of the two men, I preferred Robinson. But when they sat Callie and me down, it was Muldoon who kept drawing my gaze. He eyed us with the fixed concentration of a mind reader, and the longer he looked, the more I squirmed. You'd think *I'd* killed Ethel.

The questioning began easily enough. They just needed to confirm details, Robinson said gently, and to find out more about Miss Gail, the victim. He asked if anything had been stolen.

"Not that I know of..." Callie's voice fractured into uncertainty. Neither of us had thought to check.

"The money," I blurted out.

Callie's startled gaze met mine. "Is it there?"

"What money?" Muldoon asked.

"I don't know," I said to Callie. I turned and hurried into the bedroom. Coroner's men were going over every inch of the room. I made a beeline for the wardrobe, keeping my eyes trained away from the bed, where Ethel lay. Both pairs of Ethel's button boots—the dull brown leather pair and her slightly fancier black ones with patent toes—stood next to the wardrobe.

"The money's in the black ones," said Callie, just behind me.

I picked them up and stuck my hand inside the right one, then the left. No money.

"Let's try the others," she said.

But the money wasn't in there, either.

"How much money are we talking about?" Robinson asked as Callie and I pivoted around the room, seeking other hiding places Ethel might have used.

"I'm not sure," Callie said. "I only ran across it once by chance, when I kicked the boot over. As I bent over to right it, I saw the wad of bills inside the boot. I didn't stop to count it—but it was over a hundred dollars, I'm almost certain. That was two weeks ago."

Robinson dug his hands in his pockets. "She might've spent it."

"On what?" I asked. "She's barely left the apartment in weeks. She certainly hasn't been on a shopping spree."

Muldoon jerked his chin toward the bed. "What she's wearing right now looks expensive."

Callie paled. "Those are my clothes."

The detectives' brows raised at that, and they steered us back out to our little parlor room, giving the men left in the bedroom a specific directive to keep an eye out for a wad of money. *And what is to keep one of the men from taking the money for themselves?* Such things weren't unheard of. The papers were full of stories of flagrant police corruption.

When we were all seated again, they verified Ethel's particulars: thirty-five, unmarried, not employed, visiting from upstate. Robinson was very gentle with Callie, who began to relax a little and even smiled once at Muldoon, for all the good it did her. The man looked as if his heart, if he had one, was carved from granite.

Then again, maybe a stone heart was an asset for a man whose job was untangling grisly murders. How did they stand it? This was my first encounter with violent death, and a quivering queasiness gripped me. I couldn't imagine my life ever being the same again. Yet the detectives saw horrors like this all the time. Did they go home to their families, kiss their wives, and eat dinner just like normal people? Knowing the worst of the world, how did they carry on?

She might have been crumbling inside, too, but Callie remained surprisingly collected as she talked about Ethel and gave the detectives the rundown of the evening. She told them we'd met at my office and gone to Aunt Irene's, stayed a few hours, and then came home on the train.

I frowned.

"Miss Faulk?"

Startled, I found myself in the beam of Muldoon's dark gaze. "I'm sorry," I piped up quickly. "I just—this is all so—" I was gibbering incoherently, which was not like me at all. Why had Callie said we'd met at my office? I hadn't seen her until she arrived at Aunt Irene's, late.

"We understand," Robinson said. "On top of everything else, you young ladies are probably very tired."

"Yes," I agreed, although I wasn't tired so much as numb. I couldn't imagine how I would ever sleep this night, or ever again. Certainly not in this apartment.

"Do you often gad about so late?" Muldoon asked.

Gad about? The implied criticism in that statement focused me again. "We were visiting my aunt, and we arrived home over an hour ago," I said.

"You both have jobs, am I right?" Two lines dug in between his dark brows. "Are you in the habit of staying out until eleven on Thursday nights?"

"It wasn't ten when we left my aunt's, and we were home by ten thirty. But yes, we go out most weeks. Aunt Irene has an at-home on Thursday nights."

Robinson's face creased in puzzlement. "A what?"

"A kind of house party," Muldoon translated. "So this was a regular occurrence, leaving Miss Gail alone in the apartment on Thursday nights?"

"Yes." I shifted in my seat. I had only ever invited Ethel to my aunt's house perfunctorily, and had unfailingly felt relieved when she declined, usually claiming fatigue. Ethel was always complaining of ailments like tiredness or tummy upset. The real reason she didn't go with us, I suspected, was that Callie and I framed our nights at Aunt Irene's in terms of having agreed to help out—as if we weren't actually guests ourselves. The implication was always that it would be awkward for Ethel to tag along, and we, of course, were happy that she didn't.

My smallness of spirit toward her shamed me now. If I'd been a little more generous and made her feel welcome to join us, maybe none of this would have happened tonight, and Ethel would still be alive.

My gaze strayed to the bedroom door. Just a few hours ago, Callie and I had been talking about getting rid of her. *Anything short of murder,* I'd joked.

"Had you noticed anything peculiar in Miss Gail's behavior lately?" Robinson asked. "Anything that might explain where that money might have come from, or gone?"

"No," we both answered at once.

"The money could have been her life savings, for all I know." Callie frowned. "Her parents died when she was still in her teens. Perhaps it was her legacy from them."

"A bank would have been a safer place than a boot to keep a large amount of cash," Robinson said.

There was no arguing with that. Callie and I didn't try.

"Miss Gail never begged off engagements because she hoped someone might drop by?" Muldoon asked. "Perhaps a man? A sweetheart?"

I just stopped myself from sputtering, and Callie's "Of course not" carried a whiff of amazement that the word *sweetheart* would ever be used in conjunction with her cousin.

"She's never mentioned a man's name to us," I said. "Ever."

When I'd last seen Ethel, that morning before work, she'd been sitting in the chair Muldoon was leaning over the back of now. She said she intended to spend the evening reading. I informed the detectives of this. "Why she felt the need to dress up in Callie's clothes to read a book is what puzzles me," I added.

"She never borrowed your clothes before?" Robinson asked.

"Never," Callie said. "Louise borrows my things, but never Ethel."

"What about as you were coming home?" Robinson asked. "Did you see or meet anyone near the building?"

I waited for Callie's no before chiming in with my own. I barely knew Ford, and there also was no reason to drag Sawyer Attinger, a married man, into this mess. The detectives were suspicious enough of our morals already.

I couldn't get Sawyer's words out of my head, though. *I've just been to your apartment.* Had he come *inside* the apartment? It hadn't been locked. We rarely locked the door if someone was at home, except right before we went to bed. And when we met him down the street, Sawyer had been stirred up, tense.

But what about the envelope Wally saw in the man's hands? Sawyer hadn't been carrying anything when we saw him. Nor had I noticed any blood. The man who'd stabbed Ethel would surely have come away with blood on his hands.

The most likely reason Ethel would have been killed was if someone had mistaken her for Callie. But Sawyer wasn't demented—he wouldn't have mistaken Ethel for the woman he claimed to love. Anyway, why would he have wanted to kill Callie?

Why had Othello killed Desdemona?

"You're very quiet, Miss Faulk," Muldoon said. "If you have any information that could help us, please speak up."

I shook my head. "It's all so confusing. And poor Ethel . . ."

Callie looked at me through a haze of tears. "Poor Ethel. I'll need to let Dora know what's happened."

Robinson, softening, suggested, "Perhaps it will be best to wait until morning. We can all speak again tomorrow."

"Yes." I jumped at the suggestion. It would be a relief to have everyone gone so I could talk to Callie, and think. Much as my heart wanted to convict Sawyer, my mind kept returning to the manila envelope Wally had seen. Ford Fitzsimmons probably had several of those in his apartment.

Muldoon's forehead creased, and I guessed he wanted to argue with his partner. But he didn't. Robinson leaned forward and gave Callie a paternal pat on the shoulder. "There now, Miss Gail, what you need is some rest."

She looked about her with shining eyes. The apartment was still crowded, and there was the matter of the bedroom with all that blood in it. Neither of us would find rest anywhere near it. "How?"

Muldoon straightened. "The lady upstairs, Mrs. Freeman, has offered you girls a bed for the night."

Max and Lucia had three children and two bedrooms. Where would we fit?

But Callie and I took in all the men still lingering, and Ethel's bedroom, and without further discussion we decided to go upstairs.

After we'd gathered a few things to take with us for our night at Max and Lucia's, the coroner's men came through from the bedroom with a stretcher. A white sheet covered Ethel, whose frame seemed smaller now than it ever had in life. *All flesh is grass,* that slight figure beneath the sheet seemed to announce. Ethel's final homily.

My last glimpse of the stretcher was a piece of ivory satin hanging out below the sheet. Splattered with red, the thin material fluttered as the bearers maneuvered through the doorway.

Callie gulped. "Where will they take her?"

"Bellevue," Robinson said. "The coroner will want to look at the body."

"An autopsy?" It sounded so ghoulish. A final insult to Ethel.

The two detectives looked at each other.

"I doubt a full autopsy will be necessary. There's little doubt that the knife caused the fatal wound, but perhaps there were other"—Robinson coughed—"depredations that weren't immediately visible to us."

Muldoon glowered at the word *depredations.* They meant Ethel might have been raped. Bile rose in my throat, and for a moment I thought I was going to embarrass myself.

Callie and I edged past several shouting reporters on the landing as we made our way upstairs clutching towels, toothbrushes, and nightgowns, seeking sanctuary from all this horror.

But there was little peace at Max and Lucia's. There was no Max, either.

At our light tap, Lucia threw open the door and jerked us inside. Then, as soon as the door had closed behind us, the woman collapsed like a punctured tire and wailed at us in Italian. In moments when Lucia reverted to her native tongue, Max's interpreting skills were essential. Callie and I could only stare at her, uncomprehending, as we cast the occasional inquisitive glance around the flat. The parlor had been divided by a bed sheet to create a semi-private space next to the high front windows for Max's makeshift painting studio. The curtain was drawn, leaving just enough room for a long, narrow table and chairs—the family dining room. Paint, turpentine, and garlic mingled in the air.

"Where is Max?" I asked, attempting to hoist Lucia up from the rug.

"He go!" she cried, still on her knees. "I say to policeman he has the night work, but is no true. He just go!"

"Isn't he coming back?" Callie asked.

"*Non lo so! Non lo so!*"

That sounded like a negative to me. As quickly as we could, Callie and I extricated ourselves from Lucia and shut ourselves up in the bedroom she offered us—hers and Max's. Lucia indicated she would sleep with the bambini, but even with the door closed, we could hear her wailing through the thin wall. I doubted any of us would really sleep this night.

Callie and I changed and climbed into bed; then we lay on our backs, staring at the ceiling and trying to ignore the *basso continuo* of despair coming from the next room. The pillow slip beneath my head smelled of Max's clove-scented hair tonic. I flipped the pillow over, punched it down, and tried to relax. But when I shut my eyes, the scene of that bloody bed flickered across my closed lids.

"Thanks for not saying anything about Sawyer," Callie whispered.

I didn't mention that I was shielding Ford, too. At least until I had time to think this through. Then I remembered Muldoon's mistrustful gaze. "Maybe we should have."

"No," she said. "Sawyer wouldn't harm a fly. And why would he kill Ethel?"

"Why would anyone?" I asked. "Unless he thought she was you."

"He wasn't that drunk."

I hadn't even realized he was drunk at all. Perhaps that accounted for the feverish look in his eyes. I nearly clucked my tongue like Ethel. Men and their liquor. Sometimes I almost believed the crazy prohibitionists had a point.

"Why did you tell the detectives that we met at my office?" I whispered into the dark.

"I didn't want them going to Mr. Sanderson, the producer, and questioning him." As she spoke, her voice took on an edge. "This could be my big break—a murder could muddle it all up. You understand that, don't you?"

I was trying to, although lying seemed to be putting self-interest ahead of finding Ethel's murderer. Yet wasn't I doing that, too, by not telling Robinson and Muldoon about Ford Fitzsimmons? Omitting information was little better than a lie.

"What happened to Ethel's money?" I wondered aloud.

"Beats me. Who could have known she had it?"

That stumped me. Callie and I were the only ones who'd been aware of it, and that was only by accident. Who else could have gone looking through Ethel's boots?

Callie lifted onto her elbows and looked down at me. "You don't think *I* did it, do you?"

"What—stole Ethel's money?" I asked, surprised.

"Or killed her. Because I didn't do either, I swear."

As if I or anyone else could imagine Callie stabbing a person. "No, of course not."

She blew out a long breath and lay flat again. "It's all so awful. Why was she wearing my nightgown?"

I had no answer for that, either. Ethel had nightgowns of her own—high-necked, long-sleeved, and made from flannel so sturdy we'd once joked that her nightclothes could double as armor. All of our guffawing behind her back saddened me now.

"What will I tell Dora and Abel?" Callie whispered. "If I can't get them on the phone tomorrow morning, I'll have to send a telegram. Imagine getting news like this in a telegram. It's too horrible."

No more horrible than walking into your apartment and finding your cousin murdered. Except that Dora, no matter what kind of argument they'd had earlier this month, probably loved Ethel. You'd have to love your sister a little after living with her all that time. It comforted me somewhat to think Ethel would truly be properly mourned by someone. We certainly weren't doing a good job of it.

Through the wall came the sound of Lucia blowing her nose.

"You don't think it was Max who killed her, do you?" Callie whispered.

"No . . ." Max might not be a charmer, but he had never spoken an unkind word to me. In a building full of men, he was the most helpful of them all. And he was a family man, with everything to lose. Besides, if Max killed Ethel, who was Wally's man on the stairs?

On the other hand, Max had disappeared. Heaven knows he and Lucia were poor, and now Ethel's money was gone. And if he had murdered Ethel, Lucia's hysterics could be viewed in a whole different light. So could her offer of a place to sleep. Perhaps Max told her to extend the neighborly invitation in order to deflect suspicion.

The night was warm, but a chill worked its way right into the marrow of my bones. I pulled the covers all the way up to my chin. From the Hudson came the deep lowing of a ship's horn. Callie looked over at me in the dark, and I knew the same question held us both in its grip.

Were we sleeping in a murderer's bed?

The clopping of hooves on pavement from a delivery wagon jolted me out of a fitful sleep that had been an agony of disturbing dreams. There was no question of either Callie or me going to work that day. Our building had no telephone, so I dressed quickly in yesterday's clothes and headed to the corner candy store, which allowed us to use theirs. At first I wondered if my boss would believe me when I told him what had happened. Then I passed the newsstand.

Several papers announced the murder on their front pages, and a couple gave it so much prominence that Ethel even squeezed out General Pershing's battles in the Philippines. The Battle of Bud Bagsak was yesterday's news. What could the death of over three hundred soldiers on a faraway island be compared to a lurid local murder? One rag, *The New York World Bulletin,* featured the story above the fold along with a picture of our narrow four-story brick building, which appeared little more than a shadowy, sinister hulk in black and white. The headline screamed, BUTCHERY IN GREENWICH VILLAGE.

I bought several papers, called Mr. McChesney at home—waking his entire household, probably—blurted out my tale in only slightly less sordid language than the newspapers to a half-awake servant, and hurried back home on quivering legs. I needed to get ahold of myself. I inhaled deeply. This was the only time of day in Manhattan when a deep breath really held any appeal—just after the street-cleaning wagons had cleared the bitumen and concrete of their usual film of soot and dirt, and the traffic had yet to gin up to the point that the air was its usual choking brew of exhaust, dust, and manure. The June sky spread out overhead as clear and blue as a tropical sea.

And a woman I'd lived with for the past month wasn't alive to see it.

I'd intended to carry the milk the deliveryman had left at our door up to Lucia's, but when I reached the third-floor landing, the bottle was gone and the door stood wide open. I rushed inside, assuming Callie had come downstairs. Instead, I found myself face-to-face with Detective Muldoon.

He stood in the hallway to Ethel's room, hat tipped back, with our milk bottle in his hand. He was wearing the same suit from last night, and his bloodshot eyes spoke of an even more sleepless night than I'd had. Although at some point he'd taken the time for a shoeshine and shave.

"Detective? What are you doing here?"

He took me in without a smile. Doubtless I looked as rough as he did.

"I came to find Miss Gail, and then to speak to Mr. and Mrs. Freeman. When I discovered this apartment empty, I decided to have another look at the murder room."

I could just glimpse the bloody bedclothes in the room beyond him. Why would anyone want to look at that again?

"You're up early, Miss Faulk," he observed.

I frowned, still trying to adjust to the fact that my apartment now appeared to be police property. "Last night you were concerned that I was out too late. You seem to have an unusual preoccupation with the hours I keep."

His answer was an assessing, level stare. It was effective.

"I went to the corner store to telephone my employer," I said. "Too late I realized that the whole world wasn't up just because I was. I'm still rattled."

"Understandable." He fell silent.

"Is there some specific reason for your visit, Detective?"

He hesitated, weighing his words so cautiously that I worried something bad had been discovered overnight.

"I hope you're not going to upset Callie," I said before he could speak. "She had a difficult night." Several times I had awakened, disoriented in the unfamiliar room, to the sound of her sobbing.

"Actually, the news is good," he said. "The medical examiner found no evidence of Miss Gail's having been molested."

"I see." *Not raped, just stabbed to death.* That sunny bulletin constituted good news to Detective Muldoon.

Silence stretched, and his gaze narrowed. "Now that your friend isn't here, is there anything you can tell me that you couldn't last night?"

Tempting as it was to give Sawyer's name to the police, I'd promised Callie I wouldn't. Instead, I asked, "Couldn't the murderer have been some person neither of us knows?"

"A random madman, you mean?"

"Or a burglar, for instance."

He tilted his head. "We are considering that. . . ."

"But?" I prompted.

"Apart from money, nothing else seems to have been taken. And we can't even be sure about the money. You said it was hidden, and that only you and your roommate knew of it." He tilted his head but kept a steady gaze on me.

I swallowed. "Well, perhaps the burglar came in and forced Ethel at knifepoint to show him what money she had. She gave it over, but he killed her anyway."

"But in your random burglar scenario, it would have made more sense for the man to simply have run out of the apartment when Miss Gail called out. There would have been no reason to stab her at all." He shook his head. "In my opinion, the attack was direct, purposeful. The killer even seemed to know how to find the largest, sharpest knife in the apartment."

Not random, then. Perhaps someone I knew. I couldn't forget Callie's lie about when she'd arrived at my aunt's, even though I felt like a traitor thinking about it at all. Besides, Wally said he'd seen Ethel coming up the stairs *hours* after Callie would have arrived at Aunt Irene's. Nevertheless, I asked, "Do you know what time Ethel was killed?"

"The coroner estimated between nine and ten, not long before the body was discovered."

That squared with what Wally had said about seeing Ethel on the stairs, but I was puzzled. "How does the coroner know?"

Muldoon's brows beetled, as if this were some sort of alchemy a person like me couldn't understand. "Body temperature, and the state of rigor mortis. That kind of thing."

"Rigor mortis?"

He took a breath. "How set the muscles become after death. After about two to four hours, a rigid stiffness sets in."

"How gruesome." I was fascinated, actually, but Muldoon didn't seem interested in enlightening me further on the subject of forensics.

"Miss Faulk, how well do you know your upstairs neighbors?"

"You think it was Max?" I'd wondered the same thing last night, but I didn't want it to be him. "Max and Lucia are good people. They might not be married, technically, but what does that really matter?"

His brows raised slightly. Free love and unwedded bliss might be common in our neighborhood, but Greenwich Village wasn't the world. It wasn't even typical of New York City.

I swallowed, trying to think of a better defense. "Max was always generous. He helped us put up curtains in the kitchen and bedroom. And he and Lucia are certainly nicer than the people who lived upstairs before. When we first moved in, there were three Portuguese anarchists up there. I didn't mind that they were Portuguese, of course, and even anarchists for neighbors aren't bad as long as they keep their pamphleteering to a minimum. The worst was that they seemed to live on salt cod. The odor! I'm no stranger to fish smells, but the stink was almost enough to send me back to Altoona."

My babbling was finally halted when I caught Muldoon's unamused glower. "Better for you if it had."

"I don't think so."

"Miss Faulk, Max Freeman was once convicted of a crime. A serious crime. I need to speak to him."

What did Muldoon consider *a serious crime?*

"Did Max Freeman seem especially friendly toward Ethel?" he asked. "Or Callie?"

"So you suspect Ethel's killer thought she was Callie."

He hesitated. "It's a possibility. They had similar hair color and height. And according to you and Miss Gail, Ethel knew very few people here."

"But the lights were on," I pointed out. "In the light, no one could have mistaken Ethel for Callie."

"The lights could have been turned on after Miss Gail was killed."

"That would be a stupid thing for a murderer to do."

"Don't believe what you read. Criminals aren't masterminds."

I supposed that was good news for the authorities, because from what I'd witnessed so far, detectives weren't masterminds, either.

Without any experience or resources at my disposal, I had divined as much as they had. And, criminal record or no criminal record, the more I considered Max, the less likely a suspect he seemed. He knew Ethel—he certainly wouldn't have confused her for Callie. And even given the extremely remote possibility that he'd meant to murder Ethel, why would he have done so when his wife was right upstairs?

Except for the money. Wally had said Ethel had come upstairs before the murder. What if she'd walked in on Max stealing? But then, that wouldn't account for her being dressed in a nightgown, especially one of Callie's nightgowns.

As far as I knew, Max hadn't returned during the night. Now I wasn't sure I wanted him to. He would be an especially choice suspect when the police realized he'd hoofed it. But if he'd had a previous run-in with the police, that might be reason enough to explain his disappearance.

"What was Max's crime?" I asked.

"Assault." His lips turned down. "With a knife."

"Oh." So much for our helpful, even-tempered neighbor. I remembered Lucia's hysterics, her sobs. I just hadn't wanted to believe Max was bad. No wonder Muldoon was here so early. He and Robinson had encouraged us to accept the murder suspect's hospitality.

"I beg you, Miss Faulk, do not shield the man, no matter how much you like your neighbors."

"Of course I won't." I spoke as if such a thing would never have entered my mind, yet there were two men I was already shielding with silence.

Did I have a right to? Without the information Callie and I had, Max was the detectives' lone suspect. The story had become front-page news, which meant that there would be pressure to arrest someone and wrap up the case with a shiny, tidy bow for the papers.

Poor Max. Unless, of course, he *was* guilty.

A door slammed downstairs, followed by sounds of a scuffle. Wally's voice, high-pitched with excitement, cried out, "I've got him! The murderer! Police!"

Muldoon and I exchanged surprised looks before we raced down the stairs. By the time we reached the landing, a few saxophonists in dressing gowns or pajamas were already on the scene. Wally knelt before the closed front door, pinning down a slight blond man by the scruff of his jacket collar. An envelope lay on the floor next to them.

Wally spotted Muldoon and beamed proudly. "Got him for you, Detective! The very man I saw on the stairs last night!"

He stood and lifted his arm, drawing the man up to his tiptoes as easily as if he were a puppet on a string. When the blond man turned toward me, I gasped. I knew him—but I knew him from Altoona, not here. Blue eyes that used to gaze at me over the meat counter now bulged in panic. "Louise!" he said.

I still couldn't quite believe my eyes. "Otto?"

Chapter 3

At the precinct where Muldoon took Otto for questioning, a desk sergeant with salt-and-pepper hair and a gruff voice directed me to wait on a bench. I waited. And waited. For two hours the derelict, the drunk, and the criminal were dragged past me to areas beyond my sight. They were the ones who received immediate attention here. Others—complainants and visitors like myself—waited. Despite how difficult it was for me and my backside to endure, given how worried I was about Otto and how hard the bench was, I couldn't help being riveted by the action going on around me. I'd never been in a police station. Now I had a front row seat to the passing parade of the most immediate drama in the city.

Under feebly swirling overhead fans barely stirring up the stale air, people came and went, some meekly, but others arguing, hollering, or even weeping. A mother sought her missing son, a man complained he'd been robbed on the Sixth Avenue El, and one man arrived, head tipped back and blood down his front, shouting that his wife had clouted him at the breakfast table with a butter bell. All the while, policemen drifted in and out much the way my coworkers did at Van Hooten and McChesney, and in the background there was the familiar beehive buzz of office sounds—file drawers banging open and closed, the distant clack of a typewriter, low-voiced conversations, and even, occasionally, laughter.

All the while, I worried about Otto. Back at the apartment, events had unfurled so chaotically that nothing had made sense. Stunned to be taken for a murderer, Otto had only been able to stammer out his innocence and, more inexplicably, something about a song. Meanwhile, Wally had blustered, Muldoon barked out questions, I pleaded, and Lucia came down and burst into tears of relief and thanksgiving that it wasn't Max who'd been collared.

Frankly, it didn't help that Otto looked guilty, just normally. He was thin and nervous, with eyes that bulged slightly, like a pug dog's. But what that Cossack Muldoon couldn't see was that inside Otto's concave chest beat a heart as honest, true, and un-homicidal as they came.

What was he doing in New York? Why had he shown up at my apartment last night of all nights—and then again this morning, walking right into Wally's and Detective Muldoon's clutches? He might as well have been wearing a sandwich board announcing, "I killed Ethel." Not that he *did* kill her. I didn't believe that for a moment.

Muldoon hadn't listened to Otto's protestations or mine. No matter that the purpose of the detective's morning visit had been to question Max and Lucia. When Muldoon found a live suspect on his hook, he'd been just as happy to reel Otto in as go hunting for Max. There in the apartment building's foyer I'd felt like sinking to my knees and going into hysterics before him, but unlike Lucia I'm not the operatic type. I'm the dogged type.

Finally, a policeman informed me that I could speak to Otto. I'd heard interrogations could be rough, so I mentally girded myself to find Otto black and blue. The police were searching for a vicious killer. Every person walking past me or waiting in the station, and every copper with an idle moment, was reading about the murder in Greenwich Village. One story carried a subheading, TENANT TUSSLES WITH FAIR-HAIRED SUSPECT ON STAIRS OF MURDER HOUSE. Another more lurid one read, A BEDROOM DRENCHED IN BLOOD. Around me, lips pursed and heads shook, and mutters of outrage about the abomination perpetrated against a helpless woman hung in the air. In death Ethel had become the personification of the very perils of the wicked city that she'd been sermonizing about for the past month. The primary suspect in her murder wouldn't have an easy time of it here.

The policeman led me up a flight of stairs and we passed a police matron on her way down. I'd seen women in uniform on a few occasions but hadn't given them much thought. Now I had a hard time looking away from her in her high, starched collar, brass-buttoned jacket, and crisp blue skirt. What must it be like for her, working in this place every day? I bet it made my own job seem colorless by comparison.

My guide in blue led me through a door opening onto a large room that we entered via a waist-high wooden gate. Four desks dominated the room, a couple of them manned at the moment by men in street clothes—detectives, I assumed. I didn't see Robinson or Muldoon. At one end of the room there were several doors that appeared to be offices. File cabinets lined the adjacent wall, and directly opposite the offices was what I can only describe as a cage. Inside, like animals in a zoo, sat a couple of unsavory-looking characters and Otto.

He spotted me, hopped to his feet, and grasped the metal bars. "Louise! Over here!" He hallooed my name as if we'd been separated at a carnival. The greeting raised a few chuckles and calls for him to keep his shirt on.

At least Otto wasn't black and blue, or garbed in prison stripes . . . yet. He still wore his own clothes, a mustard brown suit that was probably a recent purchase but now looked rumpled and dusty. His straw boater was pushed far back, like a saint's medieval halo, giving a view of his freckled forehead and his hair's center part.

My policeman steered me over to a worn table near this holding pen and told me to sit down. "You get ten minutes with your pal."

"Ten minutes?" Anger rose in my throat. "I've waited two hours."

"Muldoon's orders." He pulled Otto out and locked the cage again. "No passing anything," he warned. "I'll have my eye on you two."

As if we were criminals! Rage thundered in my breast, but Otto seemed unfazed by it all. His eyes were bright with excitement to see me, and he took my hands across the table as if we were meeting at the drugstore fountain in Altoona. His lips turned down only momentarily as he regarded me with concern.

"Are you all right?" he asked.

Was *I* all right? "I'm not the one in the jail cell."

"But that poor lady, the one who was killed. Mr. Muldoon told me all about it. Was she really a friend of yours?"

"My roommate's cousin," I explained. "She was staying with us."

"That's horrible. I'm so sorry."

"Otto, why—"

Before I could get the words out, he squeezed my hand and gushed, "Gee, it's good to see you again, Louise. It's been so long. You up and disappeared so fast last year, I worried something had happened to you."

Beneath the table, my leg began to jiggle. I pulled my hands away from his. A wave of guilt suddenly hit me for how I'd treated Otto. He was right. I'd fled town leaving him nary a word, and even after he'd written I'd replied only once and hadn't sent my new address to him when Callie and I moved. It was no way to treat an old friend. "I just had to get out," I explained.

"Oh, I understand. You never did like Altoona much. Still, I was frantic those months until your Aunt Sonja finally gave me your address at the hotel. I don't know why she waited so long to tell me where you were."

I stared at the table. "I'm sorry—I should have written to you earlier myself."

"Well, never mind all that now. New York obviously agrees with you. You're even prettier than I remembered."

"Attaboy, Romeo!" one of his holding cell confederates yelled. Though policemen barked at him to shut up, several sneering glances were directed toward our table.

I glared at the sneering men and then turned back to Otto, who was still gazing at me as if he hadn't heard a thing. I wanted to shake him. "Otto, what a mess." I lowered my voice. "Why were you at my apartment?"

"I know it was early, but I couldn't wait to see you."

"I mean last night. What were you doing there last night?"

"I wasn't there last night. I explained all that to Mr. Muldoon."

I'd known Otto hadn't killed anyone, but it never occurred to me that he hadn't been Wally's man on the stairs. He'd made that protest before Muldoon had hauled him away, but I'd assumed he was just muddled, or afraid to admit it. Under the circumstances, collared by the Wyatt Earp of Greenwich Village, who *wouldn't* have been afraid?

I should have known Otto wouldn't lie.

"The man on the first floor, Wally, said he saw you last night," I said.

"He's mistaken. I was lots of places last night, but never at your apartment."

"How long have you been in town?"

"Since night before last. Yesterday"—he practically quaked with remembered pleasure, and his face broke into a huge grin—"yesterday was the most incredible day of my life, Louise. That's what I was in such an all-fired hurry to see you about. What do you think? A song of mine's been published! And it's going to be made into a phonograph record. Guess by who."

I could barely absorb what he was talking about, much less switch mental gears from police precinct to Tin Pan Alley. "Who?"

"None other than the Denver Nightingale himself, Mr. Billy Murray." He gave his head a sharp shake as if he still couldn't believe his luck. "Remember how we used to listen to his record of 'The Sidewalks of New York'? And here we are!"

There we were. In a police station. "We're not exactly tripping the light fantastic."

"Well, no. But someday soon people will be listening to Billy Murray singing *my* song."

"That's marvelous." I tried, none too successfully, to infuse my voice with enthusiasm. The song might create a sensation, but the songwriter would be in Sing Sing.

"I was bringing you a copy of the music. They gave me a whole stack yesterday." He frowned, as if he suddenly remembered what had happened since then. "Mr. Muldoon took them."

That's what had been in the envelope, then. An unfortunate incriminating detail. And yet, it hadn't been Otto whom Wally saw last night. So who had it been?

"I'm happy for you, Otto, but I'm also worried."

My anxiety didn't faze him any more than his spending a morning in a jail cell had. It was as if he hadn't heard me at all. "I dedicated the song to you, Louise."

How could someone be so unconscious of the precipice he was standing next to? He was like one of those screen comedians staring up at the sky as he strolled ever closer to an open manhole. And now I was in a conundrum myself. I always was with Otto. I'd liked him since we were kids in school, but for years now it had been clear that he wanted to be more than friends. I had rebuffed him twice, officially, but Otto lived by the maxim "Persistence pays."

"I'm honored," I said. "I really am, but—"

"Remember all the times you said that you were sure I'd make a big success with my songwriting if I just kept at it?"

Actually, *he'd* said that and I'd mostly nodded along, never quite believing his dream ever would amount to anything. When you're working in a butcher shop, achieving songwriting fame seems only slightly more likely than establishing oneself as a Bedouin prince.

"Otto, I don't think you realize the dreadful situation you're in."

"You mean the murder? Gosh, you don't think I did it, do you?"

"Of course not, but people can be convicted of crimes they didn't commit."

"Sure, but I've got all sorts of proof that I wasn't there last night."

Thank heavens! "Where were you?"

"Looking for you, mostly."

"Where did you go?"

He sighed as if he'd been over it all before, and I supposed he had. With Muldoon. "Well, first I ate supper at a café. Had a pretty darn good ham sandwich and a chocolate soda."

"What restaurant?"

His forehead wrinkled in concentration. "I've been trying to think of the name. It was smack dab in the center of town, I know that much. Are there a lot of restaurants thereabouts?"

Only a hundred or so. My heart sank. "Was anyone with you?"

"Nope, I was all by my lonesome. I stopped by that hotel you stayed at, but you'd moved, obviously, since I got that one letter, and the lady there at the desk said they couldn't just give out girls' addresses to any Tom, Dick, or Harry, even if I did have a professional connection to Billy Murray. So I wandered awhile, then went back to my hotel and fell asleep. Then, in the middle of the night, it hit me. You'd written to me about going to your aunt's house on Fifty-third Street—you even described the house with the red door and the lion carved into its pediment. I've read that letter so often in five months I practically know it by heart. So first thing this morning, I raced up there and hunted down the house." He blew out a breath. "That's a long street."

"I can imagine how showing up before breakfast went over with Aunt Irene." Not to mention Walter and Bernice.

"She didn't look happy," he admitted. "But then I told her about my song, and Billy Murray, and she perked right up and said it sounded fascinating. She even invited me to her place next Thursday, and of course she told me where you lived." He drummed his fingers on the table, looking truly worried for the first time. "You think I'll be out of here by next Thursday? I'd sure hate to miss your aunt's party."

"You'll be out of here by suppertime or a certain detective will have my claw marks all over him."

"I told Mr. Muldoon everything I could. He seems like a right type to me."

Everyone seemed "a right type" to Otto, including the bullies who'd beaten him up in grammar school. He never saw anything but the best—or the potential for the best—in anyone.

"Don't make a fuss on my account," he said. "You have enough to worry about, after what happened to your friend's poor cousin in your apartment."

"Okay, miss." The policeman who'd escorted me in stood over us. "Time's up."

I was on my feet in an instant. "I need to speak to Detective Robinson."

"He's not here."

Rats. "Muldoon, then."

The policeman pulled Otto out of his chair and locked him back in the cell. When he turned around again, he looked dismayed to see me still standing there. Had he expected me to vanish?

"I'm not leaving until I've spoken to Muldoon," I said.

The man heaved a sigh. "Follow me."

Otto clung to the bars of the cell and shouted after me. "If you pass a music store today, look for my song. Ask a clerk to play it for you."

We crossed the busy room to one of the offices. The officer rapped on the glass panel and then cracked the door open. He just managed to say, "There's a lady out here who—" before I skirted past him into the room. I had no intention of being shunted off to warm a bench for another two hours.

"You need to let Otto go," I said over the officer's apologies.

Muldoon waved the man away while keeping his eyes on me. "It's all right, Scanlon. I can handle this."

"Otto didn't do it," I said.

He seemed almost amused. "You have proof of that, do you?"

"*You* have proof. He told you what he was doing last night."

His lips turned down. "I've got an eyewitness who says he's lying."

"Wally's an idiot."

"Idiots sometimes give the most honest testimony."

"Not this idiot," I argued. "Didn't you notice that squint of his? He's half blind. Not to mention, the fathead was chomping at the bit to act the hero. Who do you think blabbed that description of the man on the stairs to the papers?"

"I never said I took the man's word as gospel."

"I should hope not. Did you look at the suit Otto's wearing? It's not what I'd call a dark suit. Would you?"

He tugged his ear in thought. "Could've appeared darker in the dim hallway." His frown deepened. "Or Klemper might've changed suits."

I was about to challenge him to go to Otto's hotel room and check, but for all I knew he already had a policeman there. And maybe Otto did have another suit. And what if he had enough money from publishing that song of his to make it look as if he'd taken Ethel's stash?

"Surely you can find out that Otto's story about last night is true," I said.

"Oh, yes. I can't tell you how much I'm looking forward to asking every waiter and waitress in midtown if they remember serving a guy a ham sandwich."

"What about my aunt?" I persisted. "She'll be able to vouch that she spoke to him."

"This morning," he pointed out.

"But doesn't that prove Otto didn't know where I live until this morning?"

"It might just show he wanted us to think he didn't. Especially after he woke up and saw the morning papers telling all about the mysterious light-haired man in the stairwell."

Frustration gripped me. I wanted to throttle Wally. "It wasn't Otto," I insisted. "Anyway, Wally just saw a man on the stairs. He didn't witness the man killing Ethel—or even notice blood on his hands."

Muldoon continued as if he hadn't heard me. "Otto Klemper was even carrying an envelope this morning, just like Wally Grimes described."

He tossed the incriminating envelope onto the table in between us.

"There are a million envelopes like that one in this city," I said. "Besides, what murderer in his right mind would show up bright and early at the apartment house where he knifed a woman in her bed ten hours before?"

"You'd be surprised at the odd things murderers do, Miss Faulk."

"It doesn't make sense," I insisted. "And answer me this: Does Otto act like a guilty man?"

He gave a shake of his head—not to agree with me, but to show his disdain for the question. "Look, it's no good your carrying on like this. It's admirable of you to stand up for him this way, but we both know you'd say anything to clear your sweetheart."

"He's not my sweetheart, he's a friend from my hometown. We went to school together, and he worked for my uncle Dolph."

"That would be your uncle the butcher."

Butcher, such a prosaic word from my past, now sounded sinister.

"Just because Otto worked as a butcher's assistant doesn't make him a murderer. In fact, my uncle nearly fired him because he broke down weeping the first time he had to dress a pig. Otto's notoriously squeamish."

"Why'd your uncle keep him on as an assistant, then?"

"Because he's dependable and conscientious, and good for business besides. He used to make up little songs about the shop and sing them for the customers." I cleared my throat and sang, as best as I could remember, " 'Brach's Fresh Meats are the best to eat,' and 'For a sausage or a ham hock, it pays to take yourself to Brach's.' "

Muldoon's face was pure bafflement. "Customers liked that?"

Evidently, my warbling didn't do justice to Otto's ditties. "The little songs kind of stuck in people's minds. Like an advertisement for the ear."

His gaze regarded me steadily. "You sound like his agent."

"I'm his friend."

"He gave me the impression that he was a little more than that."

"All right, he might be a little sweet on me—"

"A little?" He emitted a sputter, plucked up the envelope, and spilled out its contents. Sheet music fanned out onto the table. The cover was eggshell blue and bore the sepia-toned drawing of a beautiful girl with braids and a cap. Above the illustration, in fat brown letters, was the title "My Tootsie from Altoona." At the bottom left were the words *Music and Lyrics by Otto Klemper*. Then, on the right-hand side, in smaller letters, *For Louise*.

I reached instinctively for the music, surprised to find myself blinking back tears. Not because the song was dedicated to me. This sheet music, soon to be selling everywhere for ten cents a copy, represented a dream come true for Otto. No wonder he'd been bursting with excitement, even in his holding cell.

"Billy Murray's going to record it," I heard myself bragging.

Muldoon's mouth twisted. "You don't say."

Otto had already told him, apparently.

I opened it to the first page. Despite a painful year of piano lessons, I couldn't sight-read music very well, so I scanned the lyrics.

She's my tootsie from Altoona!
She's my all-time, ragtime fräulein!
And believe me, I'd as soon-a

Lose my wealth,
Even health,
Than lose that sweet, sweet gal from Altoo—oo—na!

Well, maybe the tune was catchier than the lyrics.

When I looked up, Muldoon's intent stare was an inquisition in itself. Feeling my face redden, I slapped the sheet music back onto the table. "We're just friends."

"Why?" he asked. "He's obviously devoted to you, seems like a nice young man, and you're both young."

Oh brother. "Is the NYPD going into the matchmaking line now?"

"Consider it a public service," he said. "I've spent a decade watching this city grind people up. Young men and women come here, fresh and eager, and for every one who finds success, a dozen find disappointment, struggle, and worse. Do you think Ethel Gail's the only woman murdered here this year? I guarantee you, she isn't." After this recitation of doom, his voice dropped into a concerned, avuncular tone. "You're an attractive, well-brought-up, intelligent girl. Be sensible. Go back home where you belong."

Poor Detective Muldoon. Never had advice fallen on deafer ears. If anything raised my hackles, it was a stranger telling me how to live my life. The man didn't know the first thing about me. Did he think nothing bad ever happened to girls in small towns and cities, even under the watchful eye of their families? If so, he had meatloaf for brains.

"Back to Altoona?" I asked. "And do what?"

"Marry Otto, or some other decent man who'll take care of you."

That crooked nose of his made perfect sense now. I couldn't be the first person itching to take a poke at it. Where was a butter bell when you needed one?

"You're wasted on the police force," I said. "You could make a good living writing songs yourself—maudlin ones best played to sad violins, about sadder-but-wiser girls crawling back to their dear hometowns."

His lips flattened into a mirthless line. My obstinacy bugged him as much as his arrogance bothered me.

"If Otto seems so decent to you, why are you keeping him locked up?" I asked.

"We don't want to let a suspect go unless there's at least some reason to believe that he might be telling the truth."

"Guilty until proven innocent, you mean." I was mad enough now to eat bees. "I suppose that's why you're cooling your heels around here all day."

His lips turned down. "I've been on duty since last night. Robinson is out checking your boy's story. I only stayed this long so I could speak to you."

"If you wanted to speak to me, you certainly weren't in a hurry. Or was that simply meant as another lesson about the cruel city?" Waiting on that bench had certainly been cruel to my sacroiliac.

"I had to interview Otto first. Thoroughly. You see, Miss Faulk, I sensed last night that you weren't being entirely truthful."

That penetrating gaze had my insides squirming again. Maybe he was a good detective, after all. To cover my guilty flush, I puffed up like my aunt reading a negative review. "Are you calling me a liar?"

"No—at least not a habitual one. Everyone fibs a little if they think they have good cause. Sometimes they fib by leaving something out. Last night I was interested in what you *weren't* telling us. So this morning, when your friend Otto showed up, I said to myself, 'That's it.' Was I right?"

This was tricky. If I said yes, I would be lying and implying that Otto had been there last night. If I said no, I was pretty sure I would be hounded until I gave up the names of every male between the ages of eight and eighty whom I talked to last night. After seeing the summary way Muldoon had hauled Otto off to the hoosegow, I wasn't eager to submit any other of my acquaintances to that treatment.

"Otto was not at the apartment last night," I repeated. "I never believed he was. What's more, I don't have to stand for being interrogated—unless you think *I* killed Ethel. I've wasted hours here that should have been spent with my friend Callie, who's still traumatized by what happened to her cousin. And now it appears that I'll need to spend the afternoon scaring up a lawyer to free Otto."

I had no idea how to find a good one, or how much it would cost.

"That won't be necessary," Muldoon said.

"I can't let him stay here. Or allow you to haul him off to somewhere even worse."

"He hasn't been arrested. He's just being held for questioning."

"Held in a pen with men who look like thieves and killers," I pointed out.

He shook his head. "Don't worry, Miss Faulk. You have my word that no harm will come to your sweetheart."

He was just needling me now. "I told you, he's not my sweetheart."

He crossed his arms. "I've never met a woman who pleaded for a man she wasn't either related to or in love with."

"Well, you've met one now," I said. "What's more, I will free him from this place and see him cleared, even if I have to hunt down the real killer myself."

Worry rippled across his dark features. "I don't recommend playing detective. It's not a parlor game for girls."

"Neither is seeing a butcher knife buried in your roommate's back." I'd had all the condescension I could stomach for one day. "I hate to disappoint you, Detective Muldoon, but I will find a lawyer to help Otto, and I'll prove he didn't commit this atrocity. And afterward I won't be scurrying back to Altoona so I can badger some man into taking care of me. I've been in this city six months and have managed just fine so far."

His face set into a frown. "Six months? Otto said you left Altoona at the end of last summer. Almost a year ago."

No, not such a bad detective at all. One small inconsistency and Muldoon had come as close as anyone had to ferreting out the only notable skeleton in my cupboard. My cheeks warmed. The air felt charged, and my gaze darted out of the path of his.

It's said that confession is good for the soul, and there were moments, sometimes days, when I longed for someone to whom I could confide my tale of woe. I'd almost told Callie a dozen times only to change my mind, fearing I'd see pity in her face. I dreaded that. Once or twice I'd even considered taking Aunt Irene into my confidence. But some instinct always made me pull back. *As long as I'm the only one who knows, maybe it could be as if it never happened.* The confusion inside me would settle, and I'd be myself again.

After a hiccup of panic, I fumbled for a recovery. "Did Otto say I came directly to the city after leaving Altoona?"

"No . . ."

"I took a secretarial course before I came here." It wasn't a lie, technically. I'd been at the top of my class at Central Pennsylvania Secretarial School—two years ago, after high school. "I lived with friends." That *was* a lie, and unnecessary.

Did Muldoon have a sixth sense for falsehoods? His eyes narrowed on me speculatively, as if trying to fathom my deepest secret.

A secret he had no hope of prizing from me. "Good day, Detective Muldoon." Head high, I marched out, waved a quick good-bye toward Otto's cage, and headed uptown.

For all my bluster about managing just fine on my own, I wasn't a fool. I knew I needed to enlist the aid of someone more powerful—and wealthier—than myself. Luckily, I had the perfect person to turn to.

Chapter 4

Trepidation niggled at me as I approached my aunt's house. Though nearing noon, it was still early in the day to bother Aunt Irene, who could be a dragon about her working hours. Also, although I wasn't here strictly to beg for money, hiring a lawyer to help Otto would inevitably cost more than I had in the bank, otherwise known as the Calumet baking powder tin where Callie and I kept our household money. Aunt Irene had already helped me more than I could repay—not that she would ever ask me to. To her I owed my job at Van Hooten and McChesney, not to mention all the uncountable little extras she'd supplied me and Callie with during the past months. Plus, she'd embraced me when the family I'd grown up around turned their backs. My debt to this woman I'd barely known before I'd arrived in New York was already incalculable.

Asking for help also grated at my sense of independence. I'd come to this city wanting to be self-reliant. So far I couldn't brag very much on that score, and yet if I wanted to compare myself to someone who had forged her own path, I only had to look at my aunt herself. She'd left Altoona before I was born, back when she was still my aunt Sonja's little sister Irma Mayer. Irene Livingston Green wasn't just a pen name, it was the mantle of a new persona my aunt had assumed twenty years ago. She'd arrived with only a few dollars she'd won in a magazine writing contest and a vision of herself as someone completely different from the one the family circle in Altoona expected her to become. And with some alchemy of determination, talent, and luck she transformed herself into that person she'd envisioned.

I had determination, but my vision for my future was fuzzy at best. I wasn't sure where whatever talents I had could best be applied. Van Hooten and McChesney certainly didn't seem eager to make use of them. I only knew that I wanted—no, needed—to be here. But not as a sponge. My aunt's generosity and patience wouldn't last forever.

She was still dressed in her house robe and slippers when Walter showed me into her office. Of course, Aunt Irene's robe was a garment more splendid than any dress in my wardrobe. It was sewn from a crushed plum velveteen with black piping, and a collar and cuffs of some kind of dark fur. Ermine hadn't been available, apparently, but not even Catherine the Great could have looked as queenly as my aunt did perched on her Stickley swivel chair before her hulking black Remington typewriter.

Her office was a cozy room on the second floor of her house with no window of its own. Illumination came from several lamps with lead-and-glass shades—one on the rolltop desk that dominated one side of the room, and another standing lamp next to a simple drop-leaf table holding the typewriter. An armchair draped with her favorite shawl dominated one corner, surrounded by floor-to-ceiling bookcases crowded with titles. This was her lair, her sanctum, and I'd rarely interrupted her while she was in it.

She didn't look particularly pleased to see me, but the memory of Otto behind bars gave me courage. He needed help, and I was all he had.

"I'm sorry to crash in on you like this, but I must speak to you."

One eyebrow arched a little, and my aunt swiveled away from her typewriter, not without reluctance. From the clackety racket I'd heard as Walter led me toward the study, I knew she'd been busy. My aunt in the fever of creation could manipulate typewriter keys with the dexterity of Josef Hofmann playing a Chopin impromptu on the Steinway at Carnegie Hall. On her typing table a cup of coffee in a saucer served as a makeshift paperweight to a short stack of papers, that day's output.

"I wouldn't bother you if it wasn't important," I added.

She studied me and then looked up at Walter. "Have you offered Louise a refreshment?"

"She only just arrived." His tone made clear that he doubted Aunt Irene would want me to stay.

"Bring us both some fresh coffee, then, and ask Bernice if she has any more of those cheese biscuits left over from this morning."

"You ate a plate of those already," Walter reminded her.

She drew up straighter. "Not for me, you old nag. For Louise—look at her. Pale as bread dough and clearly about to expire from hunger."

I was hungry, come to think of it. Apparently Walter agreed with Aunt Irene's assessment of my physical condition, because he gave me a brief once-over and said, "I'll bring them." Then he added, "For Louise."

Her gaze tracked him as he left the room; then my aunt leaned back in her chair with a mild huff. "I made the mistake of telling that man I needed to watch my figure, and now he's my self-anointed diet despot. Never allow servants the upper hand, Louise. First they start talking back to you, then bossing you, and soon you've lost all control. Some days I think I'm just some lunatic woman scribbling away in order to support Walter and Bernice." She grabbed a few sheets from the stack of clean paper and fanned herself with them. "Hot, isn't it?"

I nodded.

"Sit down. You look as if you expect me to bite you. What's happened? Something terrible happen at work?" Her eyes narrowed. "Ogden McChesney hasn't been chasing you around his desk, has he?"

The idea of old Mr. McChesney chasing me or anyone around a desk was so strange and unlikely that I frowned in confusion. I sank down into the armchair, because it was the nearest seat available. "No, of course not."

My aunt laughed. "Ogden chased *me* a few times—around that

rolltop desk as a matter of fact. But he was too slow even a decade ago, and his rheumatism probably hasn't gotten any better."

"Worse, according to him."

"Poor Ogden." She sighed. "But never mind him. You said you had something important to tell me?"

"It's about the man who came by this morning looking for me. Otto Klemper."

"Ah." Her eyes brightened and she scooted her chair closer to me. "I sensed a love story there."

"Unfortunately, it's more of an unrequited love story turned murder mystery." I then began to relate all the events that had happened since Callie and I had left her house the night before. My aunt listened, completely absorbed, so much so that I felt almost like an actress performing for an audience of one. Two, rather. Halfway through my tale, Walter came back in with the coffee and the promised plate of biscuits. Aunt Irene grabbed his arm before he could leave. As I told them about Callie and me sleeping in what might have been the bed of Ethel's murderer, Walter wheeled the chair from the desk over and sank into it. Both he and Aunt Irene gobbled a couple of biscuits apiece by the time I'd related my distress at leaving poor Otto in the cage back at the police precinct.

She swiveled toward him. "Ring Abraham Faber. We need to get that young man out of the clutches of the police."

I could have kissed her. I could have kissed Walter, too, because he jumped up at once and made for the door. "I'll tell Bernice to make sandwiches," he announced before hurrying away.

Within ten minutes, this was all accomplished. As I sat in the office eating sandwiches, my aunt descended to talk to the lawyer, Faber, at high volume on the phone installed in the hallway below. I could hear her relating the story all over again through the floorboards. Then she ordered Walter to fetch the papers. Finally, she came up again.

"Don't worry, Abe Faber is on the job. He promises to have Otto out of that place by suppertime."

"I don't know how to thank you," I said. "I wouldn't have bothered you if I could have found another way."

My aunt's eyes widened as if I'd offended her. "Why shouldn't you come to me at first, instead of at last?"

"Because you've done so much for me already."

"Nonsense. I've done little enough for my sister's family. And after poor Greta died, Sonja took you in, when it might just as easily have fallen to me to adopt you. But I was just starting out then. I wasn't entirely polite in the manner I left that town, either, to tell you the truth. Of course I was provoked. Sonja said some horrible things to me—you'd have thought I was moving to New York to become a fancy woman. But I shudder at some of the things I said to her, too. The phrases 'ignorant hausfrau' and 'backward Podunk town' crossed my lips, I'm ashamed to admit. It wasn't my finest hour."

"I'm sure Aunt Sonja doesn't remember it," I lied. She'd never mentioned their fights to me, but the woman had the memory of an elephant.

Aunt Irene's lips twisted knowingly. "Oh, I'm sure she does. Still, I feel better for helping you because I wasn't very kind all those years ago. But it's not just about making amends, or the memory of your mother. I'm happy to help you for your own sake."

I wondered if she would have been as eager to help if she knew my entire story. That she hadn't heard the entire truth was another testament to my aunt Sonja's tight-lipped character. Or perhaps she was too ashamed to speak of me anymore.

"But you're not just helping me, you're helping Otto," I said. "And you barely know him."

"We Altoona refugees have to stick together. Besides, he seems a very worthy young man. Imagine having worked at a butcher's shop and then writing a song that Billy Murray's going to put on a phonograph record. I've invited Otto to my next Thursday evening to play it for us all. Do you think he will?"

"Try and stop him. He was telling me about your invitation even at the police station."

Aunt Irene sat back, pleased. "I approve of him."

"I'm not in love with him," I told her, before she could get any wrong ideas.

She laughed. "Of course you aren't. No woman should be—he's as green as grass and probably doesn't even know his own mind yet."

I wasn't sure I liked the sound of that. I might not have been in love with Otto, but it was a little blow to my ego to think the one devotee I'd managed to attract was simply a case of erroneous, premature affection.

She leaned toward me. "But you show good instinct caring for him. Knowing character has served me well, and will be essential if you're going to get to the bottom of this mess."

She'd lost me. "What mess?"

"Of who killed Ethel," she answered, as if it should be obvious.

"Me? But you said Mr. Faber—"

She waved a hand dismissively. "Abe Faber will get Otto out of the NYPD's clutches, if possible. He'll make the best legal case he can for keeping him out of jail. But if he's going to prove Otto didn't commit that horrible murder—and no one with an iota of sense would believe he did—someone must find out who did kill Ethel."

"And you think I could?" For all my bluster about hunting down the killer myself in front of Muldoon, I hadn't really thought out what finding a murderer would entail.

"The police solve crimes every day, and have you ever met a policeman who struck you as a genius? Of course not. They're just normal men doing a job. You're probably brighter than the lot of them. You just need to understand character and motive, and any niece of mine should know something about that."

She made it sound as if finding a murderer should be as simple as dreaming up a plot for *Myrtle in Springtime*. "I don't know where to start," I said.

"With Ethel."

I shook my head. "You never met her. She was just an ordinary woman." I frowned. *Ordinary* didn't really tell the tale. "A moral woman," I added, "and something of a scold. She never talked about herself. I lived with her for a month, but I feel as if I barely knew her."

While I spoke, my aunt nodded at me, and as I looked into her eyes, the contradictions my simplistic statements raised came to me as clearly as if she were asking them aloud. How myopic I'd been. So far, I'd only thought about Ethel from my own perspective—that of the aggrieved roommate. Now questions leapt to my mind, familiar questions both Callie and I had asked before the murder but had never taken seriously.

What had made a woman like Ethel stay so long in New York City, a city she likened to Sodom and Gomorrah? Why hadn't Ethel gone home long before she was murdered?

A clutch of journalists loitered outside our building, smoking and talking, but when they spotted me, they became alert and swarmed.

"Miss—"

"You live here, miss?"

"Tell us about last night's murder?"

"Did you know Ethel Gail?"

I batted them away and pushed my way in the front door, then ran up the stairs as if they were chasing me. Inside our flat, Callie was draped across the lumpy sofa with one arm flung over her eyes, like a Victorian lady on her fainting couch. I deposited the pot of soup Bernice had sent home with me onto the nearest table and hurried to her. "What's wrong?"

Her breast heaved, and for a moment I thought she was weeping. Then I glimpsed her even white teeth and realized she was laughing hysterically. "How bad have our circumstances become that you can ask 'What's wrong?' the day after a murder occurred in our apartment?"

She was right. After the murder, and Otto's arrest, I was now prepared for at least one new calamity every few hours. "Did those journalists bother you?"

"Oh—yes. They're monsters, and..." Her voice trailed off; then she shook her head. "It was nothing."

"What?"

"*Nothing,*" she insisted. "After last night, my imagination is running wild."

Understandable. I looked around, trying not to let my gaze rest too long on the closed bedroom door down the hall. To be honest,

I'd expected to find Callie upstairs, at Lucia's. Our place still bore the signs of the police's search—everything was slightly askew. Knickknacks stood in different places, the furniture was at odd angles, and a lot of objects were dusted with a powder the police had used to find fingerprints. I wasn't even sure we were supposed to be in the apartment, although no one had commanded us to stay out. "Should we be here?"

"Where else can we go?" she asked. "I certainly don't want to spend another night with Lucia, do you?"

"No." With all the trouble over Otto, I hadn't given a thought to where Callie and I were going to sleep tonight. Lucia had been kind to us, but with Max gone and under a cloud of suspicion, it didn't seem right to accept her hospitality.

Callie sat up and pulled her knees to her chest to make more room on the sofa for me. "Where were you? Is your friend all right?"

I scooched over. "My aunt sent a lawyer to get him out of police custody, if possible." I studied her face. "Otto didn't do it, you know."

"I never thought he did. You're a better judge of people than I am—I doubt your oldest friend would be a murderer."

Tears spilled from her eyes, and I put my hand on her arm. "I'm so sorry."

Lacking a handkerchief, she nudged her slender shoulder up to her cheek to wipe her tears. "I called Cousin Dora," she said. "It seemed to take hours to get hold of her. First I called the drugstore in Little Falls, and then they sent someone out to Dora and Abel's place to get Dora back. By the time they called me back at the candy store, I'd read every magazine in the place and had eaten two Hershey bars out of sheer boredom and nerves. I wish Mrs. Grimes would put in a telephone downstairs."

"Fat chance."

"Oh, I know, but it's such a nuisance. If Wally would just—"

"What did Dora say?" I interrupted before we could get distracted by our dislike of our landlady and her son. "It must have been awful, telling her about Ethel."

"Awful doesn't begin to describe it. I didn't know how to break the news to her, and I made a hash of it. I expected her to burst into hysterics or faint dead away. By that time a crowd had gathered around in the candy store, listening."

"Ghouls."

"But you know the worst part? Dora didn't break into hysterics. She didn't even sound upset. I couldn't hear her crying or anything. *I* was crying."

"Telephones," I said. "It's like talking at someone on the other end of a long culvert."

She shook her head. "It wasn't the connection, it was Dora. She wasn't broken up at all. All she said was, 'Thank you for letting us know. I'll tell Abel.' And that was it. I might have been calling to tell her that Ethel had stubbed her toe. I was shocked speechless for a few moments, and then I worried she was going to hang up on me, so I quickly blurted out a question about what kind of funeral arrangements we should make once the coroner releases Ethel's body. I just assumed Dora would want her final rest to be in Little Falls. But she said to me, 'You just make any arrangements down there that you want. Abel and I'll come for the service.' "

"Come for the service," I repeated. "That's all?"

She nodded. "Can you beat that? Her own sister! Listening to her, you'd have thought I was talking about some woman she barely knew. And didn't like."

"Poor Ethel." To not be wanted back in Little Falls, the town she'd lived in all her life. What had happened?

"Ethel never mentioned to me that they'd had a falling out, but that's sure how it seems to me after talking to Dora."

Of course. We should have guessed that from Dora's brief visit. "Aunt Irene was right."

Callie looked puzzled.

"She hinted there was more to Ethel than we knew," I told her. "Think of it. Ethel must've had some motive for staying here so long. Maybe that's why she was killed."

"I don't believe it." Her brows drew together. "Why would anyone want to kill her?"

"We keep saying that. But someone *did* kill her." I drummed my fingers. "And what about that missing money? It was the only thing stolen. So whoever took it must have known about it beforehand."

"*We* were the only ones who knew," Callie said. "I certainly didn't tell anyone else about the money, did you?"

"No, but maybe Ethel did."

"Who?" Her voice rose. "She didn't know anybody here. Just us, and she didn't even tell us about her stash. The only other people she would've talked to at all were—"

"People in the building," I finished for her.

The implications of that settled uneasily in Callie's expression. "This could drive a person batty. Everybody I know is starting to look suspicious. My neighbors, my family..." She didn't go on. She didn't have to. I knew she was thinking of Sawyer. "I want to escape this, but there is no escape." She shot a glance back toward the back bedroom. "Honestly, what are we going to do with this place? We can't stay here, not in the state it's in now. Would your aunt put us up?"

"I'm sure she would if we asked." But I was reluctant to do that for some reason I couldn't put my finger on yet.

Callie sensed my hesitation. "Or maybe we could go back to the Martha Washington."

"We could... if a room were available, and if we had the means to pay for it. How much money do you have?"

She sagged. "At the moment? About two dollars and thirty cents. Oh—and the five dollars your aunt gave us... minus the charge for the candy bars and the calls this morning."

"There's three dollars in the Calumet Municipal Bank." It wasn't enough.

"I've always liked your aunt's place," she said hopefully.

"But if we leave, we might miss something."

"Like what?"

"What if the murderer is someone we know? He might come back."

"All the more reason not to be here." The afternoon was warm, but she shivered. "Have you forgotten that Ethel was killed wearing my nightgown? I haven't. The murderer might have thought she was me. And if he can read the newspapers he's figured out by now that he stabbed the wrong girl. He might come back to correct his error."

"That's what I assumed at first, too—that the killer mistook Ethel for you."

"You thought it was Sawyer," Callie guessed.

I didn't say anything. Sawyer had crossed both our minds last night. On the subject of Ford Fitzsimmons, I stayed mum. After all, the chance that a mere acquaintance would have come here was so slim. If not for Wally's description of the man on the stairs, I never would have given Ford another thought.

"It couldn't have been Sawyer, Louise. We saw him, and we both saw that bed. If he'd come from killing Ethel, his clothes would've had blood on them. But he looked as neat as a pin."

She was right. I wished I could have seen how Ford looked at ten thirty last night.

"Ethel is the key," I said, purposefully derailing my thoughts from the track they kept returning to. "She was the victim. Finding out more about Ethel will lead us to who killed her."

"You mean lead the police to who killed her," Callie said.

"The police suspect Otto, and I can guarantee he's not a murderer. I have no faith that they'll find the right person or even spend much time looking for him. Not when they have Otto to point to as the culprit."

Her eyes went saucer wide. "You don't mean to say you intend to find the murderer yourself."

"If I can."

"That's insanity! You're not a detective. You'll just be stumbling around guessing."

"Maybe. But with any luck, I'll stumble into the killer. Don't you want to find out who killed Ethel? Now that you've seen them haul Otto away, are you willing to accept whatever person the police come up with?"

Callie stared at the toes of her navy-blue shoes peeping from under her skirt. Finally, she glanced up at me. "Where do we start?"

That *we* was music to my ears. "We need to find out what Ethel was up to."

Callie laughed. "Ethel?"

"I know, I know. We used to joke about what she could be doing while we were at work. But maybe she really was involved in something."

"You think she was gambling, or sneaking off to opium dens?"

"No, but we need to find out more. It might be the key to who took her money, and her life."

I decided to start my investigation close to home. Lucia would probably be incoherent—and possibly not inclined to be truthful—so I went downstairs and knocked on the door of the Bleecker Blowers. As far as I knew, Ethel had never had many dealings with them beyond banging on the floor with a broom handle to get them to shut down their playing. But perhaps I was wrong.

A moment passed with no response. I was about to knock again when the door swung open and my knuckle rapped nothing but air.

The Bleecker Blowers consisted of five saxophone players. The group had begun life as The Five Bleecker Brothers, but one brother dropped out after falling in love with a Nebraska widow during a tour of the Midwest, and another brother had decided to join an uncle's painting business. The group scared up substitute brothers of varying talent, but since the original brothers had very distinctive red hair, the substitutes were forced to dye theirs, often with startling results. Even after the name change, the hair requirement persisted. The man standing before me now was definitely one of the recent members. His head had an artificial tangerine hue.

"Oh, hello," he said breathlessly. Something crashed behind him, and he turned to yell, "Careful with that!"

My curiosity itched to know what was happening on the other side of the door, but Tangerine Man blocked my sight. He turned back and seemed almost surprised to see me still there. "You need something?" he asked, before he remembered who I was and blushed. "That is, we were awfully sorry about what happened to that lady . . . your roommate. I'm glad they caught the bastard who killed her. Pardon the language."

"They didn't," I said.

"Huh?"

"They have the wrong man. That man they collared in the foyer this morning was just a friend of mine."

Another bang sounded from the apartment, and my orange neighbor practically quivered with impatience. "I'm sorry . . ." His eyes narrowed. "Did you need something?"

"I wanted to know if you'd heard anything last night. You or any of your roommates."

"We told all that to the police," he said. "It's not like we knew Miss What's-Her-Name, or even noticed her much. She wasn't one of those women you do notice."

"That's strange. I found her hard to ignore."

"Maybe because you lived with her." He shrugged. "She was just one of those invisible women, you know? Nothing special. I don't mean to sound callous, but we just didn't pay any attention to her."

Because she was older, I guessed. Spinsterly. She'd been no one's sweetheart, no one's mother. Mostly she'd just been in the way.

The idea unnerved me. How many years did I have before I became invisible?

I forced a smile. "Well, thank you. We were just curious to find out if you'd noticed anything. Callie is so upset, you know."

"Oh, Callie." At once, his impatience melted away, and a scrim of dreamlike desire clouded his eyes.

Callie was *not* invisible to the male sex, and I'd become used to this muddleheaded reaction from men who encountered her. It was part of the reason Ford Fitzsimmons's lack of interest in her had surprised me. Usually I was a little irritated with men for being so superficial and predictable when confronted with a pretty blonde. Now I wondered if I could use some of this Callie worship to my advantage.

"The police won't tell us much," I said, "and poor Callie is tearing her heart out with questions about what happened last night. She feels sure someone must have heard something. If I could just reassure her . . ."

"Heck, I'll reassure her," Tangerine said, leaping at the bait. He turned. "Pat, I'll be right back. Going upstairs for a minute."

"You can't leave now!" came the annoyed reply. "The car'll be here any second."

"Then the car can wait."

"Bill'll kill us."

But nothing was going to keep the orange Lochinvar from his chance to dash upstairs and comfort Callie. He pushed right past me and took the steps three at a time.

I frowned and gave the door a shove. Before I could step into the apartment, however, a natural redhead pushing an instrument case the size of a rhinoceros blocked my path. His face peeked around the top, annoyed. "What lit a fire under his tail?"

"My roommate," I said. "Would you mind if I came in and waited for him to come back?"

"You better believe I would. We gotta be in Schenectady by nine o'clock tonight. That's a long way to drive even on decent roads. If we don't leave in five minutes, we'll never make it."

I was running out of arguments to get inside. I wasn't even sure why I wanted to—except that I no longer trusted anyone.

Unfortunately, at that moment we were interrupted by Wally. "I need words with you, Louise." He grabbed my arm from behind.

With a shudder, I swiveled on him. "Miss Faulk, if you don't mind."

"It don't matter what you're called. Ma says if you and your pretty roommate can't behave yourselves, you'll have to go."

Behave ourselves! "What have we done?"

"We didn't have no murders here before."

Callie and I were somehow bringing down the respectability of the building? That was a laugh. Max had a criminal record, and the Bleecker Blowers had thrown a party the month before that had nearly shaken the bricks from the building. That had been Ethel's first weekend, and she'd sworn she'd seen two people so drunk that they had to be rolled out of the building like logs. I wasn't going to start tittle-tattling about my neighbors to odious Wally, but neither did I want to be booted out for the offense of having a visitor murdered in our apartment. As if being murdered was a crime.

My irritation boiled over, especially when the Bleecker Blower pulled his sax cases out into the hallway and locked the apartment behind him. For all I knew, there was vital evidence being hauled away inside those cases. The bass sax alone was big enough to stuff a corpse into, never mind a few bloodied garments and a wad of cash. Wally and I had to flatten ourselves against the wall to avoid being squished by the monstrous thing.

"Neither Callie nor I killed anyone," I reminded him.

"Ma says it's the kinds you attract," said Wally.

I had a sneaking suspicion that "Ma" was more interested in getting rid of us and finding a tenant who would pay more. We'd bargained her down when we moved in by promising to stay a year, paint the walls ourselves, and pay by the month.

"I refuse to discuss this with you out here on the landing," I said.

His glistening lips pulled back into a smile. "Then how 'bout we go somewhere more private? Like my office."

Not a chance. Wally's "office" was a dank room in the basement. Reversing my original intention, I planted my feet firmly and attempted a Mary Pickford–like helplessness. "You wouldn't put two girls out on the street just after they've been traumatized, would you?" He seemed unmoved. Who could blame him? I wasn't very convincing as a helpless damsel. I added quickly, "Callie was so struck by how you handled yourself this morning."

When you attacked the wrong person, I thought, bristling.

"Callie said that?" *That look* came over him, and he preened a little, which manifested itself in a sort of grotesque twitching.

"She certainly did." *Forgive me, Callie.* "You wouldn't want to put her out on the street, would you?"

"Nah, I wouldn't do that," he said. "Don't be sore at me—I'm on *your* side. I'll talk to Ma. You tell Callie she's got nothing to worry about."

The underlying message came through loud and clear: Without my roommate, my fanny would be booted out on the sidewalk.

"I'm just glad the guy's been caught," he added.

I should have kept my lip buttoned, but there was only so much of this fool I could stomach. "He wasn't the murderer."

His face scrunched like a clenched fist. "Like hell he wasn't. I caught him red-handed—the guy I saw on the stairs last night."

"That wasn't him, and he didn't kill Ethel."

"Who says?"

"The man himself. Otto."

He snorted. "Like you can believe a guy who'd butcher a woman like that."

"But he didn't. He has an alibi."

"A what?"

"He can prove he couldn't have done it," I translated.

"That must be some fancy proof, when I saw him with my own two eyes. I notice a lot that happens in this building."

"I'll bet."

He twitched again as if I'd complimented him, and combed a hand with aw-shucks modesty through hair so greasy with pomade that it looked as if his dandruff was swimming in gravy. "Have to keep my eyes open. You know. Look after things."

Looking was his hobby. Callie and I knew he was fond of looking up skirts as we went up the stairs . . . and it was only slight consolation that he was half blind. Had this predilection of his extended to watching Ethel, as well? Much as I loathed the man, I couldn't overlook anything he knew that might be useful.

"Callie and I work such long hours, you probably saw Ethel more than we did," I said.

His lips pulled down. "Not really. She was a quiet one, that one was. Sort of . . . what do you call it?"

"Aloof?"

"Nah—it was more that she was kind of standoffish."

I nodded. "That's just what I would say."

"Maybe she was snooty, or shy, or maybe she didn't like men all that much. Well, I could tell she didn't by the way she'd scurry past me, barely saying hello. Which was a damn shame. She was a fine-looking woman when she dolled herself up."

I had to repeat the words slowly to convince myself I'd heard correctly. "Dolled herself up?"

"Sure. Course, she was too old to be a knockout. Nothing she could do about that. But put a pretty dress on those skinny old bones and she wasn't too hard on the blinkers."

His eyes were worse than I thought. Ethel didn't own a dress that anyone with functioning eyesight would have described as *pretty*. I even doubted the kindness of donating her wardrobe to charity. Cutting the clothes into squares for pot scrubbers seemed the best option.

"Call me crazy," Wally went on, "but that lady had ankles almost as nice as her cousin's."

Not only was he half blind, he was cracked in the head. "Ethel wore sturdy brown boots."

He crossed his arms. "Not all the time. She had a pair of slipper-shoes—blue satin with white ribbon ties. The kind of shoe a girl wears when she wants to be noticed."

I resisted the urge to tap the side of my head to try to adjust my hearing. He sounded like Wanamaker's advertising copy. Not to mention, the idea of Ethel swanning around Manhattan in fancy, gaze-attracting togs was ludicrous. "You must have mistaken Ethel for Callie." Why not? He'd mistaken Otto for someone else.

He wasn't budging on this point, though. "No mistake."

"Ethel didn't own anything like that," I argued. "Callie does, but—"

My jaw snapped shut. The floor seemed to tilt beneath me, and I pressed a hand against the wall. I remembered Callie's puzzling insistence that I'd been responsible for an ink stain on her shirtwaist. Perhaps last night wasn't the first time Ethel had worn something of Callie's. Probably Ethel had never intended to sleep in that nightgown, but was going to change back into one of her ugly flannel ones before Callie and I returned home. But she never got that opportunity.

What else could Wally tell me?

"Did Ethel ever mention where she was going when you saw her dressed up?"

He shook his head. "Like I said, she was a real hands-off type, that one."

I looked down at his sausage-fingered hands with their dirty, ragged nails and suppressed a shudder. With some men, a hands-off policy was essential.

Outside, an automobile horn honked loudly several times. The angry goose blasts startled me, and within seconds the door to our apartment upstairs banged open and the tangerine Lochinvar galloped down the stairs. "Bill'll kill me!" He streaked past in an orange blur.

I'd forgotten he was upstairs. What had he been talking to Callie about all this time?

"Thank you for speaking with me," I told Wally. "You've been very helpful."

He laughed.

"What?" I asked.

"You sound like one of those fellows from last night—those police detectives."

"Do I?" Now it was my turn to preen. Except that I probably shouldn't want to sound like Muldoon and company. They had badges. I needed to be more discreet.

Back upstairs, Callie was pacing across our already threadbare carpet, agitated. Heaven knows a murder was enough to make anyone edgy, but there seemed to be something else that caused her to jump as I came through the door. "Where have you been?" she asked. "We had a visitor. One of the saxophone players. I can never keep their names straight."

"Me neither."

"He came in here and practically held my hand as he told me how sorry he was about Ethel, and promised that if any of them had heard her being murdered, they would have stopped it. How is anyone's guess."

"One of them almost crushed me with a bass saxophone case. That might have worked."

"They didn't hear anything, which is too bad. But get this—he told me that Ethel had asked him for directions once."

I crossed my arms. He hadn't told *me* that. "Where?"

"That's the odd part—and that's why he said he remembered it so clearly. Ethel wanted to know how to go to 115th Street and Lenox Avenue. Does that sound right to you? Why would Ethel want to venture all the way up there?"

Interesting. "I think Ethel had more going on than we knew. Wally told me she dressed in your clothes sometimes when she went out."

"My clothes?" Callie said.

"Well, he said she wore pretty dresses sometimes, and he described a pair of shoes just like your blue ones."

Her mouth dropped open. "My blue slippers? Those cost me sixteen dollars!"

I lifted my hands and then dropped them. "He swore he saw her wearing them." I told her my theory about Ethel's having worn the stained shirtwaist.

She crossed her arms. "Very handy for you to have found a scapegoat for your wardrobe destruction."

"I know I've borrowed your things before and have been careless, but Ethel really seems to have had some secret fetish for dressing up in your clothes."

"Poor Ethel. I'd have loaned her anything if she'd asked."

"Maybe it was the secrecy she enjoyed." I picked up my satchel and checked the mirror to see that I was street ready.

"Where are you going?" Callie asked.

"To Lenox Avenue and 115th Street." Not that I was completely sure where that was. Up, was all I knew. "I need to find out what Ethel was interested in up there."

Callie hopped up. "I'll go with you."

Two pairs of eyes would be better than one, and I was glad for the company. But sometime between when I crossed to the hall tree and when I turned, pinning on my hat, the color drained from Callie's face. "Oh, Louise. If Ethel was wearing my clothes often . . . like she was last night . . . isn't that more evidence that the murderer might have mistaken her for me?"

I went to her and held her by the forearms. She seemed to be in need of bracing. "Or it might mean the opposite. That more people here had contact with her than we realized. In fact, it seems likelier now that Ethel was involved with something that drew her killer here."

Callie nodded and prepared herself to leave. Looking into her tiny purse, she sucked in a breath. "Oh—I almost forgot." She brought out a key and held it up.

"What's it to?"

"The saxophonists' apartment. They're on the road for the next week and what's-his-name said that we could stay there."

Eureka! "I was dying to get in there and look it over."

"You don't think any of the saxophonists killed Ethel, do you?"

"I don't know. And until I do, I'm going to be wary of everyone."

Her brows raised. "Yet you're still willing to stay in their apartment."

"Of course." And while I was there, I intended to give it a thorough going over.

Chapter 5

I'd lived in New York for six months, but I'd never been so far north as Harlem before. "The city never ends, does it?" I said, looking north up Lenox Avenue. It seemed to unfurl into infinity—office buildings, apartments, and houses in a relentless rectilinear grid as far as the eye could see.

Callie laughed at my awestruck marvel. "Oh, it ends, all right. Somewhere beyond all this is a whole lot of nothing, and at the end of that nothing is Little Yawns."

On the corner of 115th we looked around us, getting our bearings. This far uptown there were a few more carriages and carts vying for space on the road with trams and noisy, smoke-belching automobiles. What were we looking for? To the north, I made out a tobacconist and another shop selling Singer sewing machines. An old man with a high-sided pushcart came right alongside us, bellowing, "Cash for clothes! Cash for your old clothes!"

"What are we doing?" Callie's voice was tight. "It's just a street like any other. Ethel could have had any one of a million reasons for being here."

"True. But to discover that one, we need to start looking."

We proceeded slowly, paying attention to each sign. From the names on the doors and various businesses, the neighborhood was predominantly Jewish and Italian, although we passed several Negroes working on the street, one selling fruit, another sharpening knives from a little wagon. The places we went into to ask after Ethel—tailor, pharmacy, barber, laundry, doctor, dentist—were all businesses Ethel could have found in Greenwich Village, closer to home.

No one we asked had seen her. Despair had begun to set in, when Callie stopped and pointed across the street at three golden-painted spheres swaying in the breeze above a doorway. "Look." The sign stenciled on the shop's plate glass window read: LENOX PAWN. "I bet that's it."

"Why would Ethel come all this way to visit a pawnshop? They're a dime a dozen all over town."

"For anonymity. She might've wanted to make sure to visit one far from where we live. Just in case."

"In case what?" I asked.

"In case I were to go in the store and see something of my family's for sale."

"What would she have had to sell?"

Callie crooked her head in thought. "I've been wondering about the way Dora spoke to me about Ethel. It was as if she'd done something really bad. I hate to speak ill of the dead . . ."

"I know." Although it wasn't as if we'd spoken well of Ethel when she was alive.

She continued. "But if she took something from Dora—something valuable enough to pawn—that would account for Dora's anger, wouldn't it? Maybe that's where all that money we found came from."

"It also explains why she left Ethel with us after she came for that visit, and why Ethel was so upset." Then I tried to square the image of Ethel sneaking out of Little Falls with the family silver with the woman I remembered. "I just can't see Ethel stealing, though."

"I wouldn't have imagined she'd wear my clothes, either," Callie pointed out, "but she did."

The secret life of Ethel. "But even if she did pawn something here," I said, "how could we possibly guess what that something was?"

"I know everything of value Dora and Abel own. Dora may not have a lot to show off, but what she does have she displays like the natural history museum displays its stuffed buffaloes."

Without further warning, Callie plunged into the street. There was nothing for it but to take off after her. Possessing a dancer's natural agility and timing, she was much more intrepid than I was about dodging carriages and streetcars. Darting after her felt like rushing headlong through a funhouse with things that popped out at me, only these things were horrors like buses, cars, and wagons able to flatten me under their wheels.

When I leapt onto the opposite sidewalk, I was amazed to find myself in one piece. "Are you crazy? You'll get us killed doing that!"

"Don't be a ninny. We're alive."

"Yes, but—"

Callie wasn't listening. I followed her gaze, which was riveted on a bill taped to the building's cracked window. "What if *this* was why Ethel came here?" Pawnbroker forgotten, she pointed to the hand-lettered advertisement.

Fortunes Told
Madame Serena
4th Floor

"Madame Serena?" Surely she was joking. "Fortune-tellers are charlatans."

"So are most of the peddlers who come to Little Falls, but that didn't stop Ethel from buying a lifetime supply of The Queen of Sheba's Healthful Beauty-Enhancing Cream from one of them."

Those pots of cream with an Egyptian figure etched in black against pink glass littered dressing tables and the flat's tiny bathroom shelf. Maybe Callie had a point. In unspoken agreement, we entered the building and climbed the squeaky stairs. Every floor seemed to have its own questionable enterprises—a talent agent, a novelty distributor, and a business promising IMMIGRATION—REASONABLE FEES. The hallway reeked of old sweat, cigar smoke, and disappointment.

At the top floor landing, a sign on the nearest door read:

Madame Serena
Fortunes Told, Palms Read
"Your future for fifty cents"

"Fifty cents!" I cried, outraged. "If I'd seen the price, I would've saved myself the climb." No doubt that's what this phony was counting on.

Callie shushed me. "We're just going to ask if she saw Ethel."

She overrode my grumbling with a sharp rap at the door, but no one answered. It was almost a relief not to hear any footsteps within.

I hooked my arm through hers. "Let's go to the pawnbroker's. That was a better idea."

We'd only begun to turn back toward the staircase when the door suddenly and silently swung open. Before us towered a woman with skin as black as ebony, her hair concealed beneath a turban in shades of turquoise, yellow, and bougainvillea pink. Over her royal blue dress was draped a flowing piece of gossamer cloth in the same dazzling hues as the turban. Callie and I looked like two sparrows next to a fantastic hyacinth macaw.

While we gawped, the woman inspected us through dark narrowed eyes.

"Madame Serena?" Callie's voice came out practically as a squeak.

The woman gave no indication whether she was or wasn't the fortune-teller, except to say quietly, "You'd better come in."

She turned and walked in, whispering halfway across the room before she noticed we remained motionless in the doorway. We were both staring at her feet. Madame Serena was barefoot, which accounted for her moving as quietly as a shadow. The foot peeking out from beneath her dress was arched, with toes lacquered in garish pink. I'd never seen such a thing.

"Come," the woman commanded us. We stumbled forward.

The angle of the roof, which was one wall of the garret, made the room a trapezoid. Colorful drapes over the windows blocked the afternoon sun, and in place of natural light, several candelabras stood on low tables and on the mantel over a bricked-up fireplace. A long, narrow table dominated the room, with more candelabras at both ends. Madame Serena seated herself on one side of the table in a comfortable armchair. She gestured to the three mismatched wooden seats across from her. "Sit."

Her voice resonated with such authority that it was hard not to automatically do her bidding. Before I sat, however, I wanted to make it clear that we weren't there to fall for any mystical jabberwocky. "We only want information."

One of her jet brows arched turbanward. "Of course."

"I mean, we don't need our fortunes told," I said. "We just want to ask questions."

Madame Serena nodded. "One dollar."

"One dollar!" I was ready to walk out. "Your sign says fifty cents—and even that's highway robbery."

"I see two of you."

"We only need to know if you've seen my friend's cousin," I argued.

The woman's gaze flicked to Callie. "Something bad happened to this cousin. I'm very sorry."

Callie's mouth dropped open, but she said nothing.

I shifted restlessly. Surely Callie wasn't going to interpret the woman's lucky guess as some sort of special insight. Of course Madame Serena would divine from what I'd said that something bad had happened to Ethel. For that matter, I doubted anyone came to see her when things were going swimmingly.

"Your sympathy's kind," I said, "but it would be even kinder if you'd help us with what we want to know. And as for payment—"

Before I could finish, Callie pulled several coins out of her little purse and placed them on the table. "There," she said. "One dollar."

Exhibiting the reflexes of a mongoose, the woman snatched the coins and pocketed them. "Tell me about your cousin."

I glared at Callie, but she shrugged impatiently at me and sat down. I thumped down with a huff into the chair next to her. It wasn't just the money. Part of my frustration was fear for my friend.

She was already distressed. I didn't want this woman to spout frightening mumbo jumbo at her, or lead us down a false path.

Callie described Ethel to the woman in as much detail as she could. "Believe me, if she came here, you would remember. She had a very sharp personality."

"Poor soul."

Callie scooted forward in her chair. "Then you did see her?"

"I do not think so." Candlelight shadows flickered across Madame Serena's face. "The description does not match any of the visitors I've had here."

"Good of you to tell us," I said, "now that you have our dollar."

My sarcasm had no visible effect on Madame Serena. "I will tell you that I see a tragedy," she said.

I snorted. "Oh, of course. You noticed that my friend is worried, so you inferred that some misfortune befell her cousin."

The dark eyes swung toward me. "I didn't say *whose* tragedy."

Callie gasped and grabbed my hand, and I checked the urge to fling it away. What hooey. "If you think for one moment that you're going to scare us into giving you another dollar—"

Madame Serena's voice rose. "I see much pain, smirking girl. I hear a child crying. *Crying.* It has no mother. Where is she?"

The room was stuffy from all the candles, but a cold wave washed through me. I tried to rise, but my limbs wouldn't move. My muscles had turned to pudding.

"Louise?" Callie's face twisted in worry.

My mouth opened and closed like a newly caught fish. Was this woman a sorceress, or a sadist? Did she have some secret knowledge of my life? But that was impossible. I'd never seen her, and nobody knew. Or almost nobody.

Callie took my arm. "We should go."

"Yes." I allowed her to hoist me back to my feet.

Madame Serena didn't get up. She crossed her arms, a pitying smile on her lips, her gaze never leaving mine. "I wish you good fortune."

Callie thanked her, but I was too torn to speak. Part of me wanted to stomp out, while another part wanted to fling myself back down in the chair, open my palms, and beg her to tell me what she saw in them. *A child crying.* What was I to do with just that little snippet? I needed more, or I needed never to have heard it at all. But Madame Serena was done with us. Callie's money had bought me a dollar's worth of torment.

Out in the hallway, Callie closed the door and turned to me. "What happened in there?"

"Nothing."

"Something she said upset you."

"She's a fraud." I repeated those words to myself for good measure.

"Babies crying?" Callie's smooth brow creased. "Did you have a little brother or sister once? Someone you left?"

I clutched my satchel. "The whole thing was a waste of a dollar." I wasn't going to confess my deepest secret to Callie out in this hallway—especially not because a charlatan fortune-teller had spooked me with a well-chosen sentence. Already the gears of my mind were spinning, trying to justify how she might have guessed what she could say to upset me. She was a clever one, Madame Serena. Very convincing.

"Let's go to the pawnshop," I said.

We went, and Callie inspected all the wares on display there so closely that the proprietor suspected us of having sticky fingers. He watched us like a Pinkerton man the whole time. But even after spending a half hour poring over jewelry and silver and other valuables, Callie saw nothing she recognized as coming from her cousin Dora's. When questioned about Ethel, the pawnbroker said he didn't remember her. But then, he saw so many ladies. . . .

Back out on the sidewalk, Callie sighed in discouragement. "What now?"

"We keep going several more blocks," I said.

And so we resumed our hunt. But our survey of the merchants of the area yielded nothing. No one had seen Ethel. Or if they had, they weren't admitting it.

Then we spoke to the man sharpening knives. The old man was our last stop. When we saw him, he was taking a break, sitting on his three-legged stool, eating a piece of buttered bread and reading his newspaper. He looked up when we approached and listened at first patiently and then with growing interest as we described Ethel.

"Ethel, you say?" he asked. "You mean Ethel Gail?"

Callie and I sucked in our breaths. "Yes!" she said. "You *did* see her?"

He nodded. "I imagine lots of people have." He held up the newspaper in his lap to show us. Ethel's face stared at us unsmiling from above the fold. THE VILLAGE BUTCHER'S VICTIM, the headline read.

Callie and I exchanged confused glances. The picture was one Callie had had for years in a photograph album. How did the newspapers get hold of it?

As our train barreled southward on the way home, we both sat in our own worlds, unable to talk. *A baby crying,* Madame Serena had said. I could almost hear him myself. My insides felt as if they were crumbling, as though soon my spine would be like sand, unable to hold me up. I looked over to see if Callie noticed that I was in danger of turning into an invertebrate pile of nervous rubble, but she was staring at a Cream of Wheat ad above the windows, lost in her own thoughts.

What was the matter with me? I hadn't experienced this kind of torment for months and months. I was getting better. I was forgetting. Or so I'd thought.

But then, as if to taunt me, my memory replayed it all—that afternoon over a year ago now, back in Altoona. On a fine spring Saturday, the kind of winter-finally-over sunny and warm day that tempted even grown men to skip down the sidewalks, I finished work early and returned home. Because my call of hello was met with nothing but echo in the empty house, I guessed everyone was out enjoying the glorious afternoon. I was in a hurry to change clothes after working the morning in my uncle's shop and get back out myself.

It was as I was changing that Mr. Tate found me.

Artie Tate was a young salesman, a bit flashy and loud, but very successful—at least to hear him tell it. I didn't like him a bit, but I was always pleasant to the boarders, as Aunt Sonja had admonished me to be. "We didn't expect to have an extra mouth to feed," she'd told me more than once, "so the boarders have been a blessing to us." *I* had been the extra mouth, after my parents died of typhus when I was seven. Aunt Sonja and Uncle Dolph had three sons of their own, all younger than me.

Despite all I owed my aunt, I was definitely not inclined to be pleasant to a boarder who was standing in my doorway while I was stripped down to my petticoats. Seeing him there, I lifted my dress over my corset and flashed a glare at him. "What are you doing? Shut the door."

He smiled. "All right." He slipped inside and shut it behind him.

"That's not what I meant."

"Wasn't it?" he asked, oozing toward me.

I stepped back but bumped into my dresser. The predatory way he eyed me made my stomach turn. I was used to teasing from men, even the occasional leer, but the hard glint in his eye signaled something unfamiliar, and dangerous.

"I've seen the way you look at me," he said.

I swallowed, confused. "I never did." My mouth felt bone dry—and my corset cover far too flimsy.

He reached out and ran his hand up my bare arm, ending with a tight squeeze on my shoulder. Revulsion shuddered through me, and I slapped at his arm. "Don't touch me."

I stepped around him, ready to charge out in the hallway half-dressed if I had to, but he caught me by the waist of my petticoat and yanked me back. Breath woofed out of me.

He hauled me toward the bed while I struggled and kicked. Who would have thought a hosiery salesman would have such strength?

"Oh, you're a honey." He flipped me and shoved me down so that I was pinned to the mattress beneath him. I gasped for breath. One of his hands pressed my face into the lace coverlet over my quilt. The other pushed and ripped at my clothing. The mattress muffled my cries. The shock and humiliation of it—of him, *there*—almost matched the pain. Pinned beneath the grunting, frenzied weight of him, I squirmed and thrashed, but that only seemed to make him push my head down harder till I couldn't breathe.

The nightmare seemed to go on forever, but when he was finally done, he pulled down my skirt and buttoned up as cheerily as if we'd just enjoyed an ice cream sundae together.

"You're a nice girl," he said, casually. "Shame I'm leaving today. Not sure I'll be back, but tell you what. I'll leave you some samples."

Mortified, numb, and terrified that he might come at me again, I waited until I'd heard his footsteps retreat down the hall and then down the stairs before getting up and stumbling back to my dresser. In the mirror, one side of my face was red and bore the outline of lace in my cheek. At first, in my daze of confused revulsion, I couldn't put a name to what had happened. I dressed and, not knowing what else to do, tried to continue on with my day. I got as far as the front door, but turned back. Much as I wanted to escape the house, I dreaded seeing anyone. What was I going to say?

I wound up in the kitchen, preparing supper. Aunt Sonja had mentioned having cabbage that evening. By the time she got back, less than an hour later, I'd cut up five heads of them. When my aunt looked at the mountain of chopped cabbage on the wooden counter, she demanded to know if I'd lost my mind. It took three Carusos to calm her down.

If only it could have been as easy to soothe the storm raging inside me. By then I'd conjured a word for what had happened. *Violated.* I'd seen the word in papers, and even heard the word *rape* whispered, usually in conjunction with the name of a girl who'd fallen from grace and should have known better than to . . .

But what had *I* done? That man had said I'd looked at him, but I couldn't help looking at people. If he'd interpreted my manner as leading him on, would others, too? In my heart, I knew I'd done nothing. I didn't deserve to be a girl people whispered about. Perhaps those other girls hadn't deserved it, either. Right or wrong rarely stilled flapping tongues.

Occasionally a wave of indignation would hit me and I'd determine to go to the police. But I knew only one policeman, our neighbor Mr. Meyer's annoying son Gus, who'd been a terror as a boy and hadn't matured much since. Was I really going down to the station to tell what had happened in my bedroom to smirking, sneering Gus and his colleagues? What if they didn't believe me? I couldn't stomach it.

That evening, Mr. Tate packed his suitcase, settled with Aunt Sonja, and left Altoona. So I said nothing, and continued to say nothing until three months later, when it became clear to Aunt Sonja that I was pregnant. I confessed the whole story in a rush, relieved to finally tell someone. When I was done, Aunt Sonja was looking at me with a hard, skeptical stare.

"The nice man who left you all those stockings?" she asked.

As if Mr. Tate's insulting final gesture was proof that I'd traded my body for hosiery. My heart froze. Forget policemen. My own aunt didn't believe I hadn't encouraged Mr. Tate.

I reminded her that I'd told her to donate the wretched stockings to the needy family collection at the church. But she couldn't believe I hadn't done *something* to make him think I was fast. It was as if my behavior in all the years I'd lived with my aunt and uncle counted for nothing. I had fallen, and it had to be my fault.

"You'd better write to him," she told me. "I can't say I'd want to be married to a traveling man myself, but it's too late for you to be thinking of that now."

I could have cried. *Married?* Had she not listened to a word I'd said? "Aunt Sonja, he raped me."

Her lips flattened, and she brooded in silence through "La Mia Canzone." I thought perhaps I'd reached her. Then she said, "He might be married already. In which case you're *really* in a mess, my girl."

I let her know in no uncertain terms that I wanted nothing to do with Mr. Tate ever again.

"What will you do, then?" she asked. "You can't stay here. Dolph and I have the boys to consider."

Aunt Sonja and I didn't part on the best of terms. Uncle Dolph and Uncle Luddie never said a word to me until Uncle Dolph saw me off on the train out of town. In parting, he presented me with the set of knives at the station. The cardboard box they came in was only slightly smaller than my suitcase and weighed twice as much. "I meant to give the knives to you as a wedding present someday," he said. "But now . . ."

In the weeks that followed, I tried very hard not to think too much about what he meant by *but now*. Apparently the family who raised me no longer considered me marriageable. Most days that was fine by me. I never wanted to have anything to do with men again. Marriage wasn't the be-all and end-all. The last thing I wanted to do was have to explain to some suitor what had happened to me. To apologize for being despoiled. I was done apologizing for someone else's barbarity.

Callie pinched my arm, jolting me out of my own thoughts. The train was pulling into the Thirty-fourth Street stop. Without warning, she bolted for the door, pulling me along with her.

"What is it?" I asked, watching our train—the one we were no longer on—squeal out of the station.

Callie's respiration was as quick and shallow as a rabbit's. "There was a man on that train. He's been following me."

"Are you sure?" I looked after the last car disappearing from view, as if that would be any help. "What did he look like?"

"He's about medium height, and he wore a brown suit with faint stripes, not very well cut. He has beady eyes and a bristly brown mustache. I also saw him following me this morning, and watching from across the street while I was in the candy store."

"Why didn't you tell me this earlier?"

"I hoped I was imagining things."

"He's probably one of those newspapermen." I was still incensed that they'd found a picture of Ethel—heaven only knew how. Callie's photograph album was on the bottom shelf of a table in her bedroom. Which meant that either the police had given it to journalists or someone had been snooping through our things while we were out.

"He wasn't standing with the other men from the papers," Callie said.

A maverick penny-a-liner. Even worse. "The next time I see Muldoon, Robinson, or any policeman, I'm going to demand they do something. We shouldn't have to be pestered this way—*we* didn't commit a crime."

"What can they do?" she asked. "The man following me hasn't spoken to me, or even approached me. My skin crawls when I think of him watching me, but maybe I'm making a mountain out of a molehill."

I doubted it. Men didn't usually frighten Callie. If she said this one was shady, I believed her.

We boarded the next train and once we got off again we walked with fleeter steps to our apartment, our antennae now on alert for any sign of the mustache. Callie whispered that she couldn't see him anymore, and even the flock of journalist buzzards in front of our building had thinned. Maybe this was their supper break.

At the thought of supper, my stomach rumbled. Bernice's soup was waiting for us in the icebox, which made it easier to run the gauntlet of pesky questions.

"Give us your story, girls."

"Where were you the night of the murder?"

"Why was Ethel Gail alone in the apartment?"

"Vultures," I muttered.

We scooted into the building and dashed up the stairs, mindful as always of Wally, who, happily, wasn't hovering at the bottom of the steps.

"But aren't we doing the same things those journalists are—snooping into Ethel's life?" Callie asked.

"That's different. We *knew* her. Those men out there are simply trying to get information to feed a public hunger for sensationalism. They're the lowest form of life."

As we reached the third floor, a bulb flashed, momentarily blinding us. It had come from the direction of our doorway.

"Give us a story to go with the photo, Miss Gail," a reporter standing next to the photographer called out. His voice barked as loudly as if we were all the way across a football field instead of mere feet away from him.

Once the spots had cleared from my eyes, I rushed forward. "Get out of here."

"Just a few words," the man pleaded, ignoring me. "Your angle,

Miss Gail—about how much you'll miss your cousin from the country. How 'bout it?"

"I'll call for a policeman," I warned. "You're trespassing."

The man with the camera shook his head. "We have a perfect right to be here. We got permission from the management."

Did I say journalists were the lowest form of life? My error. Landladies' sons actually took that prize. No telling how much these two had paid Wally to be let into what the papers were now charmingly referring to as "the murder apartment." Small wonder Wally had been so eager to keep us there when his mother wanted us out. He was probably raking in a tidy profit from Ethel's murder.

"Get out," I repeated. "You won't get any more fodder for your birdcage liner from us."

"Okay, girls," the scribbler said, as if I'd just wished him a good day. He and his photographer chum left, not at all out of sorts.

Unlike me. I stomped into the apartment steaming mad, my hunger forgotten. Callie sank onto the sofa. She looked depressed, which made me even madder. As if Callie didn't have enough to trouble her without Wally selling tickets to our misfortune. "I'm going to go down and give him a piece of my mind," I fumed.

"Don't," Callie said.

"We have to do *something.* Those men could have come in and taken anything. Look at this place." Our housekeeping was always a bit haphazard. We both had a high tolerance for clutter, and Callie absolutely loved to accumulate trinkets, decorative bits of material, and inexpensive objets d'art she found in secondhand stores. Now, though, after the police had been through everything, our clutter was more chaotic than usual. "How will we notice anything missing? At least until it's splashed across the front pages, like Ethel's picture. I wonder how much Wally got for *that.*"

"If we make a fuss, Mrs. Grimes will just be all that much more eager to kick us out."

"So what? This isn't the only apartment building in Manhattan."

"But it's the one where all our things are. And, as you reminded me, we've paid up for the month."

She had me there. "Next time we find a place, we pay week to week."

"At least we can go down to the Bleecker Blowers' apartment for the next few days. It'll seem like a different place."

Yes. And it was the apartment directly above Wally's. "I'm going to take up clog dancing this week," I said. "Clog dancing and bagpiping and maybe Limburger cheese making."

Callie groaned. "Take up new-roommate-finding while you're at it."

A commotion downstairs interrupted my plotting. It sounded like a riot—doors slamming, people shouting, crashes, a scream. Callie and I ran out to the landing and leaned over the railing to peer downstairs.

"This is him!" Wally cried. "The butcher!"

"Call the police!" someone yelled from outside the front door.

"I just *left* the police." Otto's voice was a muffled croak, as if someone's boot was on his throat. "I didn't do it!"

I charged down the stairs. By the time I covered the two flights, Otto was being mobbed. I jumped into the fray, taking one of his arms and trying to pull him free. The poor man looked in danger of being tugged apart like a Christmas cracker. Everyone was yelling—me louder than any of them—and the commotion didn't stop until a police constable burst through the door.

"What's going on here!" he bellowed at us all.

The dissonant, chaotic reply he received was worthy of Stravinsky. The newspaper men retreated to the sidelines, flashbulbs popping as Wally and I continued our tug-of-war with Otto in the role of rope. Sheet music papered the floor, and I nearly lost my footing when one of them slipped beneath my shoe's heel. Reporters scooped up copies.

The police officer finally pried Otto away from Wally and me.

"He's the man that murdered Ethel Gail!" Wally cried.

"I didn't do it," Otto repeated. "Ask Detective Muldoon."

"I *saw* him with my own eyes," Wally said.

I turned pleading eyes on the officer. "No, he didn't. This man was at the police station all day. They obviously let him go."

"Or he escaped," Wally said.

"Sure—and came right back here to the scene of the crime," I said with a sneer.

The policeman narrowed his eyes on Otto. "Got yourself a fast-talking lawyer, did you?"

Otto gulped. "No, sir. Mr. Faber just speaks at the normal speed."

Several reporters sniggered, which didn't help Otto. The policeman's face darkened. "A wisenheimer."

"He oughta be locked up," Wally growled. "It ain't safe with guys like this wandering loose."

The cop shook his head, disgusted. "Once these mouthpieces start getting their mitts in, there's no end to the mischief." He yanked Otto up by his coat collar until Otto was almost on tiptoe and they were standing nose-to-nose. "I'll have my eye on you, son."

"Yes, sir," Otto said.

Wally hitched up his pants and glared at Otto. "That goes double for me."

I pulled Otto free and steered him toward the stairs, but of course he had to stop to scoop up his music, minus the copies the reporters had pinched.

"What happened this afternoon?" I asked him as we headed upstairs. "When did you get out? What did they say to you?"

I could have fired off questions till I was hoarse; Otto wasn't listening. He was staring up at Callie, who was still leaning over the banister. She smiled at him.

"You're Louise's roommate?" he asked, gawking.

The day had been so long and terrible, and our situations all seemed so bound up together, that I forgot Callie and Otto hadn't met. She'd glimpsed him this morning as he was being hauled away, but the frenzy of the moment hadn't allowed for formal introductions.

"I'm awfully sorry about your cousin," Otto said, after I introduced them. "I hope you don't think *I* was the one who . . ."

Callie shook her head. "Louise explained it all to me. Now come in. I'll warm up some soup. You must be hungry if you've been in jail all day."

"They gave me a sandwich, b-but I am a little hungry," Otto stammered. "It's very nice of you to offer, Miss Gail."

"Callie," she corrected.

She ducked into the kitchenette to heat up the soup—the limit of her cooking expertise—while I got back to my questioning. "How did you get out?" I asked Otto.

He didn't hear the question. He was staring off toward the kitchen.

"Otto?"

He turned back to me, blinking. "Oh—how did I get out? Well, I don't know if I ever would have if your aunt hadn't sent Mr. Faber. Now there's a clever fellow. He told Mr. Muldoon he couldn't hold me because there was no evidence except Wally's, and that he'd have contradictory testimony from the people at my hotel." Otto frowned. "But that man Wally seems very sure, doesn't he? If I didn't know better, I'd almost believe him myself."

Even as he spoke to me, his attention strayed more than once in the direction of the kitchen.

"Wally is an idiot," I said. "So is Detective Muldoon."

"Muldoon's not so bad. He listened to Mr. Faber. Otherwise I wouldn't be sitting here. I don't know how I'll ever be able to thank your aunt enough."

I chewed my lip, wondering. Why had Muldoon listened to Faber, but not to me? Had there been some sort of payoff? I'd heard stories about crooked policemen in this town—money slipped under tables for them to look the other way. I hoped nothing like that had happened today. Otto was innocent, and it shouldn't require jiggery-pokery to prove it.

Otto, who'd been sitting in the armchair, straightened and peered around the room. "So this is where you live? It's nice. Real homey."

"It's not looking its best at the moment."

"Well, no." His gaze flicked toward the closed door down the hall. In a lower voice, he added, "Is that where . . . ?" I nodded and he swallowed, his Adam's apple leaping above his collar. "You shouldn't be here, should you?"

"We're going to stay downstairs for a few days. The neighbors are out of town for the week."

Callie darted her head into the room. "We keep coming back here, though. It seems second nature."

He nodded, drinking her in with *that look.* I shifted. Callie was smiling back at him gently, the way she might smile if we'd brought home a wounded puppy.

"What about you?" I asked him. "Where are you going to stay?"

"At my hotel, I guess," he said. "I still have money left from what the music publisher sent me. I'll need to find a room soon, though, to economize."

"You're going to stay in New York?" Otto had been so much a part of my Altoona life, it was hard imagining him here permanently.

"Of course. If I'm really going to make a go of my songwriting, I need to be where the business is."

"I thought maybe you'd want to go back to Altoona. You've had a rocky start here."

Again, that gaze strayed kitchenward. "I can't see going back to the butcher shop, nice as your uncle always was to me. And now your aunt Irene. Gosh, without your family I'd be a mess, wouldn't I?"

I wasn't positive he was out of the woods yet. There was that sheet music, for one thing. "I saw reporters picking up your music. I hope they don't mention your song in connection with the murder."

Callie zipped into the room. "I want to see your song." She picked up a sheet from the table.

"Callie might be cast in a musical revue," I told Otto.

"Oh!" He sat up straighter, his eyes brightening with a new respectful adoration that almost had me rolling my eyes. You'd think he'd just met Ethel Barrymore.

She scanned the music, smiling. "This is a sweet tune." She flicked back to the cover. "And it's dedicated to Louise!" She grinned at me.

I foolishly blushed, but not nearly as much as Otto, who was halfway to tomato on the color spectrum.

" 'She's my tootsie from Altoona,' " Callie sang in a lilting soprano. Her heels bounced a little to the rhythm, and the rest of her bounced along.

"Why, you're loaded with talent," Otto exclaimed.

Smelling soup burning, I hopped up. "Her singing's better than her cooking."

Otto had her sing a verse; then he joined in on the second. From the worshipful look in his eyes, I guessed my old Altoona beau had found a new muse.

Chapter 6

Van Hooten and McChesney was located in an unremarkable brick house on East Thirty-eighth Street, sandwiched between a brownstone on one side and a six-story apartment tower on the corner. A hundred years earlier, our building had probably been a very comfortable home for a well-to-do family. Since then, it had been converted into our inadequate offices, with the upper floor serving as a warehouse for long-forgotten titles. Mr. McChesney didn't believe in throwing anything away.

The first thing I would have thrown away was Guy Van Hooten, who, as the scion of one half of the firm, had claimed the largest ground-floor office upon his father's death. It was both the nicest room in the building and, since it was Guy's office, the loneliest. Sometimes we wouldn't see Guy for weeks at a stretch, and when he did deign to show up, it was impossible to say what he did. Right now he was on one of his greatest streaks of work-shirking yet, and my coworkers on the second floor had bets placed on how long it would last. Already Guy was the Ty Cobb of absenteeism.

Ogden McChesney could be found more frequently at the office, although he was only marginally more productive than Guy. Yet I had a real fondness for my aunt's old friend. Aunt Irene had confided to me that Mr. McChesney had proposed to her twice over the years. Mr. McChesney had also published her first book, before she'd moved on to greener pastures. To be honest, few pastures in the world of New York publishing *weren't* greener than Van Hooten and McChesney. These days Mr. McChesney did little in the business that bore his name, but he did pore over the financial accounts every day, which probably accounted for the bulk of his ulcer complaints.

The coworker I spent the most time with was Jackson Beasley, a Southern gentleman and old college acquaintance of Guy's who'd been brought in to serve as editor not long before I arrived. He and I shared the space that used to be the house's parlor. Yellow-and-white-striped wallpaper browning along the vertical seams appeared original to the house. A hideous heavy fixture like a wooden wagon wheel studded with large bulbs hung low from the center of the ceiling, and at least one bulb always seemed to be burnt out at any given moment. Against the wall opposite the foyer stood three high bookcases. Tucked in wherever convenient—and occasionally inconvenient—were five-drawer file cabinets and a small table and chair, where our office boy, Oliver, was stationed when he wasn't running errands.

My desk was wedged into the corner near the entrance hall's archway. It was a tall rolltop model in dark-stained walnut, with a handy pullout shelf for writing notes. Stacked at the back of the desktop was a matching shelf unit that reached halfway to the ceiling. I loved my desk, with its seemingly endless cubbies and little drawers. I had a place for everything. Unfortunately, one thing I didn't have was privacy, since mere feet away stood Jackson's desk, identical to mine.

He was less enamored than I of his desk and this office arrangement. At the time he'd been hired, the building had no more private offices, so he had been squeezed into this large room with the secretary. Jackson, though relieved to have a job, had never recovered from the slight. He'd attended Harvard at the same time as Guy and had probably distinguished himself academically in a way Guy never had. Yet Guy, while giving Jackson a much-needed position, had insulted him by shoehorning him in with the secretary and the office boy while his own spacious office remained empty ninety percent of the time.

My day began at nine, but I always arrived early to make some tea or coffee and to freshen up after the morning's commute. Since I was both an early bird and Irene Livingston Green's niece, Mr. McChesney had given me a key to the building. These early mornings provided blessed solitude. Although the flat Callie and I shared was a step up from life with Aunt Sonja and Uncle Dolph, where I'd lived in a houseful of family and usually a boarder or two, I still craved privacy. In New York, it was easy to feel surrounded all the time, just another ant on a teeming hill. Time alone was a luxury I didn't take for granted.

This morning, however, my mind wasn't in a relaxing mood. It flitted through all the drama of the past days, a disturbing magic lantern show constantly whirring inside my head. Ethel's horrible murder, Otto's being hauled away, Callie's tense, worried face, Madame Serena. *A baby crying . . . where is its mother?*

Why, with so much happening, did that horrid woman have to stir me up this way? I got out the broom and dustpan and attacked the floors with a fury. Fortune-tellers were frauds, of course. Clever frauds who picked up on subtle clues in a person's appearance and spun vague prophecies and predictions, trying to pass them off as meaningful. The baby crying was just in my mind, planted there by a charlatan who told lies for money.

Somewhere inside my satchel there was a torn sheet of paper with an address scrawled across it in blurred ink. The same address was written indelibly in my memory: 7 East Eightieth Street. Going there would seem wrong, I felt, but not going there tested my willpower. I'd come close. One recent Sunday afternoon in Central Park, standing at the southern edge of the museum, I'd looked longingly down Eightieth Street. I was knowledgeable enough about New York to know what I'd find there—a fashionable house on a street where even tidy shrubberies were safely encased behind wrought iron. Eightieth Street was far from the hoi polloi, a place where its inhabitants, even the children, never emerged from their doors until scrubbed, garbed, and coiffed to perfection, and uniformed nannies pushed baby carriages as elegantly designed and fitted out as the real carriages their families owned, or had until it had been traded for a shiny long automobile and chauffeur.

When the doorbell sounded, I jumped as if I'd been caught somewhere I shouldn't have been. I expected it was just a deliveryman, or possibly a boy from the Western Union office. Guy Van Hooten's cohort sent telegrams in the thoughtless way my girl-friends and I used to pass notes in school. But when I swung the door open, Ford Fitzsimmons stood before me, his face sprouting out of the enormous bouquet he was holding.

"Too early to call?" he asked.

"Oh . . . I . . ." I hardly knew what to say. "What are you—?" Were those flowers for me?

His smile dissolved into a mask of concern. "Are you all right, Louise? Your eyes are red."

"I'm fine," I piped up. "I've been sweeping, and all the dust simply . . . or I might have a touch of hay fever." Dust, hay fever . . . did it matter? I doubted Ford Fitzsimmons had come here to discuss my health and happiness. Why *was* he here? "Come in."

Once I'd closed the door behind us, it struck me more forcefully that his visit was odd . . . and early. None of my other colleagues had yet arrived. Alarm stabbed at me, but I shook it off. This was work, others would be coming soon . . . and I was curious about those flowers.

He circled the room where my desk was, recoiling a bit from the hovering light fixture, and took in the top-heavy desks and shabby walls. "Not what I imagined." His gaze rested on two framed Hogarth prints, speckled with age, and then a 1913 complimentary calendar we'd received from Gotham Printers featuring a picture of a slim-waisted damsel at a printing press and the slogan "*Just my type!*" in enthusiastic script.

"May I offer you some coffee?" It was my habitual offering to visitors to the office. "I usually arrive early and prepare some."

"I knew you'd be the first to arrive," he said. "Even on a Saturday. That's why I waited."

Waited? "You were watching the office?"

He nodded.

And yet I was here for a full ten minutes before he'd knocked.

My face must have been an open book, because he hurried to explain. "Once I saw you, I ran down to the florist and got you these." He presented the flowers to me, and I savored the riot of fragrance they lent the musty room—rose, lilac, and carnation. No one had given me flowers since . . . well, probably since Otto brought me some on some years-ago birthday.

"Thank you, Mr. Fitzsimmons."

"Ford."

"Ford." I inhaled again. A person could get drunk on that smell. "They're beautiful. Now that you've glimpsed our drab desk cave, you can see how a little nature is appreciated here."

He frowned at the room like a prospective buyer. "It could stand some new wallpaper."

He was clutching something else, I noticed. A bulging manila envelope. "Is that for us?"

He looked down in faint surprise at the envelope, as though he'd forgotten it. I doubted he had. "My second book." He held it out to me.

I had to put my flowers down on the desk so I could take it from him.

"It's called *Sun of the East,*" he said. "There's a letter addressed to Mr. Van Hooten included. I stayed up half the night composing it, like a schoolboy sweating over a love letter."

I couldn't bring myself to tell him that he'd stayed up half the night for nothing. The chance of Guy's actually reading that letter was only slightly greater than that of Henry James and Edith Wharton popping in for lunch.

"I haven't been to sleep yet," he confessed. "Too keyed up."

"Then I'm not sure whether to bring you coffee or, like a stern mother, order you to go home and go to bed."

"I'll take the coffee. Somehow I can't imagine you as a mother." I must have wobbled a little, because he hastened to add, "At least, not a stern one."

I left to work my magic in the cupboard that passed as a kitchen. When I returned with a tray bearing two cups, Ford was leaning back in my chair, his legs propped on the tall metal wastebasket, his eyes closed.

"Mr. Fitzsimmons?" No response. "Ford?"

Abracadabra. He sat up, smiling. "That's better. Oh—piping hot." He took a cup and sipped. "Perfect."

I stole Jackson's chair and rolled it over. "You didn't have to bring your book in person, you know. The flowers were unnecessary, too. I would have made sure Mr. Van Hooten saw your work even without a bribe." He would see it, eventually, but whether he would read it was another question. I would read it, but Ford already knew how little my opinion counted. "There was no reason to butter me up."

"Is that what I'm doing?" He put down his cup. "I guess it is. But not entirely for the reasons you suspect. I'm not all work and ambition, you know. Sometimes I have an urge to bring flowers to a beautiful girl."

I flushed, which was probably his intention, but I couldn't help feeling he'd just overplayed his hand. *Beautiful* was a word men reserved for girls like Callie. And though Ford was handsome—few women *wouldn't* be flattered by his attention—there was something about the role of gentleman caller that didn't quite suit him. His manner was a little too labored and, like the muscled physique beneath his best suit, seemed to be hiding something rougher.

"We're both relative newcomers to this fair city," he said. "I thought you might feel as lonely as I do sometimes."

Maybe I was being too suspicious. Men never did seem to have unselfish motives in my experience. The best man I knew was Otto—and now even he had turned fickle. Not that I wanted Otto's undying devotion. I'd had it and dismissed it. But he'd been a constant in my young life. Discovering that even he was changeable caused a pang.

Ford rolled closer to me. "What's the matter, Louise? You've had a sad look in your eyes ever since I got here."

"We've had a terrible time since I saw you at my aunt's," I confessed.

His eyes filled with concern. "What's happened?"

"My roommate's cousin was murdered in our apartment. I'm sure you've heard about it. It's been on the front pages of all the papers."

He drew back, shocked. "You mean that girl I saw at the party? Carrie?"

"Callie. Yes, it was her cousin."

His face paled. "That murder in our neighborhood? That was *your* apartment?" At my nod, he said, "I read about it, but I never dreamed . . ." He shuddered; then he took my hand and pressed it. "Why did you let me rattle on about my book all this time? You should have said something. How awful for you . . . and Callie."

"Yes." I looked into his eyes, two perfect pools of blue. Clear blue. He said just the right things, with just the right tremor of emotion. Why, then, did I doubt his sincerity? My gaze skittered to the envelope with the manuscript in it—an envelope like the one Wally had seen on the night of the murder, carried by the mystery man on the stairs.

"What do the police say?" he asked. "Have they caught the murderer yet? I read about a suspect being apprehended."

"That was the wrong man. The police seem to realize that, even if the papers already have convicted him."

"Oh dear." He drew his brows together, all concern for my well-being and safety.

I didn't believe him. He'd known my address the night of the murder, and it had been printed in the paper the next morning. He lived nearby, might even have been one of the curious neighbors who'd gathered outside our building. I'd called them buzzards and ghouls, but it was human nature to be curious about death, especially murder. It would be especially understandable if you had an acquaintance living in the murder house . . . except if you were trying not to draw attention to yourself because you knew you'd been seen the night of the murder.

"It's a strange thing . . ." I began carefully.

"Beyond strange," he broke in. "Terrifying."

"Yes, but what seemed particularly odd was that our landlady's son, who lives on the first floor, saw a man the night of the murder. The man was light-haired, of medium height, and clean-shaven."

"Like the man they arrested."

"He was just a friend of mine," I said. "The man Wally saw on the stairs was carrying an envelope under his arm—like that one." I nodded at Ford's novel.

He followed my gaze, then paled. "Louise, you don't think . . ." His hand fell away from mine. "Good God."

"I'm only curious because I gave you my address the night before last, when you were at my aunt's. And you left early."

I hadn't meant to sound accusing, but that's how he took it. He drew back, offended. "I went to a tavern," he said, emphasizing each word. When I said nothing, he blew out a shaky breath. "Well. This is quite a day. Not even nine in the morning yet and already I've been accused of murder. And by the girl I—" His voice broke off, and he snatched his hat off the top of my typewriter.

I stood when he did. "I'm not accusing you, I'm just . . ." I didn't know how to finish, and bitter laughter met my fumbled words.

"Oh no, you're not accusing," he said. "You're just asking if I was the suspicious character seen the night your housemate was brutally murdered."

"The man might have seen something," I said. "He wasn't necessarily the killer."

"It makes no difference. I was not the man. Do you understand? It wasn't me."

I nodded. I wasn't convinced, but I wasn't going to call him a liar. In fact, I suddenly realized the difficulty of my position. I was either foolishly accusing and alienating a man who'd been nothing but friendly, almost affectionate, toward me, or I was even more foolishly accusing a man who might be a murderer when I was shut in an empty office with him. Alone.

His eyes widened. "Stop looking at me like that!"

"I'm sorry." I must have been sizing him up as a murderer.

"For God's sake, do you really think I could be such a monster?"

Did I? I looked into those eyes again, and my doubts tumbled and looped and then faded. I remembered Ethel on that bed, that hideous tableau of violence. The man before me couldn't have done that. "No," I said. "I don't."

He shook his head. "Damn. This visit hasn't gone at all according to plan. I'd hoped . . ."

He turned toward the door, but I stopped him with a hand on the arm of his jacket. "Hoped what?"

"To discover that your feelings were running in the same direction as my own. That our minds were on the same track."

And there it was. He cared about me, but my suspicions had probably snuffed that out. Yet I wondered if I would have found a pretext for being wary of him, or any man. Maybe I was hopelessly damaged when it came to trusting the opposite sex.

"I'm sorry," I said. "This past day has been . . . well, I can't put it into words. Callie and I found Ethel that night, Ford. Every minute since then has seemed like a waking nightmare. If I've offended you with my questions, please understand where my morbid paranoia is springing from. Our conversation at the party seems a lifetime ago now, yet I remember going home that evening thinking it was one of the nicest things that's happened to me since coming to New York."

A little of his tension seeped away. "I was beginning to think I'd dreamed our connection that night—or that I'd simply drunk too much."

"You *had* drunk too much."

He smiled. "I need the love of a good woman to reform me. Like in one of your aunt's books."

"I didn't know you'd read any of them."

A hint of red stained his cheeks. "I might have gone to the library yesterday and checked one out. *Violet in the Shade*. I wanted to read it so I could have something to mention when I wrote your aunt a note of apology for my boorish behavior at her get-together. What do you think she'd make of that?"

"She'd call it handsome of you," I said. "So would I."

He stepped closer. "Louise, I—"

The front door swung open. The moment Jackson Beasley appeared in the foyer, he had a perfect view of Ford and me standing together beneath the pendulous light fixture. We sprang apart like guilty lovers in a melodrama.

Jackson, who was carrying a handled case and a newspaper, recovered from surprise faster than I managed to. He rushed forward. "Louise—I never expected you to come in this morning," he said in as rapid-fire a manner as the remnants of his Alabama drawl would allow. "Are you sure you should be here?"

"It's a relief, to be honest," I said. "The flat's not exactly comforting right now."

"Of course." He turned a curious, expectant stare on Ford. "You aren't alone, at least."

"Ford Fitzsimmons." Ford offered his hand and gave Jackson a firm shake. "I'm very pleased to meet you, Mr.—"

"This is our editor, Mr. Beasley," I said, worried he'd mistaken

Jackson for Guy Van Hooten. As if Guy would ever grace the office with his presence on a Saturday morning.

My coworker crossed to put his briefcase on his desk and removed his hat, his attention seizing on the large bouquet on my desk and the fact that his chair had been moved. The trespass caused his shoulders to stiffen. "Ford Fitzsimmons . . . that name sounds familiar."

"Mr. Fitzsimmons is an author," I said. "He's submitted his second book to us."

Jackson's big dome of a forehead, which gained new territory every day as his hairline retreated, crinkled into a mass of lines. He wasn't fond of authors—at least not our authors. In his university days he'd imagined hobnobbing with the literary giants of his age, not writers of books on the salutary digestive effects of pickle juice tonic and other gems like that.

"His first novel was very promising," I said. *Please don't remember that you hated it.*

Ford smiled at Jackson. "I'm mostly here as Miss Faulk's friend."

"She needs friends, I think." Jackson unfolded his newspaper, which featured another headline about the murder—this time with an accompanying picture of Otto's sheet music on the front. My heart sank. Poor Otto. His big chance was being undermined by forces out of his control. It was so unfair.

Ford's lips turned down as he studied the front page. " 'My Tootsie from Altoona,' " he read aloud. " 'For Louise.' " He looked at me. "Aren't *you* from Altoona?"

"So is Otto—the songwriter." My face heated, but I soldiered on. "We've known each other for years."

His expression clouded over. "I see."

He obviously didn't. He looked almost angry, as if I'd led him on. "Otto worked for my uncle. The one I lived with."

"Even better," Ford muttered.

"Your uncle the butcher?" Jackson squinted at the paper. "The newspapermen are calling the barbarian who did the murder the Village Butcher."

"Otto might have been a butcher's assistant, but he's the gentlest soul you can imagine."

"Well." Ford took a step back. "I suppose I should leave you two to your work."

I trailed after him, frustrated. Before Jackson had come in, it seemed that Ford and I understood each other. Now things were all muddled up again. From Ford's expression you'd think I was the Village Butcher's moll-accomplice.

"I'll read your novel soon," I promised.

He murmured a good-bye and headed out the door.

When I turned back, Jackson was rolling his chair back to his desk. "Curious fellow."

"I wish he hadn't left in such a strange mood," I said.

"Don't worry your mind about that one," he said. "Writers make the worst husbands."

I scowled. "I don't think of Mr. Fitzsimmons as a matrimonial prospect."

He frowned at the paper. "I doubt songwriters are much better."

Oh, for Pete's sake. "Can't a woman just exist in the world, making friends and living her life, without everyone assuming she's on the constant lookout for a husband?"

Jackson's brows arched toward that big dome of his. "What do you intend to do with your life, then?"

"I'm doing it."

He seemed genuinely perplexed. "You want to be a secretary, forever and ever? That's all?"

No, that wasn't all. But apparently it never occurred to Jackson that I might be capable of more. Of doing what he did, say. Most days I wasn't even sure myself. I'd taken the job that was offered through my connection to my aunt—much as I'd accepted the work that my uncles had offered me in Altoona, managing accounts at their butcher and fish shops. Despite the fact that I'd just drifted into this job, I was essentially doing many of the same tasks Jackson performed. But I lacked a college degree, and I was the wrong sex.

"Well, I suppose an *exceptional* woman might feel called to a profession as a man naturally is," Jackson allowed. He gestured toward my typewriter. "But is that what you consider a calling?"

Was it? I'd spent several months trying to believe it was. I'd worked hard, yet apparently those I worked alongside saw little value in what I did, at least compared to their own worth.

Jackson sighed and pulled his chair up to his desk to begin his day. His eye fell on Ford's discarded coffee cup. "Fix me a cup of coffee, won't you, Louise?"

I never realized how exhausting the news could be. Back in Altoona, scanning my uncle's *Evening Mirror* after he was done with it had kept me reasonably well informed. But in New York the newspaper business was a relentless hour-by-hour concern. No sooner had my fellow Manhattanites put aside their morning papers—they had about fifteen to choose from—than the afternoon editions hit the street. Editions were staggered, too, so that there was always a newsboy somewhere braying the latest headline. When I'd first arrived, the local obsession with being au courant seemed invigorating. Now as I scuttled past brass-lunged newsies shouting about the Village Butcher, my enchantment with the fourth estate was at an end. Forests in Washington were being reduced to stumps so hacks could spread lies about poor Otto.

A slightly smaller group of scribes and gawkers loitered around our front door today. They swarmed me, but I was used to battling my way inside now. At the sound of my feet on the stairs, a door far above me opened. "Max? Max?"

Lucia's mournful wail tore at me, and I looked up to see her leaning over the banister, peering down the stairwell. "It's me, Lucia," I said.

"Oh." She disappeared and a short silence followed, heavy with disappointment. Max had not come back yet. "*Buongiorno,* Louise."

"*Buongiorno*."

Her door above clicked shut. Were the police still looking for Max? I supposed they were, which was why he could probably never come back until the true killer was caught and convicted. But what if they never found the killer?

Poor Lucia.

Callie and I had spent the night in the saxophonists' second-floor flat, but it was empty now. I wandered upstairs to see if Callie had returned to ours. The saxophonists, we'd discovered, lived in primitive conditions. The apartment was the same layout as ours, but they used it in an odd way. The larger bedroom seemed to be where they stowed their musical gear, although with them on tour now it was practically empty except for an old saxophone that seemed to be used for spare parts and a trunk holding various brass fittings, tools, oils, solvents, and glues for repairing instruments. The small bedroom contained only one rather high bed. This puzzled us until we pulled back the moth-eaten wool blanket covering it and discovered three thin mattresses piled atop the bedsprings.

"The boys must spread the top two mattresses on the floor each night and sleep that way," I'd surmised after studying the mattress pile.

"Do you think they draw straws every night for the bed?" Callie had wondered aloud.

"Or maybe the real brothers get the bed and the fake ones are relegated to the floor."

Another puzzle was how they survived almost entirely without furniture. A few mismatched wood chairs littered the main room, none of them the slightest bit comfortable, along with three metal music stands. There was no table, yet we could tell that they cooked because the kitchenette boasted two battered pots, and grease and various food splatters created a disgusting varnish on the surface of the cook top, counter, and walls. A fine layer of dust covered the floor everywhere except a few patches where the mattresses were dragged out to the living room every night. Which didn't make us any more enthusiastic about sleeping on those mattresses, I can tell you.

I laughed to think how I'd imagined myself combing through the place in the saxophonists' absence, hunting for evidence that one of the Bleecker Blowers was a murderer. Nothing had been cleaned in the apartment in—well, perhaps forever. Any trace of the murder would have been obvious. Nor was it likely that evidence had been hidden in the apartment, for the simple reason that there was nowhere in the apartment to hide anything. There were no bureaus or wardrobes. The one small closet held a knee-high stack of old sheet music, two men's overcoats, a box containing a jumble of bed linens and towels, all dirty but nothing bloodstained. There were no clues to be found in that apartment. No comfort, either. Perhaps one murderous saxophonist might have possessed the foresight to dispose of all the bloody evidence, but I doubted he could have managed to do that right under the noses of his roommates.

As I entered our flat, a figure rising from the sofa startled me.

"Otto! What are you doing here?"

"I came in and no one was here," he said. "It was so much bother getting in past the policeman, the reporters, and then crazy Wally, I decided to stay put until you came back instead of battling my way out again."

That made sense. My heartbeat slowed to normal again. "It's not that I mind your being here, but you scared me silly."

"Sorry. Callie told me I could visit anytime," he said. "She said the key was under the mat in the hall."

It was. It probably shouldn't have been, but Callie had the bad habit of forgetting her key. She said no one in Little Falls locked their doors. Come to think of it, I couldn't remember Aunt Sonja and Uncle Dolph's house ever being locked, either.

"Where is Callie?" he asked, peering over my shoulder as if I were hiding her.

I flopped onto the sofa and slipped off my shoes. Not exactly delicate behavior, but my dogs were killing me. Besides, it was just Otto. "I'm not sure. When I left for the office this morning, she was still asleep. She must have gone out on some errand or another."

"I've been here an hour," Otto said.

So Callie had been gone at least that long. Worry gnawed at me.

"You wouldn't believe what happened to me today, Louise. I walked into a Kresge's and in the music department they were playing my song." He beamed. "Actually playing it without my having to ask them to."

"Really? I worried, with the headlines . . ."

"That's what *I* thought, but I asked the lady at the register about the song—not telling her I was the author, you understand—and she said they'd sold five copies already. Five! And that's just in one morning, in one store."

"That's good." Perhaps the publicity hadn't harmed him—or at least not yet.

"If they keep on selling, I'll be on my way. And then maybe—"

Whatever he was about to say was lost. The door jerked open

and Callie scooted in, slammed it behind her, and leaned back against it, panting. "He's back!"

"Max?" I guessed, dread filling me.

"What?" Her eyes focused on me, confused. "No—the man who's been following me."

"There's been a man following you?" Otto asked, alarmed.

"He trailed me all the way back from"—she gulped, then continued—"I worried he would walk right into the house after me."

"The man with the mustache?" When she nodded, I ran to the open front window and stuck my head out, peering at the smattering of people below. "I don't see a man with a mustache . . . oh, except him." I drew back and pointed him out to Callie, who was hovering at my shoulder. Behind her was Otto.

Her breath hitched in frustration. "That's not him."

"Who is following you?" Otto asked.

"I don't know. Some man." She crossed the room and flung herself onto the sofa. "I swear I'm not imagining things. He followed me twenty blocks, at least, always a half a block behind. I even stopped at several stores and when I came out, he was still behind me."

"We need to tell the police," I said.

She let out a groan. "I've just been to the police this morning, to see about Ethel." My confusion must have shown, because she explained, "Her body, I mean. I need to arrange for the burial, and tell Dora when to come."

"Did you mention the man following you to the police?"

"No—at that point, I hadn't seen him since yesterday. I was beginning to think I'd just imagined it. And then I wondered . . ."

"What?" I asked.

"Oh, nothing." She rubbed her palms together, then blurted out, "Only I wondered if it could have anything to do with Sawyer. He always acts—acted, that is—so jealous."

Otto glanced from Callie to me. "Who's Sawyer?"

My God. Why hadn't I thought of that? "You're right. We should tell the police about him, Callie."

"No," she said quickly. "Sawyer wouldn't be involved in this. He knows having a shadow would frighten me. And drawing attention to himself is the last thing he wants now."

And why would that be? I frowned. Was I imagining things, or did something in her tone ring false? "We should talk to Sawyer, then."

"Who's Sawyer?" Otto asked again, impatiently.

Callie was shaking her head. "No, I told him it was over, and I won't go knocking on his door now pestering him. It's best just to forget about him."

As she spoke, Otto's features took on a glum cast. "Oh, a beau."

"Not anymore," Callie said.

He brightened. "You gave him the brush-off?" At Callie's nod, he said, "Then you're right to forget all about him. Say, I was just telling Louise about what happened to me today. I was walking down a street and I saw a five-and-dime . . ."

As Otto related his Kresge's triumph again, my mind whirred. Was I mistaken, or was Callie holding something back? If there was even a possibility that the mysterious man was someone Sawyer had sent, wouldn't she want to do something about it?

Even if she didn't, *I* did. Callie might be content to leave Sawyer alone, but I decided to pay a call on him just as soon as I could.

CHAPTER 7

Newsprint isn't kind to the complexion. On Monday morning, seated on the crowded train on the way to work, I found myself staring back at me. *Is this the Village Butcher's "tootsie"?* read the caption below my picture. One of the photographers had caught me on the stoop, and now I was gaping in outrage at commuters all over the city. My mouth was opened in an O of anger, and my face in black and white was mottled gray. The hat shading my eyes enhanced my dark, sinister look. One consolation was the probability that no one would recognize me, unless they went out of their way to read the *Sun-Herald.* And who did? It was obviously an inferior, gossipy rag.

Oliver, our office boy, practically tackled me as he came through the door that morning brandishing three copies of the *Sun-Herald.* "Toots, you're famous!"

Jackson scolded him. "Her name is Miss Faulk to you." But even Jackson was eyeing the photo with more than passing interest.

"Aw, Louise doesn't mind." Oliver tossed the newspapers down on my desk and pulled a wax-paper-wrapped donut out of his pocket. "Do you, Toots?"

"You can call me anything you want," I told Oliver, "as long as you promise to get rid of those awful papers."

Jackson clucked at me. "You'll regret those words."

Oliver hiked a hip onto the corner of my desk and inspected me with new curiosity. He was a boy of fourteen—the nephew of a friend of our proofreader's wife. His tendency to pudginess, nut-colored eyes, and brown bristly hair gave him the look of an energetic woodchuck. "Who'd've guessed from looking at you that you're sort of interesting?" he said.

"Sorry to disillusion you," I answered, "but newspapers lie. I'm not interesting, at least not in the way they're insinuating. Otto is my friend, but only a friend. And he's not a murderer."

Oliver sagged in disappointment. For a few glorious moments, he'd been in the presence of a scandalous woman. "Well, you're still the first lady I ever met who got her picture in the paper."

I leaned toward him and whispered confidentially, "Just between you and me and the desk lamp, it's not the first time."

His eyes went wide. "No foolin'?"

"No foolin'. I was plastered all over the front page of the *Altoona Evening Mirror* a few years back."

"How come?"

"I won the elocution prize at the city's all-school symposium."

When he realized he'd been had, he snorted with laughter. "Yeah, that fits. I bet your *Hiawatha* knocked 'em cold."

"Would you like a sample?"

"Don't you have work to attend to?" Jackson made shooing motions at Oliver, but I sensed the question was meant for me, too. "You're dribbling crumbs everywhere."

Oliver hopped to his feet and lifted his half-eaten donut to his forehead in a mock salute. "Aye-aye, Cap'n."

After Oliver clomped upstairs—probably to hand newspapers around to the staff on the second floor—I informed Jackson that I needed to take a longer lunch break than usual that day. Jackson was not, technically, my boss. But since Guy Van Hooten's absentee streak was still holding strong and even dyspeptic Mr. McChesney seemed uninterested in how anything was actually getting done these days, Jackson had assumed the role of de facto manager of everyone.

He opened his mouth to question me and I cut him off with the ominous sounding, "Police business."

Mr. McChesney was just coming in the door as I walked out at eleven o'clock. His tall figure stooped slightly forward, so that his walking stick sometimes appeared to keep him upright. As always, he was impeccably, if slightly unfashionably, dressed, with dark tweed coat, vest, and a high, starched collar. He'd obviously shrunk since the clothes were new, because they now hung loose on his bones. A gold tie pin and the heavy watch fob spanning his waistcoat pockets were his two extravagances.

Seeing me, he grabbed my elbow. "Poor Louise! You shouldn't be here. Take the week. There's nothing here for you to do that can't be put off, surely?"

"I'll be back this afternoon," I assured him. "I just have a bit of police business."

Police business was a magic phrase. I probably could have told him I needed a two-year paid vacation and received it as long as I claimed it on behalf of police business. Unfortunately, it was a lie. I was going to see not the police, but Sawyer Attinger.

When I emerged from the subway thirty minutes later into the canyons of Wall Street, how little I knew of the island I now called home became clear to me. Here was a place mere minutes by subway from my flat in Greenwich Village, but it was an entirely different world. Austere buildings of granite grayed with coal soot loomed close and imposing, temples of finance and insurance modeled in the Greek revival fashion. At first glance, I couldn't see that there was any life here besides finance—no homes, no schools, no groceries—yet it was teeming with people, mostly men. Only the old spire of Trinity Church seemed to remind one that there was any purpose to the world apart from business.

I'd hunted down Sawyer's business, Attinger and Beebe, in our office's city directory earlier that morning, and after meandering the wrong way down one street, I found the correct building. I tried to practice what I was going to say in the elevator up to the seventh floor, but the truth was I was unsure. I had no authority to question Sawyer, even as Callie's friend. She would kill me if she found out what I was up to. But I had to know if he was involved in the strange goings-on of the past few days.

Upon pushing the brass bar to let myself through the oak doors of Attinger and Beebe, I was confronted by a roomful of desks, most empty, with men clustered around a clacking stock ticker, watching the tape with the avidity of eagles circling a fish pond. A few men held desk phones and bellowed instructions into them. I approached one of them and asked for Mr. Attinger.

"Over there." He rolled a shoulder toward some double doors at the end of the room.

Going through those doors felt like passing from chaos to sanctuary. The sound from outside was muffled by the private office's reception room. A thick Turkish carpet lay on the floor, and on the dark walls hung paintings of tall ships on turbulent seas.

Sawyer's secretary, a round-faced man no older than me, frowned when I told him I needed to speak to Mr. Attinger. He gave me a cautious up-and-down look and then slid an anxious glance toward the closed door to his right. "Mr. Attinger is very busy."

"As am I," I replied. "But it's imperative I see him today."

He gestured to a leather upholstered chair in the corner and advised me to take a seat. I did, and as the minutes ticked by on the clock behind the secretary's desk, I grew more restless. The secretary made no move to inform Sawyer that I was waiting. When the inside office door swung open at last, I stood to remind the secretary of my existence. Sawyer appeared, more handsome than ever in a perfectly tailored suit the gray hue of a pigeon's back, guiding a handsome blonde in her thirties out of his private office. He caught sight of me and his eyes flashed in momentary alarm. He then steered the woman more forcefully toward the outer door, although she glanced back at me in curiosity.

"We'll talk more about it this evening, Margaret."

Margaret. Sawyer's wife. I knew her name from Callie. Margaret Attinger was very striking, with ash-blond hair peeping from under a voluminous hat that looked as if half a rainforest of birds had been defeathered to adorn it. She resembled Callie a bit. A slightly older, richer version.

After escorting his wife through the outer office and to the elevator, Sawyer returned and greeted me almost as if I were a stranger. As if his wife were still watching. "Miss—?"

"Faulk," I said, playing along.

His genial smile was more for the secretary's benefit than mine. "What a pleasure to see you. Come in, come in." He kept a formal distance as he led the way into his private sanctum.

My gaze strayed around the room lined in rich walnut wainscoting. Behind the desk hung a portrait of a man who resembled an old, whisker-laden Sawyer—father or grandfather Attinger, no doubt. The view from the high windows was blocked by inside awning shades covering the bottom pane. Through the upper half I caught sight of a seagull swooping past. I always forgot how close we were to the ocean, and frankly I'd never felt farther from it than in this austere, manly room in the ventricle of America's financial heart.

Sawyer gestured to a chair opposite his desk and shut the door. Then, crossing the room, he growled in low tones, "You fool! Have you lost your mind? What in God's name brought you here?" His eyes snapped with irritation and suspicion. The mask of civility had dropped.

"Don't people come to see you in your office?" I asked, sitting.

"Clients do. And friends. Are you either of those?"

He had me there. "I'm here as Callie's friend."

He circled to the other side of his desk and seated himself. "She sent you, too?"

"No . . ." *Too?* Who else had been by? "She'd probably have my hide if she found out I was here."

"Then why are you here?"

"To tell you to call off whatever goon you've hired to follow Callie."

His hostility faded. "What goon?"

His voice struck just the right note of alarm, but I doubted his sincerity. "A short man, with a mustache, usually wearing an ill-fitting brown suit?"

If he knew whom I was talking about, he did a good job of concealing it. "I have no idea who you mean. If there's someone following her, why doesn't she tell the police?" He added petulantly, "She obviously has no qualms about talking to them."

Whatever was meant by that remark escaped me. I crossed my arms. "The night Ethel was murdered, you were following Callie."

"I most certainly wasn't. I was *waiting* for her."

"Lurking around the corner from our apartment," I reminded him. "Lying in wait for her."

His face crimsoned in irritation. "All right. I lost my head. I've got it screwed on again now. I might have been crazy about Callie once, but that's done with. Completely over. And I just told the police all this, so you don't have to go blabbering about it to them."

His words threw me. "You went to the police?"

"The police came here—as if you didn't know."

"I didn't." Why would the police have come to see Sawyer? How would they even have known of his existence? "Was it a detective?"

"Yes—two fellows named Robinson and Mulrony."

"Muldoon."

His face darkened. "You know them well, then. I might have guessed. They were waiting for me when I arrived this morning, like cats stalking a mouse. They knew Callie and I . . . well, they assumed we had a liaison. You know how the minds of that type of men work."

"You think Callie told the police about you?" I was sure she hadn't.

"How else could they have found out about us?"

"Not through Callie, or me. From the very first, we agreed not to mention you."

He didn't look convinced. No wonder he'd seemed so rattled when he'd spotted me in his outer office. I'd assumed it was because he hadn't wanted his wife to see a young woman waiting on him, and maybe that was part of it. But he obviously believed Callie or I had sent the police after him. And then Margaret had appeared.

"Did the police speak to Mrs. Attinger? Is that why she was here?"

"Good heavens, no. Margaret knows nothing about—well, about anything. She only happened to come downtown this morning by chance. Unhappy chance. At least the detectives had already left." Judging from the film of sweat beading on his brow, the prospect of the police telling his wife that there was cause for suspicion in Sawyer's activities—activities involving an attractive young blonde—was what he dreaded most. "There's no reason for those damned detectives to bother Margaret. No reason at all," he continued. "I'll tell you what I told them. I lost my head over Callie for a few weeks."

"Months," I corrected.

"Well—all right. Yes, Callie is very pretty, very charming. Even the detectives allowed how a man might forget himself over her. I'm hardly the first man to behave foolishly over a pretty smile. But she never meant anything to me, and now it's over. Completely over."

"Just like that?" I was offended on Callie's behalf. Thursday night he had been professing undying love.

"You heard Callie give me the gate. I'm not going to make an ass of myself. I'm a happily married man."

"Good of you to remember."

"A family man," he continued, as if he hadn't heard me. "I've got two lovely children. You think I would really jeopardize their happiness for a girl like Callie?"

"I think you did." His tone riled me more than his words. He made it sound as if Callie were some bug under his boot, to be scraped off and flicked into the gutter. "Last week you claimed to love Callie."

"She bewitched me."

The more he explained himself, the more I disliked him. "And now the spell's been broken?"

"I was out of my head," he confessed, "and last Thursday I was a little worse for drink. It wasn't until the next morning when I read about the murder that I realized what a sordid element Callie was mixed up with."

"The murder had nothing to do with Callie."

He shook his head. "*Someone* in that apartment brought a murderer to the door. If it wasn't Callie, then who? You?"

I sputtered in anger.

He lifted his hands. "Never mind. It's of no matter to me. I'm well out of it. As I said, I'm a family man. I've learned my lesson—and by the way, I told the detectives all of this. I confessed all that happened last Thursday night to them, and they believed me."

Wonderful. Now Muldoon and Robinson knew Callie and I had been shielding Sawyer.

"Did you confess to your wife?" I asked.

"Confess what?" he asked with a straight face. "Evenings at restaurants, a few cheap gifts, some words thoughtlessly spoken? There's not a man in my position who hasn't made a bigger fool of himself over a woman than I did with Callie. Besides, my wife is a wise woman. Doesn't ask too many questions. She knows a henpecked husband is more apt to stray permanently than one who's given a little freedom."

My jaw clenched tight enough to crack Brazil nuts. The man had a heart as hard and cold as the granite blocks this building was made of. And poor Margaret Attinger. How many more times would that unquestioning attitude result in Sawyer's pursuing women who were a fresher version of the woman she'd once been?

I stood to go. I'd heard enough. "I won't waste any more of your time."

Sawyer escorted me to the door—or rather trailed after me as I stomped out. *Family man, my eye.*

Before we reached the beehive of the outer office, he caught up and stopped me with a hand to my elbow. Unless I wanted to make a scene in front of his secretary, I had no choice but to turn and face him. I braced myself for the expected warning to stay away from his place of business from here on. But that wasn't what he said.

"Is she all right, Louise?"

The misery and worry in his expression nearly knocked me on my heels. So much for the dedicated husband and father. The family man. I shook my head in disgust. Was there anything more pitiful than a man who didn't know his own mind? "She'll be fine. Callie's strong." *Unlike you,* I added silently.

As I rode down in the elevator, I shook off my annoyance with Sawyer and sifted through our conversation for whatever useful nuggets I could glean. Why had the police gone to Sawyer this morning? They'd found out all about his relationship to Callie, but how?

Callie had been on edge all weekend, which was perfectly understandable given that her cousin had just been murdered and a strange man was following her. And yet, there had been absences she hadn't explained. I knew she hadn't gone to the police—not to talk about Sawyer, at any rate. She'd never do that. But I was beginning to sense that there was something she had neglected to tell me. Something had led the police to Sawyer.

The single bell tolling from Trinity Church told me that it was time to go back to work. Mr. McChesney might not care if I returned or not, but Jackson would be watching the clock and noting every minute I was gone. And yet my feet didn't take me back in the direction of Van Hooten and McChesney. I needed to talk to Muldoon.

This time I wasn't kept waiting forever. After ten minutes, a policeman with ginger red hair appeared to escort me up to see Muldoon. As we were walking up the stairs, we met the policewoman I'd seen before on her way down. She was tall, and her long legs made brisk work of the steps.

"Afternoon, Cliff," she said with a breezy smile.

My escort beamed genially. "Hello, Mary."

As soon as the woman was out of earshot, I asked, "What does Mary do?"

"She's a police matron."

She didn't look very matronly. "How did she get a job here?"

"Her father died, so the poor thing was forced to find something to help feed what was left of the family."

He made it sound as if having to work for the police was an ongoing tragedy for Mary, but she'd looked perfectly happy to me. "But how did she get the job?"

It took him a moment to understand me; then he just shrugged. "Same as the rest of us."

"And how is that?" I persisted. "I really want to know."

"First, there's an examination. No piece of cake, that. And then, if you've done well on the test, you're told to come back."

That was it? Just a test? I'd assumed there were all sorts of cronyism and corruption even in the lower levels of the police force. Most of the policemen I'd met looked as if they'd been recruited from the same Irish county, which couldn't be a coincidence. But if it really was all predicated on a test . . .

I was good at test taking. "Are there any female detectives?"

"Ay, one." He shook his head. "Though what the use of that is, I'll never know."

A female detective. Being paid to do what I was doing . . .

I gave myself a shake. *You have a job.* A good one. Reading books and working in a publisher's office was much more desirable than being around cops and criminals all day. And night.

Still, I asked, "Do you enjoy being a policeman?"

From his expression, you'd think I'd asked how he liked breathing. "It's my life."

"Yes, but do you like the work?"

"My da wore the blue. And three of my uncles."

"But haven't you ever dreamed of being anything else?"

"What, I'd like to know."

I thought of my uncles. "Well, just for instance, you might have become a butcher."

The suggestion, which didn't seem at all outrageous to me, nettled my escort. "Nobody in my family was a butcher."

"That doesn't mean you couldn't have been."

He frowned at the unthought-of possibility, then admitted warily, "I had an uncle once who ran a grocery."

"There," I said. "Wasn't he just as contented as a policeman?"

"He died." Cliff shook his head, as if shopkeeping had been responsible for the man's demise.

We approached the room where I'd spoken to Muldoon before, but as Cliff reached for the doorknob, my gaze strayed back to the cage where Otto had been held that day. And now I saw someone else I recognized—Max.

With a gasp, I broke away from Cliff and threaded my way through chairs and desks to reach the cell. As I closed in on the cage, my outrage grew. Max was slumped against the wall, and his face was a mess. A busted lip bloomed with dried blood, and his head sported a lump the size of a goose egg.

"Max!" I said the name forcefully, both from shock at his condition and to wake him up.

His eyes opened, bloodshot and wary. At the sight of me standing there, they blinked. "Louise?"

At least he was still in good enough shape to recognize me. The state he was in and his rasping voice brought me to a boil. "How long have you been here?" I asked.

"Since last night." He lurched to his feet, none too steadily, and gripped the bars. "I didn't do it, Louise. I never harmed Ethel Gail. I barely knew her."

So he was now the police's pet suspect in the murder. "I know."

"I never was down in your apartment that night until you girls came home and Lucia heard all the ruckus. But now they've got all sorts of ideas, because of my paintings . . ."

What did his paintings have to do with anything? That head wound obviously had him rattled. "Why did you run away?"

"Because of that other time," he said. "I worried I'd get blamed."

Worried rightly, as it turned out.

Cliff the policeman grabbed my arm and attempted to steer me away, but I planted myself. "Does Lucia know you're here?"

Max's expression hardened. "You tell her not to come, you hear? Especially not with the children."

"But someone needs to straighten this out."

He shook his head. "I won't have my children in a police station, or a jail."

"Come on, miss," the policeman insisted.

I shook him off. "I'm a citizen. I have a right to talk to this man."

His eyes widened in shock. "That's the one who murdered your friend."

"In a pig's eye, he did," I said.

The other policemen who'd been eavesdropping laughed, and

even some of Max's fellow detainees chuckled. It was hard to tell what amused them more—a young woman standing up to a policeman, or the policeman's face blazing red.

I steamed back across the room to Muldoon's office and stormed in without knocking. Cliff puffed in behind me. "The young lady, sir."

Muldoon was dressed in a dark suit and wore a snow-white collar. I wondered if he'd dressed with care that morning to visit Wall Street. He was just rising to his feet as I let fire with the questions. "Why is Max's lip broken? And why are you holding him?"

"She asks a lot of questions," the policeman, still behind me, said.

If I hadn't been so focused on Muldoon's face, I might have missed the barely perceptible twitch of his lips. "I know," he said.

"She just ran over and started talking to one of the prisoners."

Muldoon nodded curtly. "Doesn't surprise me a bit."

"No doubt you'd prefer to hide him away so no one can see how you treat prisoners in your custody," I said.

Ignoring me—except for the stain of red that leapt involuntarily into his cheeks—Muldoon said, "You can leave us, O'Connor."

O'Connor backed toward the door but eyed me suspiciously. "I'll be just outside, sir."

"Thanks."

Even before the door had shut, I repeated my question. "What's Max doing here?"

"You know the answer to that."

"Where did you find him?"

"Officers were called to a brawl at a tavern near the Bowery. That's where Max was found and arrested, and that's where he got the knot on his head."

I folded my arms. "And the busted lip?"

"He resisted arrest."

A likely story. "Max didn't kill Ethel."

"Tell that to the man he knifed in the side almost five years ago."

"*Five years ago,*" I repeated. "Max has a wife and children now."

Muldoon let out a sputter of mirthless laughter. "Would you like a list of the men I've arrested for murder who have families?"

"I'm not interested in those people. I'm thinking of my neighbor, Max."

"We've talked to his wife and been through his flat. *Not* the model husband and father, I'm afraid."

My certainty wavered. What did he know that I didn't? "I've never heard him so much as raise his voice to Lucia. And as for that knife fight five years ago—was it unprovoked?"

"It was a fight in a bar."

"Do you think Ethel and he were involved in a brawl?"

"She was knifed to death, and Max ran."

"Because he was afraid of just this—that you would jump to conclusions. Tell me, did you find Ethel's money on Max?"

"No," he admitted.

"There."

"It's been three days," he pointed out. "He might have spent it, or hidden it."

"I assume you searched their apartment."

"Oh yes." Again there was that infuriating knowingness in his tone—as if he wasn't telling me something. "We'll be holding Max Freeman for further questioning, and if we aren't satisfied with his answers, in all likelihood we'll arrest him for the murder of Ethel Gail. He'll be transferred to the Jefferson Market Courthouse cells pending trial."

"You sound awfully certain of yourself. Friday you thought Otto was the murderer. Now Max. Who will it be tomorrow?"

"If he's guilty, it'll still be Max."

His implacable confidence left me exasperated. "Am I going to have to arrange a lawyer for Max, too?"

"You might not want to once you've heard all the facts. And seen them." He paused to let the ominous note he'd struck sink in. "When we went to speak to Mr. Freeman's wife and search the apartment, we of course came across the paintings in his studio."

"I've seen some of his canvases. They're modern."

"*Modern* is one word for it. Your artistic neighbor has been paying his bills by selling pictures of nude women."

I gaped at him. Was he serious? "So has practically every artist from cave painters to Matisse. Didn't you go to the Armory Show?"

For a whole month that winter, the armory building on Lexington Avenue had been the center of an exhibit of the most modern art of Europe and America. Callie and I had gone through twice, exploring the endless mazes of paintings and sculptures that were by turns breathtaking and perplexing. Matisse's blue nude had been one of the most shocking and daring of the whole exhibit—a great primitive reclining figure of a woman.

"I heard about it." Muldoon's sneer told me all I needed to know of his thoughts on cubists, fauvists, or anything that wasn't *Washington Crossing the Delaware.* "I'm not talking about so-called avant-garde art." He held my gaze a moment before adding, "And, as far as I know, none of the painters at the Armory Show was using your roommate as a model."

He turned and lifted a piece of butcher paper from a frame in the corner leaning against a file cabinet. I hadn't noticed it before, but now, with the paper gone, I saw Callie, draped across a chaise longue in the nude, her lips turned up in a lascivious, come-hither smile.

Heat washed over me. I wanted to shout at Muldoon to cover the painting up. How many policemen had been sniggering over this since it had been brought into evidence? Yet, despite my instincts, I forced myself to eye it objectively. Lurid as it was, the painting was not badly rendered. The composition might be unimaginative, but the figure was realistically done.

And yet not real at all. It was a dream of Callie—but not her.

"Callie did not pose for that," I said.

"That's what she told us."

Callie saw the painting? She must have been mortified.

"Well, then," I said, "she didn't. But even if she hadn't denied it, I would know she didn't pose for Max."

"How?"

"First, because it takes hours to model for a painting like that. I would have noticed if she'd disappeared for that long." But even as I said it, I wondered, *would I?* She had been out of the flat often lately, but I hadn't questioned where she'd been. I added, "And technically, that's not a true likeness."

"Looks like her to me."

"Her face, perhaps, but the proportions of her body don't look right. The"—I forced myself not to blush—"bust is exaggerated, and the legs are too plump. Callie is a dancer, and lithe. Also, she has a wine-stain birthmark on her hip."

Muldoon frowned at the peachy-smooth nude hip where I was pointing. "He might have painted an ideal instead of the reality. Isn't that what you'd call an artist's prerogative?"

"I don't care what you call it. If Callie said she didn't pose, she didn't. Max obviously just used her face. Why shouldn't he?"

"Or she might have modeled for him. And maybe while they were together, she mentioned the money her cousin had stashed away."

"No," I insisted. "She wouldn't have told Max about the money."

"Whether she did or didn't, this picture indicates an obsession. Callie and Ethel Gail shared certain physical characteristics."

I caught his drift and dismissed it for the foolishness it was. "Any man obsessed with Callie wouldn't have mistaken Ethel for her."

He eyed me steadily. "You sure seem to want Max to be innocent."

"I just don't want Ethel's killer—the *real* killer—to go free."

Muldoon leaned on his desk. "Do you know the killer's identity?"

"Of course not."

"Then stop trying to thwart my investigation."

Calling what he was heading an investigation struck me as rich. And as for my thwarting it—that was a knee-slapper. "Is having Callie followed part of your investigation?"

His jaw remained rigid, but the flicker of respect I detected in his eyes told me I'd guessed correctly.

"I just came from Sawyer Attinger's office," I explained, unable to keep from boasting a little. "I assumed *he* was the one having Callie followed. But when he revealed that you'd just spoken to him this morning, I realized you could only have found out about Sawyer through Callie. And since Callie wouldn't have mentioned him to you, I knew that that brown-suited mustached man following her had to be one of New York's finest."

He listened to me patiently, not at all impressed by my powers of deduction. In fact, by the time I was done he was practically vibrating with anger. "If you thought Sawyer Attinger was desperate enough to have your roommate followed, then why for the love of Mike didn't you tell us about him from the very beginning?"

I shifted, knowing how feeble my answer would sound from his point of view. "Callie asked me not to."

His anger vented in a gust of irritation.

"If I'd suspected there was the slightest chance that Sawyer was guilty," I said, "I would have convinced her to tell you. I swear it. But I saw Sawyer that night not far from our apartment. His clothes were neat as a pin. You remember the murder room. If Sawyer had just come from killing Ethel, he would've had blood on him somewhere, wouldn't he?"

His lips flattened. "Maybe, or maybe not. He might have changed clothes. There could be any number of reasons the results of the murder might have escaped your eagle eye. Sawyer might have hired someone else to do the murder. Did you ever think of that?"

I was forced to admit I hadn't.

"But as it happens," Muldoon continued, "Mr. Attinger was drinking in a bar called McGrath's not long before he saw you on the street. The bartender and another witness confirmed his story, and the time he left. He would've had to be the world's fastest killer to have managed to murder Ethel Gail in the short window of time between when he left the bar and when you saw him."

So the police hadn't just taken Sawyer at his word. That was gratifying. Of course, they were probably all the more eager to dismiss him as a suspect knowing they now had Max in custody.

"None of this changes the fact that you should've told us about Attinger from the beginning," Muldoon said. "Instead, we wasted manpower having Miss Gail followed."

"For no reason," I pointed out.

"For the very good reason that I could tell you were both hiding something." His eyes narrowed on me. "My question now is, was Sawyer Attinger the only one you were protecting, or are there others?"

I wasn't going to give up Ford's name, especially now that I'd seen how Max looked in their custody. "Are you going to have me followed now?"

He gave his head a derisive shake. "Why should I do that? You just keep coming here."

Very funny. "Of course you won't have me shadowed," I said. "You already have your case sewn up. You have Max."

"You seem awfully certain he's innocent."

"Because there's no evidence he isn't. All you have is a coincidence or two."

"You'd be surprised how many murderers are tried and convicted on a few coincidences."

As if that was any comfort. "I wonder if that number has any correlation with the number of men who are wrongly convicted?"

Muldoon's face reddened. "Why is it you're always eager to tell us we've got the wrong man but strangely reluctant to help us find the right one?"

"Why do you seem so keen on arresting all the men we know? Why couldn't the attacker be a stranger?"

"Because we're fairly certain it was someone familiar with your apartment—familiar enough to know when only one of you was home, and where to find a murder weapon."

"Knives are generally kept in the kitchen," I said.

Nevertheless, I thought about Sawyer, who had been in the apartment a few times. And Max. He had been there, too. That big butcher's block was hard to miss.

"You look worried, Miss Faulk."

"I need to get back to work." Moreover, I needed to get out of Muldoon's office. The thing I'd come to find out, I now knew. Sometime this weekend, Callie had met with Sawyer. What else hadn't she told me?

"Work is a good idea," Muldoon said, seeing me to the door. "Attend to your typing and filing and leave detecting to the police."

Of all the advice he could have given me at that moment, *that* was the most injudicious. I left the station more determined than ever to find out who killed Ethel. And then, when I was done, some able, obedient police officer—maybe even Muldoon himself—could type up the paperwork and file it away.

Chapter 8

"Were you with the police all this time?" Jackson asked me when I returned.

"Just about." Amazing how easily little lies and half-truths were starting to come to me.

Was that the case with Callie, too? All the way back uptown I'd pondered what could have been in her head, meeting Sawyer clandestinely again after the murder. What had been the purpose of the meeting, and why take such a chance? Of course, she hadn't guessed that the police had been following her, so perhaps she'd assumed, as I had, that by speaking to Sawyer she would figure out who the mustached man was.

My mind sifted through other problems. They were adding up. Max, for instance. Poor Lucia would be frantic. How would she and the children live if he ended up in jail? And there was that painting. I sent up a prayer that Wally and Mrs. Grimes hadn't seen it before the police took it.

Could Max have killed Ethel? Muldoon hadn't convinced me. But my trip to the police precinct and Max's bloodied appearance did persuade me that I'd been right not to mention Ford.

On my desk lay his manuscript. At the moment, fiction seemed like a lifeline to sanity. I fixed myself a cup of tea and pulled the stack of papers out of the envelope. The novel was short enough that I would be able to finish it in an afternoon, especially since Mr. McChesney had left early, claiming his ulcer was acting up.

I knuckled down to the task of reading the manuscript and put my worries about Callie, Max, and Lucia aside for a while. To be honest, it wasn't difficult. I'd liked Ford's first novel, but this one was even better. The prose was stripped down, direct, with none of the obvious flourishes and indulgences that had occasionally bogged down the other manuscript. The story about a young man from a patrician family in Boston who went down to work on the Panama Canal and fell in love with a local girl drew me in at once, and for a few blissful hours my worries drifted far away.

I didn't finish the book until six o'clock; then I stayed another half hour to type up a recommendation to Mr. Van Hooten. True, it might take weeks for Guy to actually see the report, but Jackson had nixed Ford's first book, and I was sure Mr. McChesney would declare the spare style and daring material too newfangled. By the time I was finished, I was so wound up by the story that I almost dreaded going back to my own life, and to my troubled building. Instead, I jotted down Ford's address and before I could talk myself out of it went straight to his house. After all, it was practically on my way home.

Greenwich Village was a neighborhood of hardworking families of all stamps, but its affordable rents also attracted artists, freethinkers, and people who didn't quite fit in comfortably in other neighborhoods. Even within my little patch of the neighborhood, its character changed from street to street, or even building to building. It wasn't until I was climbing the staircase of Ford's building that I realized I'd fallen into a seedy pocket. Empty liquor bottles were piled outside one doorway, and the reek of alcohol mixed with the other smells of poverty—years of boiled dinner odors, bad drains, and stuffy flats with too many bodies. In front of another door an unwashed little boy squatted, constructing a skyscraper out of matches. He must have been hoarding matches a long time, because it was already almost a foot high.

"That's impressive," I said.

"When I'm done I'm gonna light the whole thing up." He made a sound to illustrate the coming conflagration.

Oh dear. "That's not a good idea. Fire is very dangerous."

Still concentrating on placing his matches, he merely repeated the noise.

So much for safety lectures. "Do you know where I could find Mr. Fitzsimmons?"

The dirt-smudged face looked up at me. "Who?"

"Ford Fitzsimmons. A young man with blond hair who lives here."

The boy's eyebrows scrunched together. "The one with the typewriter?"

"Most likely."

"He ain't young."

"Well . . . not as young as yourself."

The boy puffed up. "I'm six."

"Imagine that." Six, and already well on his way to a career in pyromania. "Where can I find the man with the typewriter?"

He jerked his tiny chin in the direction of the stairs leading to the next floor. "He don't like me to go up there. Maybe you shouldn't, either. He walloped me once for going into his room."

"Thanks for the warning. I'll try not to get walloped."

The boy lifted his shoulders in a suit-yourself shrug.

I climbed another level, the worn wood of the old stairs groaning and protesting each step. At the top floor I stopped and caught my breath. Laughter came from beyond one door and I scooted past it to what I hoped would be Ford's room. I knocked, and waited.

And waited.

"Mr. Fitzsimmons?" I called.

Suddenly, the door I'd passed jerked open and the laughter from within rose in volume. Ford's head poked out.

"Louise! What are you doing here?"

"Who're you talking to, Fitz?" a gruff voice called from inside the apartment.

Ford flicked a look back. "Never mind. Deal me out." He closed the door behind him and, taking my elbow, steered me to the next door. "Come in."

His Spartan garret was covered in hideous wallpaper in brown and blue torn off in chunks in places, revealing bare boards beneath. The wide plank floors were warped, which made me peer up at the yellowed ceiling plaster overhead. Ford was neat—a thin blanket was pulled over the bed, and the only other furnishings—an old metal trunk, a table and chair, and a make-do shelf fashioned out of a board and two crates—were all tidily arranged. Yet there was no tidying up the shabbiness of it all.

"I've christened it Xanadu," he said with only mild embarrassment. "What do you think?"

"I can't believe you write such magnificent things in these shabby surroundings."

His expression brightened. "You read my book? Already?"

"I did."

"And you really thought it was magnificent?" His boyish eagerness was hard to withstand, so I didn't try.

"I wrote a long note to Mr. Van Hooten telling him I thought so."

He slapped his hands together. "At last—someone who agrees with my high opinion of myself."

"I also admire your modesty." But his palpable happiness infected me, too. I couldn't help smiling.

"What writer ever got ahead by showing modesty?" He turned to his little trunk and picked up a bottle. Amber liquid filled the bottom fourth. "Just enough here to celebrate."

Call me foolish, but it took that whiskey bottle to make me question my actions. Rushing here without thinking to visit a man I barely knew alone in his room was the most reckless thing I'd done. I tensed, looking at the ropy muscles of his forearms where he'd rolled up his sleeves.

"Something wrong?" His face screwed up in puzzlement. "Don't tell me you're a teetotaler."

His teasing made me get ahold of myself. Every man wasn't Arnie Tate. "No, but I'm not much of a whiskey drinker. And I skipped lunch today."

"All the better—the liquor'll hit you faster. I don't have much of the stuff, so we need to optimize, as the businessmen say."

He poured a generous amount of the whiskey into two mismatched, cloudy glasses and handed me one. "To you, Louise," he said. "My patroness."

I drank, then tried to mask my shudder as the liquid burned its way down to my empty stomach. It was no use. I coughed until he came and pounded me on the back. The stuff was like drinking kerosene.

"Did you really like the book?" he asked.

I cleared my throat and waxed enthusiastic for several long minutes, going on at length about the story and the parts I'd liked best, and how much more forceful his writing seemed than in the last book, and how original it was. "Even if the book doesn't get taken on by Van Hooten and McChesney, some smart editor will see your talent. I know it. You're on the brink of success."

"That calls for another toast," he said.

Before I could demur, the door opened and a burly man broke in.

"Why'd you run off, Fitz?" A split second later the man noticed me. Some half-dead instinct awoke him and he pulled his blue cap off his head, revealing a thatch of oily hair. "Who you got here?" he asked with a half leer.

"I'm entertaining, Mug," Ford said, not introducing me.

Mug's lascivious up-and-down stare made me cringe. The man was as thickset and sweaty as a stevedore. Not to mention, it was only suppertime and he was clearly drunk. Was this one of Ford's friends?

"How long's she gonna be?" he asked.

"She's a lady," Ford said. "You don't give ladies the bum's rush. Don't you know that?"

His friend snorted. "Nah, I dunno a lot of ladies."

When he was gone, I said, "You need to find another place to live."

Ford shook his head. "Mug's not so bad. He and his brother saved my life once."

It was hard to keep the amazement out of my voice. "How?"

"I had a little run-in with the law in Boston. Before I came here."

"You mean they came to New York with you?"

"No, but they found me when they got out."

I was afraid to ask, but I did anyway. "Out of where?"

"Jail." My silence made him smile. "Don't look so appalled. I was in jail with them, but only for a night, because of a fight. Trouble over a lady. I was charged with being drunk and disorderly, and Mug and his brother were in the same cell for the same offense, with theft added to it."

"Thieves," I repeated.

"Sailors get accused of all sorts of crimes. I don't think they really did anything so awful." He finished off his glass. "You see, I'm not like my book's protagonist. A patrician." His lip curled. "I knew that type at the university. I worked in the dining hall's kitchen after the check my father gave me to cover my tuition turned out to be bad. My old man—he never failed to disappoint. After two years, I dropped out, worked on the docks, wrote when I could, and started to hunger. A man like me needs friends of all sorts. Believe me, Mug and Red aren't bad types to have on your side when you need them."

"Why would you possibly need help of that sort now?"

"You never can tell." I must have looked appalled again, because he reached out and took my hand. "Don't worry—I don't court danger. And I only play cards with Mug and Red because I get bored here all on my own. Think of them as my Callie."

I knew he had a bad opinion of my roommate, but that was taking things too far. "Why would you say that? What do you have against her?"

"I've known her type before."

I crossed my arms. "What type?"

"A vivacious taker. She'll charm you until she's got you where she wants you—but then something will happen to make you realize that she *feels* nothing. She only wants." The bitter flash in his eyes, which I'd noted at Aunt Irene's house, made me suspect that

Callie reminded him of the woman who'd been at the center of his troubles in Boston.

"Something will happen . . . like jail?" I asked.

He polished off another glass. "Exactly."

I remembered moments when I'd felt at odds with Callie. Like when she'd said she *would* marry Sawyer, even knowing he was a cheater. Didn't that make her seem like a taker?

One of his brows arched. "Something the matter?"

"No." But doubts whirled in my mind. Callie's secret meeting with Sawyer. Her lateness the night of the party. Even that horrible painting and Muldoon's suggestion that Max and Callie had somehow conspired to kill Ethel and steal her money. *Where is that money?*

My disloyal thoughts made me ashamed. "You're wrong about Callie." There were explanations for all of this, I was sure.

"I hope so." Ford stood and crossed to his typewriter. "Say—how tired are you of reading the oeuvre of Ford Fitzsimmons?"

"Not a bit," I answered truthfully.

"I had something else I wanted to show you last week, but I changed my mind. It's only a long short story—I'm not even sure such an animal is supposed to exist. I doubt your publisher would have anything to do with it. That's why I gave you the novel instead."

I glanced around the room in amazement. "How many unpublished pieces do you have lying around?"

"Too many. I write stories and then I feel as if I've just wasted my time. Some days I'm not sure if I'm a writer or just a very accomplished typist."

"You're a writer," I assured him.

"When you say it, I almost believe it." From a stack on his typing table he unearthed a manila envelope. "It's a little different than the book. It hasn't got a bit of romance in it."

"I'm not so fond of love stories that I can't appreciate something a little more realistic."

His gaze met mine. "Isn't love real?"

I couldn't help remembering Sawyer's fickle vacillations, and Otto's, never mind my own limited experience. "I suppose it can be."

"Do you have someone you're in love with now?"

Despite my best efforts, a flush crept into my face. "No."

"That fellow the police picked up—"

"Otto's a friend." Would I ever meet anyone again who didn't think I was Otto's *tootsie?* That awful word. "And he's a good songwriter. Next time he publishes a song, though, I hope he keeps me out of it."

Ford walked me to the staircase. It was only a polite ritual—escorting the guest out—but I savored every detail like a girl at her first dance. The slight pressure of his hand at my lower back. The almost shy way he glanced at me. The warm pressure of his hand squeezing mine as he sent me on my way.

"I'm glad you hunted me down in my burrow," he said. "You've lifted my spirits more than a winning bet." His lips brushed my cheek. Although I tensed in surprise, even the liquor on his breath didn't repulse me.

I pressed his envelope to my chest and hurried down the stairs much more quickly than I'd come up them. The matchstick urchin was gone, and the smell of the place didn't offend my nostrils so much. I hadn't reached the front door before a swell of laughter rose from above. Ford had returned to his cronies. Maybe Mug and Red were ribbing him about me.

I hated to think of him being mired in such rough company. But perhaps even if I wasn't rich or influential enough to really be Ford's patroness, I could at least be the gatekeeper who opened a way out of this squalor. That thought lightened my steps during the short walk home. The sun was disappearing behind the tallest buildings to the west as I approached our place. A miracle had occurred. For the first time since the murder, no reporters waited outside our door, and I could detect no sign of a police detective lurking on the street, either. Wherever they'd all gone, I was glad to no longer be forced to bushwhack my way into the building.

Wally, unfortunately, was still with us. He attacked me the moment I crossed the threshold. "I can't take another day like this one, Louise. You tell your friend I can't stand the racket."

"What racket?" I tilted my head, listening. A thump or two

came from above, but for our building it was surprisingly quiet. Once you were used to the bone-shaking blare of a bass saxophone, nothing could rattle you. Or so I'd assumed.

"Those brats of Lucia's!" he yelled right into my face. "Callie's got 'em on the second floor. How can little feet clomp so loudly?"

I lifted my eyes to the ceiling. I could hear footsteps and childish voices, barely. "You think that's louder than saxophone players?"

"I don't mind music," he grumbled, "but those shrieking, squeaky voices get on my nerves."

I wondered if his mood didn't have more to do with the defections of the journalists than his tiniest tenants. Both his brief fame and source of graft were gone.

"I got half a mind to tell Ma to chuck everybody out and start over," he grumbled. "Painters, musicians, kids, working girls, Italians—you're all nothing but trouble. After seeing what Max and that roommate of yours was up to, it's a lucky thing the police didn't toss us all in jail on indecency charges."

So much for the hope that Wally hadn't seen the painting. "Callie had nothing to do with that."

"Sure looked like her to me," he said, practically licking his lips. "Bad enough we got murders here and people being arrested for killing each other without pornographic kind of doings. Ma don't like it."

I walked away.

"Ma said there'd be trouble with yous girls," he called after me.

Upstairs, I soon discovered why the sound of the kids was as muffled as it was. Callie had laid the saxophonists' mattresses across the floor, and now the two oldest children were tumbling about like tiny acrobats while the baby crawled after them. In the center—in the role of the frog being leaped over—was Callie. When she looked up at me, her eyelids sagged with exhaustion.

"Louise—thank heavens!" She got to her feet, taking the little girl clinging to her back with her. "Where have you been?"

Guilt for staying away for so long made me turn away slightly. "I worked late." It wasn't entirely a lie.

She frowned at the envelope I carried. "And you brought work home, too. You—" Whatever she was going to say next was lost to me when I was tackled by Lucia's three-year-old son, Charlie or Carlo, depending on which parent was talking to him.

"Louise! Play a game with us!"

When I refused, he simply climbed up me as a monkey might swing up a tree.

"Did you hear about"—Callie looked down at the boy and spelled it out—"M-A-X?"

I nodded.

"And the painting?" she asked.

"I was at the police station earlier. I saw it."

Her voice rose in alarm. "They have it on display?"

"It was in an interrogation room," I said. "Covered."

Her blue eyes grew big. "Why were you being interrogated?"

"I wasn't. I was there for . . . other reasons."

"Max evidently painted several like it to sell to bars," she said. "No telling where I'm hanging in this town. Me and the Miller High Life girl. He might as well have painted me on a crescent moon."

"I saw M-A-X at the station, too. He seemed very sorry." I wasn't certain how much consolation that would be.

"Oh, I know he did it for the money. And for them." She nodded toward the baby yanking on my skirts. "Lucia was beside herself. I thought she'd never stop apologizing."

"She knew?"

"She was the model. But the bar owners said they preferred a blonde. So he stuck my head on her body."

I spent the next five minutes untangling myself from children; then Callie and I prepared something for dinner.

"Wally was complaining about the noise," I told her once we were huddled together over the burner. We had canned soup and bread. It would have to do.

Exasperation sighed out of her. "He was up here earlier. Honestly, what was I supposed to do? I don't know anything about children, so I was teaching them a little soft shoe."

"The way he was carrying on, you might have been teaching elephants to polka."

Callie lowered her voice. "Why were you at the police station this afternoon?"

"Just checking on something—a hunch I had." I told her about her faithful shadow.

"The police were following me?" She reddened, and I guessed why.

"They were watching when you paid your visit to Sawyer this weekend."

"Muldoon told you that? You two must be chums."

"Hardly," I said. "He didn't have to tell me anything. I spoke to Sawyer this morning because I thought *he'd* hired the man who was following you. But when he told me the police had just left his office, I realized the only way they could have found out about him was if you'd led them to him."

The fact that the police had spoken to Sawyer seemed to distract her from the fact that I also had. "They don't suspect Sawyer, do they?"

"He denied any involvement with the murder, and according to Muldoon they believe him. A bartender at McGrath's vouched that he was there."

Callie started hacking through the hard loaf of bread with the saxophonists' dull knife. I considered running upstairs to get one of our sharper ones, but the thought of that butcher block with the murder weapon missing stopped me.

"Sounds like *you're* not convinced Sawyer's innocent," she said.

"I don't think he murdered Ethel. But I still don't understand why you went to see him."

"I wanted to protect him." She blushed. "That sounds silly now, but I didn't know the cops were following me. I worried he'd read the papers and would think he should come forward, for my sake. I had to warn him not to volunteer any information, or to go to the police on his own."

"Fat chance of that."

"I also wanted to assure him that I was keeping his name out of it. He worries so much about that precious name of his."

"What did he say to you?"

"He swore that he had nothing to do with the murder, of course, and then . . ." She bit her lip. "Well, he said that I'd been right and that we shouldn't see each other anymore. He said that he loved his children and he intended to be faithful to Margaret."

Ah. So that was why he suspected Callie had sent the police to his office. He'd told Callie he'd decided to give her up. Reading what had happened to Callie's cousin in the newspapers had put the fear of scandal in him. But when the police came knocking, he must have imagined that she'd felt like a woman scorned and so had sent them after him.

"Why didn't you tell me about all of this?" I asked.

"That's a fine question, coming from you."

I drew back. "I tell you everything."

"No, you don't." I must have looked incredulous, because her expression hardened. "You think I don't ever notice you looking off as if you're miles away? Whenever I ask what you're thinking, you always say nothing." She crossed her arms. "That's a lie, isn't it?"

I said nothing, even though I knew exactly what she was talking about, and where my mind disappeared to in those moments. I could even give her a specific address. *7 East Eightieth Street.* Only I'd never been there. I'd never worked up the courage.

She laughed mirthlessly at my silence. "Don't lecture me, Miss Enigma."

"I don't lecture," I said. "Do I?"

"Well, no. But I knew if I said anything about Sawyer you'd think I was being a sap. And maybe I was—I honestly thought he'd be mad with worry about me because he still cared for me so much in spite of all I said to him last week. Fine blow to my conceit to find how easily a man can set me aside."

She sounded depressed. I remembered the look in Sawyer's eyes when he was showing me the door. *Is she all right?* It hadn't been easy for him to renounce Callie, but he'd managed to hide that fact from her. Maybe Sawyer possessed more maturity than I'd given him credit for. When one was trying to break off a relationship, making a show of lingering emotions was the same as leaving the other person fettered. He'd had the wisdom to free her. Following his lead, I held my own tongue.

"Did Lucia say when she'd be back?" I asked.

Callie shook her head.

We were both anxious about Lucia and Max, but we tried to

mask our worries as we fed the children. They attacked the food with gusto, and Callie and I collapsed on a mattress and watched.

"Early this afternoon—before Lucia came by—I went out and ordered a new bed," Callie told me in a low voice.

The new bed would replace the one upstairs. I should have thought of it myself. But where had Callie found the money for a new mattress? Our meager cash supply wouldn't cover that.

"We can't stay down here," she said. "The Blowers will be back before long, and anyway, we have our own place."

"Mm . . . and this apartment is revolting," I agreed, distracted. Muldoon was in my head again—insinuating that Callie might have had something to do with that stolen money.

"Dora and Abel will be here soon," Callie reminded me. "For the funeral. I can't let them see that mess up there."

The task of cleaning up our place had been hanging over our heads all weekend. Neither one of us had wanted to face it.

"Where did you find the money for a new bed?" I asked.

"I sold the bracelet Sawyer gave me." Before I could say anything, her eyes flashed as if I'd accused her of something—and not the thing that had actually been plaguing my thoughts. "He wouldn't take back the jewelry. What else could I do? I didn't want to keep it, so I sold it." A little red appeared in her cheeks. "All but my brooch."

The brooch, an amber butterfly with diamond eyes, was her favorite.

I breathed out, expelling the last of my suspicions. Of course she hadn't used Ethel's money. How could she? She'd never had it. "I understand."

Even though I'd been living through them right alongside Callie, I kept forgetting how awful these days were for her. And here was I, her best friend, letting people who didn't know her plant doubts in my head. I gave her a hug, and I thought she might break down. But she stepped back and straightened.

"That miser at the jewelry store only gave me eleven dollars for the bracelet."

She'd been swindled, of course. That was how those places operated. I doubted Callie had been in a bargaining mood.

"The man said they'll deliver the mattress tomorrow morning," she said.

So she'd have that to tend to, plus funeral arrangements to manage, and Dora and Abel's arrival to prepare for. It didn't seem fair for her to be trapped doing all the grim tasks. "After supper I'll go upstairs and clean a little," I said. "I haven't stepped foot in that room since . . ."

She worried a nail. "Neither have I, except to gather some of my clothes that first night."

Later, a mournful Lucia came to fetch the children. Max hadn't wanted the little ones exposed to what had happened, and Callie and I had both tried to avoid any mention of jail around them. But Lucia exhibited no such worry. Luckily, the children had fallen asleep on the pallets on the floor after their meal.

Dressed all in black, Lucia sank onto one of the wobbly chairs and buried her head in her hands. "What I will do?" she wailed.

I had no answer. With Max gone, even his meager income wouldn't be available to her. I doubted the family had any savings. "Does Max have any paintings you could sell?" Callie asked. "I mean, besides the ones . . ."

Tears streamed down Lucia's face. "I don't think so. There's not hope. *Nessuna speranza. Nessuna speranza.*"

We bucked her up the best we knew how, giving her the last of the bread and soup and mouthing optimistic platitudes to counter her *nessuna speranzas*. I doubted she believed us, but as she mopped up the last of the soup with her bread, her tears had dried, or maybe she'd just finally run out of them. She frowned at the bowl. "Your soup is not so good."

Callie nodded. "I made it."

"How you burn soup?" Lucia asked. "Is mostly water."

"Oh, we burn everything," I said cheerfully.

We helped her carry the little ones up to the fourth floor. Lucia thanked us. "Soon I will not bother you no more."

"You don't bother us," I assured her.

Callie hugged her. "Come down anytime you need to talk. Or if the children need minding."

When she added that last, I knew she must have been as alarmed as I was by Lucia's ominous words. *Soon I will not bother you no more.* What was she planning?

Both worried, we went down to our own apartment. I set Callie to dusting the parlor while I filled a bucket with soapy water and tackled the dreaded bedroom. Three days—three warm summer days—had not improved the room's condition. Nor had time dulled the shock of seeing that dried, rust-colored stain blooming across the bedclothes. I stripped the linens, which had dried stiff, bundled them, and then doubled the mattress over so I wouldn't have to stare at the equally large stain on it. Hopefully the deliverymen could be convinced to haul it away tomorrow when they brought the new mattress.

As for the sheets, there wasn't enough bleach in all of Manhattan to clean those stains. And would we really want to use them again? I bundled them for the incinerator. Maybe Aunt Irene had an old set of bedding she could spare. If not, I would simply have to buy some new.

I surveyed the floor for other items in need of cleaning. The night of the murder I'd been appalled at the state of the room. When we'd found Ethel, clothes had been lying on the floor, along with her stockings and a pair of blood-spattered gloves. Some of the clothes were still there—moved by the police, I assumed, who'd dropped them on the stool in front of Callie's bureau, which was now dominated by Queen of Sheba cold cream. I went through the clothes. Everything I remembered was there except for the gloves.

Curious, I rummaged through the bureau's drawers. Although Callie had several pairs of gloves—at least one without a match—I couldn't find the ones I was looking for. Probably the police had taken them as evidence.

I spent the next hour cleaning everything I could—every surface got wiped down with soapy water, bloodstained or not. But blood seemed to be everywhere. I discovered drips on the floor, the woodwork, the wallpaper. It all got scrubbed. When I was done, I emptied my pail, refilled it, and went over the room once more. When I emerged from the room the second time, Callie was asleep on the sofa. I woke her up and we returned downstairs, unpinned our hair, changed into nightgowns, and prepared the beds. It was Callie's turn for the real bed, so I took one of the lumpy mattresses on the floor.

Ford's envelope lay nearby where I'd dropped it when I came in. A hazy memory of wanting to spend the evening reading came back to me, but I was too bushed to keep my eyes open. One Ford Fitzsimmons work per day was enough. I turned over the envelope and saw a note he'd scrawled to me.

Louise—I hope you meant what you said this evening.

"Night, Louise," Callie called out, snapping off the light.

"Good night." I was smiling. Even the prospect of a stiff back in the morning didn't put me out of humor now. I didn't entirely trust Ford's flirtation, but the memory of his blue eyes buoyed me, and I settled onto my thin pallet as if I were sinking into half a foot of goose down. I went over our conversation at his apartment again, word by word, gesture by gesture, glance by glance. I could almost feel his lips on my cheek.

I hope you meant what you said . . .

My eyes popped open. I sat up, knees to my chest, frowning. A moment later I was kneeling by the window, examining the handwriting on the envelope in the scant light coming through the dirty panes. *Louise—I hope you meant what you said this evening.*

Ford hadn't written anything on that envelope while I was with him this evening, and he hadn't been out of my sight the whole time I was in his room. And of course he'd had no way of knowing in advance that I'd visit him. Which meant that the note had been scrawled on the previous evening we'd met. The night of Ethel's murder.

My hands shook, and I put the envelope down. My stomach gnawed, reminding me that I'd skipped dinner. There was no more food, but food would have just made me queasier anyway. I wasn't sick to my stomach. I was sick at heart.

But why should I be? This was what I'd suspected all along. Wally hadn't seen Otto on the stairs the night of the murder—he'd seen Ford. Ford had been carrying that manila envelope with its message to me. I could imagine it all clearly. He'd left Aunt Irene's, gone home, dug up his story, and then, deciding to strike while the iron was hot, walked the several blocks to leave it at my door. But then . . . what had happened? Had he happened upon the murder scene . . . or was he the murderer?

The contempt with which he'd stared at Callie last Thursday night chilled my blood now. Could Ford have killed Ethel?

It didn't take much for my ghoulish imagination to gallop away with me. I gulped in a deep breath and thought again, more logically. Contempt wasn't murderous rage. And he'd taken a long look at Callie at the party. He wouldn't have confused her with Ethel . . . if Ethel had come to the door. Especially since he would have assumed that Callie and I were still at Aunt Irene's. He'd probably written the note on the envelope before he'd left his flat, knowing I wouldn't be in.

And what about the money? He certainly didn't live like a man who'd just stolen a bundle. Besides, he wouldn't have known to look for it, and wouldn't have reason to suspect that there was money hidden to begin with. The apartment hadn't been ransacked. So unless he tormented Ethel with that knife until she handed over anything she had of value . . .

That was another thing—the envelope had no bloodstains on it. If Ford had killed Ethel and then left with the envelope, chances were it would have a bloody mark on it somewhere. He clearly hadn't been the one to knife Ethel. So what had happened?

All I knew for certain was that Ford hadn't left the envelope at the flat. Ethel must not have come to the door. If she had, he probably would have handed her the envelope and gone on his way. Most likely, she was already dead, and he'd given up when his knock wasn't answered. And so he'd walked away, and when he saw the news the next morning, he'd decided not to mention the incident.

It made sense that he didn't want to place himself at the murder scene. I remembered his neighbor, Mug, the one with whom he'd spent an evening in jail. Like Max, Ford had apparently had run-ins with the police. And look how Max had ended up, beaten and bloodied.

For a long time, I lay on my pallet flat on my back, gravity pulling my spine into the floorboards. It was amazing what a difference the lack of a bedstead made. I blinked at the ceiling, unable to shake the sinister sensation of being tugged down, down. *It's all in your mind,* I assured myself. I only hoped that my fears about Ford were unreal, as well.

Chapter 9

The next day, Ethel's murder was blasted off the front page by a grain elevator explosion in Buffalo that killed sixteen and sent sixty men to the hospital "burned and blackened." The dramatic stories of those poor men filled column after column. *The journalists have a new tragedy to chase,* I thought, and yet I was as drawn in by the Buffalo drama as anyone else. Every newspaper featured acts of heroism—from the firemen, policemen, and also fellow workers, many of whom were suffering from burns and injuries themselves but pitched in to help rush their friends to safety.

The preoccupation with the Buffalo story provided me with a distraction from the dilemma of Ford's envelope, which I'd slipped into my satchel. I debated whether to show it to Muldoon. I knew I should. Ford had been Wally's man on the stairs, I was ninety-nine percent certain of that now. Though Muldoon had warned me not to play detective, even he would admit I'd uncovered a vital clue about the events of the night of Ethel's murder.

But what would he do with that clue? The specter of Max's face never left me—the purple flesh and the matted blood. I would hate to see Ford's face end up a ruin. I believed he was guilty of Ethel's murder even less than I believed Max was. And it wasn't just naïveté or starry-eyed admiration that convinced me of his innocence. It was the envelope. Closer inspection by daylight had verified that the envelope had not a drop of blood on it. Except for the scribbled note to me, it was clean as a whistle.

Ford hadn't killed Ethel. Perhaps he'd seen something, but if he had, wouldn't he have spoken up? He wasn't a monster. My guess was he'd gone to the apartment, knocked, and found no one home. So he'd left. End of story. Just because Wally had seen him didn't mean Ford witnessed anything. One thing was certain, however. If I convinced Muldoon of the envelope's significance, the police would descend on Ford's flat like flies on horse flop. How long would it take them to discover he had a police record, like Max?

Ford's hurt look on Saturday morning when he realized I'd suspected him of murder haunted me. He'd forgiven me that. I doubted he'd forgive me if I sent the police after him. I needed to speak to him first. I resolved to do just that after work.

Having settled on that course, I fidgeted through the rest of the day, watching the clock, barely able to concentrate on whatever I was doing. It took me nearly half an hour to type a letter to an old man who had resubmitted his autobiography, *Fifty Years a Barber,* this time with a revised and expanded section covering his childhood. Later, Mr. McChesney dictated a few peevish letters to suppliers about costs. When I stood to leave, he waylaid me.

"How are you, Louise?"

"Just fine, sir." I should have asked how he was. His eyes had bags beneath them like a bloodhound's.

"When will the funeral be?"

"Thursday, we hope."

His lips turned down. "You must take the whole day."

"Thank you."

His face sank into a deeper frown. "Don't let yourself get run down with worries, that's the important thing. I envy you young ladies sometimes—you don't have the weight of the world on your shoulders. Enjoy youth and the bloom of health."

Did he not realize that my roommate had been murdered in my apartment, and that the police were looking at practically everyone I knew, and that my childhood friend had fallen under suspicion? I was fairly certain he did. He still had dinner or at least tea with

Aunt Irene once a week, and she wasn't exactly close-lipped when it came to gossip. "Just this week, it's hard to believe I'm in the bloom of anything," I said.

"Well, don't brood," he counseled. "Once you start brooding about life, you're closing the blinds against fresh air and sunshine."

He wasn't a man who took his own advice, evidently.

"Has Guy come in today?" he asked.

"No, sir."

"Worthless young ne'er-do-well." He drummed his fingers. "How many days does that make?"

"Twenty-six."

He raised a brow. "Did you wager anything?"

I shook my head. "I'm not a gambler."

He sagged. "Me neither, more's the pity. Probably was my best chance to come out ahead this month."

I left him with his mental blinds closed against the sunshine and quickly typed up the letters so I could get them in the last post.

That evening as I entered Ford's building, I was almost knocked over by two miniature tough guys barreling down the stairs, screaming like Rough Riders storming San Juan Hill. I recognized one of them as the boy with the matches. I called out a greeting, but he banged out the front door without answering.

Nearby, an eye peeked out at me through a partially opened door. Squinting, I stared back, and the door slammed shut. I continued my climb up the protesting stairs to the top floor. A child's wails echoed down the stairwell, and on the third floor a door stood open, revealing a woman inside an unkempt room, slumped in a chair over her nursing baby. I glanced away and hurried up to the next floor. A series of squeaks and moanings coming from Mug's apartment made me move quickly to Ford's and knock. Perspiration trickled down my back, and I fanned my hand in front of my face in the vain hope of stirring the hot, stinky air.

When there was no answer, I knocked again. No sound came from within, but the carnal noises next door grew louder and more vigorous. I could hear a woman crying now, and Mug's grunts. Tasting bile in my throat, I gave up waiting and fled down the stairs.

"Some likes it rough," the nursing woman said to me as I flew past.

I didn't stop until I was a full block down from the apartment house; then I leaned against the side of a building, sucking in deep breaths. What was the matter with me? A year had gone by. A year, yet it still took only a few overheard grunts to send me reeling back to the worst moment of my life.

I gathered my breath again, stood straighter, and hiked my satchel more firmly on my shoulder. The sidewalk jostled with people on their way home from work. A couple of young boys with pails whizzed past me toward the corner tavern, rushing the growler for their father's supper. Another boy, alone, played a solitary game of kick the can. Nearby, an organ grinder churned out a tinny version of "The Sidewalks of New York," while a tiny monkey in a fez begged passersby for tips. It was impossible not to smile.

Even in my lowest moments, I gathered perverse comfort in New York's chaos and bustle—the immigrants fresh from who-knows-where, the fresh kids who'd only stepped off the train from Iowa or Oklahoma, old tramps, loose women, housewives calling their kids in from the street, the kings of capital in their carriages and automobiles. Everyone on this ten-mile stretch of island and all its boroughs beyond, working, struggling, and somehow surviving, whatever their troubles. I fed off this spirit. My struggles were real, but my past was my own business and the future was what I could make of it.

I considered going back and leaving a note for Ford, but my footsteps turned toward home. I would seek him out later. Right now I needed rest and a little dinner. A note asking, *Were you a witness to a murder?* might have seemed odd to Ford anyway.

At home, Callie heard me on the stairs and called down from the third floor. "Louise? Finally! Keep your hat on—we're going out."

"Where?"

"Downtown. I'm craving chop suey."

I never made it to the landing before I was swept back out again—not only by Callie, but also by Otto, who was with her.

"I didn't know you'd be here," I said.

Callie put a hand on his arm. "He's helping me."

He ducked his head modestly as we ambled toward Sixth Avenue to catch the train downtown. "I didn't do much."

She laughed and took his arm and mine. "Not much—just saved me. I never knew how hard it was to deal with these mortuary men. You wouldn't believe how much they were going to charge for Ethel's funeral."

I had to step ahead to make way for someone coming in the opposite direction on the narrow sidewalk. "How much?"

"Three hundred dollars."

I almost tripped. "Three hundred? Did Ethel have insurance?"

"No, but even if she did—three hundred dollars! I nearly fainted."

"You have to dicker with these people." Otto puffed up, a savvy businessman.

Authoritative wasn't exactly the word that usually came to mind when I thought of Otto, but apparently he'd talked the mortuary man down to two hundred and forty dollars. That sum still astounded me.

"I paid twenty dollars down," Callie said. "I'll have to ask Dora for the rest."

Where had she come up with the twenty dollars? I only had to look at Otto's worshipful expression for the answer.

When we got off the train and walked down crowded Canal Street, Otto was more like his old wide-eyed self. By Mott Street he was gaping openly at the Asian men standing in doorways, some in long jackets, loose pants, and queues of various lengths down their backs. Then he turned his attention from the men to the paper lanterns strung across the street, and the colorful banners depicting dragons and horses and rats. At least the skinned carcasses hanging in some of the restaurant windows didn't seem to bother him. More likely it made him feel right at home.

"It's like being in Hong Kong." He shook his head. "Or how I imagine it is over there."

"It's a lot easier to get to, I know that," Callie said, pulling him into the restaurant.

There was a long menu, but none of us could read the characters it was written in, and the man who brought us tea only offered us chop suey with soup or without. We all ordered without.

"Have you heard from Dora and Abel?" I asked Callie as I lifted my hot tea. The small cup without handles was hot to the touch, so I sipped fast. "Shouldn't we be worried they might arrive tonight?"

"They sent me a note," she said. "They'll be here tomorrow night. They're staying at a hotel called the Seasbury. They said they'd meet us out front of their hotel Thursday morning so we can go to the cemetery together."

"Seems odd," I said.

"That was part of Otto's bargaining—no funeral carriage for us."

"I meant it seems odd that they'd stay in a hotel when we can offer them a room."

"Maybe they didn't want to put you to any trouble," Otto said. "If you look at it that way, it's kind of nice."

"It would have been," Callie said, "except we already went to the trouble to clean the place up and get new bedding. Not that I wouldn't have had to do that anyway." She remembered something and touched Otto's sleeve. "Otto helped me put it all together. He's been my hero."

Otto nearly choked on his tea. "Hero? Gosh, after all you did for me . . ."

I narrowed my eyes. "What did she do for you?"

"Just helped me set up my new flat," he said.

I nodded, pretending I'd known about his flat and trying not to feel slighted that I hadn't. I'd barely heard of his plans to move out of his hotel.

"Don't be a dope—you didn't have anything to set up." Callie turned her gaze to me. "Honestly. I had to take him shopping just so he'd have the basics."

They'd had a busy day, apparently. My mind had been so focused on other things—the police investigation, mostly, and Ford—that I'd almost forgotten about Otto.

Now as I looked at him staring adoringly at Callie and spinning the red lacquered lazy Susan that held little jars of Chinese spices and sauces, a pang of fear for my old friend struck me. Not because of the police investigation. With the help of lawyers, I could protect him from the Muldoons of the world. But he was an innocent young optimist in New York City, and I couldn't think of anything that would safeguard him from inevitable disillusionment. He was a toy balloon floating through a roomful of pins.

Though Ethel's death had been front-page news, the same could not be said for her burial.

On Thursday morning, we met Dora and Abel at their hotel, not far from Grand Central Station. It wasn't much of a family reunion. As promised, the two of them were standing underneath the hotel awning, on the lookout for us. Dora I had glimpsed before, but I don't think I'd noted how much she resembled an older, stout Ethel. She and Callie didn't embrace, merely exchanged awkward hellos. After that, the three relatives stood mute.

"I'm so sorry about Ethel," I said, for lack of anything else.

Dora's lips dipped into a tight frown. "So are we."

I glanced up at Abel, who reminded me of a daguerreotype of young Abraham Lincoln—tall, with a head that was all cheekbones and ears. If it bothered him to have his wife speaking for him, he didn't show it.

To fill the void, I took another stab at paying tribute to Ethel. "She was such a strong woman. I doubt if I'll ever meet anyone quite like her again." *Except you,* I amended silently.

In response to my little eulogy, Dora pivoted to Callie. "How long will it take us to get to the cemetery?"

The answer was nearly an hour. All Faiths Cemetery was across the river, and it took a train and a horse-drawn omnibus to get us there. Saving sixty dollars didn't feel like such a bargain when you were forced to listen to Dora's terse griping all the way to Queens. When we arrived, not five minutes before the appointed time for the start of the graveside service, the other mourners there were Otto and Detective Muldoon. A wreath sent by Aunt Irene provided the only flowers.

Otto I knew was there for Callie's sake. He stood like a nervous, vertical question mark next to Muldoon, looking as if he feared he'd be hauled off to the hoosegow at any second. He clearly wished he'd stayed home.

In this he was not alone. Although perhaps I was reading too much into Dora's and Abel's dour countenances. I don't know what I'd expected of them—people more like Callie, maybe. But Dora turned out to be Ethel's sister to her fingertips. She stood by her sister's grave garbed in solid black from her veiled hat down to her high-button boots, yet she was dry-eyed and seemed almost impatient with the entire ceremony. God knows she looked appropriately grim and funereal, but I suspected this was simply how she looked every day of her life.

The preacher Callie and Otto had scared up, who of course had never met Ethel, struggled against the small, unresponsive audience. After a few generalities about the deceased and then some assurances that God would soon set to work binding up the wounds of the brokenhearted, he seemed at risk of running out of steam. But then he reminded us of the gruesome circumstances of her death and launched into a sermon on the vice of the big city, the senseless waste of Ethel's life from an earthly perspective, and the work ahead in trying to make the world clean for decent people. Once started, the man delivered a stem-winder probably not heard since Reverend Parkhurst's crusade against crime in the 1890s.

Those of us standing around the grave began to shift uncomfortably. My feet ached. But I knew that if anyone would have appreciated the long-winded oration, it was Ethel, who, if there was a heaven, was nodding her approval at every outraged word. I looked over at Callie, who had tears streaming down her face, and I knew she was thinking the same thing.

She'd brought a tiny velvet bag with her but had obviously forgotten to put a handkerchief in. She patted the small pocket of her suit jacket in the hopes of finding something there. Instead, she fished out a scrap of paper and stared at it. I searched in my own black bag, which was daintier than my satchel but still a suitcase next to Callie's. When I handed her my handkerchief, she passed me the paper, which had an appointment written on it.

May 27, 10:30. Dr. A. 112 Lenox Ave.

I recognized Ethel's handwriting, but it took me longer to understand the significance of what I'd read. This was the appointment she'd had uptown. As the preacher droned on, I ran through all the places we'd visited in Harlem, trying to place Dr. A. Then I remembered that a dentist office I'd looked into had belonged to a Dr. Albe-something. Alberink. But Dr. Alberink's reception nurse had told me that there was no record of Ethel's having been there. Had Ethel been unable to find the office? Or perhaps she'd changed her mind and decided not to go.

If she'd changed her mind, why would she have put that note in Callie's pocket? That note showed Ethel had gone to the trouble to get dressed in Callie's best dark jacket and skirt. Why wouldn't she have gone?

But why hadn't she mentioned needing to go to a dentist? Wouldn't she have asked us to recommend someone to her?

The preacher, finally winding down, asked us to join him in prayer. I bent my head, looked at Callie, and mouthed "the dentist." Her frown deepened. No doubt her mind was sifting through all the same questions and coming up with as few satisfactory answers.

We each sprinkled earth over Ethel's coffin. Dora slung the dirt in as carelessly as one would toss a pebble into a lake. Abel wound a long, thin arm about her waist, but she stepped decidedly away from this gesture of comfort.

After we thanked the preacher for stepping in on such short notice, our small group migrated toward the cemetery gates. "Won't you come back to the apartment with us for a while?" Callie asked Dora and Abel, without too much enthusiasm.

Judging from their demeanor, they only wanted to get away as fast as they could. "We'll just return to our hotel till it's time to catch the train," Abel explained. "Got to get back to the farm, you know."

"Of course," Callie said.

I was incensed. Their train didn't leave till after supper. Also, if it were my sister we'd just buried, I'd have wanted to talk to Callie and find out more about how she'd died, no matter how painful the details. I'd also want to learn if the newspaper accounts were true, and if the police were any closer to capturing the killer.

I was not Dora, obviously.

Dora nodded a curt good-bye to Detective Muldoon. "Very thoughtful of you to come, Detective."

"I'm sorry for your loss." I was struck by how gentle his voice sounded then, and how earnest he seemed as he took her gloved hand. "I promise I'll do my utmost to achieve justice for your sister."

Dora withdrew her hand. "The reverend said it best. Vengeance is God's. His justice is assured."

And with that, she said a general good-bye and simply walked away, as if the rest of us weren't all heading in the same direction.

Abel turned to us. "Dora's not herself. This has cut her up something awful."

His words, unfortunately, carried a vivid echo of what had befallen poor Ethel herself. He paled. "That is . . . um, what I meant to say was, she's very sad."

"We know." I felt sorrier for him than anyone, even Ethel herself. Ethel, after all, was beyond worldly cares now. Abel had to live the rest of his life with Dora.

"I'd better go," he mumbled. His wife was already halfway to the bus stop. He leaned in and gave Callie a quick kiss. To me, he said, "It was a pleasure to meet you, Miss Faulk." He blanched again. "Or it might have been, under different circumstances. That is—"

"Abel!" Dora thundered from down the street. "Come on!"

He jumped. "Good-bye." He cast a last anxious look at us and tore off after his wife.

Muldoon's thoughtful gaze followed him down the street. "There goes a very nervous man."

Now I saw his presence for what it was: detective work. Even with Max under lock and key, he was still on the lookout for suspects. I supposed I should be glad for his perseverance, but to me suspecting Abel seemed almost as preposterous as suspecting Otto, or Max.

"They never went to your apartment?" Muldoon asked us.

Callie also divined the direction of his thoughts and jumped to the defense of her family. "They're farm people. They don't know their way around New York City. Besides, they're nervous about catching their train."

Their train that didn't leave for six hours yet.

"Really? Judging from the way they bolted out of here, they seem pretty confident about navigating their way back to Manhattan," Otto observed.

Callie glared at him.

His bug-eyed gaze darted from me to Callie in what-did-I-say confusion.

"Didn't you mention having to get back to town right after the service?" she asked him. "You said you had that important meeting with that fellow. . . ."

His brows knit in confusion. "What fellow?"

"That music publishing fellow," I said, fearing we were going to have to step on his foot or something.

"Oh!" Finally, the actor heard his cue. "Yes! I need to get back. Right away. Shall we go?"

"Louise and I aren't leaving just yet," Callie answered quickly. "But you should get back, by all means. If you hurry, maybe you could catch up with Dora and Abel. With three of you there would be less chance of getting lost."

"Oh. Sure." He clearly didn't relish making the trip back with Callie's relatives instead of Callie herself.

I was a little puzzled at her sending Otto away, but I assumed she'd tell me why when we were alone. Alas, even after Otto left, hands buried in his pockets, Muldoon was still with us, hovering by my side.

"Do you know of a florist nearby, Detective?" Callie asked him. "I can't bear leaving poor Ethel without a few more flowers. I'm not certain when we'll be out this way again."

The question surprised me. When I'd asked her about flowers this morning, she'd dismissed the idea. "They'll only die," she'd said. "And then I'll have to think of a bunch of dead flowers on Ethel's lonely grave and be even more depressed."

She'd changed her tune now.

Muldoon frowned in thought. "I'm afraid I can't help you."

"Never mind." Callie bestowed her most winning smile on him.

"You've been so much help already. Dora was right. It was so very kind of you to come out today."

That tough mask of his softened again. "Perhaps I should catch up with your cousin and her husband. That way *I* won't get lost on the way back, either. Are you sure you won't return, as well?"

"No, thank you," she said. "Flowers first, then home."

After Muldoon had left, Callie said, "We'll just wait for the next bus and then go."

The whole florist question had been a feint. "Nothing makes a man squirm with impatience more than shopping for fabric or flowers," she said. "Look how quickly the detective cleared out."

"He probably hurried off to catch up with your relatives. He seemed suspicious of them."

Her jaw tightened. "Oh well. Dora could stand interrogating, I guess. The woman has ice in her veins."

I couldn't contradict her. "At least it frees us to go see Dr. Alberink." I frowned. "Why would his receptionist have told me he'd never seen Ethel?"

"Did she?" Callie shrugged. "Maybe she didn't remember. If Ethel simply wandered in off the street, for instance."

I brought out the paper again. "But there's a time written here. She had an appointment."

It took us longer to get to Lenox Avenue this time because we started out from the back of beyond. I worried that the dentist might be closed by the time we got there, but his office was still open. And busy. A haggard woman with a flock of children occupied a bench along the wall of the tiny reception area, but I wasn't in a mood to sit and wait. A drill whined somewhere down a hallway, a noise that was the equivalent of chewing metal on my nerves. The receptionist I'd spoken to last time, dressed in starchy, professional whites, squinted at me as I approached her desk in my funeral clothes.

The woman was obviously trying to place who I was, so I helped her out. "I came by last week to inquire after someone who was a patient of Dr. Alberink." I stepped aside so she could see Callie. "This is my friend Callie Gail."

At that moment, Callie was turned away from the receptionist, picking up a filthy rag doll that one of the woman's children had dropped. But the receptionist had seen enough, or perhaps it was just Callie's name she reacted to. She jumped up from her chair. "Miss Gail, you shouldn't have come back. Dr. Alberink told you—"

Callie turned. The woman's voice broke off, and her face contorted in confusion. "You're not Miss Gail." She glanced anxiously between Callie and me. "Who are you? What is this about?"

"I am Callie Gail," Callie said. "I believe Dr. Alberink saw my cousin Ethel. Ethel Gail."

By now I was bristling. "Why did you lie to me when I was here before?"

To say the woman was flustered was putting it mildly. She hurried back to her post and knocked over her pencil cup with her sleeve. A great deal of fidgeting was required to put everything to rights again. "Lied? I-I don't think that was . . ." Before she could reply, she nearly tumped over the candlestick phone. "The woman you mean, the one who came in earlier this month, gave the name Callie Gail. That's why I was confused."

Callie looked at me. "She lied about her name. And wore my clothes. Why would she have done that?"

"And why would she have come so far to see a dentist when there are several in our neighborhood?" I wondered aloud.

"I believe she might have said something about Dr. Alberink's being recommended to her," the receptionist said.

I looked at the closed office door. The drilling had stopped. "What did Dr. Alberink do for her?"

"Nothing," the woman piped up quickly.

Odd. "Ethel came all this way for nothing?"

She shrugged. "To be honest, I'm not certain what he did. Miss Gail wasn't here long. I don't always know what goes on between the dentist and his patient."

"Then may we please speak to the doctor?" I asked.

"As you can see, young lady, the doctor's busy today. If you have questions, perhaps you should speak to Miss Ethel Gail herself."

"Ethel's dead," Callie said flatly. "We just buried her."

Was it my imagination, or did the woman tremble at this news? Her face went slack, and she made an effort to swallow. "Dead! Oh dear. I'm sure it wasn't . . . when did . . . when did she become ill?"

"She was murdered," I said.

"You must have read about it," Callie added. "Ethel Gail. She was killed last Thursday night. It's been in all the papers."

The woman's eyes bugged. "*That* was the lady who came here? That poor murdered woman?" She shook her head. "I did hear about it, of course."

Strangely, the news that one of the doctor's patients had been killed in cold blood had a calming effect on the woman. She finally stopped gulping and knocking things over and looked Callie in the eye. "I'm very sorry."

"You see, we found Ethel's appointment written on a scrap of paper in my pocket," Callie said.

I added, "Ethel never mentioned having toothaches."

"It probably came upon her quickly," the receptionist said. "Toothaches do sometimes."

The door to the dentist's office opened and a man shambled out, teary and dazed. I understood his pain. There were few things worse than submitting to the horror of the dentist's chair. Which made it all the more strange that Ethel would have done so in complete secrecy. She hadn't been one to suffer in silence.

The door remained ajar, and I glimpsed a man in a white smock within. Sensing that this might be our best chance to talk to Dr. Alberink today, I darted toward the room. As soon as she saw my intent, the receptionist whooped at me to stop.

"You can't go in there!"

But that's exactly what I did do. The room was large. Electric lights illuminated the dental chair—so much like a barber's chair, only sinister. I looked across a wheeled metal table containing the gruesome tools of the dental trade before I caught sight of Dr. Alberink half hidden behind a cabinet door, knocking back a belt of something. I doubted it was lemonade.

"Get out of there," the receptionist yelled as she barreled in behind me.

Dr. Alberink clearly thought she was shouting at him, because he slammed the cabinet shut guiltily and turned to us.

"Dr. Alberink?" I said.

The receptionist grabbed my shoulder in a deadly strong pinch. "You had no right to—"

"She only wants to speak to him," Callie said, skidding in behind us both.

Dr. Alberink's eyes widened. He was a small, mousy man, with thick glasses inside round, wire frames. A strange map of birthmarks showed on his scalp through his thinning gray hair.

"What's the meaning of this, Miss Crombie?"

"They've come about Callie Gail," she said.

"Ethel," Callie and I corrected in unison.

"I'm Callie," Callie said.

The doctor suddenly took on the same edgy demeanor that had caused Miss Crombie to start knocking things over. "I don't understand. . . ."

I explained it all over again—Ethel's death, and our finding the appointment written on the note in her pocket, and the strange fact that Ethel had given a fake name.

The more I told him about Ethel's death, the calmer he became. "Oh my word. I had no idea—both that she wasn't who she claimed to be, and that she was that poor soul the newspapers have written so much about. I'm very sorry for you, my dear," he said to Callie. "But I'm afraid I can't help you. Miss Gail had a cavity. A very small one. I filled it for her, and that was the end of the matter."

"She never told us anything about a cavity," I said.

"No reason she should have." The dentist shrugged. "She wasn't here twenty minutes. She didn't even let me apply Novocain."

His explanation seemed plausible . . . except for one thing. Why had Ethel come here, of all places? "Have you ever practiced in Little Falls?" Given how few people Ethel knew in New York City, I didn't see how she could have found this dentist unless he'd had some connection to her hometown.

The man's forehead scrunched into a mass of lines. "No—is it near here?"

"It's a small town upstate," Callie said. "Ethel and I came from there."

He shook his head. "I don't know it. And, of course, Miss Gail was only here once. We didn't chat about anything besides that tooth that was deviling her. So I'm afraid I can't be of much use to you."

"No, you're no use." From the flat tone of Callie's voice, her dissatisfaction matched mine.

Miss Crombie herded us out. "The doctor is very busy. The next patient has been waiting a long time. Doctor?"

He nodded. "Just give me half a minute, Miss Crombie, and send Mrs. Johnson in."

That thirty seconds was probably the time he needed to get back to his cabinet and take another slug of the hard stuff.

It was also the time Miss Crombie needed to personally escort us past the unfortunate Mrs. Johnson all the way to the door, which she shut firmly behind us.

Out in the hallway, I tapped my foot in irritation. My whole body was vibrating from the encounter. Something was not right.

"A tooth filling," Callie said.

"Baloney." I stomped down the stairs. I needed to move.

Callie hurried after me. "You think the dentist was lying?"

"Of course he was. He and that dragon of a receptionist. Ethel didn't have a toothache. We would have heard about it day and night if she had."

Callie agreed.

"And why would she have come all the way up to see this half-blind lush of a dentist? If he'd said he'd ever even been through Little Falls, or even knew someone from there, I might have swallowed it, but—"

"He was telling the truth about that. I could see it in his eyes. He'd never heard of the place."

"He'd never heard of Ethel, either," I said. "Just you. Why would Ethel give a false name to a dentist?"

Above us, a door opened and closed, and footsteps clattered toward us. The steps sounded so urgent, Callie and I fell silent and looked at each other, afraid it was Miss Crombie coming after us. But when the owner of the footsteps appeared, it was only one of

Mrs. Johnson's girls. The oldest one. She wore a dress two sizes too small for her, a limp ribbon in her unwashed braid, and the most fretful, careworn expression I'd ever seen on a girl her age.

"Excuse me—miss?" The girl's anxious gaze moved from Callie to me. "Misses?" She wiped a patched sleeve across her brow.

"Is anything wrong?" I asked.

"You were talking about a lady, the one who died?" She noted Callie and I exchanging glances, and she blurted, "You can't blame me for overhearing, can you? You weren't exactly whispering."

"She was my cousin," Callie said.

The girl's worried gaze strayed up the stairs. She was still holding the newel post as if she might flee. Her tight dress, which squeezed her flat chest, gave her the impression of being about to burst. She chewed her lip, deliberating whether she should say anything to us.

She's just curious about the murder, I decided.

Callie looked at me impatiently, shrugged, and turned toward the door. I was going to follow when the girl suddenly asked, "Are you sure the doctor didn't do her in?"

The question stopped us cold. "Dr. Alberink?" I asked.

She lifted her finger to her lips to warn us to keep our voices down.

Callie looked skeptical, whereas I was busy convicting the doctor in my mind, comparing his appearance to the photos I'd seen of the infamous Dr. Crippen, the doctor who'd hacked up his wife in England and fled with his mistress to Canada a few years back. At the time, I'd avidly followed the transatlantic chase to catch him in the newspapers. The police had apprehended him, but it just showed how dangerous a mousy man with a little medical knowledge and a motive for murder could be.

Except what would have been Dr. Alberink's motive to kill Ethel? "Why would you suspect the doctor?" I asked. "Is he a lothario?"

The girl blinked. "A what?"

"Is he a masher?" Callie translated, flicking an exasperated glance at me.

She shook her head. "I'm not supposed to know, but I hear things. Ma'd slap me silly if she even knew I was talking to you, and I bet that lady upstairs would, too."

"Why would either of them care?"

"On account of the doctor. I hear it's dangerous."

"Dentistry?" I asked.

"It's not Ma's teeth he's working on."

"Then what—"

Before I could finish, Callie punched my arm. "Don't be a clunk, Louise."

Understanding dawned. "You mean he . . . ?"

"Stops babies," the girl said.

Her matter-of-fact tone shocked me. At her age, I'd still half believed that babies came from cabbage patches.

And look how that turned out.

"Ma said she can't have any more," the girl said. "We're already six, and some days Ma don't even eat. So a neighbor lady told her to see Dr. Alberink and he'll fix it so's she won't have it. I wasn't supposed to hear what they were talking about, but I did."

I remembered seeing a room off the dental treatment room. I'd assumed it was Dr. Alberink's private office. Probably that was the place where he performed his secondary trade. Stopping babies.

No wonder the girl was nervous. Abortionists killed as many women as they "fixed." At least, that's what I'd heard. Could Ethel have actually come here for an abortion? When? It was hard for me to wrap my mind around.

In any case, Ethel was gone. Mrs. Johnson was still up there.

"We've got to stop him," I told Callie.

The girl hopped onto the first step and thrust her hands out to block me. "You can't! Ma'd kill me."

Her mother had looked tough, but I imagined there was still a higher probability that Dr. Alberink would kill Ma.

Callie restrained me. "Why are you telling us this?" she asked the girl.

"I only want to know if he's a bad doctor."

"Are you crazy? Of course—"

Before I could finish, Callie shot me a warning glance.

"Did he do in your cousin?" the girl finished.

Callie pushed past me and took the girl's arm. "My cousin was murdered in our home. It was awful, but it wasn't Dr. Alberink's doing."

"That we know of." Sordid scenarios reeled through my mind, with evil Dr. Alberink playing the villain in all of them. "What if—" Callie kicked back, and the direct hit her boot heel landed on my shin made me wince. But it shut me up.

"Go back upstairs," she told the girl. "Take care of your brothers and sisters—and your mother, when she's done. And if she has any trouble when you get home, you send for a doctor right away. Dr. Alberink will tell you not to, but don't you listen to him. Right away, do you hear?"

The girl's eyes widened, but she nodded.

Callie reached into her bag and pulled out a five-dollar bill. "Keep this in case you need anything."

I wasn't sure whose eyes were rounder—mine or the girl's. For the split second the child's proud gaze fastened on the bill, I half expected her to refuse it. Then, fast as a frog's tongue flicking out to catch a fly, her hand darted out and took it. "You won't tell, will you?" the girl asked.

Callie shook her head. "We won't tell."

We wouldn't?

Without another word, the girl turned and ran up the stairs.

Callie pulled me outside.

"Five dollars?" My voice practically squeaked. There went the Calumet savings bank.

"It's only money," Callie said. "Did you look at that poor girl? I would've given her the dress off my back, except for the small difficulty of having to make the trip back home naked." She laughed dryly. "Not that half of Manhattan hasn't seen me that way already, for all I know."

Her generosity made me feel petty. It hadn't occurred to me to offer the girl anything. "You shouldn't have lied to her about going to the police, though," I said. "We have to tell them."

"Like hell we do," Callie said.

"I've heard about these doctors." I lowered my voice. "Most of them are butchers, and he's not even a real doctor to begin with. Mrs. Johnson might die."

"Do you think she doesn't know that? Did you get a look at those children? It isn't just the mother who's been going without food. They were starving, and in rags."

"Even so . . ."

"We don't know what it's like to be in Mrs. Johnson's shoes," Callie said. "Besides, if it weren't Dr. Alberink, it would be someone else. Or maybe the woman would try to take care of it herself."

She didn't seem to notice that I'd stopped arguing with her and was intently studying the sidewalk beneath our feet. A year ago I'd been desperately trying to think of what to do with myself. I even considered finding a Dr. Alberink . . . but I hadn't known where to start, and had been too afraid.

And to think, I prided myself on being observant, but Ethel had lived with us all those weeks, grappling with the same agonizing thoughts I had dealt with, yet I hadn't guessed a thing.

I leaned against the side of the building. "How could Ethel have gotten herself into that situation?"

"It's hard to imagine her in the throes of passion," Callie agreed.

"Maybe there was no passion," I said.

She looked even more alarmed.

"Don't you see? We *have* to tell the police. Ethel might have been attacked."

My voice was shaking, and Callie looked at me as if I were half mad. "If she was, we'll never be able to prove it now."

Yes, I knew that. "All right, but what if Dr. Alberink was somehow connected to the murder?"

"How? Her appointment was weeks ago," Callie said. "Whatever happened in that office, Ethel recovered from it. She seemed fine those last days. Didn't she?"

Those wild scenarios came to mind again. "What if Ethel threatened to expose the doctor?"

Callie shook her head. "That would have meant exposing herself. I'd lay money that this was a secret Ethel intended to take to her grave."

And, in fact, she had.

As astonishing as this news was, however, it explained so much. Why Ethel had acted like an invalid. Why she'd stayed with us so long . . . and even why she'd come to New York City to begin with.

Where better to hide her sins than in the city she assumed was full of it?

It also explained something else. I touched Callie's arm. "The money—I bet it wasn't stolen at all. She probably paid it all over to Dr. Alberink."

"Of course," Callie said.

"But where did she get it?"

Callie's frown deepened. "What day did Dora visit us?"

"Wasn't it near the end of last month?" I remembered our happiness at the idea of her taking Ethel back to Little Falls with her . . . and how crushed we were when she disappeared after one day, leaving Ethel more entrenched in the apartment than ever. Ethel had said she was too unwell to travel.

No wonder.

Callie's eyes met mine, the blue in them hardening to ice. "You're right. Dora knew. She must have known."

"Well . . . it's the sort of thing sisters would tell each other, isn't it?"

"Yes, but then why would she have abandoned Ethel with us and then never contacted her again? And then not have shown a scintilla of emotion at her death?"

I bit my lip, imagining Aunt Sonja at my funeral. Would she shed a tear? *Concentrate, Louise.* "I suppose the father was someone back in Little Falls."

"She didn't go to the police, so that makes it likely that it was someone she was fond of."

That wasn't necessarily the case, I knew. "I wouldn't go to the police, would you? I mean, if I were ever in the situation Ethel was in. Probably she was just too mortified."

"Why is it always the woman who should feel ashamed?" Callie's lip twisted in disgust. "And if Ethel was a victim of a random attack, why would Dora be so mad at her?" I could have told her my thoughts on why, but she shook her head. "No, my hunch is, to cause such a rift between sisters, it had to be someone both she and Dora knew. But who?"

"Someone Dora wanted her to stay away from, apparently."

Suddenly Callie's thoughts and mine joined. We stared at each other for a moment, stunned by the possibility taking root in our minds.

The color drained from Callie's cheeks. "And to think—I felt bad that Detective Muldoon suspected them."

"Do you really think it could have been . . . ?" I asked, not quite believing it.

"I'm not sure, but would you mind if we make a stop before going home?" she asked. "I need to speak to Dora and Abel before that train departs for Little Falls."

CHAPTER 10

The Seasbury Hotel was located east of the new Grand Central Terminal, past Second Avenue, just at the point where Forty-second Street's commercial buildings gave way to several blocks of brownstones that had seen better days. The afternoon had grown warmer, and a slaughterhouse toward the river emitted a noxious smell that had Callie and I wrinkling our noses as we hurried into the lobby.

Maybe at the dawn of the Gilded Age the Seasbury had been a stylish establishment, but now its décor managed to appear both garish and threadbare. Crimson wallpaper had sun-bleached to a pale plum, clashing with mustard-colored drapes that I assumed had once been gold. Up close, leather-upholstered furniture showed crazing from age and wear. And even inside we hadn't entirely escaped the *eau d'abattoir* stench.

Callie surveyed the lobby. "When do you think this place was considered fashionable?"

"Eighteen seventy-never."

I approached the bored-looking clerk at the front desk and asked for the room of Mr. and Mrs. Abel Chandler.

"Four eleven." The man added, as if he'd said it a thousand times, "Stairs at the back, elevator's out of order."

We made our way toward the stairs, but halfway across the lobby Callie tugged on my sleeve and motioned me toward an anemic potted palm. "We shouldn't pounce on them all at once," she said.

"Pouncing wasn't my intention."

"Sometimes you lose your temper and pop off, Louise."

"I'm just interested in hearing what they have to say for themselves."

"Do you think we should send for Detective Muldoon?" she asked.

Muldoon had accused me of not keeping him informed, but how could I inform on people before I knew if they were culpable of anything? My latest attempts to find Ford at home had failed, and for two days I'd agonized over not telling Muldoon what I knew about him. But if Callie's and my suspicions about Abel and Ethel were correct, Ford had nothing whatsoever to do with Ethel's murder. It just proved I shouldn't rush to judgment of anyone.

"Contacting the police would be premature." Imagining Muldoon's disapproving scowl, I continued. "We don't know for sure if Dora and Abel have done anything."

"True. After all, how could they have come here and killed Ethel without our knowing?"

I frowned. "The same way they came to the funeral. By train." I glanced at her. "Of course, you telephoned them early the next morning and spoke to them."

"Just to Dora. Abel might have been in Little Falls, or he might not have. Dora didn't say."

This was why we needed to speak to them. With so little information, it was easy to assume the worst. Our new theory would explain a lot, though. Such as why he and Dora were so emotionless during the entire ordeal. And why, after hearing about Ethel's death, they'd never even bothered to come to New York until last night.

"Abel just doesn't look like a murderer to me." Although it dawned on me that *no one* I knew looked like a murderer. Either I was too trusting or killers were hard to spot.

"He doesn't look like anybody's dreamboat, either, but we both think he and Ethel were having an affair," Callie said.

It was still so hard to believe. Yet Ethel and Abel had lived in the same house, under Dora's boot. It wasn't inconceivable that a sympathy would spring up between them and develop into something deeper—or that the discovery of the affair would result in Ethel's exile.

We started up the stairs. "We need to act as if nothing is wrong so they'll let their guards down," she said in a low voice. "Then we can ferret out how much they knew about Ethel's condition."

How did one rationally ask another person if they'd committed murder? I hadn't gotten the trick of that yet. Nevertheless, I agreed with her.

"We need to use finesse."

"Finesse," she repeated. "Exactly."

We made it to the fourth floor and I followed her down the hallway to room 411. She rapped on the door and stepped back, hands at her sides, waiting.

When Dora opened the door, her face registered surprise. I was just about to speak when Callie bellowed, "MURDERER!"

Dora immediately moved to shut the door. I shot my hand out to stop it, and Callie bulled her way in. All I could do at that point was bolt after her, feeling as if I'd grabbed a tigress by the tail. What had happened to finesse?

"How could you?" Callie demanded when we were all inside.

Abel, standing in the center of the room in his shirtsleeves, suspenders drooping around his hips, turned the same drab hue of green as the room's color scheme. He couldn't have looked any guiltier if he'd blabbed out a full confession.

Callie pivoted back to me. "I told you we should have brought the police. Send for them now."

"No!" Dora threw herself against the closed door, almost making an X of her body. "You'd just be wasting their time. No one could convict Abel of anything."

"Killing someone isn't murder?"

Dora's eyes bugged. "Have you taken leave of your senses? He didn't kill Ethel!" She threw back her head in contempt. "Abel? He won't even wring the neck of a chicken."

"Louise and I just came from Dr. Alberink's office," Callie said. "We know all about what happened there."

Up to that moment, we hadn't known anything for a certainty, but after seeing the look of Dora's hard, implacable expression, we did. "Ethel got herself in a mess. What else could be done?"

She spoke as if Ethel had impregnated herself.

"You could have raised it," Callie said.

"And told our neighbors what, exactly?" Dora shook her head. "I wasn't going to let Ethel cast her shame over my whole life. She had no right to have that child."

I shook my head. "So you took her to a dipsomaniac butcher? How did Ethel even find Dr. Alberink?"

"I found him," Abel confessed, red-faced. "Man I met in Utica gave me his name. Said he was okay."

Callie scowled. "Okay if you didn't care whether the person he operated on lived or died, which you obviously didn't."

"Don't you talk to my husband that way," Dora said. "It was me that took her there. You remember my visit. You saw it all and you didn't say a word that I recall."

She spoke accusingly, as if we had been a party to the whole episode. "We didn't know what you'd done, or why you left Ethel with us," I said. "We assumed you'd had a quarrel."

"Of course we did. I never wanted to speak to her again—and I never did. She threw herself at Abel just like a Jezebel. I hate to say it of my own sister, but that's what she was. And after I'd let her live in my home all those years. Imagine how betrayed I felt." Although Dora's blazing fury commanded our attention, it was hard to ignore the elephant in the room, which was Abel. He stood there, silent and ashamed. I had a hard time imagining how this unassuming man had become the center of a domestic hurricane.

I almost blurted out, *And what if Ethel had died?* But of course that was ridiculous. Ethel *had* died, but it wasn't Dr. Alberink's illegal work that had done it. "Neither of you heard from Ethel after Dora went back to Little Falls?"

Abel shook his head. "I swore to Dora I'd never so much as look at Ethel again, and I've kept that promise."

Dora glared at him. "If you'd stayed true to your vows to begin with, we wouldn't be in this mess."

Callie was indignant. "Would you stop calling it a mess? Your sister is dead."

"That's not my fault." Dora's chin jutted forward. "I gave her a good home. Our parents raised us to be decent women, but Ethel resented my happiness. She always was prone to envy, even when we were girls. I couldn't keep her out of my hair ribbons until I put poison oak in my ribbon box. You should've seen the state of her hands the next day! *That* cured her."

I never expected my heart to be so filled with sympathy for Ethel, but at that moment I could have gladly strangled Dora. I turned to Callie, but she had sunk down on the bed and now sat there, tears in her eyes. "I misjudged her," she said.

"No more than I did," Dora said, but I didn't think she meant it in the same way as Callie. "I should have known, though—'The evil person out of his evil treasure brings forth evil.' "

I couldn't take any more. "You talk about evil? You hated your own sister. Did you hate her enough to kill her?"

Indignation snapped in Dora's eyes. "I told you—neither of us ever saw Ethel again. It was her own doing that got her killed, I've no doubt. Once a woman loses her character, there's no telling what she'll get up to."

"It didn't happen like that." Not that I knew how it *had* happened.

Dora leveled a disdainful glare at me. "Then you'll have to look to your own lives for the answer. Abel and I weren't involved. We told that detective who was at the funeral all about where we were the night of the murder. We were at a church supper in Little Falls. About fifty witnesses saw us there. So don't go blaming us for what happened to Ethel. This town's probably full of murderers and heaven only knows what-all."

"There's plenty of what-all in small towns, too," I said.

Dora's eyes narrowed to slits. "You know nothing about us."

Callie stood. "I've heard enough. Louise and I are leaving now." I could see what an effort it was for her to maintain her composure. She kept her head high, but she didn't seem quite able to look either of them in the eye. "Have a safe journey back to Little Falls."

I was as glad to get out of that hotel room as a traveler would be to flee a city of contagion. Yet the encounter left me unsatisfied. Could we trust what they'd said? If they'd told Muldoon they had an alibi for the night of the murder, they probably had one. That would be easy enough for the police to check. But Muldoon had suggested to me once that Sawyer conceivably could have hired a professional killer. Couldn't Dora and Abel have done the same?

I kicked the idea around for a block or two, but it seemed too unlikely. Yet, so was the thought of Dora, Abel, and Ethel being involved in a sordid love triangle. If Abel could manage to drum up the name of an abortionist, he was more resourceful in the ways of lawbreaking than his Honest Abe appearance had led me to believe.

Callie was so shaken that we barely spoke all the way home. What we'd just learned wasn't the kind of subject you could talk about openly on public transportation. At one point she did say, "I guess this solves the mystery of Madame Serena."

The jolt I felt had nothing to do with the lurching brake of the conductor pulling into Twenty-third Street. "What?"

"Don't you remember? She mentioned a crying baby. You seemed bothered enough at the time. I assumed it was still worrying you."

"Oh . . . yes. I suppose that's true."

She sighed, already thinking of something else. "I was going to ask Dora and Abel to pay for the funeral, or at least help. Not now. I'll hock everything I own and pay installments till I'm gray rather than ask them for a penny."

"I'll help you."

"Thanks." She crossed her arms. "Our generosity's a little late, isn't it? If only Ethel had told us!"

If only.

At home, we both dropped onto the sofa. I felt like dough that had been squeezed through Aunt Sonja's noodle press, and Callie groaned with exhaustion. She looked profoundly sad. Of course she would. These were people she had known all her life.

"We should tell Muldoon about this," I said.

"What good would that do?" Callie asked. "Apart from soiling Ethel's memory a little more."

It would soil Dora and Abel, who deserved it. Yet I couldn't quite bring myself to advocate dragging Callie's family through the mud just to appease my righteous indignation. The goal was to find who'd killed Ethel, and to make sure the wrong man didn't pay the penalty for that crime.

"Do you still think they were involved in Ethel's murder?" she asked.

I made myself look at the matter logically. The hows and whys didn't add up. "Dora confessed that they were involved in getting rid of the baby, and that happened weeks *before* the murder. Why would either of them kill Ethel after she was no longer carrying a child? She did what they wanted."

"What *Dora* wanted," Callie said. "To clean up 'the mess.' "

I sank farther down into the lumpy cushions. My heart itched to convict them, and I could tell Callie's did, too. At least Dora.

"I feel almost sorry for Abel. Why is that?" I wondered aloud.

"Because he has to live with Dora." She shook her head. "A girl who'd poison her own hair ribbons to punish her sister's petty theft probably knows how to make her husband plenty uncomfortable for cheating on her with that same sister."

"Forgiveness doesn't seem to be in her nature."

"It's awful to think so bad of your own family, isn't it?" Callie asked. "I grew up around those two. Now I wouldn't weep to see them behind bars."

"Dora was in Little Falls the very next morning," I reminded her. "Given the logistics, it's unlikely she killed Ethel."

"It's an age of wonders. Late trains and automobiles . . ."

"But she practically dragged Ethel uptown to get rid of the baby and then banished her from her own hometown and family. Why kill her?"

"Maybe she decided no punishment was bad enough."

"It would have been taking a big chance, with no benefit. Abel was and is under her thumb, and *the mess* had been dealt with." I couldn't believe that *I* was standing up for Dora. But I wasn't, really. I was advocating for the truth.

Callie continued to brood as I fixed a pot of tea for us.

"It was nice of Otto to show up at the funeral," I said, trying to make her think of something else.

Her mouth tilted up in the hint of a smile. "I'm not sure he would have if he'd known Muldoon would be there."

"No, probably not."

"Not that he has anything to hide," Callie added quickly.

I cut a glance at her. "He seems very fond of you."

"Oh!" She rolled her eyes. "He's a good person. I think he's one of those young men who feels a natural sympathy toward a woman in distress. A knight on a white charger."

"Do you need a white knight?" I asked.

"Everyone does, sometimes." When she caught me eyeing her, she added, "Well, don't they?"

"Otto's not like your usual beaus," I said.

"He's not a beau, he's just being nice. And in return, I showed him a few secondhand stores in his neighborhood. Is that a crime?"

"Of course not."

She sat up straighter. "You act like I'm a corrupting influence because I've paid him a little attention. Meanwhile you've been ignoring the poor fellow since he got here."

Everything she said was true. It had been a strange week, and now I didn't seem able to stop suspecting everyone around me. "I'm sorry if I insinuated—"

She collapsed again. "Oh, don't mind my temper, Lou. I'm all keyed up and bushed at the same time. Otto's grand, but you're my best pal."

We sat in silence a moment, until music filled the air. Not saxophones. The opera teacher next door, Mr. Weiss, was singing a duet with a student. I knew the song from one of Aunt Sonja's records, but my neighbor's rendition made it sound even more stirring, as if the mournful notes were drifting through the window directly into my bones.

"What is this?" Callie asked.

"*The Pearl Fishers,*" I said. "Bizet."

"It's beautiful." She hummed a few bars of chorus, but I could tell she was still distracted. I should have tried to figure out why.

My own thoughts were going over everything we'd just said. Did I think Callie was a corrupting influence on Otto? I was sure she didn't mean to be, but she was so different from other women he'd encountered. He was susceptible, and she couldn't have missed the signs that he was smitten with her.

And in return, I showed him a few secondhand stores. In return for what? For helping with the funeral . . . or something else?

The baritone and tenor didn't skimp on the duet's finale, and the last rousing notes raised gooseflesh on my arms.

"I wonder what that song was about," Callie said.

I remembered Aunt Sonja's battered copy of *Stories from the Opera,* which sat on a shelf between the Bible and the dictionary. "It's a song sung by two friends. It's about friendship."

She stretched and sighed, as if still savoring those last notes. "I don't ever want to live anywhere else, do you?"

I wasn't sure if she meant New York City, or Greenwich Village, or this apartment, but I shook my head, agreeing. No matter the horror that had happened, I felt that same willful contentment I'd had since I'd stepped off the train at the Pennsylvania Station on a frigid January morning. I was where I wanted to be. And no matter their faults, my circle of friends here made me happy. I was in a city I loved, with my people.

That night as I was nodding off, however, I wondered if I'd been right about that duet from *The Pearl Fishers*. Was it really a song about friendship . . . or about one friend deceiving the other?

"Oh, it's you."

It wasn't quite the reception I'd expected when I'd decided to pay my impromptu visit to Otto's apartment. I'd left work early again, hoping to swing by Ford's to have that conversation about the envelope. It was long past time I told Muldoon about it. But after my conversation with Callie last night, I was also curious to see Otto's new flat, and to talk to him.

He glanced expectantly over my shoulder.

"Just me," I confirmed.

His disappointment gave way to eagerness to show off his new place. The apartment, he told me, had been used for years as a music teacher's studio, which explained the grand piano taking up half the main room.

"Mr. Kesdekian, the old music teacher, left it here because he couldn't afford to move it. Isn't that sad?"

"Lucky for you, though," I said, edging around the behemoth.

"Oh sure. I don't even have to worry about playing it at night. The hardware store downstairs closes at eight, and there's only an accountant's office on this floor and an old deaf man up above me. Isn't that great?"

"Maybe you can find some high stools and make it double as your dining table."

"No need." Otto practically danced over to the corner, where a wobbly gateleg table in desperate need of refinishing stood next to two chairs, one with a frayed cane back and the other with the words *Marvin is a dunce* carved into the backrest. "I found these after I came back from the funeral yesterday. The chairs were a steal."

"Unless you actually did steal them, you might have paid too much."

He laughed and pulled one of the chairs out for me with the formality of a maître d'. "Have a seat, madam. I'll make us some coffee."

After I sat, he bustled over to the corner of thc room where the makeshift kitchen was only half hidden behind a striped wool blanket serving as a curtain. He filled his percolator's pot with water from the tap, then began manipulating the one-burner contraption that was the stove. At times like these it seemed a miracle that the whole city hadn't burned down yet.

"I think I'm finally getting the hang of this thing," he said, referring to his coffeemaker. "I was completely flummoxed until Callie showed me how to work it."

I peered around me, wondering what my roommate had made of this place. The apartment faced Union Square, and the noise and dust from Fourteenth Street came right in through the high transom-topped windows. He had no curtains or shades, either, so the glass had the effect of a greenhouse. I felt hot enough to start sprouting.

A few minutes later Otto presented me with a mug of coffee, which, now that I was holding it, I realized was the last thing I really wanted. Yet he seemed so happy playing host, I couldn't disappoint him. Though steam plumed in warning from the black brew, I took a tentative sip. The liquid was inky, boiling acid.

"Is it strong enough?"

"Delicious," I rasped.

He produced a china sugar bowl whose red-and-white old-fashioned pattern made me do a double take. The busy pastoral scene of a castle and a footbridge in the foreground looked just like something out of Otto's mother's kitchen.

"I saw it in a secondhand store and couldn't resist," he explained. "I guess I get a little homesick sometimes."

"We all do."

"Not you, I bet. You never did like Altoona all that much, or living at your aunt Sonja's."

"Oh, I've discovered myself missing things I never dreamed I'd ever give a second thought. One day I found myself with tears in my eyes, and I realized it was because our office boy at work was crunching on a huge dill pickle. Remember Mr. Meerfeld's All-Day Nickel Pickles?"

" 'The Best Dill in Town!' "

The slogan had been on a sign outside Meerfeld's, five doors down from Uncle Luddie's fish shop. It wasn't easy to tempt me to forego stick candy and lemon drops, but those gigantic garlicky pickles were worth saving pennies for.

When I looked up from my cup, Otto's face had gone deadly serious. "I'm glad to finally talk to you alone, Louise. I was so worried about you. One minute you were there, and the next you weren't. I know you hadn't seemed happy for a while before you left, but you never said why."

I swallowed. "It doesn't matter now."

"Every time I tried to talk to your uncles or your aunt about you, it was like you'd died. What happened?"

I forced myself to choke down more coffee. "Aunt Sonja and I had a disagreement. You know how she is—life is work, dreams are frivolous, content yourself with listening to Puccini while you scrub the floors. I had to leave."

His brow puckered. "Sure, but . . ."

"What good does it do to look back?" I asked. "Especially now. Aunt Sonja said it best—'Sufficient unto the day is the evil thereof.' "

"So you ran away from her, but you're trying to be like her now?"

I crossed my arms. He was more right than I wanted to admit—but maybe sharing the same genes as my aunt was my salvation. I'd become almost as expert as she was in stifling the urge to look back, to dream too big, to regret.

"Well, if you don't want to talk about yourself," Otto said, "what about Callie? Something's been worrying me."

His face was so deadly serious. He hadn't looked this grim even when he was in jail, or at Ethel's funeral. Had Callie confided something to him? "What is it?" I braced myself.

He gulped in a deep breath and blurted, "I think I'm in love with her."

Before I could school my reaction, a nervous laugh escaped me. *Love?* Part of me wanted to sag with relief and say, *Is that all?*

"I knew you'd be surprised," he said. "So am I. My whole life's topsy-turvy now. Everything that was fixed in my mind—you and me—has been shattered. You must feel it, too."

"Not exactly," I said. "We were never fixed in *my* mind."

He nodded. "I can see that now—all those refusals you gave me, and leaving town without warning . . ."

"We've always been friends," I said. "That's what's important."

He blew out a long breath and sank into the chair next to mine. "I'm so relieved to hear you say that. And I hope this won't affect your and Callie's friendship."

"I don't see why it would, but—"

"It's good you're not the jealous type."

"Is there anything to be jealous of?" Before he could answer, I added, "You've only known Callie a week, and this hasn't exactly been a normal week for any of us."

"I knew from the moment I saw her, though. She's the most perfect girl I've ever met. More perfect even than you."

"You need to stop romanticizing people, Otto. Everyone has faults. Even Callie."

He crossed his arms. "All right, Miss Wet Blanket, name one."

"Well . . ." I hated to disillusion him, but what were friends for? "She's fickle. I've known her six months, and she's been in love twice in that time."

"Oh, I know all about that. At least, I know about one of them. Sawyer Attinger." His expression hardened. "I'd like to knock his block off."

If Callie had told Otto all about Sawyer, maybe they knew each other better than I'd assumed. I looked around me. "What did Callie think of your apartment?"

His glance cut away from me, staring at a dust patch on the floor illuminated by sunlight. "She liked it well enough, I guess, but she didn't stay long. I think she was distracted by the funeral and all. I wanted her to visit awhile, but she couldn't." He released his breath in a rueful laugh. "I even asked if she wanted to play cards. She bolted like a rabbit."

Otto and I had been card fiends since our teens. I nudged his leg with the toe of my shoe. "A little bird might have told her what a card sharper you are."

"Ha! Look who's talking. I've never seen a person just so happen to drop cards under a table so regularly in my life."

"I'm a butterfingers."

"There are better words for it than that."

I laughed. "Okay, here's your chance to get even. Where are your cards?"

His face brightened. "You really want to play? Now?"

I looked out the windows. It wasn't even four o'clock yet. Plenty of time. "Why not?" I suddenly had a craving for the competitive nonsense Otto and I used to engage in during our stolen hours of free time. I'd missed my friend. "It'll be nice to think about something besides murder for a change."

"I'm starving, though," he said. "Would you like a sandwich?"

I swiped a dubious glance toward his sad excuse for a kitchen. There was no icebox, and I spied nothing on the single shelf but two tins of sardines, condensed milk, a can of tomato soup, and soda crackers.

"Don't worry," he said. "I'll just run downstairs to the delicatessen and buy us something. How about pastrami on rye? I'll even spring for a pickle."

He seemed so giddy at the prospect of playing Mrs. Astor, I couldn't have refused even if my stomach hadn't been gnawing with hunger, which it was. "I wouldn't say no."

He was out the door like a shot. I stood and idly circled the room once, admiring the busts of famous composers obviously left behind by the previous occupant, and also the way Otto had tacked up sheet music to cover holes in the plaster. Deciding I could make better use of my time, I set the table with the paltry utensils and plates I scrounged up in the kitchen and then started hunting for the cards. The main room was so sparsely furnished it echoed, so I peeked into the bedroom.

It was actually little more than a large, long closet, and looked about as spacious and comfortable as a Pullman berth. I sidled along the length of the narrow bed to reach the dresser, which abutted the footboard. The dresser had five drawers—three large ones and two half-size ones side by side at the top. The top drawer on the left contained socks, so I tugged on the rusted shell drawer pull on the right. The contents there were much more promising. At a glance, the drawer held scissors, a rolled-up belt, and a glass ashtray containing eighteen cents in change. I pulled it open farther to reveal a few family photographs, a small ball of string, a knife, the sought-for deck of cards, and a pair of women's gloves stained with blood.

Sharp on the heels of my mind's registering that last item came an intense longing never to have seen it. In fact, I wished I'd never have opened the drawer at all. If only I could have reversed time, I would have waited patiently for Otto with my now-tepid but still undrinkable coffee. Instead, I stood there, transfixed, unable to breathe. All my mental effort focused on trying to make sense of those bloodstained gloves—surely the ones I had seen by Ethel's bed the night of the murder. What were they doing in Otto's drawer?

Blood pounded in my ears. I refused to believe the explanation that leapt to mind first. *Otto is not a killer.* How many times had I repeated those very words to Muldoon? I couldn't be wrong. I knew Otto as well as I knew anyone. Didn't I?

Slowly, I backed away until a body behind me stopped me. I cried out.

Otto grabbed me by the shoulders and whirled me around. "What's the matter?" When I failed to find my voice, his gaze traveled to where I'd been standing and the opened drawer. His face tensed. "What did you see?"

"Enough." A wave of sickness hit me. And fear. Not just for myself, but for Otto, as well. "Why did you lie?" Unable to contain my emotion, I thumped my fist on his chest. "I stood up for you. I swore up and down to Detective Muldoon that you had nothing to do with the murder."

His hands dropped away from me. Across his features—his familiar, dear, bug-eyed face—understanding dawned. "But I *didn't* have anything to do with it!" An incredulous sound barked out of him. "You know me, Louise."

That was the trouble with murder. One life was taken, and a dozen others were damaged in the aftershocks. Doubts about everyone rumbled into my thoughts. A week ago I would have sworn I trusted Callie more than anyone else in the world, but now I sometimes wondered if I knew her at all. None of us seemed completely innocent anymore, or completely clean.

"Why are those gloves in your drawer?" I asked. "Are you saying you didn't put them there?"

"Of course I did. Callie gave them to me."

So the two of them were colluding now. Tears filled my eyes.

Seeing my distress, Otto took hold of my arm. "Come on. Let me explain. I'll make you some more coffee."

"No, don't," I said quickly.

A blond brow arched. "Afraid I'll poison you?"

In spite of my confusion, or maybe because of it, I smiled. "Maybe not intentionally."

We returned to the gateleg table—there was really nowhere else to go unless we wanted to sit on the bed or at the piano. The chair I sank into had one leg that was too short. I wobbled back and forth, tapping out a Morse code of frayed nerves.

Still standing, Otto said, "It's nothing like what you're thinking. Honest. Callie just brought the gloves and asked me to keep them for her. That's all there was to it."

"Why did *she* have them?"

"She found them the night of the murder and grabbed them before the police came."

Yes, that's when I last saw them—before the first policemen had arrived. She probably picked them up when I ran to call for help. "She must have been out of her mind! Those gloves are evidence."

He shook his head. "She thought they'd make her look guilty."

I remembered Callie's plaintive question to me that first night when we were up in Lucia's. *You don't think* I *did it, do you?* It had seemed so absurd. I'd seen the gloves lying next to the bed, but it had never occurred to me that they might tie Callie to the murder.

"Now she looks guilty for hiding them," I said.

"That's what I told her when she brought them here. But by then it was too late. She'd been hanging on to them for days."

"There was no way the police would have thought *she* committed the murder," I said. "Why would they? She was the one who discovered the body."

"That doesn't mean anything," Otto said.

No, I supposed it didn't. "But I could vouch for her. I was with her."

"The entire night?"

I remembered that Callie had been late to Aunt Irene's party, and a chill went through me. But that was ridiculous. The coroner might have done a slapdash job, but surely he would have known if Ethel had been dead several hours before the police arrived on the scene. In fact, Detective Muldoon had mentioned something about . . .

I dug through my memory for the term I was looking for. "Rigor mortis!" I cried, in the way a miner might shout "Eureka!" on discovering the big strike.

"What?"

"Detective Muldoon told me Ethel couldn't have been dead too long, because the body hadn't reached the stage of rigor mortis, when it goes stiff."

He frowned.

"So Callie couldn't be guilty," I explained. "If she'd killed Ethel before arriving at Aunt Irene's, the body would have been stiff. But it wasn't, so there's no way anyone could think she did it."

"She said she was worried that the police might think the two of you were in on it together."

Provided with a little evidence, the police might have imagined some scenario of two roommates killing an inconvenient guest. And what a heyday the press would have with that idea. I could just see the headlines. MURDEROUS ROOMMATES RUN AMOK!

"But we'd been at my aunt's," I said.

Otto proved himself an able devil's advocate. "You might've fudged the time when you left."

"But what about Sawyer?" I asked. "He met us coming home."

"She worried the police wouldn't believe him." He blew out a breath of exasperation. "Besides, he's no help. She showed him the gloves."

I choked, took another sip of coffee, and then choked some more. "Why?"

"She wanted his guarantee that he would stand up for her if anything went wrong, and also to assure him that she wasn't going to tell the police she'd seen him that night. I told her I thought it was crazy, but she'd already spoken to him by then."

His account squared with what Callie had told me about her meeting with Sawyer over the weekend. She hadn't told me about the gloves, though. "What did Sawyer say?"

"He told her to destroy the gloves and to keep him out of it."

"But by meeting with her, he'd become involved. The police found out about Sawyer through Callie. They followed her to their rendezvous."

Otto's eyes bulged. "Do you think they followed her *here?*"

"I doubt it. Muldoon told me on Monday that they weren't following her anymore."

"He *would* say that, wouldn't he?"

True, if he wanted us to let our guards down. And yet I'd believed him. I still did. "I think it had more to do with having Max in custody. There are only so many resources they want to waste on an old spinster's murder, after all."

My words did little to soothe Otto. Judging from his stiff posture, he expected the men in blue to bust down his door any second now. I hated to see him dragged into this more than he already had been.

I stood. "Give me the gloves."

"Why?"

"Because it makes no sense for you to have them. If the police ever do search this place, their finding the gloves here would simply drag you under suspicion again."

He chewed over my words. "We should destroy them. That's what I told Callie the moment I saw them."

It's what Sawyer wanted, too. Which convinced me they needed to be safeguarded. "They're evidence."

"Callie was hesitant to destroy them, too. But at the same time she was afraid the police would jump to the wrong conclusions if they got their hands on them."

At least Callie and I were on the same page, even if she was afraid to tell me what she'd done. The gloves were evidence.

But of what? Something about them bothered me. I frowned, trying to think. Callie's gloves . . . I pictured them again on the floor by the bed. They were soft leather, reaching just beyond the wrist.

"If you take the gloves, what will you do with them?" Otto asked.

"Hide them with someone who's not in danger of becoming a suspect in Ethel's murder."

"Who?"

"Aunt Irene." No chance of the police suspecting her. An entire houseful of guests were witnesses to the fact that she'd been at home all of Thursday night.

Given how afraid he was that the police would raid his house, I assumed Otto would hop at the chance to have the gloves taken off his hands, so to speak. I assumed wrong.

"I told Callie I would hold the gloves for her," he insisted. "I promised."

Callie had not mistaken her Galahad.

"Don't worry," I said. "I'll explain it all to her."

"A promise is a promise."

"I'll sort this out," I assured him. "But for now, I'd feel better if you didn't have the things here. They'll be safer at Aunt Irene's. Callie will understand that. This evidence could send you to the electric chair, Otto."

He remained stubbornly silent. I nodded at his hands. They were delicate, small—not only for a butcher's assistant, but also for a piano player. When he played, they moved fast, hopping across the ivories "like fleas on the keys," he'd joked once. "Not many men could wear those gloves," I pointed out to him. "But they would fit you."

He stared at his hands. Swallowed. Red flashed into his cheeks. Reluctantly, he stood, retrieved the gloves, and gave them to me. Dried blood had stiffened the butter-soft leather, so that taking them from him was like grabbing hold of desiccated flesh. It took all my composure to slip the gory relics into my satchel without gagging. I could see why Callie would be frightened witless by the things. It was impossible to forget how so much blood had gotten on them. Ethel had not been wearing them when she was found, and she certainly hadn't been in any shape to sit down and remove her gloves after she'd been attacked with a knife. So unless the gloves just happened to be lying next to the bed and were soaked with blood accidentally, that meant the murderer had worn them.

Who besides Callie or myself would have known where to find the gloves in Callie's drawers?

I froze. Was this why Callie had been so quick to condemn Dora? Perhaps Dora had borrowed the gloves when she'd visited Ethel earlier in the month. And then knew where to find them when she sneaked into the apartment to murder her sister.

Whether or not Dora was guilty, the gloves changed everything.

Otto looked at me. "What is it?" he asked, sensing my shift in thought.

"A woman killed Ethel."

"Who?"

"I can't be sure," I said. "But I think I know someone who can tell me."

Chapter 11

At Ford's apartment I knocked and received no answer, but his neighbor, Mug, jerked his door open. "Whaddaya want?"

I wish I could claim I didn't tremble a little to see him hulking there like a gorilla in a stained undershirt. "Do you know if Mr. Fitzsimmons is in?"

"This about money?" He swaggered closer. "If so, hand it over. He owes me."

I eyed the calloused outstretched palm in disgust and clutched my satchel a little tighter. "I'm not here for money. I only need to speak to him."

The door at my back yanked open suddenly. I pivoted toward it, and there was Ford, grinning at me. "It's okay, Mug. Remember? She's a friend." He took my arm and pulled me inside as his goon of a neighbor continued to give me the cold eye.

"What was that about?" Annoyance spiked in my voice.

"Mug and I have an arrangement. When someone knocks at my door, he asks if they've come for money. If they have, I'm not at home and Mug can get rid of them in any way he sees fit. If the person doesn't want money, then I'm able to hear their voice through the door and know if I really do want to speak to them."

"Should I feel honored?"

"A man needs a stratagem to keep the wolves at bay," he said.

"I'm not a wolf. I just came for some information." His smile faded as he sensed my change in demeanor from the last visit. I hadn't come to flatter or to be flirted with. I put my hand into my bag and pulled out the gloves. "About these."

Ford eyed them curiously and then, realizing what the stains were, recoiled. "Good God! How'd you wind up with those gruesome things?"

"They're Callie's gloves," I said. "They were found at the scene of the murder."

"Well, put them away. I don't want them."

I stowed the gloves back in my satchel and snapped the clasp shut. "I just wanted to be sure you didn't notice them last Thursday night."

"I never went inside—" Whatever he was about to say, he doubled back and started over, more carefully. "Do you mean at your aunt's party? Was Callie wearing those gloves there?"

He wasn't fooling me. I shook my head, crossed to the cane-backed chair at his typing desk, and sat.

"Oh yes," he mumbled with a dollop of sarcasm, "please make yourself at home."

"I may as well, since this is obviously going to take a while." I eyed him closely. "I know you were at our flat that night, Ford."

"How could you, when I was never there?"

"You were. The last time we talked, you gave me an envelope with a note scrawled to me on it, expressing your hope that I'd meant what I said that evening when we talked."

"So?"

"You wrote it the evening of my aunt's party, not the night you gave it to me. You never wrote anything on the envelope the evening you gave it to me, and you were never out of my sight when I visited you here."

Heat flamed in his face, but he continued to stonewall. "Bunk."

"I doubt the police would think it was bunk if I showed the envelope to them."

"Then why don't you?"

"For the same reason I didn't the moment I realized you were Wally's mysterious man on the stairs. I don't think you're a murderer, and I don't want to get you involved with the police."

"Thank God for that."

"If I don't have to," I added.

He glared at me. Then, sighing, he threw himself onto his bed. "All right. I was there. What of it? *I* didn't kill your roommate."

The legs of my chair shrieked across the floorboards as I scooted toward him. "But you might have seen who did."

"Don't you think if I'd seen a murder taking place I'd have said something? Your opinion of me must be pretty low if you think I'd let a woman be killed before my very eyes."

"Just tell me what did happen."

He sucked in a deep breath. "Well, as you'll recall, I was drunk, so I staggered home from your aunt's, never really intending to go back out. But then I saw a freshly typed story sitting there on the table and thought it would be a fine trick to have it waiting for you before you got home from your aunt's. So I scribbled the damned note and set out to the address you'd given me. As I said, I was the worse for drink. I was fairly certain you'd mentioned the third floor, so I went straight up and knocked. Of course I wasn't expecting an answer—not unless you'd sprouted wings and flown home from Fifty-third Street. I was just about to slide the envelope under your door when it swung open and a woman appeared. I'm afraid I made a fool of myself—I yelped in surprise like a girl. The woman seemed startled, too."

"What did she look like?"

"I hardly noticed, except that she wasn't you. Or Callie."

"Was she blond or brunette?"

"Impossible to tell. She was wearing some kind of scarf on her head—you know, like ladies do sometimes when they're out. She had light eyes, I think, but it was dark. The lights were off in the hall and if there was a light on in the apartment, it was dim, and behind her."

A scarf? "What was she wearing?"

He gestured vaguely at my attire. "Some kind of dress."

"Not a nightgown—ivory, rather sheer, and low-cut?"

He exhaled a silent laugh. "Even in the state I was in, I think I'd have noticed if the woman at the door had been wearing something like that. But to be frank, there wasn't time to take in much. I started backing away almost immediately, believing I'd blundered into the wrong apartment, maybe even the wrong house. You never told me there was another woman living with you."

"She was only supposed to be visiting."

"Well, visiting or not, there she was, glaring at me as though I were a burglar or worse. 'What are you doing here?' she asked. I said I'd only meant to drop something off, and she asked who it was for. 'For Louise,' I said, 'but I think I've made a mistake.' 'Yes, you have,' she said. And then she slammed the door in my face."

"Did this woman look like Callie?"

He frowned. "I've only seen Callie once, but this woman was older."

"How much older?"

"Mid-thirties?" he guessed.

It wasn't out of character for Ethel to have chased off a stranger bringing me a package instead of telling him to leave it. But this would have been so close to the time of the murder. She would have been wearing the nightgown, surely. "You're sure she was alone?"

"Not sure at all," he answered honestly. "She blocked the doorway, and I can't see through walls. You have to understand, I was only there for a matter of seconds. It was late and the woman didn't know me from Adam, so I skedaddled. I didn't give the encounter another thought till the next day, when I saw the papers."

I was now fairly certain it was the killer he'd seen, not Ethel. "Why didn't you say something about this earlier?"

He shrugged. "I didn't see how my account added to the story. And when the papers reported that they were looking for me after your landlord saw me . . . well, I decided to stay out of it."

"So you lied to me."

He lifted his shoulders in negligent dismissal. "No harm done."

No harm? "My friend Otto spent a day in jail because the police mistook him for you."

"A day?" A laugh sputtered out of him. "I've survived worse than that."

"Now one of my neighbors, Max, is in custody. He has a family. His wife is frantic."

"Well, if he didn't do it, I'm sure they won't keep him locked up forever."

His blasé attitude about other people's misfortunes bore a stark contrast to his lingering resentment of having been arrested once himself. I felt incensed, but I was also preoccupied with trying to fit the pieces of the puzzle together. Ford's woman at the door confirmed my hunch—the killer hadn't been a man. Had Ford seen Dora? Maybe Callie had been right. Dora could have come to New York, killed Ethel, and left before we got back from Aunt Irene's. If she'd caught a night train, she might have traveled back to Little Falls in time to intercept Callie's call the next morning. Or perhaps she'd had Abel drive her, as Callie had hinted.

I now understood why Callie had been so quick to attack Dora. Knowing about the bloody gloves, she'd probably been mulling over the possibility of her cousin's death for days, and she didn't even have the information Ford had just given me. That was the trouble. All of us were missing pieces.

I wondered if Callie had a picture of Dora that I could show to Ford. I doubted it. The only one I recalled seeing was ancient, from when she and Ethel were girls. That would be no help.

I remembered Muldoon urging me not to play detective. Maybe he was right.

"I need you to come with me," I told Ford.

"Where?"

"To the police."

"Like hell I will."

"You must. Don't you see? Either Ethel was alive when you arrived, or there was someone else in our apartment who shouldn't have been there. Either way, what you saw puts Callie in the clear."

"Bully for her." Ford lifted his chin in defiance. "But if you think I'm going to the police to prove your roommate didn't commit a crime—which I can't see that anyone even thinks she did commit—only to put my own head in a noose, you've got another think coming."

His selfishness astounded me. "They might not suspect Callie now, but after Max clears himself—*if* he clears himself—they'll start hunting for other suspects."

"Precisely. Leave me out of it."

"But if they discover the bloodstained gloves, which Callie has taken pains to conceal . . ."

"So burn them."

Everyone wanted to destroy the gloves, apparently, except Callie and me. "I can't do that."

"Of course you can. It's easy enough—a little kerosene and a match will take care of the problem. The police will have no reason to suspect Callie, and you'll have no reason to run to the police. Perfect."

But they were evidence. Evidence that pointed to a woman—certainly not Max—having committed the crime. Just the thought of destroying evidence rubbed my fur the wrong way. The gloves might even prove important in some way I couldn't perceive now. Those disgusting scraps of once-beautiful leather in my purse were as sacrosanct in their own way as a famous historical document.

"I would no more burn them than I would put a match to the Magna Carta," I declared.

Ford looked at me as if I should be carted off to an asylum. "The Magna Carta? What the hell are you talking about?"

"Something important that shouldn't be destroyed."

"Then keep the damn things hidden and tell your friend to relax. Surely she's got plenty of witnesses to say she couldn't have murdered her cousin. If what I saw at your aunt's party was any indication, Callie's hardly inconspicuous. She's got nothing to worry about."

"We all have something to worry about," I said. "Have you forgotten? There's a murderer prowling around Manhattan."

His lips twisted in a sneer. "Oh, more than one, I'd be willing to bet."

"But it's only in our power to help the police catch this particular one. Wouldn't that be worthwhile?"

"It'd be peachy if I didn't risk the police turning their attention to me."

I slapped my hands against my knees in frustration. "You act as if you've got something to hide."

"Everyone has something to hide." He tilted a speculative glance at me. "What if detectives started poking around in *your* history. I wonder what they'd discover."

"Nothing like murder."

"But a few details you don't want them to find out, I bet. You've got spirit, sister, but that's the kind of thing that gets people in trouble. You'd be better off keeping your head down and minding your own business."

"I never would have pegged you for such a coward."

His gaze darkened. "I'm not. But I've had my share of hard knocks and I'm ready for something better. Something easier. You read my book and liked it. But what publisher's going to buy a book by a fellow suspected of being the Village Butcher?"

"Notoriety hasn't hurt Otto."

"Songwriting." He stretched out the word like taffy, pulling as much disdain as possible from each syllable. "Entertainment in this town's practically run by gangsters, but publishing's as much a gentleman's game as the Harvard-Yale football match. You think the patrician types who publish your aunt's verbal swill would take on a book by a murder suspect?"

"Verbal swill!" I stood.

His eyebrow crooked. "Don't pretend a similar thought hasn't crossed your mind."

"What's crossing my mind is to go to the police and tell them what you said about the night of the murder. And then to head straight back to the office and tear up the recommendation I wrote for your stupid book. That's one piece of evidence I wouldn't mind destroying."

He shot to his feet and grabbed my forearm. "I wouldn't do either of those things if I were you."

The pressure of his grip made me wince, although I tried my damnedest not to show it. Shame filled me that I'd ever considered this person to be appealing. A diamond in the rough. How could someone create beautiful works like his novels and yet be so malevolent? It was like discovering a bluebird was a vulture in disguise.

I yanked away from him. "Don't worry. I'm too busy at the moment to sabotage your career."

"Good girl," he said.

But for once I celebrated the fact that projects proceeded through our office with the headlong speed of a molasses spill in an ice storm. The first chance I had alone at the office, I would make a beeline to Guy Van Hooten's office and rip that recommendation into little bits. Petty and vindictive? Oh yes. I didn't care. I didn't want to be the least bit of use to this bully.

That secret vow gave me satisfaction enough to lift my head. "If you should change your mind about going to the police and you need someone to hold your hand, you can find me at my aunt's."

"Don't hold your breath," he said.

I didn't intend to. Instead of going straight to Aunt Irene's, I stopped by our building to talk to Callie and then give Lucia a word of encouragement. These gloves, plus what Ford said he saw that night, surely would convince the police that Max hadn't been the murderer. If only I could convince Callie to talk to Muldoon, and Muldoon to talk to Ford.

I took the stairs two at a time but stopped cold on the third-floor landing when I saw a woman standing in my doorway. She was stout, dressed in dark clothing, and wore a scarf over her head. The woman who answered the door Thursday night was wearing a scarf, Ford had said. My mouth went dry. Then the woman turned, and I exhaled a sigh. It was only Mrs. Grimes. Our landlady was old and as deaf as day-old cod, as Uncle Luddie used to say, and her brown wrinkly skin made her look like a walnut. What was she doing up here? Wally handled most day-to-day matters in the building.

She saw me and her frown deepened. When she spoke, it was practically a bellow. "Son—one of 'em's here!"

Wally was in the apartment? I rushed forward. "What's going on?"

Mrs. Grimes had a disarming way of looking at you while you were talking. She couldn't understand much, but her beady brown eyes widened to show their whites, as if she were trying to make her eyeballs absorb the sound her ears couldn't. Meanwhile her wrinkly lipless slash of a mouth tightened. "What?" she yelled.

Wally lumbered out from the hallway that led to our bedrooms.

By now I was practically vibrating with impatience. "Why are you in my apartment?"

Mrs. Grimes turned to her son. "Is this one the nude model?"

"No, Ma," he said. "This is Miss Faulk."

"Oh!" She pivoted back to me and foghorned, "The police have been in. I wanted to make sure *someone* was left up here."

"What?" No matter how loud she spoke, none of her words made sense to me. *The police?* "I don't—"

"What?" she hollered back.

The two of us might have stood in the hallway yelling "What?" at each other all evening if Wally hadn't interceded. "Lucia's gone," he said.

"Gone where?" I asked. "When?"

"The police came by after noon, and she wasn't there. Just took her kids and"—he snapped his fingers—"twenty-three skidoo. Up and disappeared. Left all her stuff excepting her clothes."

"Owed two weeks' rent!" the old lady thundered.

I wasn't about to cry for the Grimeses' lost income. They'd make a profit selling Lucia and Max's belongings. "Why were the police here?"

"Didn't you hear?" Wally's face perspired with excitement. "He escaped."

The hallway seemed to spin. I grabbed on to the banister behind me. "Max escaped the police?"

"From the jail." He scratched the bristle of his five o'clock shadow. "I guess he figured it was either bust out or be sent to the chair."

But he wouldn't have been sent to the chair. If only the police had known about the gloves earlier . . .

Now that Max was a fugitive, they probably assumed they'd been right all along about him. His running made him look guiltier than ever. And with Lucia vanishing, too, there would be no hope of contacting him.

Frustration swamped me. "I was just going up to see her."

Wally's squint narrowed. "Why?"

"You say you've seen her?" Mrs. Grimes yelled. "When?"

"I haven't seen her," I explained. "I was—"

"Of course not," Mrs. Grimes interrupted. "How could you? She's run away—foreign baggage!"

"I figured you and Callie wouldn't clear out so soon after buying that new mattress, but Ma wanted to be sure." Wally lowered his voice. "She thinks the Bleecker Blowers have ducked out, too. But they'll be back. I made 'em leave a saxophone with me as security."

"Good riddance!" the old lady piped up. Impossible to tell who she was talking about. But it was clear from the way that her eyes bugged out that she didn't like the way Wally was leaning toward me. In that, Mrs. Grimes and I were in accord. "C'mon, son! I told you to leave these girls alone. They're bad."

Yes, listen to your mama. Leave us alone.

I waited until they were gone, locked the door, and put the key under the mat. Then I went upstairs, just to see for myself. Sure enough, Lucia had stripped the beds but left everything else except clothes—Max's included. The furniture was there, and Max's canvases, too, both his modern pieces and a nude no doubt meant to hang in a Tenderloin bar. Now the latter was probably destined for Wally's basement lair. I shuddered. At least this one didn't have Callie's face.

Where was Callie? I needed to talk to her, but I didn't have the patience to wait around the apartment.

I left the building and walked toward Sixth Avenue. Out of curiosity, I went by the Jefferson Market Courthouse, where Max had been held. Standing on Sixth, in the shadow of the El rumbling by above me, I tried to make out where to enter. The courthouse's red-brick edifice with its white stone rings, clock tower, and churchlike roof had always made it my favorite building in the neighborhood. I'd never expected to have to go there, though. Especially to the adjacent prison. Police precincts, prisons . . . what a week I was having.

The place seemed awfully calm considering that a prisoner had escaped just hours ago. After pushing through a glass-paned door, I didn't get far before I was stopped by the largest policeman I'd ever seen. The man was Taft sized—a wall of walrusy flesh covered in blue wool and brass buttons.

"What're you doing here, miss?" he asked.

"I wanted to find out about the escaped man, Max Freeman."

"What about him?" He sized me up. Wrongly. "You a reporter?"

"No, just a friend of the family."

"Then you have fewer friends now than you did a few hours ago. He and his family have all run off."

"He hasn't been found, then?"

"Would I be saying he ain't here if he had? His escape's a black eye on all of us."

It certainly was. The guard was apparently more effective at keeping people out than keeping prisoners in. "Is Detective Muldoon here, by any chance?"

"Why? Are you a friend of *his,* too?"

"I just wanted to talk to him."

"Listen, sister, if you're a scribbler and I pick up a paper tomorrow and read that Sergeant Flynn said Freeman's escape was a black eye on the department—"

"I don't work for a newspaper," I interrupted. "I just wanted to talk to Muldoon, if he's here."

"Well, he ain't. It's been a busy day. No telling where he is now. Try the precinct."

I nodded and left. I intended to try the precinct—sooner or later. First, I needed to have a powwow with my aunt.

"I knew there was a reason I didn't like that young man," Aunt Irene said after I'd told my tale of the afternoon. Maybe I should have held my tongue about Ford, but once I'd started talking I couldn't help venting it all.

"I didn't realize what he was until today," I said.

One sweep of her hazel eyes, the only distinct feature we shared, showed she understood all I'd felt. "Don't let it make you miserable, Louise. The world's full of people who are boundlessly talented and utterly despicable. It almost makes me glad to be a mediocrity."

"You're not," I said, remembering how angry I'd been when Ford insulted her.

Her dismissive wave sent the fringe on her sleeve fluttering. "I'm no Tolstoy and we both know it. For that matter, I believe readers have grown a little weary of my plant-based heroines. Or maybe it's I who has wearied of them. Althea might be my last."

"What would you do instead?"

She stroked Trollope absently. "I'm not sure. Travel, I suppose. Isn't that what people of leisure do these days?" She tilted her head and then grunted in amusement. "I can just see Bernice, Walter, and me ascending Pikes Peak on donkeys."

Give up writing? I could just as easily have imagined her traveling up the Nile on a barge à la Cleopatra, or taking up polo. Her life had been so ordered around her work, it was difficult to envision her doing anything else.

"But let's not get sidetracked," she said. "You haven't spoken to Callie, and your neighbor is now a fugitive. How do you know he *didn't* murder Ethel?"

"It was a woman. The gloves," I reminded her, "are ladies' gloves."

"Perhaps Lucia, his wife, wore them."

Lucia, a murderer? "I saw her the night Ethel was killed. Her horror at what happened couldn't have been an act." I frowned. Hunches weren't good enough. I needed something concrete and persuasive. "Plus, her eyes are dark. Ford said the woman had light eyes."

"After how that man treated you, you'd believe his word?"

"Why would he have given that detail? He didn't have to. I think he was telling the truth at last, as grudgingly as he could." For that reason I also put Mrs. Grimes out of my mind as a suspect. She might wear scarves, but her eyes were also dark, and that face of hers wasn't something Ford would have forgotten.

"We must figure out what to do with this evidence of yours," Aunt Irene said. "You say you brought it with you?"

She reached over, opened my satchel, and rummaged around. "Honestly, Louise, how do you find anything in this mess . . . ?" The dogs perked up, tails wagging. I was so tired, I was happy to lean back, shut my eyes, and let her fish the gloves out herself.

My rest was short-lived. Barely had my lids closed when Aunt Irene let out a bleat of dismay. One of the dogs growled, my aunt shouted, "Bad Trollope, bad!" and by the time I opened my eyes, the small mass of fur was tearing out of the room with my aunt fluttering after him. I'd never seen her move at anything above a saunter before.

"He has a glove!" she cried. "Stop him!"

I leapt to my feet and chased after them. To my surprise, Aunt Irene was fast, but neither of us was a match for Trollope. Something about the scent of those gloves had revived the spirit of his long-ago ancestors, and now he was the wolf with his kill, charging up the stairs, growling ridiculously, blue satin ribbons streaming from his floppy ears.

Aunt Irene called for Walter, and he joined the pursuit, overtaking us in the upstairs hallway. We finally cornered the little spaniel on his pillow at the foot of Aunt Irene's bed. Walter, brave man, prized the glove from Trollope's jaws, earning a nip. He held up the glove—it was only one—pincering it between his thumb and forefinger.

"Bad dog!" Aunt Irene said.

Trollope met the stern scold with an unrepentant display of panting tongue.

"Is there a reason you wanted this . . ." The disgust on Walter's face would have been amusing, if I hadn't been so confused. "This object?"

"It's evidence," Aunt Irene said.

But it wasn't. "May I have it?" I asked Walter, who gladly relinquished the glove.

Aunt Irene shut Trollope in the bedroom and we all went back down. I kept staring at the glove in my hand. It was just a white glove. One I'd borrowed from Callie, I remembered now. It had no blood on it at all.

"At least Dickens didn't behave like a beast," my aunt said, carefully holding her skirt as she made her way down the stairs.

She spoke too soon. Entering the parlor, we stepped into a crime scene. The criminal, Dickens, had dug into my satchel and emptied practically everything onto the settee and the floor. In the short time we'd been gone, he'd also managed to eat the lion's share of a pastrami sandwich on rye—the one Otto had bought for me, which I'd forgotten about—and was now gnawing on something else. One of the evidence gloves.

Aunt Irene shrieked. Saliva had mixed with the dried blood, and now the puppy's neat muzzle was a horror.

Walter was already trying to tidy everything, picking up bits of sandwich and putting them on the half-chewed waxed paper, along with several pencils, scraps of paper, a comb, a toothbrush, paperclips, hairpins, a dollar and change, a library copy of the latest P. G. Wodehouse—now stained with grease—a handkerchief, a scarf, an apple, several loose lemon drops covered in lint, and the second glove covered in blood.

I snatched the glove from his pile, studying it next to the glove that we'd rescued from the jaws of Trollope.

My aunt, bedraggled after having fought Dickens to retrieve the half-devoured glove, stood next to me. Her nose wrinkled in disgust, but she held the bloody object, unflinching. Then she glanced at the ones in my hand. "So now we have a mystery of the third glove."

"The glove without the bloodstains was one that was already in my purse."

"I'm glad you brought the gloves here and not to the police, then. Otherwise they might have arrested you."

"You mean Callie."

"No, bunnykins, I mean you. Didn't you notice? The glove you say is yours is a dead ringer for the ones with the blood on them."

We laid them out side by side on the table next to the settee. I'd forgotten the glove—no telling what had happened to its mate—was in my purse. Or that I'd had it at all. "I haven't worn those gloves in weeks and weeks." In summer I usually went without gloves, unless I needed to camouflage my ink-stained hands. I'd worn gloves at the funeral, black ones, but I hadn't been carrying my satchel that day.

Aunt Irene turned the bloody glove partially inside out. "It's the same mark."

She was right. The embroidered tag, bearing the maker's name Ogilvie, was identical.

"I borrowed the gloves from Callie."

"When?"

"Maybe . . . in April? I don't remember. She probably forgot all about them." As I had.

"Until she saw the bloody pair on the floor." Aunt Irene's brow furrowed. "Does Callie own two pairs of identical gloves?"

"I doubt it. She doesn't own two of anything. She gets so many free things through modeling, and as gifts—"

A startling thought broke off my words. These gloves *had* been a gift, one of the first things Sawyer had given Callie, before the bracelet and her pin. Gloves of the softest kid. She told me so when she'd lent them to me.

My skin felt clammy.

Aunt Irene turned to Walter, who was finishing his cleaning up. "Ask Bernice to fix us some tea. My niece is about to faint."

"No—I'm fine," I said, attempting to rise. Walter gave me a skeptical once-over and then poked me back down to sitting with a stern finger on my shoulder. He skipped my aunt's instructions and crossed straight to the brandy decanter. A moment later, he put a short glass in front of my nose. I had no intention of drinking it, until the bracing smell reached my nostrils. I needed a little reviving so I could get back downtown and talk to Callie.

I belted down the drink and then stood up, sweeping all the gloves—bloody and clean—back into my satchel, along with most of the other items except the sandwich remains and the lint-covered lemon drops.

"I thought you wanted me to hide those gloves here," Aunt Irene said, seeming to forget that the dogs had almost eaten the evidence.

"On second thought, I'd better keep them with me." I bent down and kissed her on the cheek. "I should be going. Maybe Callie's home by now. I'm worried about her."

"Wouldn't you like to have Bernice send you home with some food?"

Thirty minutes ago I might have welcomed some leftovers, but now impatience to get back downtown overrode even hunger.

Walking as fast as I could without breaking into a trot, I made my way toward the El. My legs were tired—my whole body craved a good long rest—but my mind was full of questions. I had to keep going. Hopefully Callie would be back at the apartment by now.

Hurrying up the covered steps at the El stop, I couldn't help thinking about taking this route just a week ago with Callie, before we'd known what horror awaited us at home. That night seemed as distant now as the days when I wore pinafores and braids and begged my uncles to carry me on their shoulders. Last Thursday night I'd just met Ford and had a head full of vague romantic notions that turned my stomach now. Some weeks felt as if they could stretch on for a decade, and age a person at least that much. This had been one of those weeks.

The platform was middling crowded—everyone wanted to get to their Friday night entertainments, or were just eager to get home after a long workday. The breezeless warmth of the evening lent the air an added hum of impatience. I was perhaps the most impatient of all. I wanted to talk to my friend—to assure myself that what seemed true in my heart was true in fact.

The rumble of the planks beneath my feet signaled the train's approach, and I moved toward the edge of the platform. I looked left. The train careered toward us against the third-story backdrop of the buildings along the avenue. Closer, closer. And then, with a sharp shove from behind, I felt myself falling forward, stepping off into air, right into the path of the oncoming train.

Chapter 12

How does it feel to die? I mean that moment when the will is forced to bow to the unavoidable, the inevitable. Surely that's what we all fear most about death. It's the jolt from our world to the next that's so frightening—being that little mouse the instant the owl's talons sink into its flesh. A beating of wings, a flash of terror, pain, and then . . . borne through the air toward the unknown.

The moment after I felt the shove to my back, I was airborne yet too surprised by my predicament to feel terror. The fall to the wooden slats supporting the track was not far, so I reckoned my landing would probably result in a minor injury, at worst. The oncoming train, however, was a lethal inevitability. I saw light—not the glorious light of Heaven, but the lights of the first train car powering down the track toward me. I wish I could say I scrabbled to escape, but at best I flapped my arms as if that would somehow save me. The miracle was, it did.

Rescue came by way of an excruciating wrench of my arm. A burly man who'd been standing next to me on the platform caught my forearm and hauled me back with such force that a blinding white pain tore through me just as warm wind from the train blasted us. In an instant, I thumped to safe ground with a shriek that almost drowned out the metal-against-metal scream of the train's brakes.

As I sat, dazed and hurting, the train doors opened and people coming off the cars had to veer around the startled group huddled over me. Everyone was yelling—at me, at each other, to the world at large.

"Thief!"

"Call a policeman!"

"Are you all right, miss?"

"Is she drunk?"

"She was pushed!"

"He took her purse! I saw it!"

When that last exclamation registered, I gasped. My satchel, which had been looped over my right shoulder, was gone. My senses crashed back to life. *Gone.* My shoulder throbbed so sharply that it took my breath, but my missing satchel was like a gaping wound. The thief must have held on to it at the same moment he'd bumped me forward. And then he'd run, taking my bag. With it went the gloves.

I let out a yowl.

"She needs a doctor!"

"I saw a guy running after the man—"

"Can you stand, lady?"

"Is there a doctor?"

"Did she jump?" someone from inside the car asked.

The train's doors were still standing open, and I could hear another voice, farther away, grumble at high volume, "Crazy woman holding up everything."

I wanted nothing more than to stand and sprint after whoever had attacked me, but every time I moved, my head reeled with the pain. I could only hope that the man who did run after the robber was fleet of foot. Without those gloves . . .

"Say, that arm doesn't look good, does it?"

"It's all whopper-jawed," someone agreed.

"You ripped her arm out, Ed!"

"Man doesn't know his own strength."

Ed, I gathered, was my rescuer. The man was built like a mountain and his craggy face, which featured a nose like the flat side of a shovel, gazed down at me apologetically.

"Can you talk, lady?"

I gulped, intending to use my first words to shout for them all to stop talking and pursue the thief who had run off with my bag. But when I opened my mouth, the only words that croaked out of me were, "My arm."

"Here comes a policeman," someone said, and the crowd parted to let the officer through.

The cop, a solid fellow in his forties at least, scratched at his sideburns as he looked at me. "What happened here?"

A man in a dusty suit and a conductor's cap came from the opposite direction. "This lady here jumped in front of my train."

"She was pushed," my rescuer said, contradicting the motorman.

"It was a thief," someone called out.

"Ay, I saw a man chasing him," the cop told me. "He's long gone by now."

"He has my satchel—I need to get it back."

The policeman shook his head. "You need a doctor, young lady. That arm of yours looks bad. Can you move it?"

I tried, and winced.

"Dislocated," he declared. "I've seen it before."

"Can you yank it back in place?" the man named Ed asked him.

I didn't like the sound of that. "Now wait a minute . . ."

"Maybe I could," the cop said, "exceptin' it's a lady's arm."

"Is a lady's arm so different from a man's?" a third man asked.

The crowd was thinning, and passengers in the stalled train grumbled more volubly. Most people would rather be on their way than witness the drama of my arm. I couldn't blame them. Given my druthers, I'd have skipped it, too.

"I've never manipulated a lady's limbs," the cop said primly.

I laughed, but it came out almost as a gasp.

"Heck, Bellevue's just a few stops down the line," the motorman said.

"I'll take her there and let the docs tend to it," my rescuer said. He hauled me to my feet, earning another shriek from me, but I was better off standing. I might be unsteady on my feet, but at least I wasn't stuck helpless on the ground like a maimed bug.

"Name's Ed Blainey, ma'am," he said.

"Louise Faulk. Thank you so much."

"Wasn't nothing—I saw you go forward and just reached out. It was like what you call a gut reaction."

"Well, it saved my life."

The cop, growing impatient and more unsure of what he should do, nodded to the motorman. "You can move the train again, Conductor. I'll escort the lady."

I got on the train with my policeman and Ed Blainey, who wasn't going to let me out of his sight. It was like having a benevolent bear watching over me. I winced as the train got under way. Every rattle and shake sent a jolt of pain through me.

Once we got off at Twenty-eighth street, it took a long time for me to critch down the steps from the platform. We made the long block between Second and First in about ten minutes because I was moving so cautiously. It was a relief to turn and see the brick buildings of Bellevue ahead. Before we entered the hospital's interior quadrangle, the cop stopped at a call box on the street to tell his precinct what had happened, and where he was.

"Once you're done at the hospital, we can take you back to the precinct and report your little robbery," he announced when his telephone call was completed.

The idea of going to the police station panicked me. "I can't do that. I live downtown. I'm halfway there now."

"Don't you mind that," he said. "It'll just take two ticks to make your statement and you'll be on your way again."

"But I don't have anything to report—I didn't even see the man who pushed me. I don't even know if it was a man."

"It was a man, all right," Ed said. "One of the others on the platform saw him and ran after him."

"Yes, but *I* didn't see him," I said.

"But you know what was in your bag." The policeman shook his head. "Not much chance of it turning up, but if it's found, you'll surely want it returned. You'll have to tell us what was in it, so it can be identified."

Money-wise, I probably hadn't lost much. But the bloodstained gloves . . . I could hardly mention *those* in a police report, could I? And now they were gone, perhaps for good. I could have wept, but not from pain. I'd been on to something. I'd had proof, such as it was, to back up my developing theory of what had happened, but now . . . nothing.

Could it have been a coincidence that I was attacked on this of all evenings? I doubted it. Of course, robberies of this type were not unheard of. Purse snatchers and pickpockets and other sneak thieves were almost as common on the streets of Manhattan as newsboys and bootblacks. People idling on crowded El platforms were especially easy marks, because the thief could melt into a crowd or disappear onto a train car—or the person being robbed could step onto the train before noticing anything amiss.

But how many of these robbers actually took the extra step of trying to kill the person they were stealing from? Because no matter how I tried to deny it, a clear memory of a hand against my back was imprinted on my mind. I'd been pushed. Someone wanted me dead.

The hospital's teeming waiting room filled me with dread. It reminded me of the pictures I'd seen of Ellis Island, only these huddled masses had more pain and less hope. I would be there all night. Fortunately, my police escort seemed to work in my favor. The charge nurse gave my arm a brisk inspection and waved us in through the double doors and down a hallway to an examination room where a young doctor waited. Tall, pale, and thin, he looked undernourished and dog-tired. Yet he sat up a little straighter when he saw the askew angle of my arm.

The process involved in getting my arm back into the correct position in the shoulder socket was probably no different at the hospital than it would have been on the subway platform, performed by the cop. As I lay back on an exam table, the doctor fretted his hands about my shoulder and collarbone for a few minutes—watching me grimace in pain each time he tried to manipulate the arm—and then asked me, "Would you like a bit of laudanum for the pain, Miss Faulk?"

I hesitated.

"I recommend it," he said.

Laudanum. I'd had it once for a toothache and would dearly have welcomed a little of the oblivion an opiate could deliver. Except that the policeman was still waiting to take me to the station, and someone had tried to kill me. I needed to be on guard.

"No, thank you," I said.

The doctor's brow crinkled in worry. "If you prefer . . ."

Prefer suffering, he meant.

I wish I could claim to have stoically endured what followed. I can't. I doubt that poor young doctor's eardrums have been the same since. But the end result was successful—my arm no longer looked like a broken limb after a tornado. It ached something fierce, but the doctor put it in a sling, had the nurse administer two aspirin, and then sent me on my way.

I had endured the worst, I was sure. While I was gritting my teeth in agony on the doctor's table, I'd prepared a strategy for how to deal with my kindly policeman. I would simply give him the bare facts of what happened on the subway platform without letting him know what was in the bag—in other words, keeping the gloves out of the story.

That, at least, was my plan until I walked out the door and saw the policeman and my rescuer chatting with Detective Muldoon.

My feet froze even as my stomach somersaulted. What was *he* doing here? Had he come looking for me? I glanced around, desperately seeking exits, but the corridor had no visible outlets. Behind me were the surgical rooms, ahead of me stood The Inquisition.

Ed Blainey, who'd taken off his cap to reveal an even bristle of jet black flecked with gray, grinned when he caught sight of me. "There she is. Right as rain."

Hard to believe I looked right as rain or anything else when it felt as though all the blood had drained out of me. Good thing I'd passed up that laudanum. I'd need my wits about me to wriggle past Muldoon. Unless . . .

A troubling thought occurred to me. Perhaps something had happened to Callie, or Otto . . . or was this about Max's escape?

Muldoon's gaze followed Ed Blainey's. From the way his dark

eyes bugged, he was as surprised to see me as I was to see him. That put some of my fears to rest, at least. He hadn't come looking for me, and now my appearance had caught him left-footed. I walked toward them, resolved to brazen this out.

"*This* is the girl you brought here?" Muldoon asked.

"A young lady, I'd call her," Ed Blainey said.

"Thank you, Mr. Blainey." I would've liked this man even if he hadn't saved my life. "It was kind of you to wait for me. And you, too, Officer—?" I'd never caught his name.

"MacDougal."

"Officer MacDougal, you've been so kind. But now I'm perfectly fine, so no harm done and—"

"You were attacked, Louise," Muldoon said.

MacDougal gaped at him. "You know her?"

"She's involved in a case," Muldoon told him. "The Greenwich Village murder."

Ed gaped at me. "The Butcher?"

"My roommate was killed."

His jaw dropped. "And now someone's tried to kill *you!*"

Muldoon turned to MacDougal. "You said the girl's purse was snatched."

"That's what I was told," MacDougal said, almost apologetically. "I didn't figure it for attempted murder."

Ed scratched his stubbly jaw. "Me neither, at first, but something's been bothering me. See, I was standing on the platform, waiting." He squared himself to reenact the incident, indicating an invisible line between himself and the policemen to be the platform's edge. "And as the train's approaching the station, this young lady comes and stands right next to me. Not pushy or anything. But I notice her because . . . well, because she's pretty, ain't she?"

MacDougal looked me over as if he was trying to decide. Indignant heat filled my cheeks, and Muldoon's lips twisted. "Go on," he told Blainey.

"Not that I was going to get fresh—I'm a married man. But even married men notice things, you know?"

MacDougal nodded. "I've heard that rumor."

Ed frowned at his sarcastic tone, and I liked him even more. "Well, so this young lady's standing there, same as me, sort of glancing down the track expectant-like, when all the sudden she just jerks forward."

"Did you see anyone shove her?" Muldoon asked.

Ed shook his head. "No, sir, I didn't. I was too busy watching her flying out over the track. I used to play baseball—maybe you wouldn't know it to look at me, but back in the day I was a quick man on second base. So I darted my hand out and yanked her back by the arm." He shrugged sheepishly. "Guess I yanked a little too hard."

"I'll never think so," I said.

MacDougal considered the man's words. "I still don't figure it for attempted murder. Just a purse snatch. She lost her balance."

"That's what I thought, too, at first," Ed said. Bless the man, but I dearly wished he'd let the subject drop. "But I been standing here thinking. A thief would grab her bag—here, I'll show you." This time he moved me over to demonstrate, while he played the part of purse snatcher. He mimicked stealing up behind me and grabbing the bag off my arm—luckily, my good right arm. When he tugged at my sleeve, I turned a little. "See? Doing that would spin the lady around so's she'd see him. But this thief was tricksy. He didn't want her to see him, so he grabbed her purse"—Ed took hold of the sleeve covering my forearm—"then he pushed her forward." With a shove—almost from the same place in my back that the attacker had used—I was propelled forward, coming to a halt just a few inches from Muldoon. "See?" Ed asked. "She never saw who did it."

"And neither did you," MacDougal said. "You're just slinging hash."

Muldoon wasn't so scornful, though. His gaze never left my face. I tried to keep my expression neutral, but I could feel my color rising again.

"Were you pushed?" he asked me.

Practiced as I was becoming at skirting the truth, I simply couldn't bring myself to look him in the eye and tell him a bald-faced whopper. "I might have been," I admitted. "But perhaps the purse snatcher just hit me by mistake and—"

"What did the thief steal?" Muldoon asked.

"My satchel."

"What was in it?"

"Oh, the usual things. A little money. My comb, a handkerchief. A library book . . ."

"Do you have any reason to think you might have been followed?" he asked.

Was I so transparent? I attempted an innocent shrug.

His face darkened. "Louise, what else was in your purse?"

I swallowed. "Nothing of any value."

"Are you sure?"

"I'll have to think." I'd wanted to talk to Callie about all this before I spoke to the police about the gloves. I owed her that, surely.

Muldoon sighed and turned to MacDougal. "I'll take her off your hands. This is a matter for downtown, I think." He took my arm—my good one. "Come on."

"Hey now," Ed Blainey protested. "This young lady's done nothing wrong."

"I just need to ask her some more questions and get a description of this purse snatcher," Muldoon assured him.

"I didn't see him," I said.

"Maybe not, but I suspect if we jog your memory, you might realize you didn't need to see who it was to know who it was."

To MacDougal's amusement, and over Ed Blainey's protests, Muldoon began to tug me away from the others.

I resisted. "Is anyone in your family an avid reader, Mr. Blainey?"

It was a shot in the dark, but the man's craggy face broke into a smile. "I got one daughter. Always has her nose in a book."

"My aunt is an author. If you go to her house on Fifty-third Street, I'm sure she'll be more than happy to sign a few books for your daughter. And perhaps you could tell her what happened, and that you saw me being dragged away by Detective Muldoon?"

Muldoon made a disgusted sound, but Mr. Blainey nodded and

then winked at me for good measure. "I've got to head back uptown anyway." I could have kissed his bristly cheek for that lie. Instead, I gave him Aunt Irene's address.

"Who's this aunt?" MacDougal demanded. "Famous author?" He pivoted to Muldoon. "Sounds fishy to me, sir. Could be a newspaper scribbler."

Muldoon shook his head to warn MacDougal off any conspiracy theory that might be brewing in his noggin. "She writes novels. Irene Livingston Green."

"*Myrtle in Springtime*? *Shy Fern*?" The officer's face went slack. "*That* Irene Livingston Green?"

My astonishment was only slightly less than Muldoon's. Or slightly less obvious.

"My ma's a bookworm," MacDougal added sheepishly.

Muldoon snorted. "Sure she is."

I gave Ed Blainey Aunt Irene's address, and MacDougal said he'd go, too—"just to show him the way."

Mixed feelings warred within as I watched those two men stroll away. At least I wouldn't disappear into police custody with no one knowing where I was. On the other hand, I was now alone with Muldoon. And he didn't look pleased.

"Wait here," he said, and darted into the street to hail the black cab chugging in our direction. The driver pulled up and yanked the brake, then hopped out. He wore a duster and cap and opened the door for Muldoon, who waved me over.

"A taxi?" I asked.

"You're hurt, in case you haven't noticed."

"I'm also penniless, now that my satchel's gone."

He stopped short of rolling his eyes. "Just get in." He turned to the cabbie, who was still holding the door. "Charles Street. Sixth Precinct Headquarters."

I climbed into the cab and pushed myself toward the far side. Muldoon came in after me, shut the door, and placed his hat on his knee. He seemed larger in the small space. We both faced forward, stiff and formal in the dark interior.

A block or two of silence was all I could take. "If I didn't know better, I'd think you've been following me, Detective. Your being at the hospital was quite a coincidence."

"Nothing really seems like a coincidence where you're concerned," he said. "You appear to be tangled up in all sorts of troubles. I imagine you're no stranger to hospitals."

"I'll have you know I haven't been to one since my uncle chopped his pinky finger off with a meat cleaver."

"Your uncle the butcher?"

"I suppose it's a professional hazard." I frowned. "Why were you at the hospital?"

"Robinson got stabbed. That's *our* professional hazard."

A horrible possibility struck me. "Was he hurt while you were hunting Max?"

"You heard about the escape?"

"I was at the flat this afternoon. And then I went to the Jefferson Courthouse jail to see what had happened. I asked after you, but some big galoot named Flynn said you weren't around."

"You were looking for me? Why?"

I wasn't certain how much I should tell, so I deflected his question with one of my own. "Was Detective Robinson working on my case—I mean, Ethel's murder?"

He shook his head. "Yours isn't the only criminal case in town, unfortunately."

The cab made a sharp right turn, and my free hand pushed down on the dimpled upholstery—inadvertently mashing Muldoon's hand. I withdrew mine quickly, as did he.

"Is Detective Robinson going to be all right?" I asked.

"The doctors think so. They sewed him up and are keeping him there awhile."

"Maybe we should buy him some fruit."

"I took him a sack of oranges." He must have noticed my blink of surprise. "You think a detective can't be thoughtful?"

The memory of his speaking so kindly to Dora after the funeral came back to me. "I know you can be. You only act gruff."

"It's not an act." His lips turned down. "Most of the time."

I smiled.

"Who pushed you, Louise?"

The question caught me off guard, as it was intended to. My smile faded. "I don't know." Not that I didn't have suspicions. "Why would I necessarily have known the culprit?"

"You really believe a man just so happened to target you as a good candidate for purse snatching?"

"Why not?"

He gave me a shrewd up-and-down glance. "You don't wear jewelry or particularly fashionable clothes. That shirtwaist looks fine on you, but your skirt has the look of something you sewed yourself, assuming you're not a very able seamstress. Your hem's wavy."

I touched my skirt self-consciously. His assessment should have ruffled me, but I was fascinated. Everything he said was true. The shirt was a Callie cast-off, and the skirt was one I'd made the spring before I'd left home. I'd had to adjust the waist twice, but I hadn't thought to fix the hem, even though Callie had complained about it. I would never have expected Muldoon to notice such details.

"When was the last time you carried any more than a couple bucks on you?" he asked.

"On payday I do. Maybe the robber thought Friday was my payday."

Muldoon frowned.

"Also, I wasn't alert to my surroundings," I said. "That's part of a thief's strategy, isn't it? They probably seek out people who seem preoccupied."

"What was bothering you?"

"Why would anything have to be bothering me? I probably just looked absentminded. It was the end of the day and I was tired."

"I don't know you very well, Miss Faulk, but I'm familiar enough with you to say you're not a scatterbrain. And your words usually mean something."

"So it's Miss Faulk again, is it?" I asked, trying to change the subject.

"You said preoccupied."

I shouldn't have said anything. I should have run the moment I saw Muldoon standing in the hospital, even if I'd had to duck into a broom closet or crawl out a window. But no. I'd thought I could outsmart him.

Too soon, we were back in Muldoon's stomping ground, and I was running out of steam. It had been a long day, I hadn't eaten much, and I was worried about Callie. What would she say when she found out I'd lost the gloves? In retrospect, I should have left them with Otto, except Otto had become too involved already. And how was I to know that someone would steal my satchel?

"All right," Muldoon said, sitting opposite me, a hawk in human form. "Let's go over this again. Where were you coming from when you were attacked?"

"Aunt Irene's."

"And you saw no one following you."

"No. Why would anyone follow me?" He kept returning to this point and I became more uneasy each time he voiced it. Who had been following? I could think of only one person—Ford—and that possibility sickened me.

"Where were you before your aunt Irene's?"

"I visited . . . friends."

"Which friends?"

"A writer I know."

"Who?"

"A novelist. He's a realist, and yet his books are filled with wild adventure and heartbreak. If he ever finds a publisher, I'm sure he'll do well." *If* he found a publisher. I renewed my vow that it wouldn't be Van Hooten and McChesney.

"I just wanted a straight answer, not a literary critique," Muldoon said. "Would it be asking too much for you to supply this man's name?"

"I was only at his apartment for a half hour."

"Fine." His expression darkened. "Where were you before you visited James Fenimore Cooper?"

"At Otto's. He recently moved into a flat right by Union Square."

Muldoon tapped his pencil against the tabletop. "Are you in the habit of visiting several men in their apartments every time you have a free evening?"

I stiffened. "You don't have to make it sound immoral."

"I've been dealing with the vice in this city for ten years. I've seen people get up to things I never would've dreamed of before I joined the force. The bad, the corrupt, the degenerate. It's a different world from what most people are used to. So forgive me for being disturbed when nice girls start romping around the city as if visiting a man in his flat is no different than attending a tea party."

I supposed I should feel grateful that he still categorized me as a nice girl.

"Sometimes there *is* no difference," I said.

"Suppose I ask one of the officers here to find Otto and bring him in," he said. "Would he tell me the same story—that the two of you just chatted?"

I swallowed. "Yes."

"Of course," he continued, "I'd have to tell him that I'd been talking to you. And that you'd been attacked. What do you think he'd say to that?"

Otto would go wild. He'd spill everything he knew about the gloves—probably in the way most likely to incriminate himself.

"You're a fiend," I said.

"What was in your purse, Louise?"

I told him. Everything. About the gloves, and Otto, and my conversation with Ford. I told him Ford had been the man on the stairs. I even told him about the dogs chewing the gloves . . . before they were stolen. And as I spilled all this information, I consoled myself with the fact that the story of the bloodstained gloves really exonerated Callie. Her gloves had been in my purse since May, so the bloody ones couldn't have been hers. To truly bring that point home, I reminded Muldoon that Ford had seen either Ethel alive or Ethel's killer at the time Callie and I were still on our way home from Aunt Irene's.

While I spoke, Muldoon jotted notes down on a sheet of paper before him, tapped his pencil in irritation, and asked just enough curt questions to elicit specific information—times, addresses, basic descriptions. Then, before I was quite finished, he got up and stepped just outside the door, whispering to a policeman.

All this time, I'd expected to see my aunt's lawyer, Abe Faber, waltz into the interrogation room to rescue me. Perhaps Ed Blainey hadn't made it to Aunt Irene's house—or she was out. In which case, I was on my own.

As Muldoon came back in, I concluded, "So you see, Callie is wholly innocent. She only *thought* the gloves incriminated her. But since I had her gloves in my purse all along, the bloody ones must have come from the killer."

I assumed Muldoon would at least give me a little credit for piecing this all together. It had been a long, exhausting day, and I could have used a little validation that my running around town and almost being killed hadn't been in vain.

Instead, he gazed at me with a disturbing level of calm. Almost a minute ticked by before it dawned on me that what I was looking at was actually barely suppressed fury. "Do you want to help us find out who killed Ethel Gail?" he asked in a tight rasp.

"Of course," I said.

"You could've fooled me. You should have come to me the moment you saw that glove. And as for hiding the identity of a witness for *an entire week*—"

"Ford wasn't a witness, exactly—that is, I didn't know he was. I wasn't certain he'd seen anything at all until this evening."

"But if you'd told the police of his existence as the man Wally Grimes had seen on the staircase, maybe we could have found out that information earlier."

"But you were so unreasonable about Otto, and then Max had been beaten."

"Injured during the course of an arrest," he corrected.

"So you say."

His fury grew. "Look, if we had this writer's evidence earlier, we might have easily deduced, as you have, that the killer was a woman. Max Freeman would not have been held at all." The man's whole demeanor was spitting righteous outrage. He looked like a Roman candle about to pop off. I expected him to blow his stack or order me carried off to a cold, dark cell somewhere, but instead he fisted his hands in front of him and eyed me grimly. "What other information are you sitting on? How far would you go to shield your friends, and your roommate?"

My roommate? "You're not listening," I said. "The things I found out are all evidence that Callie is *innocent*."

He took a deep breath and held it a moment before exhaling. "I asked you before to leave the detective work to us. You can also leave the misconstruing of evidence to us, if you don't mind. Your so-called non-incriminating evidence doesn't exonerate your roommate as thoroughly as you'd have us believe. Or at all, in my opinion."

"I knew you'd say that. You see? You're making my argument for me."

"Louise, you have no argument. We're the police, you're not. You shouldn't be hiding things from us. When you do, it leaves us with an incomplete picture and puts you at risk. You do realize that someone tried to kill you tonight—and that it was probably the man whose identity you were protecting."

"Actually, I suspect it was his friend in the next apartment. His name is Mug. I believe that's a nickname, not a surname."

Muldoon looked up from his paper, his face a blank wall of disbelief. "This writer, this paragon of literary genius, has a friend named *Mug?*"

"You'll have to let Ford explain it."

"Oh, I will."

I shook my head. "But this is all beside the point. *I* had Callie's gloves, so the bloody ones couldn't have been Callie's."

"She could've had two pairs of the same make of gloves. It's only practical, isn't it? A woman likes a pair of gloves, so she buys two pairs. My sister does that all the time."

"You have a sister?" It was the first time he'd offered up any personal information.

"Don't look so shocked. I have all sorts of family."

I leaned forward. "Is she older or younger?"

"Nothing could matter less to this case," he said wearily.

"I'll bet older—practical and frugal."

"As a matter of fact, she's younger, practical and frugal."

"Well, Callie's not that way. What's more, the gloves were a gift, and good quality. Buying a duplicate pair would have struck her as throwing money away."

"Who was the man who gave them to her?"

"I shouldn't say without asking her permission first."

"Dollars to donuts it was Sawyer Attinger."

My silence was all the affirmation he needed.

He clasped his hands on the desk in front of him. "Louise, I need your solemn vow that you will stay out of this investigation from now on. Otherwise, I'll have no other choice than to lock you up."

"On what charge?"

"Anything I can come up with. How about obstructing justice?"

"But I just told you everything I know." Nearly everything. I whisked the information about Ethel's abortion to the back of my mind.

He shook his head. "I've got a hunch that the minute you leave here you'll be up to your same shenanigans again."

"What shenanigans?" I asked, offended.

We were interrupted by the entrance of an officer in uniform. "MacNamara telephoned, sir," he announced. "The girl wasn't at home."

Girl? Fear pierced my heart. "Callie? Does he mean Callie?"

"The landlady's son says she hadn't been around all day and didn't come home this evening, either."

Muldoon eyed me skeptically. "Where has she gone, Louise? Did she know anything about Max's escape?"

I could tell which direction his thoughts were racing toward now. Max had escaped. Now Callie was gone. The old artist-and-model collusion theory was percolating afresh in his fevered brain. I might have been suspicious myself, except that Lucia had also disappeared. And the children. Two might be company, but six was definitely a crowd. Callie considered herself a modern woman, but she wasn't *that* modern.

I stood. "I haven't seen her since this morning. For all I know, she had a date with someone. Her not being at the apartment isn't necessarily connected with the murder, you know. And certainly not Max's escape." But where was she?

"Not necessarily," he agreed, in a tone that made it clear he *didn't* agree.

"I'd like to go home now," I said. "I'm tired, and hungry." And I needed to track down my friend.

Muldoon's expression softened. "All right. O'Malley, escort Miss Faulk home."

"That's not—"

He cut me off. "Yes, it is. Someone tried to kill you and now your roommate's gone missing. I'll feel better if a policeman sees you to your door."

O'Malley saw me to my building without incident. In spite of the many troubles I had jostling for space in my head, I was able to keep up a conversation with the police officer, who was interested in my work at Van Hooten and McChesney.

"I've often thought I should write a book," he said.

"I'm sure you could."

"*Twenty Years on the Beat,* I'd call it. Of course, the brass downtown might not appreciate the unvarnished truth, and I wouldn't want to tell it any other way," he confided. "We aren't always heroes, I'm afraid."

Whether or not they were heroes, I was beginning to envy these men their jobs. It had to be interesting, if not always rewarding, to deal with the nitty-gritty bits of life. With problems that mattered. With life and death, right and wrong. This past week had been horrible, but I couldn't remember feeling so deeply immersed in anything in my whole life.

At my doorstep, "You Made Me Love You" floated down from the second floor. The Bleecker Blowers were back from their upstate tour.

"Nice band," O'Malley said. "Must be a treat having them right here."

"Oh yes, it's like having a dance band in your living room." Whether you wanted them there or not. "Good night," I told him, and he tipped his hat back at me and backed away from the door. Thank heavens.

I whisked up the stairs briskly and entered my apartment, hoping against hope to find Callie there, lounging on the lumpy sofa. But the place was empty. Or so I assumed. When I peeked into her room—which I was trying not to think of as *the murder room*—a hand darted out from behind the door and covered my mouth. My heart stopped.

"Don't scream," a voice whispered.

Chapter 13

After I recovered from my heart attack, I knocked Otto's hand away and spun toward him. "What are you doing?"

"Keep your voice down, will you?" he said in an urgent whisper.

I did, without quite understanding why. "I wouldn't have made a peep if you hadn't been stalking around here like—well, like the Village Butcher."

"Don't say that, even in fun." He gaped at my arm in its sling. "What happened to you?"

"A near miss and an exuberant rescuer."

His hand tapped impatiently against the door frame. "This evening's been confusing enough without you speaking in riddles."

"I had a little accident. I'm fine. But what are you doing here? Have you seen Callie?"

"Not exactly. I had to find you, and I was hiding in case more police came in."

"More?" I asked.

He proceeded to dart around the apartment, peeking out windows before flicking curtains closed. Only then did he turn on two lamps so that we weren't talking at each other in the dark. "There was one here before."

Of course. Muldoon had sent someone to look for Callie. "And where were you?"

"Across the street, in a doorway, waiting for you."

Another evening I might have laughed at the two of us criss-crossing the city on our various missions. But nothing about this evening seemed humorous anymore. Where was Callie?

"You could have waited here," I said. He obviously didn't have any compunction about coming in uninvited.

"Your aunt told me to keep out of sight. She said you'd come back here eventually."

"You talked to Aunt Irene? When?"

"I went to her house this evening, looking for you. You said you were going to give your aunt the gloves. When I got there, she was in a state. She said two men had come by—"

"Ed Blainey and a policeman?"

He nodded. "That's right. She was trying to get in touch with Mr. Faber, and sent Walter to fetch him after she couldn't reach him on the telephone. But Walter came back and said that Mr. Faber was fishing at Lake Placid."

"Good thing I managed without him."

"Your aunt figured you'd talk your way out." He smiled. "She's so fond of you. She was telling me how clever you are—as if I didn't know."

I didn't feel clever, although at least I'd wriggled away from Muldoon. I blew out a breath. "Well, all's well that ends well, I suppose." Except that nothing had ended. "Where's Callie?"

"Oh! That's why I was at your aunt's. I was trying to find you, because I had a note from Callie."

"What did it say?"

He pulled a small envelope from his vest pocket, then hesitantly handed it over. "You're not going to like it."

The sheet of paper I removed from the envelope had been folded several times into a square. Callie's tiny cursive filled the light pink paper.

> *Dear Otto,*
>
> *When you receive this, I'll be in Little Falls. I didn't tell Louise because I didn't want to be talked*

out of going. You know how she can be. She would either have stopped me, or insisted on coming with me. Louise might be good at nosing around, but nobody knows Little Yawns like I do. We need to find out whether Dora and Abel were truly there the night Ethel was killed, and I know the people to ask.

If Louise corners you, tell her the truth—I know you hate to lie—but make it clear that I don't want her to follow me. I'm only writing you because I don't want anyone to think I've disappeared, or worse. And frankly it feels better having people know what I'm up to, just in case. I don't expect anything bad to happen to me, but I never expected anything bad to happen to poor Ethel, either. Try not to worry, Otto. I'll be back in a day or two.

Sincerely yours,
Callie

Sneaky Callie. I should have known she wouldn't accept Dora and Abel's word concerning their whereabouts the night of the murder. For that matter, maybe I shouldn't have, either.

As I reread the note, Otto's face hovered so close I could smell the wintergreen of the Teaberry gum he favored. "What should we do?" he asked.

"Nothing."

"But she's up there all alone."

That worried me, too. On the other hand, I was almost certain Callie wouldn't be tangling with a murderer in Little Falls. If Dora had felt homicidal against her sister, surely she would have killed her *before* Ethel got rid of the baby. For that matter, if she was prone to murderous rages, she would have killed Ethel when she'd first discovered the pregnancy.

"Callie's safer where she is." I prayed I was right about that. "Muldoon's on the warpath," I explained. "My fault. He winkled the information about the gloves out of me, and now he wants to talk to Callie. And you, too, I assume. I'm sure that's why Aunt Irene told you to stay out of sight."

My aunt surprised me. Even without knowing what happened at the police station between Muldoon and me, she grasped enough to send Otto after me here, not at the police station. She was a step ahead.

As I freshened up for what was sure to be a long night, I filled Otto in on all that had happened since I saw him that afternoon. He was distressed about my encounter with Ford, and even more upset about what happened on the El platform.

"Who did it?" he asked. "It can't just be a coincidence that you were shoved while you were running around with those gloves."

"Of course it wasn't. Like an idiot, I told Ford I'd be at my aunt's. He probably sent that goon next door to get rid of me."

Otto thought about that. "Then *he* has the gloves. He could use them to incriminate Callie."

"He'd have no luck with that. I've already told Muldoon about them. The police believe the gloves were stolen by someone who wanted to kill me, so Ford's having them would make him a suspect in my attack."

"But he could decide not to go to the police and blackmail Callie with them instead."

"Let's hope he doesn't have that chance. Muldoon sent an officer to his apartment while I was talking to him, I'm fairly certain. He sent one after Callie, and probably another after you, too."

"Good." He shook his head. "I mean about his sending someone to get that Ford fellow."

"Even if Muldoon interrogates him, I doubt he'll be any closer to finding Ethel's killer when he's done. Ford didn't kill her."

"But he engaged some goon of a neighbor to push you in front of a train. Why would he have done that if not to cover up evidence of his crime?"

"He saw me as an obstacle."

That was what gave me chills. Ford hadn't threatened my life to save his skin. He'd only wanted to safeguard his career. Anything that got between himself and a book contract needed to be eliminated—even if that something was me, the fool who'd recommended his book in the first place. There was writerly gratitude for you.

Otto reddened. "I hope Muldoon locks him up. He deserves the electric chair."

I shook my head. "Ford will deny everything, and I didn't see the man who pushed me."

"But what about the night of the murder? He was the man I was mistaken for. The killer! Wally saw him."

"Ford wasn't the killer." It would have been so satisfying if only I could have convinced myself that he was. At this point, there was no one I would rather see behind bars.

Except for the real killer, of course.

Otto tossed himself onto the couch in frustration. "Life was simpler in Altoona."

No. Even now—even after a murder and an attempted murder—I wasn't willing to concede that point. Bad things happened everywhere. I hadn't been safe in Altoona, in my own home. In sleepy Little Falls, a sordid melodrama had played out that had ended in Ethel's murder. Sure, she'd been killed in New York City, but it had all started in a quiet upstate burg, with a forbidden love affair and a jealous woman.

I straightened. *A forbidden love affair and a jealous woman.* "Good Lord."

Otto blinked. "What is it?"

"I've been such a dunce. I understand it all now."

"You're *too* understanding, Louise. Taking the psychological view is one thing, but sympathizing with a man who had you flung off a train platform is taking compassion too far."

"It's not the train platform I'm thinking of," I said.

It was a jealous woman. And I didn't mean Dora.

I brought my aunt around to my way of thinking before I was able to convince Otto.

"A respectable woman would never do anything so awful, or so cold-blooded," he argued, his mouth full of cake. "Would she?"

Bernice had made one of her unforgettable coconut cakes, and Otto and I were on our way to demolishing a quarter of it. I'd been famished, and was so energized now by having put my finger on the culprit that I was stuffing forkfuls into my mouth without even thinking.

My aunt watched us chow down with a considering look on her face. "Margaret Attinger." She said the name slowly, as if trying it out as a possible character in one of her books.

"Whenever I thought about who might have killed Ethel, what puzzled me most was lack of motive," I said. "Maybe Sawyer could have killed Callie for his own twisted reasons—passion, guilt, and jealousy can create a monster—but he wouldn't have mistaken Ethel for Callie, not in a million years. And although Ford disliked Callie's type, that alone didn't seem to justify killing a woman he'd never spoken to, unless he were a true maniac like Jack the Ripper."

Otto put down his empty plate with a clatter of fork on china. "What exactly is your definition of a maniac, if not someone who would have a woman shoved in front of several tons of rolling metal?" he asked.

"For starters, it would be someone who doesn't hesitate to commit a crime with his own hands."

"But you said yourself you didn't see the man who pushed you, so for all you know it *was* him."

Aunt Irene interrupted us. "The police have been looking for a butcher-knife-wielding maniac. A man. But a woman who came to confront her rival and was met by a hapless woman who denied everything while playing dress-up in a risqué negligee might be frantic enough to grab the nearest weapon she could think of—a kitchen knife—and run her down."

That memory of the bedroom came back to me in all its horror. Had it happened the way Aunt Irene imagined?

She continued. "Ethel wasn't Callie—but their family resemblance has distracted us because anyone who would have wanted to kill Callie specifically would have been able to distinguish between the two."

"Unless they wanted to kill her but hadn't actually met her," Otto said, understanding.

My aunt nodded. "Exactly."

"A woman who knew that her husband had cheated on her, who perhaps had only glimpsed the other woman from afar, might have been fooled by the similarities between the cousins," I said. "Especially since Ethel had used our absence from the apartment to engage in an activity she seemed to have developed a secret fetish for—dressing up in Callie's clothes. She'd put on Callie's most alluring nightgown and even her slippers. Perhaps she'd fallen asleep accidentally and only woke when Margaret Attinger had knocked on the door."

"She needn't have knocked at all," my aunt reminded me. "Didn't you say you girls kept the door unlocked when you were in?"

"That's right. Poor Ethel. From the way her body was positioned on the bed, she'd flung herself toward the bedroom window to cry out for help, but she received the fatal stab in the back before she could reach it. The Bleecker Blowers would have drowned out the sound to all but Lucia, who was directly above."

"Very likely," Aunt Irene said. "That also explains the matter of the glove, which worried me all evening. To be frank, I'd begun to wonder if Callie was as innocent as she claimed to be."

Otto's eyes bugged. "You thought Callie was the murderer?"

"Well, not really." Aunt Irene pursed her lips. "She'd been here the night of the murder. I saw her with my own eyes. Nevertheless," she continued, "one thing puzzled me—those gloves. I assumed they were Callie's, but how had Callie's gloves ended up with blood on them? They aren't the kind of gloves Ethel would have worn with a negligee—unless they're even more backward in Little Falls than Callie has led us to believe. And, of course, a murder victim wouldn't stop to take off her gloves as she's dying. So we know Ethel wasn't wearing them. But even if Louise was wrong and Callie *did* own two pairs of the same style and make, why would a killer have taken the time to go through a bureau to find gloves? Especially a man for whom the gloves would have been too small."

"Margaret must have been given a duplicate pair by Sawyer," I said.

A tut of disapproval accompanied my aunt's nod of agreement. "Men are so lacking in imagination. And so calculating. Sawyer might even have bought both pairs at once—one to give to his wife, and the other for his girlfriend. Imagine." She seemed to find the duplicating of gifts almost as distasteful as the murder.

Did Margaret know about Callie's pair? After she'd plunged the knife into Ethel's back and dropped the bloodied gloves, did she realize she was leaving a clue that would create such confusion?

Of course not. Because at that moment she'd assumed her rival was dead.

"Poor Callie." Aunt Irene snapped open a fan and twitched it vigorously. "She hid those gloves fearing they implicated her. Instead, hiding them simply camouflaged the actual murderer."

Margaret Attinger. I was still trying to square the elegant woman I'd seen at Attinger and Beebe with the kind of maniac I'd imagined the killer to be.

I could almost pity Sawyer. He'd been terrified when his relationship with Callie threatened to bring bad publicity down on him. Being the husband of a convicted murderess would be even worse for business. Did he have any idea what a monster he was living with? He'd spoken so proudly and pompously about being a family man, but his family needed protecting from an enemy within.

Otto crashed his coffee cup down in its saucer. "We need to go to the police and tell them about Mrs. Attinger."

Had he lost his mind? "I spent much too long with the police already, thank you."

"But they need to know about her. She could kill again. She might want to attack Callie—the real Callie."

Another reason to be glad Callie was in Little Falls.

"Haven't the police already spoken to Sawyer?" my aunt asked. "And presumably his wife, too?"

I tried to remember. "They interviewed Sawyer at his office. Muldoon told me he had an alibi from drinking at a nearby tavern. They never seemed to suspect him at all, unless he was working in cahoots with Callie. And they had no cause to suspect Mrs. Attinger because Sawyer probably pleaded with them not to let his wife know about the other woman."

Margaret had the perfect blind—a husband trying desperately to hide his own secret. By asking—probably begging—the police not to tell his wife of his infidelity, he'd unknowingly given her cover. If the police assumed Margaret was ignorant of her husband's mistress, they wouldn't think she had a motive to kill anyone.

"But when they interviewed Sawyer, the police didn't know about the gloves," Otto said. "It's different now. The gloves point to a woman being the killer."

"Muldoon knows about the gloves," I said, "but instead of thinking of Margaret, he suspects Callie."

Worry clouded Otto's features. "We need to warn Callie to stay in Little Falls."

That wasn't a bad idea, but how could I let her know she was better off where she was? "She's checking to find out whether Dora and Abel were in Little Falls the night of the murder, so I doubt she's staying with them. Trouble is, I don't know her family's address. Or even her father's name."

"Can't you send a telegram to her care of The Gail Family, Little Falls, New York?" Aunt Irene suggested.

I considered this. "Dora and Abel are also part of the Gail family, through Dora. In a small town where everyone knows one another, there's a chance the message might be passed to them."

My aunt sipped her tea thoughtfully as she mulled over the problem. We seemed to have run out of ideas, unless I were to go back to the apartment and rifle through Callie's things in hopes of finding an address.

"I'll go," Otto piped up.

"To the apartment?" I asked, still following my own line of thought.

"To Little Falls," he said. "It's only a few hours away by train. And if I need to stay over a night, what of it? If Little Falls doesn't have a hotel, I'm sure Callie's family could put me up. It's not as if I have to report to an office." He bounded to his feet. "If I hurry, perhaps I can make it to the station before the last train leaves."

My aunt stopped him. "Don't go scudding off quite yet, young man. You can leave just as easily tomorrow morning. We still need your help here."

He stopped, taken aback. "With what?"

"Formulating a plan," she said.

"What kind of plan?" Otto asked.

I immediately grasped what she meant. "How to catch a murderer," I said.

The plan took us hours to hatch, develop, and sort out. At first I was all for charging right up to the Attingers' door and pointing an accusing finger. But as Aunt Irene suggested, all that would do would be to make the woman deny any involvement and then clam up defensively. And if we were to do something that unsubtle, Margaret might convince Sawyer they needed a vacation; then the Attingers would soon be summering in some exotic locale, far from the reach of the NYPD.

"We should let Muldoon handle it," Otto suggested, after my idea of going in guns blazing was struck down. "He's a right type."

I did give that possibility some consideration. But Muldoon had never taken my ideas seriously before now. And he'd warned me off playing detective. I didn't want to be told I was *playing* at anything. I wanted to deliver a murderer right to the precinct.

Aunt Irene seemed to be of the same mind. "First we must find incontrovertible evidence that Margaret Attinger is our murderess. Then we can go to the police."

"But we *have* evidence," Otto said. "The gloves."

"We don't have them anymore," I reminded him.

"Oh, right." His face fell. "I keep forgetting."

It was all my fault. My instinct to protect Otto and then accuse Ford had done nothing but complicate matters. Not to mention, running around with those gloves had almost gotten me killed. Perhaps I should have gone to Muldoon straightaway. But all the what-ifs in the world couldn't change how things stood now.

"I keep thinking that having right on my side means I'll prevail," I said. "But it doesn't. The important thing is to find some way to prove Margaret killed Ethel."

Otto's face fixed into a painful study of concentration, and I'm sure mine looked similar.

Walter sailed into the room to refill coffees. "What's needed, if you don't mind my saying so, is a little invention."

It didn't surprise me that Walter would know what we were talking about—Walter always knew everything. But what did he mean? "Invention?"

"Isn't someone in the room a fiction writer?" he asked.

All eyes turned to my aunt, who steepled her fingers and smiled in approval at her butler. "You've hit the nail on the head, Walter. We need to be as crafty as the killer was herself."

Hope budded inside me again. "But she wasn't crafty, was she? She dropped an incriminating piece of evidence, and she allowed herself to be seen."

Otto, slumped in his chair, sat up straighter. "By whom?"

"First by Wally, the troll. He's a great one for staring up skirts, but he obviously wasn't looking clearly at Margaret. He told me that Ethel had been out earlier in the evening because he'd glimpsed her going upstairs just a short while before he saw Ford on the stairs. My guess is that he actually saw Margaret going up, but he missed her coming back down again because she probably slipped out in a big hurry."

"Wally's not a reliable witness anyway," Otto pointed out. "He thought *I* was that writer."

I nodded. "But there was another person who saw Margaret, and that was Ford. He was lucky he didn't end up another fatality. Although Margaret probably judged that she would do better by brazening out her encounter with Ford at the door than by attempting to commit a second impromptu murder in the hallway."

"So Ford Fitzsimmons is a witness," Otto said. "All we have to do is have him confront Margaret—"

I stopped him before he could become too invested in that idle hope. "He's already shown what lengths he'll go to in order to avoid becoming involved. An evening at the precinct isn't bound to make him feel any more cooperative toward helping me or Callie."

"Then it's hopeless," Otto said. "Our witnesses are no good, and we've lost our evidence."

I'd despaired over that, too. But all at once another possibility struck me. "Margaret doesn't know we've lost our evidence."

My aunt's breath caught. "Of course!" She smiled at Walter,

who was still standing by, arms crossed, practically bobbing on his heels.

An idea formed rapidly in my mind. "Do you think it could work?"

Otto glanced from me to my aunt to Walter. "Could what work?"

"Using a little pretend crime to catch a murderer," Walter said.

Otto sat up, alarmed. "You want us to pretend to murder somebody?"

"Not murder," I said. "Blackmail."

Chapter 14

I spent the night in Aunt Irene's spare bedroom, where I'd passed my first weeks in New York six months earlier. All through the night, I didn't sleep more than twenty minutes at a stretch, and that was usually followed by an equal amount of time lying wide awake, blinking at the ceiling, and worrying about the scheme we'd hatched. Among other things.

That spare room had a strange effect on me. The last time I'd slept here I was new to the city, traumatized by recent experiences, and unsure what my future would be. Now, half a year later, my subconscious was telling me how little I'd progressed. Nightmares yanked me out of sleep. I dreamed of being in a free fall, arms whirling frantically as a train barreled toward me. In another dream I found a body on a bloody bed, only it wasn't Ethel lying there, it was Callie. Several times a baby's crying woke me, but when I sat up, tensed, to listen, the only sound in my aunt's house was the intermittent chiming of the grandfather clock in the downstairs hall.

Daylight creeping through the windows came as a relief. I popped out of bed and changed from the frill- and lace-bedecked nightgown my aunt had lent me into my clothes from the day before. My shoulder ached, but I left the bandage the hospital had given me looped over the back of the dainty armless chair in the corner. With so much to accomplish today, I didn't want to be encumbered by a sling and the questions it would raise. Fresh clothing would have been nice, but going downtown to the flat would take too much time. I was eager to get to the office before anyone else. I did as much freshening up of my skirt as I could with gentle sponging and brushing. Its uneven hem reminded me of Muldoon, and our taxi ride.

Downstairs, Bernice was already stirring. Literally. Her elaborate, set-in-stone porridge method involved a double boiler and a solid hour of careful monitoring. The end result was creamy, oaty perfection, but the labor required astounded me. With Bernice nothing was easy and shortcuts were deplorable. The coconut cake Otto and I had partially scarfed down in minutes the night before had no doubt been the result of hours of grating, mixing, and baking.

She eyed me without surprise but with a hint of exasperation, perhaps because a scruffy stranger with a drooping mustache already sat at her breakfast table. Where had he come from? Clearly, this was not a normal morning. I approached the table warily. The man slouched in his chair, his legs stretched out, boots scuffed and dull next to Bernice's polished kitchen floor. Details of his appearance puzzled me—the cap worn inside, the ill-fitting small-checked jacket, the pants like something a bellhop would wear.

And yet it was me to whom Bernice said, "You look like something the cat dragged in."

I didn't have time even to mutter my wry thanks before the man at the table added, "But chewed up first."

His voice jarred me. It took me a moment to realize the visitor wasn't a visitor at all. "Walter?"

As the question came out, it sounded absurd. Fastidious Walter, scruffy? And yet it *was* Walter. I would have bet my first cup of coffee on it—and I needed that cup of coffee.

I made for the pot and poured as Bernice glowered at both of us in turn. "Whatever's going on in this house," she said, "I don't like it. First the police come knocking at the door yesterday with a story of you being knocked off a train platform, and now Walter here is telling me he can't fetch groceries because he's on some kind of mission. What kind of mission requires a decent man to wear old moth-eaten clothes and paste that ugly hank of fur on his lip?"

Walter lifted his hand to his lip to make sure his mustache was firmly in place.

I knew exactly what his mission was. "I think your disguise is marvelous. I didn't recognize you at first."

Walter preened at the praise. "I've been a thespian at heart since I played Malvolio in *Twelfth Night* at my school." He lifted his hands and recited, " 'Some are born great, some achieve greatness, and some have greatness thrust upon them.' Alas, I achieved no greatness of my own, although I tried to make a go of a stage career for a short while."

"What happened?"

"I played Merriman in *The Importance of Being Earnest* and felt I'd found my true calling. When I looked into the matter, I discovered being a real butler in New York paid better and more steadily than playing Wilde on tour in Idaho and South Dakota."

"Yet you kept your actor's kit."

"One never knows when a little spirit gum will come in handy," he said.

I looked him over again and for the first time I felt more confident about what we'd dreamed up last night. "It's wonderful."

Bernice leveled a look a shade short of a glare at me. "Wonderful? Is that what you call all these doings around here? Murders, police, and you getting yourself shoved in front of trains? And now him dressed up like I don't know what. I hope you two haven't got Miss Irene mixed up in something shady. If I wanted to work for someone in jail, I would've stayed with my husband."

I filed that last morsel away for future inquiry. "You don't have to worry about Aunt Irene. Once Walter does his bit, her involvement is finished." Walter cocked an eyebrow at me, and I added in a lower voice, "At least, the dicey part."

"And what about you?" Her expression hadn't budged from outright skepticism.

"I'll be fine." I wasn't sure I sounded very convincing, even to myself.

Walter and I sat in subdued silence as Bernice slammed bowls in front of us and refilled our coffees while muttering about fools, police, trouble, and actors. Walter was clearly put out by the grumbling, but I couldn't help seeing Bernice's point. Our plan might work splendidly, or it might blow up in our faces like a vaudevillian's trick cigar.

"Where is Aunt Irene?" I asked.

"Where she's supposed to be—asleep, until it's time for her to work," Bernice said. "That's the only normal thing going on in this house today."

I bolted my oatmeal and then stood, wishing Walter good luck.

"Don't worry," he said. "My part's a breeze."

"It's the most important bit, though." If Walter wasn't successful, our whole scheme would stall out.

We'd decided last night that I would spend the morning at my office, awaiting word of Walter's success or lack thereof. I also had private reasons for wanting to be at work, and to be there early, so I set off immediately after breakfast without disturbing my aunt.

As soon as I stepped outside, I wrinkled my nose at the heavy air. The sun was struggling to break through a dull haze. The overcast sky didn't seem threatening, only oppressive. Rivulets of sweat trickled down my back after just a few blocks, but I didn't let the warm sponge atmosphere slow me down. A hint of fear lurked in the back of my mind, yet my senses were sharp and my mind clear. I had objectives. First I was going to sabotage Ford; then I was going to catch a murderer. A cakewalk.

For the first half of my walk from Fifty-third Street to Thirty-eighth I really did feel invincible, almost heroic. Was this how the policewoman I'd seen at Muldoon's precinct felt every day? To make a real difference in the world, to be in control, must be a grand thing, I thought, envying her.

Then I crossed Lexington and turned south, and for a few blocks the dizzying gothic tower of the Woolworth building spearing into the sky came into my direct view. The stone edifice against the blue-gray haze made it seem even taller, almost part of the sky itself. Months ago I'd read all the details of the building in the papers during the week of its grand opening. It contained two miles of elevator shafts, twenty-seven acres of office space, and its steel piers were sunk 130 feet into solid bedrock. At night, 80,000 bulbs made its summit a blazing landmark able to be seen by sailors forty miles at sea. The copper-roofed tower soared 792 feet and 1 inch above the sidewalk. It was colossal. Awe-inspiring.

Fear flapped in my chest like a moth in a jar. *What are you doing, Louise?* This was madness. Muldoon was right: I wasn't a detective. Nor was I invincible, brave, or heroic. I was Louise Faulk, secretarial school graduate who, so far in my twenty years, had only worked jobs found through the grace of family connections. Hardly the sign of an intrepid character. The mere thought of going to the top of that building turned my legs to jelly.

Last night, I'd argued for holding the meeting at a different landmark. Washington Square, for instance. Or Grant's Tomb. Someplace on solid ground. But Aunt Irene and even Otto had pointed out that those sites were open, which created difficulties if one wanted to trap another person. The observation gallery of the Woolworth Building was both public and enclosed. The only way out was fifty-eight flights down an elevator. Finally, I had agreed. A phobia of heights was a small matter compared to the importance of catching Ethel's killer.

Eyes trained on the sidewalk, I hurried down the midtown streets starting to perk with another day of commerce. The newsstands were busy, and neither I nor anyone I knew was on the front page. That was something to be thankful for. Nearer the office, a grocer was arranging his fruit displays in eye-catching pyramids. A tower of peaches made my mouth water and my pace slow . . . until I remembered I lacked the means to pay for anything. My money had been snatched along with my satchel. Then an even more distressing realization struck me: *No keys.* Those had been in my bag, too.

Peaches forgotten, I covered the last few blocks to Van Hooten and McChesney in a few minutes, anxious about what I would do if I couldn't get in. Jackson sometimes arrived early, but never as early as seven thirty. What would I do if I had to wait? I didn't even have a nickel for a cup of coffee at the Automat.

I climbed the stoop to the building with a sense of frustration, but when I pressed the brass door handle, the latch clicked open. Who had arrived before me? I crept inside, peering about furtively, half expecting one of Ford's thuggish cohorts to jump out at me.

No lights were on. I called out a tentative, "Hello?"

Only the ticking of a wall clock answered me. I looked over both my desk and Jackson's. Nothing was amiss there. Had someone forgotten to lock the door the previous evening?

A moan rent the air, and I jumped like a rabbit. Then the piteous sound repeated itself, coming from Guy Van Hooten's office.

I rushed toward the sound but stopped momentarily at the threshold of his office. Guy was slumped over his desk. To see him here at all at this time of day was startling enough, but his appearance—facedown on his desk blotter—sent a shiver of apprehension through me. What had happened?

Closer up, he looked even worse: a ghostly pale, greenish complexion beneath a thick stubble; bloodshot eyes covered by half-closed lids; forehead crinkled in pain. His jacket lay on the floor, a discarded necktie trailing it across the carpet like a tail. I picked my way across loose change and crunched over some fallen papers. My progress wasn't silent, but Guy still lay collapsed over his desk in his shirt sleeves and suspenders. And the smell . . . The putrid odor made me hold my breath and then fling open the blinds and window behind us.

Despite my revulsion, I leaned close and gave him a firm shake. "Mr. Van Hooten?" My voice quavered. "Guy?"

I was wondering if I should call a doctor when his head snapped up. He weaved in his chair and groaned.

I held his shoulder to keep him vertical. It took effort to prevent his torso from crashing back down onto the desk. "Mr. Van Hooten, what happened to you?"

Blurry red eyes blinked at me out of his round face. "Myrna?"

Heaven only knew who Myrna was. Maybe one of my predecessors—even on his best days, I sometimes detected the struggle to recollect my name in my boss's face. Understandable, really. We met so rarely.

"I'm Louise, Mr. Van Hooten. Louise Faulk. Your secretary."

His gaze remained bleary, but he said, "Oh right. The new one."

"Six months new," I muttered. "But never mind that. What happened? Who did this to you?"

"Did what?"

I gestured with my free hand at his person. A stain trailed down his front, and an imprint of typewriting had transferred itself from something on his desk to his sweaty cheek. I looked down. My report on Ford Fitzsimmons's book, right where I'd left it days earlier, had served as his pillow. The manuscript itself was fanned out unevenly across the desk and accounted for a few of the papers strewn across the floor. His pencil cup had been knocked over, and several desk drawers gaped open, their contents spilling out onto the floor. It looked as if he'd been knocked out and the place ransacked. My mind whirred. My missing key . . . Ford . . . Mug. What if they'd discovered the office key in my bag?

"Should I call the police?" I asked.

That word—*police*—worked on Guy like a tonic. His eyes cleared. "Good God. What for?"

"So they can get to the bottom of this."

He laughed, then regretted it. He lifted his fist and pressed it against his brow. "Honey, the only thing responsible for *this* is a bottle of whiskey, and there's no point in asking the police to get to the bottom of it. I already have."

With his shiny leather boot, he toed the metal wastepaper basket next to him. A tall bottle stood in it, drained dry.

I dropped my hand from his shoulder. "You mean you're only drunk?"

He thumped forward again, but this time his fall was broken by his elbows bracing on the desktop. "There's no *only* about it. I might not be dying, but at this moment there are a thousand angry Irishmen step dancing on the inside of my skull." He stilled, taking inventory. "Maybe a few dozen in my stomach, as well."

Now I understood the putrid smell and the stain. I frowned, shoved the waste basket closer to him, and then backed a safe distance away.

He crooked a brow at me. "What did you think had happened?"

Now probably wasn't the time to tell him that I'd imagined an angry author had come to—to what? What could Ford have done? Forced Guy to buy his book by violence?

As he looked at me, his slight sneer collapsed. "Say—you're the girl who knew that poor woman who bought it in Greenwich Village, aren't you? I heard about that. No wonder you're so jumpy." He laughed. "The police!"

As if it were all a fine joke. "You were moaning," I pointed out.

He nodded and lurched forward again, propping his head in his hands. "My head. It's going to split open like the Grand Canyon did."

I moved over to tidy Ford's manuscript pages . . . the better to whisk them away, I hoped. "The Grand Canyon was formed by erosion."

His hand shot out and grabbed my wrist. "Never mind geology. I need chemistry. You must know a remedy for this sort of thing."

"When my uncle overdoes the schnapps, he swears by tomato juice, lime, and egg."

He considered this combination with horrified awe. "That sounds revolting. I'll try it!"

He meant that he'd try it after I made it for him. I cast a reluctant glance at the manuscript. Perhaps I could just snatch it on my way out.

"Get going." He clapped me away. "Chop-chop. Fetch me a Louisa's Uncle's Special."

I stared at him.

"What's the problem?" he asked.

"First, the name's Louise, and second, I don't have any money. Last night my purse was—well, I don't have it today."

His lips curled in annoyance. "Girls are confounded things. Never have any money." He picked his jacket off the floor, hunted through the pockets for his wallet, and fished out a fifty-dollar bill, which he tossed onto the desk. "That should cover it."

I gaped at the bill. I'd rarely seen one that large. "A fifty for tomato juice and an egg?"

"If the grocer raises a stink, tell him to keep the change. I'm a desperate man."

I took the fifty and hurried out. The man at the corner store didn't rejoice at the large bill, but he said nothing and I returned with the ingredients within twenty minutes. Back at the office, I nearly bumped into Guy coming out of the washroom, freshly shaven, and, disturbingly, shirtless. He'd obviously attempted a rudimentary sink bath, because he was patting his glistening torso with a handkerchief.

"Bring it to me when you're done," he said.

I reddened, both from coming across my boss half naked and being ordered about like a servant. But I proceeded to the office's little kitchen area and mixed the concoction. Guy was in the last stages of buttoning a clean shirt when I brought the glass in. Heaven only knew where the shirt had come from. I supposed that was what he thought desk drawers were for—to keep an emergency change of clothes in.

He swept a glance my way. "On the desk, please."

I made a show of placing the drink and all the change from the grocer next to the smudged desk blotter. He picked up the glass immediately and jeered at me between gulps. "A smart girl would have kept the change and blamed it on the grocer."

I edged toward the manuscript. "What if you'd found out?"

He started to laugh, but then his face became a frightful mask of bulging eyes and gaping mouth. A tear or two streamed down his cheeks. I worried he would pass out. Then a belch loud enough to rattle the building's foundation rumbled out of him, followed by a whoop. "Damn! That uncle of yours knows his stuff."

I picked up the book and turned to go.

"Leave that," he said.

I froze.

"I read it last night," he added.

Unable to contain my amazement, I blurted, "You read a book?"

His expression darkened. "Maybe you think I'm as much a no-hoper as old Grandpa McChesney does. Imagine—that old geezer hunted me down at the club where I was having dinner yesterday to tell me that I was a drag on the firm. Said the paperweights were doing more work around the office than I was, among other insults. What do you think about that?"

I shifted. What *could* one think? It was true. Guy was obviously waiting for me to echo his outrage, however, so I offered a lukewarm, "No one likes to be compared to a paperweight."

"Damn right, they don't. I told the old fossil I'd show up at the office when I was good and ready, and then he'd see what I could do."

"So you got drunk?" *That would show him.*

He shrugged sheepishly. "I might have already been a bit ripped when I talked to the old man. And then I was so mad I stumbled back here and polished off my friend there." He nodded toward the bottle. "But I *did* read that book you'd put on my desk." He frowned and craned his head to look at the memo I'd written. "Louisa. That's you, right?"

"Louise."

"Right. Well, the book seemed quite good—especially after I'd had a few snorts of the hard stuff. I might not have been entirely lucid by the end."

That "not entirely lucid" gave me hope. "To be honest," I confessed, "the more I've considered it, the less the book appeals to me. The writing is good, but the story is a little far-fetched, don't you think?"

He shrugged. "You're a woman. You probably don't appreciate action and so forth."

"I do, usually. But this story—that coincidence of the two men meeting on the boat, for one thing. It seemed amateurish."

Guy finished tying his tie. "I got the impression from reading your memo that this writer was something of a protégé of yours."

"I do know him, but only a little. He's a rather unsavory character, to be honest."

"Fascinating."

"No, criminal," I said. "The police were searching for him last night."

"How do you know?"

"I was at the police station."

His eyes narrowed on me. "What for?"

I swallowed, considering. Should I come out and tell him the whole story?

Guy wasn't interested, anyway. He eyed me with a crooked

smile. "By God, you're a dark horse, aren't you? Mousy on the outside and all the while consorting with cops and murdered people." He sighed. "Well, *I* liked the book, and if the man has a colorful persona, perhaps we can exploit it." He sank into his chair and tossed his head back, looking like an entirely different man from the one I'd discovered half dead an hour ago. He thumped his hand on the arm of his chair. "Yes—I'll make a success of it! And then Old Gramps will have to eat his hat. When was the last time *he* found anything with real potential? Eighteen ninety-two or thereabouts, would be my guess. If it was up to him, this firm would publish nothing but sermon collections and quack remedy pamphlets from pickle juice pushers."

"I still don't think that story's quite—"

A gushing, irritated sigh cut me off. "For God's sake stop yapping and get me some coffee," he said. "My head's still shaky."

"Of course." I took two steps before turning back around. "But about that book. I really don't think—"

"Never mind the book. I'll have Jackson look it over. Big Baldy ought to be good for something."

I skulked out, fuming both at him and myself. Of course, I could simply march back into his office and announce that Ford Fitzsimmons had had me tossed in front of a moving train. But I didn't have proof, and I might never have any unless Muldoon had brought Ford into the precinct last night and succeeded in making him crack, which I doubted. Ford had mendacity, and he probably hadn't done the deed himself. There would be no witnesses who could point a finger of blame at him. If I told my tale, Guy Van Hooten would likely write me off as a hysterical woman.

While I was making coffee, the others trickled in. Usually Jackson arrived first, but he was late this morning. A few fellow workers murmured hello and went to the offices on the second floor. John Philpott, our reader and copy editor, noticed the light from Guy's office and blinked. Eyes bugging, he mouthed Guy's name at me. I nodded.

He scurried upstairs. Within moments, everyone on the second floor found an excuse to come downstairs and pass by Guy's office on their way to the kitchen, just to see for themselves. The coffee disappeared quickly, and I was overseeing a second pot when Jackson came in.

"I had the most extraordinary encounter this morning . . ." Before he could elaborate, his attention honed in on Guy's office like a bird dog scenting quail. His voice lowered. "Did I hear a cough coming from there?"

I nodded.

"It sounded almost like Guy."

"It is. He slept here last night. He and Mr. McChesney had an argument, and then Guy started drinking and came back here and read a book."

Jackson's dark brows leapt into his vast expanse of forehead. "Read a *book?*"

When I explained what had happened, up to and including our discussion of Ford's manuscript, Jackson became agitated. He poured himself a second cup of coffee even though there was a full cup right at his elbow. "If he wants me to look over the manuscript, he must respect my opinion." He lifted his chin. "Well, of course he does." He tapped his fingers nervously against his saucer, as anxious as a girl awaiting an invitation to the big dance. How heartbroken he would have been to know Guy had called him Big Baldy. "Well, well. I suppose I should go talk to him. What an extraordinary day."

While Jackson was closeted with Guy, I received a phone call. I answered, prepared as usual to summon a colleague to the phone.

The familiar voice startled me. "Louise?"

It was Aunt Irene. "Yes," I said expectantly.

"I wanted to let you know that *everything's all right.* You know—as I said I would."

Guy Van Hooten's appearance at work had taken me so by surprise that I'd almost forgotten about last night and the plan. We'd agreed Aunt Irene would send me word at the office if Walter had been successful. "Everything's all right" meant Margaret Attinger had received a note, which Walter—in disguise, so no one would be able to trace him back to Aunt Irene—had been given the task to deliver to her door with a bouquet of flowers. The card accompanying the flowers read:

I know you did it. You were seen, and now I have your gloves, stained with your victim's blood. If you don't want me to go to the police, meet me at the observation gallery on the fifty-eighth floor of the Woolworth Building at 8 p.m. tonight (Saturday). For $500, the gloves will be yours.

So the plan had been set in motion. Across town, Margaret Attinger would be pacing. Worrying. Wondering what her bank's Saturday hours were, or if Sawyer kept that much cash in their house's safe. Perhaps she would have to hock a jewel or two so her husband would never know.

I checked the clock. It wasn't even ten in the morning yet. Ten hours to go. Time crawled. I regretted not sleeping the night before.

Jackson finally came out of Guy's office, and soon afterward, Guy himself emerged, spinning his bowler on his index finger. Oliver hopped up from the stool he'd been dozing off on and hurried ahead to open the door for Guy, who had that confused crinkle in his brow when he looked at the boy. We'd had several office boys this year.

"If old McChesney finally makes it in," he told me with a smug look, "tell him I was in this morning, early, and couldn't wait for him." He popped his hat on, tapped his hand to the brim in a jaunty salute, and strolled out.

Several people had filtered down to see Guy Van Hooten again in the flesh in the office on a Saturday morning. Debts were settled to the grumbles of some and the amazed jubilation of the winners. Bob Wagner, our accountant, seemed crushed by his loss, especially when he saw that Oliver had come out on top. "The rich get richer," he groused.

After the excitement died down, Jackson rolled his chair near my desk.

"I'm surprised at you, Louise. This business about the book—I know you're just a secretary, but you can't just go around changing your mind about things. Recommending a book one day and then unrecommending it the next. I've never heard of such nonsense! It's unprofessional."

So was having your potential publisher's secretary pushed off a train platform. "I decided I'd let my personal feelings get the better of me and estimated the book too highly."

He regarded me almost sorrowfully, like a parent catching a child in a lie. "Wasn't the situation in fact almost the opposite?"

"What do you mean?"

"This author, Ford Fitzsimmons, met me just outside this morning and asked to take me to breakfast. He said you'd hurled the most extraordinary accusations at him—that you'd even gone to the police."

"Of course I went to the police. He tried to have me killed."

His gaze grew several degrees more pitying. "There was no proof. Even the police said that. Just your word—*after* you sought the man out in his flat and he"—he hitched his throat—"rejected your advances."

My jaw dropped. "That's a lie."

"So you didn't go to his flat?"

"Yes, but only because I thought—well, it was to do with Ethel's murder. Ford was at my apartment the night it happened. He might have seen the murderer. I had to ask him about it."

Jackson's face screwed up into a skeptical frown. "And while you were there you told him you meant to sabotage his chances of being published. What did *that* have to do with that poor woman's murder?"

He had me there. "Ford said he wouldn't help me because there might be bad publicity if his name was connected to a murder case. *That's* why he had me pushed off the train platform."

"So you say."

I folded my arms. "So I know."

Jackson clucked. "It's hard to know whom to believe." But it was clear he didn't believe *me*. "You have to admit, it seems odd for a girl to visit an author—an attractive young man—in his flat. Twice."

I quaked with anger. Ford must have laid it on thick. Now *I* looked like the unbalanced one.

"This has shown very poor behavior from you," Jackson continued. "It's a good thing Guy had me to turn to."

He looked so absurdly pleased to have been singled out by Guy, I almost pitied him. His already giant head had grown a few hat sizes in one morning.

Someone else was having a good day, too. Oliver had made out like a bandit in the Van Hooten Absentee Stakes, and now he sat on his stool, counting bills and coins. If only I'd placed a hefty bet myself, I would now have a nice cushion in the Calumet bank.

Or a little legacy to leave Aunt Sonja's boys in case tonight's plan went disastrously wrong.

CHAPTER 15

I could have left work early, but I didn't. I wasn't sure what to do with my afternoon. Go to the picture show? A stroll? It was too hot and humid to enjoy either activity, and walking felt especially inadvisable. I lingered at the office and read a story about a spirited girl with three sisters during the Civil War. It kept me absorbed until I realized it was *Little Women* with the names changed. I wrote Miss Not-Alcott a polite rejection and went home.

Wally pounced as soon as I crossed the threshold. "You girls've been gone forever. Ma was convinced you skipped out, too, like Lucia."

Ma hoped *we had skipped out,* he meant. "No, we've both just been staying with relatives for a day or so."

He flicked something out from between his two front teeth with his thumbnail. I flinched left to avoid its trajectory. "Guess you girls need to remind yourselves what real homes feel like from time to time."

I glared at him—not that he noticed. "Is there something you want? The rent's not due for a week yet," I reminded him.

"Ma just wants to know your intentions, is all."

"Tell your mother we're very happy here. After all, we signed a lease till next January." The more fools us.

I continued upstairs, jittery with exhaustion. I regretted not sleeping last night. Of course sleeping was out of the question now, but maybe if I took a hot bath, that would relax me and help pass the time until I needed to head downtown. It would also get rid of the accumulation of perspiration and dirt I'd acquired on my way home. The sky had darkened up since this morning, and while I and everyone else welcomed the prospect of rain washing away the heat and grit of a warm June day in New York, the increasing clouds created a dome over the city, holding all the heat in. I felt washrag limp.

One of the reasons Callie and I had rented the flat, and part of the reason we were loath to leave, was that we had our own bathroom. While the tiny room with its rattling, leaky plumbing and ancient zinc-lined tub couldn't be labeled anything more than adequate, exquisite privacy compensated for its deficits. Having grown up in a house full of family and usually one or two boarders, I couldn't get over the thrill of sharing facilities with only one person. To Callie, former farm girl that she was, anything that wasn't an outhouse was opulent.

I filled the tub partway from the tap and then started boiling water in the kettle to add to it. Firing up the kettle, of course, just made the air in the apartment more stifling. I'd planned to soak for just a little while, but I kept dozing off right there in the tub, my knees drawn halfway to my chest, my head lolling back against the hard edge. I glanced down through the water at my middle, which still seemed a little poochier than it used to. Evidence.

Some days I could almost convince myself that I never had a baby on the 29th of December, 1912. Four and a half months before that day, Uncle Dolph had seen me off at the station and given me the knives. Aunt Sonja had found the name of a home for unwed girls outside Philadelphia, and I could think of no other solution. The route Ethel had taken terrified me, and I knew I would never have the ability to pass myself off forever as a young widow in some West Coast city. My biggest worry was that I couldn't love a child conceived in the worst moment of my life—and that I wouldn't be able to hide my aversion. My baby deserved love, even if his or her own mother couldn't provide it.

But of course he wasn't my baby. The people who ran the home—the directress and all the staff, even the kindly doctor who attended us—were careful to emphasize this to us every day. The baby I was carrying was meant for a worthy couple who'd been carefully scrutinized for means and moral character; we girls possessing neither. It—to us, the babies in our wombs were always spoken of as *it*—would have nothing but the best, and I would be able to forget and to forge ahead with my own life with a clean slate.

We were allowed to stay in the home for a week after giving birth. The directress presented this as the height of generosity, and in truth I was glad for the grudging boon. The birth had gone easier for me than for some—a month earlier, one girl had died—but I needed the time. My body needed to recuperate, but my mind needed that week even more. Some girls left as soon as they could move, intending to return to their hometowns and explain they'd been on holiday or an extended visit to relatives in far-flung places. Others spent their grace period lying in bed almost catatonic. But I was restive. I paced every inch of the old farmhouse and grounds, turning questions over in my mind. Where would I go? More important, what could I do that would make me feel as if I were of some use in the world?

I'd had months to plan my future, yet my time in the home was remarkable for how thoroughly I'd avoided thinking about anything substantive. I'd played cards with my fellow inmates and read every novel I could lay my hands on. I'd knit the world's longest, homeliest shawl—we girls were discouraged from knitting baby things specifically for our *its,* but encouraged to knit for the charity box. During those months, the constant refrain of my thoughts was that I simply wanted the ordeal over with, and to forget.

Now I had to plan a future for myself double-quick.

During one night's perambulations I found the directress's door wide open. I never considered myself a sneaky person. I'd signed an agreement and I intended to abide by it. The agreement emphasized that I renounced all rights and responsibility for my child, and that the adopting couple would remain anonymous to me. Forever. But was there really any harm in my knowing? Or in my discovering whether the baby had been a boy or girl? For that matter, would it hurt anyone if I knew who had taken the baby?

I closed the door, turned on a lamp, and rifled through a cabinet until I found my file. And that's where I saw what had become of *it:*

Child's date of birth: December 29, 1912
Sex: Male
Weight: 7 pounds 2 ounces
Receiving family: Mr. and Mrs. Richard W. Longworth
7 East Eightieth Street
New York City

How long did I stare at that sheet of paper? Perhaps a minute? I was trespassing, after all, and welshing on my agreement with the home. But that minute changed my life. I knew then where I was going. I had an aunt in the city—famous Aunt Irene. For all I knew, she lived in the same neighborhood as these Longworths.

Six months later, I almost laughed at the naïveté of that girl who didn't understand what living in a city of five million people meant. A brisk twenty-minute walk in Manhattan could be the equivalent of traversing several different towns in the rest of America. And as for forgetting . . . After I'd settled in New York City, all the questions and issues I'd pushed to the edges of my consciousness swirled at me in a confusing rush, like leaves picked up by a whirlwind. Had I made the right decision? With a bit more courage, I *could* have gone west. But could I have ever loved *it,* and what if I'd risked that I could and then failed? I knew what it was to be considered another mouth to feed.

If only I could be sure I'd done right. I just wanted proof. The address was etched in my brain. But if I saw something at that house on Eightieth Street to convince me I'd made a mistake, what then? Around and around I went, trying to decide whether I'd been generous or selfish. Brave, or the world's biggest coward.

I must have fallen into a deep sleep in the tub, because a blast from below woke me, followed by the opening bars of "When the Midnight Choo Choo Leaves for Alabam." I jerked back to consciousness in a slosh of tepid bathwater. The Bleecker Blowers were celebrating their return with a Saturday night at home—thank heavens. Otherwise I might have slept till kingdom come.

I dressed quickly for my rendezvous with Margaret, swallowing back my nerves as I laced, buttoned, and hooked. The apartment seemed darker than it should have been at seven in the evening, and one glance out the window showed why. While I'd slept, a roiling swamp of clouds had continued to gather and fester till the sky above Manhattan resembled a painting by El Greco.

I debated wearing a coat—or, more accurately, borrowing one of Callie's. But even the light waterproof coat she had would probably feel sweltering in this weather. Her yellow umbrella leaning against the door appealed to me more. It had the added benefit of heft. I wouldn't be marching unarmed up to the top of the Woolworth Building to meet a murderess.

Not that I imagined myself in armed combat with Margaret Attinger. The observation gallery of the Woolworth Building was a public space, the whole point of meeting there, and Margaret didn't strike me as a woman who would make a spectacle of herself by brawling with another woman.

Of course, she hadn't struck me as the type of woman who would bury a butcher knife in Ethel's back, either.

I won't be alone. That thought comforted me. She couldn't very well knife me there in the middle of the Woolworth Building—Aunt Irene had been right about that. And reinforcements would arrive soon after I did. My aunt's part was to summon the police. I might have to take the bear by the tooth, as the saying went, but my hand wouldn't be wrapped around Margaret's bicuspid very long.

Otto had been for telling the police of our plan upfront, but Aunt Irene thought that was naïve, and I agreed with her. If forewarned, Muldoon would never go along with our plan and would—rightly—accuse us of criminality for blackmailing Margaret. And if he interviewed Margaret based on our speculations, she would simply deny her guilt. Only believing she was trapped might make her act rashly and give herself away. That was our hope, at any rate.

Worst case, we would come out looking like fools. Best case, Ethel's killer would be off the streets for good and all.

I arrived a few minutes early and waited behind the entrance columns of the city hall post office across the street to see if I could glimpse Margaret going in. I'd never been in this part of town at night. Though the Woolworth Building was lit up like a Christmas tree, there was little traffic on the streets around it. Perhaps this business area was always a bit deserted on Saturday nights, but the weather didn't help. Unruly winds created miniature cyclones of dirt and garbage, and a newspaper blew past my feet like a tumbleweed. As I craned my neck, the uplit heights of the Woolworth Building's tower caused my stomach to knot. The bright summit was haloed in clouds. How could an elevator carry a person all the way to the top of that? I'd never been higher than eleven floors on an elevator, and that had been nauseating enough.

I thought longingly again of Grant's Tomb—so compact, so not fifty-eight stories high. Too late now. I couldn't stand across the street forever, either. Either Margaret was already inside waiting for me, or she intended to be fashionably late, or she had decided not to come at all. For all I knew, she'd torn up our blackmail note as soon as Walter had delivered it.

Finally, a clock struck eight. I squared my shoulders. Standing out here wasn't making me any braver. The sooner I went in, the sooner it would all be over.

Once I'd passed through the arched entrance, however, I had to stop a moment to gather my breath. Though I'd read descriptions, nothing had prepared me for the lavish richness before my eyes. The veined marble, the great vaulted ceiling with its elaborate, colorful mosaic, the grand staircase with the amber glass above it made me feel as if I'd stepped into a palace. Everywhere were artistic touches—intricate carvings and tracery; rich, polished wood and gleaming metal. I couldn't help gawking around me like a tourist.

At the bank of elevators, a crimson-uniformed man poked his head out.

"Going up, miss?"

The question goosed me forward. Gulping, I stepped in. I was his only passenger. "Observation gallery, please," I said.

The young man stared at me as if he'd misheard. "Are you sure? Kind of blustery out, isn't it?"

My feelings exactly. "I need to go to the fifty-eighth floor, please."

"Customer's always right," he muttered.

The floor lurched upward. My tummy lurched right along with it.

"Not often a person gets a private ride," the operator said. "Must be your lucky day."

I tried to feel lucky instead of petrified. I regarded the young man through the mirror of the polished metal panel facing him. "Is there anyone else up there now?"

"Night like this? Not many."

Not many people that stupid, he meant. "I'm supposed to be meeting a friend. You might have noticed her. A pretty blond woman, alone?"

He frowned. "Hasn't been a lone rider like that in my box tonight. But I see lots of people all day. Up and down, up and down. I stop lookin', you know?"

The climb seemed to take forever, and every creak made me queasy. Was it my imagination or was the building swaying? How strong would a wind have to be before the entire building went over like a felled tree?

One hundred and thirty feet into bedrock, I reminded myself. That was quite an anchor. No one would construct a building that couldn't withstand a breeze or two. Of course, the *Titanic* had been unsinkable, yet just over a week ago I'd served sandwiches to a lady who'd spent a tooth-chattering night in one of her lifeboats.

When the elevator finally stopped and the doors slid open, the elevator boy nodded across the hall. "Take the elevator to the fifty-eighth floor."

Another elevator? I wanted to weep, and cursed the name of Cass Gilbert, the architect of this crazy structure. What kind of lunatic designed a building that required two elevators to reach the top?

"You mean this isn't it?" I asked, not wanting to believe it.

"This is just the fifty-fourth floor. The view's okay from here, but the real observation gallery's on the fifty-eighth floor. You can take the elevator, or there's a staircase."

I knew what my choice would be. I took a moment to look about the room here. The booths selling picture postcards, souvenirs, and ice cream were shuttered for the night, but there were still a few people scattered about. It wasn't hard to see why. Just the sight of the city stretched out before me made me gasp. A streak of lightning lit the sky and I pivoted; then I was looking out over the lower island, the bay, and the Statue of Liberty. I swayed and stepped back, seeking the safety of the wall behind me. A man alone and a couple nearby were looking west toward the Hudson and the piers along the island's edge. Further on a group of women faced a north view. The lights of the city stretched toward midtown, the Bronx, and beyond. I walked close enough to each to discern that none of the women was Margaret. No doubt she'd followed my instructions and was waiting upstairs.

The spiral staircase was a steep, narrow affair, without adornment. Clearly it was assumed that most visitors would opt for the elevator. The passage continued up to some unknown height, but the fifty-eighth floor was clearly marked, and I stepped off there.

The door opened onto a single room with arch-topped viewing windows. The floor was tiled in geometrical mosaic, and the rest of the finishes reflected the ornate care taken with the building's spectacular lobby. Outside, an open walkway encircled the entire floor. The doors to the catwalk were closed tight at the moment. No one was foolish enough to go out there now—certainly not me. I doubted Margaret was lurking out there, either. As far as I could tell, I was alone.

Perhaps she had torn up the note. Or she wasn't guilty at all and was sitting at home in her cozy parlor wondering why such a strange message had been delivered to her door this morning. It was entirely possible, after all, that Dora really had killed Ethel and I was on a fool's errand.

With something akin to relief, I turned back, looking forward to being at ground level again. The downside to our bungled plan, and it was a big one, would be that Aunt Irene would have already alerted Muldoon, so the cavalry was coming whether Margaret was here waiting to be arrested or not. Muldoon's ire would land squarely on my head. For all I knew, he was already in the building.

As I was mentally preparing myself for that confrontation, I glimpsed a statuesque woman watching me from the other side of the elevator. Where had she come from? Recognition set off a nervous quake inside me. I walked toward where she waited, beautiful and stone-faced. She wore a dark suit and a wide-brimmed summer straw hat to match. Not a hair or pleat was out of place. She looked tense but perfectly, eerily poised.

"Margaret?" I said.

For a fraction of a second, her eyes flared in surprise. She knew me from that brief glimpse at Sawyer's office; clearly I wasn't who she'd expected. Puzzlingly, her gaze fastened on a point beyond my shoulder. I wondered if she was under the influence of some narcotic. Then she nodded—more as if giving a direction than in answer to my question. My bafflement grew, until from somewhere behind me a hand reached round to cover my mouth.

I gasped and inhaled only leathery palm. The gloved hand also muffled my subsequent scream. Nothing could mask the sound of my umbrella clattering to the floor after it slipped from my fingers, but there was no one to hear. The last I saw of the fifty-eighth floor was Margaret Attinger kicking the umbrella toward the wall and strolling away to take in the view, calmly, like a tourist.

In the next instant, my own view became the narrow passage containing the spiral staircase, which my captor proceeded to drag me up. *Up.* Where did the stairs lead? I was almost afraid to find out.

I tried to crane my head around to see him, but he had the bend of his arm crooked around my neck, choking me, while his other arm around my torso squeezed off my breath as he dragged me backward. I kicked my legs out, which was no help since he was behind and slightly above me. I was like some dumb farm animal being dragged away to the slaughter. *Again,* I thought, angry at my helplessness.

So much for our—laughable, I now saw—planning. So much for cutting off routes of Margaret's escape. All we'd done was cut off my own. As we reached a sharp turn I was able to glimpse him, and it was as I expected. "Sawyer," I croaked into his palm. His fair cheeks were stained scarlet with the effort required to haul me up the stairs.

His elbow squeezed tighter around my neck. "Shut up! Another word out of you, you die. Do you understand? *You will die.*"

Did he mean that there was an iota of a chance that I *wasn't* going to die? Maybe there was a way out of this. I kept my mouth shut.

It wasn't until we finally reached another, smaller landing and Sawyer banged open a door that I realized that, threat or no threat, I should have been screaming my head off. A gust of wet air slapped my face, and Sawyer dragged me onto the slick, rain-splattered cement of a narrow walkway. This was a sort of partially open-air crow's nest encircling the building's copper cupola, just below the lantern at the top. The walkway area available was no more than a few paces, and rectangular open-air viewing windows were cut into the metal wall at regular intervals. My heart banged against my ribs. Get too close to those windows, and a six-hundred-plus-foot plummet to the ground would be a matter of a shove. There was no Ed Blainey to save me now, and the bottoms of those windows were low. Too low.

Another miscalculation in our brilliant plan: There *was* another way out of the building besides the elevator—a straight plunge down fifty-eight-plus floors. Although with any luck one might land on one of the decks below. I wouldn't be any less dead, although perhaps marginally less gruesomely so.

I dug in my heels, desperate to scramble back to the staircase. Then the door blew shut again, and Sawyer slung me forward. I screamed, expecting to go flying over the rail, but instead I fell to ground. I scrabbled backward at once and leaned all the weight I could against the metal wall in the vain hope that I could make my body cling to it, as if I had barnacles.

He loomed over me, eyes blazing, blond locks unmoored by the wind from their Brilliantine neatness. Beyond him was an equally angry sky, the city view obscured by clouds. That's how high up we were. A flash illuminated us. I'd never seen lightning so large before, but I'd never been so close to its source.

"The gloves," he barked. "Give them to me."

Thunder clapped and the sound jolted through me. "I don't have them."

"Liar! I saw the note you sent my wife."

"It was a bluff." My teeth chattered as I spoke. "T-to scare her. I thought she'd killed Ethel . . ." Had I been wrong? Right now, it was Sawyer who seemed murderous. Yet Margaret had been in the observation gallery, and had directed him with a nod. The perfect puppet master.

His face, tense and distrustful, didn't change. Yet he didn't deny his wife was a murderer.

"Sawyer, I know you didn't kill Ethel. It was Margaret. She mistook Ethel for Callie, didn't she?"

He answered mechanically, like a child who'd been too well coached in his lessons. "Callie nearly destroyed our home."

No, you *nearly destroyed it, you bastard.* I gulped back my outrage. Anger wouldn't help me here. "But now you don't have to worry. Callie hasn't bothered you again, has she?"

"You or she could go to the police with the gloves."

"But we won't. We can't. The gloves were lost."

"I have to protect my family," he said, not hearing me. "I have two children."

"Then go. Now. Leave here. The police are coming."

His lips twisted into a sneer.

"They are," I insisted. Unfortunately, when and if they came, they wouldn't find me where I was supposed to be. The way things were going, they wouldn't find me at all until I was splattered all over lower Broadway. "My aunt's bringing Detective Muldoon. Did you think I would come up here on my own?"

He grabbed my arm in a circulation-killing grasp that had me keening in pain. "If what you say is true," Sawyer growled close to my ear, "then when the police arrive they'll find the first woman to commit suicide by jumping from the Woolworth Building."

"No one will believe it. Why would I commit suicide?"

"Why not? A woman alone, depressed over her roommate's death—no family, no children, no one to care about her at all, really. That's what the papers will write."

He dismissed my whole life with such conviction, I could almost believe him.

Lightning flashed again, and I shook my head in hopes that I could talk him back to sense. "The papers would be wrong. I have family, and friends who care for me." *I even have a child.* Suddenly a vision of that typed form I'd glimpsed just once flashed through my mind as clear as the lightning that bolted across the sky. "Detective Muldoon knows me, and he'll never believe I jumped."

"The police are idiots."

They certainly are slow. Perhaps they wouldn't be coming at all. Maybe Aunt Irene couldn't convince them and they'd written us all off as crackpots. Who could blame them? Muldoon wasn't kidding when he'd warned me not to play detective.

How was I going to save myself? I had nothing to work with. A mere three feet of area between the wall and the window. I swallowed and glanced up, but there was nothing over my head but metal roof. There was nothing to grab for, or hang on to.

The door, I thought. Getting back inside was my only hope.

I lurched toward it. Sawyer grabbed my other arm and yanked. If not for the events of the night before, I might have been able to stand it. But intense pain shot through my shoulder, and I let out a mighty howl that grew even more agonized as I realized I was being dragged again toward that window. Closer to that sharp drop to oblivion. I made myself a dead weight. If Sawyer was going to kill me, I wasn't going to let it be easy for him. He loosed a string of curses that a gust of wind carried off.

Fat drops of rain created an irregular drumbeat against the copper. Some drops blew in on us, and Sawyer's hand slipped enough that I was able to scramble back toward the door, screaming my head off. I'd never be so foolish as to remain silent again. He seized hold of me before I reached the door, but I tried not to feel too discouraged. *Delay.* If I was growing tired, so was he. Every moment of delay was a little victory.

"Let me go," I pleaded. "Please, Sawyer. This wasn't your crime. It was Margaret."

"She's the mother of my children."

"Your children need you," I argued. "If you do this thing, you'll both be murderers. Your children will have no one."

We'd reached the window ledge. I leaned as far away from him as I could and tried to tuck my free hand at the metal edge on the right of the window. I gasped for air against the pelting rain. Most of all, I tried not to look at what was beyond, at that empty nothing, that drop that would be my end. Here I was at the top of the most brightly lit beacon in the most populous city in America, and my struggle might as well have been invisible. Those sailors forty miles out to sea, or however far the blazing tower could be seen on this blustery night, would have no idea they were witnessing a death scene.

Sawyer pushed my head down until I couldn't help but see over. A slender gargoyle protruded below us. My view was northeast now, and in the distance I glimpsed the bridges draped across the East River. The cloud-blurred lights of the city stretched on and on. The whole world seemed topsy-turvy, as if I were looking down through the clouds at the stars.

I blinked, shuttering out the lights, the amorphous buildings, the distant bridges, and the fear rising inside me. Instead, my mind's eye saw Callie laughing, and Otto in a white butcher apron, entertaining customers by making a plucked Cornish hen sing like Al Jolson. My parents' hillside grave, Uncle Luddie's kind old face, Aunt Irene on the sofa with the dogs. All the people I loved. Even Aunt Sonja, who I loved in spite of everything. And I sensed someone else, too, a young boy's face that seemed almost like a mirror.

A last scrap of determination surged inside me. "Sawyer"—I gulped—"you can't do this. Don't make yourself a murderer."

"You should have left us alone." His face twisted in an anger that was almost despairing. "What did it matter to you? Margaret didn't kill Callie—just that cousin Callie was always complaining about."

Just Ethel. An old spinster. A woman without a home, one of those undesirables who seemed to be both invisible and at the same time always in the way.

"She was a human being," I said. "She didn't deserve to die."

"All right!" he bellowed. "It was a mistake!"

Confusion only agitated him, making him both peevish and enraged. I wondered how far I could argue the point before he pitched me out the opening just to shut me up. It didn't really matter. At this point, all I had left were words. "What if Margaret decides to correct her mistake and goes after Callie again?"

"She won't. We agreed—just the blackmailer. That'll be the end of it."

How reasonable of them. Breakfast conversations at their house must have been interesting lately. "But Margaret assumed Callie was the blackmailer, didn't she?" I asked. "She thought she'd be getting rid of the threat to her purse and the threat to her marriage. But Callie knows nothing about the blackmail, Sawyer." At least, she hadn't known about it when Aunt Irene, Otto, Walter, and I had cooked up this scheme. "Margaret will always resent her. You know that. Don't you still care enough about Callie not to want to see her killed?"

His face twisted in anguish. Rain had plastered his hair against his temples. "God, yes. But Margaret promised."

"I saw Ethel's body, and the blood. Margaret buried a butcher knife in Ethel's back, thinking it was Callie."

"Because she was so angry. She was trying to save our family."

"And now she's making you do this. And what if the next time she's angry, it's with *you?* Will she bury a knife in your back?"

"No! She loves me. She's loyal. Nothing means more than family to her, and to me. Nothing."

His grip was so tight, my arm went numb. I was soaked and trembling. We were talking in circles, and I couldn't see a way out. Sawyer's every argument came out by rote. When he got tired of repeating what Margaret told him to say, it would be over for me.

"Please listen to me—"

"Shut up!"

Behind us, a door banged open. We both tensed, me in hope, he in fear.

"It's me you want, isn't it, Sawyer?"

Callie stood in the stairwell doorway, the wind whipping her hair that had escaped its pins. She wore a light cape over her dress, and when lightning cracked across the sky I wondered if my terrified brain had conjured her. She looked like a phantom standing there. Or an angel.

"Let Louise go." Her voice sounded loud and authoritative, despite a slight quaver.

Sawyer's grip loosened, but a new panic surged through me. *Is Callie crazy?* Why had she come here? We might both be killed now. And where was Margaret?

"Callie!" Sawyer's eyes were frantic, and suddenly he gave me a shove and sent me sprawling to the flooring again. He scrambled toward her. "Callie, get out of here. Margaret's downstairs. She might have seen you already. She'll kill you like she did that cousin of yours."

"I know." With a sad smile, Callie stepped aside.

Muldoon emerged first, holding a revolver; then a uniformed policeman pushed Margaret forward. The little area felt too crowded. I crept as close as I could back to the wall.

If Muldoon noticed me, he didn't show it. All his focus was on Sawyer. "Your wife told us that *you'd* done the murder, Mr. Attinger. She claims you're insane."

Sawyer's face collapsed as water poured down. "Margaret?"

Her expression hardened, and her chin notched a fraction higher. "Just confess, Sawyer. For the children's sakes."

He took another step toward her, disbelief warring with anguish. "Margaret . . ."

Hadn't I told him so? "She's sticking the knife in, Sawyer."

"Shut up!" Margaret barked at me. "You're a filthy blackmailer."

"And you're a cold-blooded killer," I taunted back. "A woman who sacrificed her family's future to get revenge. You couldn't even kill the right woman."

"I didn't kill anyone," she said, more desperately. "*He* did it. Tell them, Sawyer. Would you have the mother of your children go to prison?"

He dropped his hands to his sides and gulped in a breath. *Don't confess,* I silently begged him. *Don't let her win.*

I don't know if he heard me or not, but when his words finally came, they were barely audible over the tempest around us. "My wife killed Ethel Gail."

Margaret's face filled with rage and she surged toward Callie, claws out. "It was your fault, you whore!"

I leapt to my feet and rushed to Callie's side. But before I could get to her, Muldoon's hand clamped down on my arm—the bad one. I groaned. My arm would be ringed with bruises tomorrow... but right now I was too relieved that there would actually be a tomorrow to care.

He nodded curtly at Margaret. "Officers, take Mr. and Mrs. Attinger into custody. Miss Gail, you're free to go."

"What about Louise?" she asked.

"I need to have a few words with Miss Faulk," he said. "Choice ones."

He didn't wait long to say them. As soon as the others had left, he rounded on me. "Have you lost your mind?"

I edged toward the stairwell. "Would it be all right if you yelled at me where it's dry? And safe?" Now that the danger of being hurled off the side of the building was past, the sight of that void beyond the window turned my knees to pudding. My stomach roiled as Muldoon led me back in, blasting abuse at me all the while. The words "cockeyed scheme," "idiotic," and "one-way ticket back to Altoona" echoed around the stairwell.

I met every blistering word with an understanding nod. But all I could think was, *It worked... and I'm alive.* Despite everything, a glimmer of satisfaction stirred in me.

Water dripped off his hat, and though he took it off and shook it in disgust, his diatribe didn't stop. "I should have let that maniac Attinger push you off the building. Maybe sometime during the sixty-story drop you would have realized how imbecilic this plan you and your aunt cooked up was."

"And Otto," I said.

His face tensed, as if his jaw were the dam holding back the tide of anger he longed to unleash. "All this city needs right now is a crime-fighting songwriter-crusader."

"And yet you now have Ethel's killer in custody, whereas the man you suspected has escaped." Letting him digest that, I reached up to straighten my own hat and touched only a mane of sopping tangles and runaway pins. Heaven only knew where my hat had gone—the Statue of Liberty might be wearing it now.

"Blackmail is a crime," he said.

"We weren't really attempting blackmail, though. It was a... what do you call it?" I searched for a word I knew only from the papers. "A sting?"

"God help us," he muttered.

"Don't police do things like that?"

He rubbed a hand over tired eyes. "Like what?"

"Stings?"

"*Police* do. Publishing secretaries do not."

I rocked on my heels. "Maybe I should be in the police, then. I caught the murderer."

"Did you? Funny, when I peeked out the door, it looked very much as if the murderer had caught you. Do you understand how many ways your plan could have gone catastrophically wrong? You might have ended up in a bloody heap on the sidewalk. You could have guessed the wrong culprit and ended up going to jail yourself."

"But I wasn't wrong," I insisted.

"You were lucky."

"I was right."

He nudged me toward the stairs. "All right, Miss Sherlock. You can explain exactly how you came to all your brilliant conclusions in a formal statement at the precinct."

So much for dreams of dry clothes, a hot mug of tea, and bed. Muldoon marched me down to the fifty-fourth floor. I stepped away from him to look around the room again, now deserted except for a uniformed policeman who stood alert by the shuttered souvenir booth.

I'd expected to find Otto, my aunt, and Callie here. "Where is everyone?"

"We cleared the area. The last thing I wanted was a pack of journalists up here."

Journalists. I hadn't thought about them. I made another effort to put my hair in some kind of order. My reflection in one of the windows reminded me how much work was needed. I tried to concentrate on my drowned-rat appearance and not the dizzying, magnificent panorama beyond. Rain splattered and dribbled across the vast panes, turning the city unfurling below us into a sparkling blur.

The elevator doors slid open and Muldoon took my arm. "Some view," he said.

"Spectacular," I agreed without enthusiasm. Nothing would please me more than never to have to see the city from this vantage again.

He treated me to another fifty-four-floor harangue during the elevator ride down. After that, it was jarring to step out into the sumptuous lobby and be greeted with such joy by my aunt, Otto, and Callie. A flashbulb went off, blinding me temporarily, and Muldoon hustled over to the gathered journalists to push them back from our reunion.

Exuberant, Aunt Irene cocooned me in a hug. "You did it, Louise!" She soon pulled back, frowning at me. "You're dripping wet."

"It was raining." As if I'd been out for a stroll in a summer shower, instead of up in the clouds at the heart of a tempest.

Aunt Irene took off her wrap, a cape of crimson crushed velvet trimmed in black fur. She snapped it over my shoulders and fastened the furry ends across my front, then pulled the hood over my messy, bedraggled hair.

Callie looked at me gravely. "I could kick myself for having left you. Dora and Abel *were* at their church the night of the murder. Half the town saw them there."

I nodded. "Just as they said."

"I should have taken their word for it. I shouldn't have gone at all. When Otto told me your plan, I was terrified Margaret would figure out some way to kill you."

"She did. She turned her husband into a weapon."

"Callie was so frantic about you, I couldn't keep her in Little Falls," Otto said.

I smiled. "Nothing could ever keep her in Little Falls."

A hint of a smile tilted Callie's lips, too. "When Otto and I talked our way up to the fifty-eighth floor, Muldoon was already speaking to Margaret. She denied that you were ever there, but I knew something was wrong, and I saw her glance a few times at that stairwell door—and then I spotted my yellow umbrella lying near the stairwell. I told Muldoon and after we hurried up the stairs, we could hear some of what you were saying. Muldoon was ready to run out with guns blazing, but when I saw Sawyer holding you so close to the edge, I convinced him to let me go out first and try to talk to him."

"I was never so glad to see anyone in my life," I said, "except I worried he'd kill both of us. I didn't know you had backup."

Otto bobbed on his heels. "I would have gone up, too, but they said there were too many people in the stairwell already. And then they shunted me off down here."

He looked genuinely disappointed to have been deprived of the opportunity to play the hero.

"You can write a song about it," I said.

Someone tapped me on the shoulder. I turned and realized Muldoon had been standing behind me. His anger had given way to weariness. "Go home and get some sleep," he said.

"You're letting me go?"

"Tomorrow afternoon will be soon enough to give a statement."

"Thank you." I truly was grateful. Despite the adrenaline pumping through me, I was ready to drop.

We ran the gauntlet of the press to get to the sidewalk. My aunt reached into her bag and fished out five dollars. "You all take this and cab home."

I accepted the bill and gave her another long hug. Before I could break away, she held my forearms in a tight grip and pulled me aside. Thinking she probably wanted her cape back, I started to take it off, but she stopped me.

"You should have seen that man's face when I told him you'd gone up there to confront that woman," she confided.

I frowned. "What man?"

"Detective Muldoon. He positively panicked. I thought the poor fellow was going to come unstrung."

"He thinks I'm an idiot, and who can blame him? Our plan was more foolhardy than foolproof."

Aunt Irene shrugged. "True, but it all worked out in the end. That's what I aim for in all my books, and it's not a bad goal in life, either." She tilted her head and looked back at the great arched entrance through which Muldoon had disappeared again, back into the Woolworth Building. "There's something about that man . . ."

"Something irritating?"

"Fascinating." Her face brightened with a sudden notion. "Do you think you could convince him to come to one of my Thursday nights?"

"I'll try." If nothing else, I wanted to see the look on his face when I asked him.

For once, Callie and I decided not to economize and found a cab for ourselves and Otto. Inside, we all collapsed against the cushions, exhausted. Callie was silent but still tense. Maybe she was still living through that experience at the tower's pinnacle. I didn't doubt the horror of it would be a prominent feature of my own nightmares for years to come.

Once we were under way, however, she rounded on me, glaring over Otto, who was squeezed between us. "Louise, you idiot! You could have been killed!"

"I've heard that song before," I said. "Muldoon sings it particularly well."

She exhaled in exasperation. "It's all my fault. If I hadn't gotten involved with Sawyer, none of this would have happened. You warned me."

"I warned you because I didn't want you to be heartbroken," I pointed out. "Not because I thought his insane wife would try to kill us all."

"Why be angry at yourself?" Otto asked her, his face set into a rare expression of bitterness. "It was Sawyer. You can't blame yourself for being misled by a man."

"Can't I?" she asked, without humor.

"If he hadn't led you astray . . ."

"Oh, Otto." A pained sound tore out of Callie—something between a laugh and a wail of despair. She turned to look out the window at Houston Street passing quickly by.

Otto blinked, finally understanding that his idol had feet of clay and a heart that wasn't his. "Oh. Well, we all make mistakes."

"Louise doesn't," Callie said.

"Not true," I said. "Not even remotely true."

He twisted and looked at me, not with his old blind devotion, but with an expression much dearer to me. The clear-eyed affection of an old friend. "You were wonderful tonight, Louise. I always said there was nothing you couldn't do if you put your mind to it."

Oh, but there was. Specifically, there was one thing that heretofore I hadn't been able to bring myself to face. I intended to remedy that at the earliest possible opportunity.

CHAPTER 16

Sunday dawned clear and bright. Not that I saw the dawn. I slept fitfully but woke late, finally roused by the peal of church bells and the aroma of coffee brewing in the kitchen. Callie and I ate a solemn breakfast. She announced that she was going to spend a quiet day writing letters and washing out some clothes.

Callie staying home on a perfect Sunday in June? What a difference a few weeks could make.

"If I don't return to work this week I might never work again," she said.

"I doubt that." But I could see how she might worry. Solomon's probably had girls knocking on their door every day hunting for modeling work.

"I suppose you have to go to the police station again," she said.

"I don't mind. It's starting to feel like a second home." I sipped my coffee, watching her. Callie never looked haggard, but she had shadows beneath her eyes, and her shoulders sagged in exhaustion, or sadness. Maybe both. "But if you rather I stayed home . . ."

"Nah," she said. "I just need to shake this blue mood away. Maybe Otto'll come by—if he doesn't consider me a scarlet woman now."

"He doesn't," I said. "You're not."

"Just wait and see if I have to testify at Margaret's trial. Then the whole city will think I am."

"Then the whole city will be wrong," I said. "*You* didn't chase after Sawyer. It was the other way around, and he deceived you about being married. You gave him the brush-off after you found out." When she didn't look convinced, I said in frustration, "We can't go trailing our mistakes and misfortunes around with us all the time. If we do, then we might as well have let Sawyer shove us off the top of the Woolworth Building."

Her eyes widened at the vehemence in my voice. "What's eating you?"

"What I mean to say is . . ." What *was* I trying to say? "Give yourself a break. And don't hole up here all day on a gorgeous afternoon. If Otto comes by, you should take him to the Hippodrome, or Coney Island. The poor boy hasn't seen anything of the city so far but police stations and the music departments of five-and-dime stores."

I could tell from the tilt of her head that she wasn't averse to the idea. "Wouldn't you like to come with us? After Muldoon's finished with you, that is."

"I have someplace else to go." I got up to take my cup to the sink, and to hide my face. This was one errand I needed to run alone.

The rain the night before had worked a miraculous change on the city. The very air seemed scrubbed clean. I took my time going uptown, jumping off the Sixth Avenue El and crossing over to Times Square and then to Fifth Avenue. The air in New York rarely smelled so fresh as it did after a cleansing downpour, and the morning sun had already dried the sidewalks. For a few hours, at least, the pavement would look bleached and clean.

I wasn't the only one who'd had the idea of a long stroll. Half of New York was out in their summer colors, parading up and down Millionaires' Mile as if it were a second Easter parade. In my robin's-egg-blue linen dress, my Sunday best, I didn't feel out of place in the fashionable procession.

Walking past the grand residences of the Astors and the Vanderbilts provided me with good mental preparation for what I assumed was ahead. I'd seen the mansions before, of course, first gaping in wonder and then later treating them as just part of the city's landscape like my jaded fellow citizens who'd become inured to such opulence. Some of the houses spanned entire city blocks. Given the number of new churches and hotels that had sprung up around them, these great family piles seemed to serve as the generators for entire neighborhoods.

When I'd first arrived in New York City, I'd considered my aunt's townhouse the height of elegance and luxury. I laughed at my naïveté now, or I would have if my stomach hadn't tightened into a ball the closer I came to Eightieth Street.

It was almost a relief finally to turn onto that street and discover that Number Seven, the home of Richard and Julia Longworth, was a relatively modest five-story row house of white stone and beige brick in the Italianate style. Two wide windows dominated the second floor front—the living room or parlor, I guessed. Above that, each story boasted three windows of equal size. My head tipped up to eye the third and fourth floors, where the family bedrooms would be, and the nursery. Of course there was no chance of seeing a little face pressed against the pane. The son of the house was just six months—still at the crawling stage, I assumed.

As I stood there, Number Seven's front door opened and the end of a black perambulator poked out the front door like a clumsy bear backing out of its winter den. A stout girl wearing a dark blue dress, white apron, and cap wrestled the contraption down to the sidewalk, twitched her shoulders straight, then pointed the buggy toward the park.

My heartbeat picked up, and before I could talk myself out of it I set myself on a course parallel to hers, arriving at my corner just ahead of her. I darted across Eightieth Street in front of an automobile only slightly smaller than a steamship. The chauffeur honked his disapproval. The *ah-yoooo-gah!* of the horn hurtled me the last few feet onto the opposite sidewalk. I nearly plowed right into the nanny.

Apologies spilled out of me in a gush of nerves. "I'm sorry—so absentminded. I hope I haven't disturbed—" Though I was speaking to the woman, it was the carriage I was attempting to look into. At first I glimpsed only a yellow-and-blue blanket and a green knit cap.

The woman, who had been pursed up in displeasure, softened a little as I gaped at her charge. "It would take more than a bump to upset the little mite when he's out for his walk," she said in a British accent. "He's that fond of the outdoors, is Master Calvin."

"Calvin!" I was too aghast to hide my surprise. Outrage bristled through me—as if I should have been consulted in the naming of young Master Longworth.

"Seemed a little peculiar to me, too, at first," the young woman confided. "But I suppose there are worse. I had an uncle named Obadiah. Imagine having that pinned on you for good and all."

There was opening enough in the traffic for us to scurry across Fifth Avenue toward the park. I continued to walk with her, and she didn't seem to mind the company.

I was trying to adjust to the idea of a family choosing such an unexpected name for my baby while at the same time craning my neck as I walked to get a long glimpse of him. He was also dressed in his Sunday best—a starched white jumper, stockings, and booties. His limbs seemed well-fed and pudgy, and his cheeks were rosy with good health. I hesitated to look too closely at his face for fear I'd see the arrogant countenance of his father. But what I saw was almost as eerie. Eyes that I knew only from the mirror stared back at me, brown flecked with green. His soft downy hair was also strikingly similar to my mouse brown. *Better for a boy,* I thought.

"Is everything all right, miss?" the nanny asked.

"Wha—?"

My voice couldn't squeak past the baseball-sized lump in my throat, but she didn't seem to notice that. "Your face looks reddish and queer. That was a near miss you had with that automobile."

I shook my head, gulped, and nodded toward Calvin, who was kicking impatiently inside his little chariot. "He's very sweet, isn't he?" I choked out.

"And why shouldn't he be?" she asked, almost as if offended. "He's the luckiest little boy in the world."

"Is he?"

"Certainly. His parents might not be quite as rich as the Rockefellers, mind you, but he's the apple of their eyes, and he'll have everything his heart desires."

That knot was back again, but I managed to nod and mumble, "Lucky."

She leaned toward me and said in a low voice, "Especially since the poor mite was a little foundling."

"He wasn't!" I couldn't check the anger in my voice. She made it sound as if I'd abandoned my child in an alley.

She nodded, and kept her tone confidential. "Adopted. No telling who his people were—and now look at him." She chuckled. "Like a little prince."

For months I'd feared this encounter, yet held out hope that finally setting eyes on the child I'd given away would give me reassurance and resolution. The effect fell short of what I'd hoped. Frustration filled me. If he grew up and discovered he was adopted, what would he think of me? Clearly mothers who gave up their children were seen as only one type of woman.

But he *was* better off. *Like a little prince.*

It was only Madame Serena who'd confused me, with her talk of the forlorn baby crying for its mother. Mrs. Longworth was the mother—not me.

Unexpectedly, envy for the Longworths hit me in a wave, like a fever. It frightened me. I shouldn't have come.

"I have to go," I said.

The nanny nodded, as if my leaving were just a matter of course. She hadn't realized how close I'd come to grabbing the buggy and running. Or just dropping to the ground and sobbing.

"Take good care of him," I said, backing away.

The woman probably thought I was a lunatic. I was beginning to wonder myself.

For months I'd dreamed of viewing the Longworth house and catching a glimpse of the baby, and now I had. It had accomplished nothing.

And everything.

As I made my way back down Fifth Avenue, I felt bound to this city more than ever. The world might not know it, and *he* certainly never would, but my son lived here.

I expected more hullabaloo after Margaret Attinger's arrest. A few papers reported what had happened Saturday night, some with quite a few dramatic details. Happily, my name was only mentioned far down in the articles, and my picture never appeared. News of a war breaking out in the Balkans hit the headlines Monday morning, along with a report of an entire game between the Cubs and the Reds in which only one baseball had been used, and so interest in the Attingers and Ethel's murder began to fade away.

At home, the mood continued to be more somber than usual until midweek, when Callie received an offer from the old producer to join the chorus of his show. I'd never seen her so jubilant—she practically danced through every mundane activity. She also began a strict regimen of "shaping" exercises and eating. "You'll blush when you see my costume," she said. "It shows every curve and bump."

I was happy for her. We'd needed good news.

On Thursday, at work, I was typing a letter for Mr. McChesney when Ford Fitzsimmons strolled into the office as if he owned the place. At the sight of him I tensed in my chair, eyeing him warily over the top of my typewriter. What was he doing here? The possibility that he'd come to finish off what a shove in front of a train hadn't accomplished crossed my mind. But why would he? Margaret's capture meant there would be no more suspicion cast on him. In fact, if she pleaded innocent to the charges, he would be a star witness at the trial.

Yet aside from a brief, wry glance, Ford barely acknowledged my presence. He didn't have to. Jackson was already hopping up with obsequious eagerness.

"Fitzsimmons—how wonderful that you could come so soon!" He clasped Ford's hand, shook it, and then led the way directly to Guy Van Hooten's office. "Guy's eager to meet you." He knocked at the door and then turned back to me. "Fetch us some coffee, won't you, Louise?"

They went inside and I stewed in my chair for a good two minutes before standing to do as bid. I deduced that Jackson, who had nixed Ford's first book, had undergone a change of heart with the second. Naturally, Guy's opinion had nothing at all to do with the recommendation.

When the coffee was brewed, I carried it inside on a tray, doing my best impersonation of Walter as I passed cups around. The men were being especially effusive in their admiration of each other.

"Guy's got an eye for quality," Jackson was saying—and, I assumed, lying. "It's what people always said of him, even back in our university days."

"You're old school chums, then?" Ford asked.

"Back in Boston." Guy and Jackson laughed with immodest modesty. You could always tell a Harvard man.

"It's really Jackson you owe your good fortune to, Fitz," Guy said. "He gave the manuscript a glowing recommendation. Called it a taut, raucous drama."

Actually, *I* had said that—before I had tried to *un*say it. But I was now invisible. "Will you be needing anything else?" I asked.

Guy glanced up as if he'd barely noticed me till then. "No, thank you, Louisa."

I gritted my teeth.

Jackson cleared his throat. He had enough decency to look abashed. "You know Louise, don't you, Ford?"

"Of course." Ford's blue eyes settled on me with what I could only describe as triumphant amusement. "She's been indispensable to me."

Except that time you decided to dispense with me altogether with a fatal shove.

"Indispensable—that's just the word," Guy said. "Makes a mean hangover cure, too. What would we do without her?"

I smiled. He would have the opportunity to learn the answer to that question in the not-too-distant future, I hoped. When Aunt Irene had secured this job for me, I'd been so grateful to have a place in New York City. But now I knew it wasn't enough to accept whatever was handed to me—or taken from me. I intended to forge a path of my own.

Imagine my surprise that evening when, at Aunt Irene's at-home, Muldoon walked in. With his black suit, dark features, and grim look, he seemed more like an undertaker arriving for a pickup than a party guest, but Aunt Irene greeted him with the zeal that she usually reserved for the local luminaries who stumbled into her orbit. "Detective!" she exclaimed. "Come in. So nice of you to join our soirée. Have you met Madame L'Huillier of the Metropolitan Opera?"

I amused myself a full quarter hour watching the detective's discomfort as he was passed along the room from opera stars to actors to city councilmen to a Russian painter who didn't speak a word of English, who I suspected only came for the free food. I handed the painter my sandwich tray and plopped down in a chair next to Muldoon.

"This is quite a gathering." He eyed Callie laughing among a group of young men. "Your friend seems in better spirits."

"We all are." I nodded toward Otto playing a rag on the piano. A young lady had sidled up close to him on the bench. By the weekend, perhaps *she* would be his muse.

"And you?" he asked.

"I'm doing fine," I said. "I've made some resolutions this week."

"Let me guess—to never again visit the observation deck of the Woolworth Building."

I laughed. "I'm considering avoiding five-and-dime stores altogether."

The comment earned a rare smile. "I don't blame you."

"I've also decided to join the police."

His smile faded. "Is that joke meant to needle me?"

I folded my arms. "Who's joking? There are women police officers, aren't there? Why not me?"

"We have police matrons who watch our female prisoners," he said. "You wouldn't enjoy the work."

"I wouldn't enjoy it more than being an office drudge?"

"You say that now. Spend a day around the jail cells and then report back to me."

"I've spent a bit of time there already, as you know." I smiled. "I think the NYPD could use me."

He shook his head.

"Was I or was I not key in capturing Ethel's killer?" I asked. "The NYPD has one woman detective, why not more?"

"She doesn't work homicide."

"Why not?"

"The brass would never assign a woman to homicide."

"*Now,* you mean."

He sputtered. "The department isn't going to change just because you want it to, Louise."

"It might. Someday. It's had to make changes before—ask Teddy Roosevelt. He was the one who put women in police jobs."

Muldoon's expression said clearly that he gave the man no thanks for that. "Why would you want to be around crime and corruption all the time? Girls should have higher aspirations than that."

"Like marriage and babies," I guessed. "Maybe I should ask Otto to play 'Home Sweet Home.' I sense one of your stirring soliloquies on old-fashioned girls in small towns coming on."

"Are you telling me that you don't want marriage and family for yourself?" he asked. "I thought every girl had a loving, protective instinct inside her."

The image of little Calvin Longworth kicking in his baby carriage came to me. He would have everything a little boy could dream of. And I would do my part to make sure the world he grew up in was as safe and just as I could make it. Perhaps Muldoon wasn't wrong about that protective instinct. I couldn't watch over the child I'd brought into this world, but I could watch over his city.

At my lack of response, Muldoon took a breath. "I see. Well, don't worry. I won't try to talk you out of anything."

"You couldn't if you tried."

He laughed, showing even white teeth, and his dark features became a shade less forbidding. "Believe me, Louise. I know."

A sharp hitch in my chest caught me by surprise. My aunt was right. There was something about him.

ACKNOWLEDGMENTS

"Write the book you'd like to read" is the writer's advice I've tried to follow for most of my career. But two and a half years ago, after the sudden loss of my middle sister, Julia, who was also my lifelong confidante, my first best friend, and sometimes coauthor, I'd hit a wall. I'd never written anything without having Julia as my sounding board. Half the joy of it all was writing a book she would like to read, too.

That I kept writing at all is thanks to some wonderful people. First, John Scognamiglio, my editor at Kensington, who knew just the right moment to nudge me in a different direction. Without his encouragement, I'd probably still be staring at a blank screen in Word. I also owe a special debt of gratitude to Annelise Robey at the Jane Rotrosen Agency, for seeing me through a period of trial and error—lots of error—with unflappable humor and good advice. Endless thanks to my husband, Joe Newman, for proofing and being my partner in crime, and to my sister, Suzanne Bass, for reading and critiquing this manuscript, and listening.

I ended up writing a book I hope Julia would have wanted to read. She loved a mystery.

Connect with Us

Visit us online at
KensingtonBooks.com
to read more from your favorite authors, see books by series, view reading group guides, and more.

Join us on social media

for sneak peeks, chances to win books and prize packs, and to share your thoughts with other readers.

facebook.com/kensingtonpublishing
twitter.com/kensingtonbooks

Tell us what you think!

To share your thoughts, submit a review, or sign up for our eNewsletters, please visit:
KensingtonBooks.com/TellUs.